RAVENBLOOD

AMBER & GLASS

LUKAS MAERTENS

FOREWORD

This is the second and final book in the Ravenblood duology.

If you're returning, welcome back. If you're new, you've skipped some scars, but I'm not stopping you.

The story picks up in the aftermath of Shadows in the Stone. The stakes sharper, and the people are still painfully human.

That's all I'll say. You'll find your way, or you won't.

D/2025/Lukas Maertens, Lukas Maertens

PROLOGUE

The wind howled across the land, scraping over the ruinous plain until it gathered and sang around the black tower. The stone rose like a wound against the dying sun, too smooth and cold for this world. Its outline resisting the dusk as if refusing to decay. The world here was empty except for the shriek of air and the scatter of old bones at the tower's feet.

Samric walked alone, boots silent against the frost-hardened earth. His cloak, a battered drape the color of dried blood, trailed behind him, restless in the wind. He felt the weight of the satchel at his side with every step, old leather with its buckled shut, heavy in a way that had nothing to do with its contents.

He did not hurry. There was a rhythm to this moment, a ritual in the way the last light bled across the threshold. The tower called to him. Each time he neared it, the air seemed to sharpen, the cold tightening around his ribs. Tonight the sensation was different.

When he reached the base, the doors were already half-open. Massive slabs of stone, blacker than night, groaned on unseen hinges. No hand guided them. Dust spun in lazy circles, rising up to catch the light like motes of ash. The tower felt alive, responding to his presence, the old rune wards quivering as he passed.

Samric entered without pausing. Darkness closed around him, thicker than outside, but alive with motion. With each step, the tower seemed to notice him, the floor hummed with buried power, a low, ancient pulse that resonated up his legs and through his bones. The stone underfoot was flawless, seamless even, no sign of tools or mortar, only the feeling of something grown.

He climbed. The spiral stair was steep, the walls pressing close, every echo swallowed before it could return. Here and there, the stone emitted a faint, sullen light like a pulse, dim and rhythmic, as if the tower itself was breathing. Samric's hand traced the wall for balance, fingers tingling with static. In the half-dark, the marks on his own skin, old sigils, burns, the memory of bonds long since broken stood out pale and stark. Every step he took, the hum grew warmer, brighter. Somewhere above, something was waiting to wake.

He didn't look back. The wind battered the doors behind him, but he pressed on, climbing toward the top.

The stairs spat Samric out onto the rooftop, the last step rising straight into open air. Up here, the sky was impossibly clear, no haze or color left from sunset, a vault of night settling black over the ruined world. Stars blinked awake, hard and cold, shining even as the last edge of daylight clung to the west. No wind reached him now. The tower's peak seemed to exist outside weather and season, detached from the slow decay below.

The roof was a wide circle, broad enough to hold a muster of men, but empty except for the runes carved in a double ring at its edge. Each sigil was cut deep, filled with what looked like old blood gone black and glassy. The symbols pulsed, catching the faint starlight and bending it along their edges, making the rooftop seem to float apart from the world below.

Samric paused at the threshold, feeling the strange pressure in the air, the thinning, the chill, the brittle tension of power waiting to be called. He looked out over the broken plains, the scattered scars of old villages, the shadows creeping out from ruined woods. The lands stretched as far as he could see. It would not remain so for long.

He drew a slow breath, tasting the metallic edge of the air, and stepped into the center of the rooftop. Here, the floor rose slightly, a raised circle of bone-pale stone, worn smooth by centuries, yet untouched by moss or decay. It looked like an altar, but there were no marks of worship, only the lingering intent of all who had come before.

He knelt and set the battered satchel on the altar. The leather creaked as he unfastened the buckle. Inside, wrapped in a strip of old velvet, was a single, slender bone: the color of old ivory, smooth and fragile, stained at one end as if it had once been scorched. The phalanx of a finger, or perhaps a piece of the jaw. A true relic of the First King.

He held it in both hands, reverent, feeling the weight of history and expectation settle onto his shoulders. The runes on the rooftop flared, their dull glow shifting to a cold, clear blue. For a moment, the night seemed to hold its breath.

Samric bowed his head, whispering words no language had held for centuries, and began the ritual that would break the silence and summon what slept beneath the world.

Samric placed the bone with care, centering it in the hollow at the heart of the altar. The stone felt cool beneath his fingers, too cool, as if it drank the warmth from his skin. He closed his eyes and let his hands rest at his sides, palms flat against the ancient circle. The rooftop's runes, still dull with age, waited.

He began to speak, but the words were a murmur, half-prayer, half-command, old syllables rolling over his tongue like the last echo of thunder. The wind quieted, as if it, too, was listening. Each phrase was spoken not for the world above, but for what moved beneath the stone. The bone at the center of the ring seemed to blur, haloed in a trembling light that was not reflected, but born from within.

Above, the sky pulsed, soft at first, then stronger, like the slow inhale and exhale of something vast and sleeping. The constellations flickered, their shapes distorting as if viewed through a layer of water. Shadows crawled across the edge of the rooftop, drawing closer with every heartbeat.

The runes glimmered, faint amber, lines brightening as Samric's voice faded to a whisper.

Samric's fingers tightened around the relic bone. Then in a single, decisive motion, he snapped it in half. The crack rang sharp and final, slicing through the tower's hush. He crushed the fragments in his palm, feeling the brittle shards grind to powder against his skin.

Beneath him, the altar stone moaned, a trembling resonance that ran through his bones. Hairline fissures crawled outward from the ritual ring, fracturing the rooftop's smooth surface. The runes spat light, first amber, then violet, then a sickly white before the center split open.

A wound in the world opened. The world struggled to reconcile what it saw. The gap flickered between realms. Unfamiliar constellations writhing and shuddering, hints of steel and bone, the glint of blades, the flicker of impossible shapes. Cold poured from the rift, bitter and dry, carrying with it a scent of burnt metal.

From that gash, three shapes pulled themselves through; their limbs too many, too long, bodies half-clad in bony armor and veined with oozing black. They were void ravagers, but every joint bending as if remembering how to walk. Black ichor dripped from their jaws. Their eyes fixed on Samric with hunger and confusion.

The creatures lurched forward, claws scraping on stone, their mouths splitting open in soundless screams. One surged ahead, maw distending, a razor-rimmed void set to devour.

Samric stood unmoved, the wind flattening his cloak. He lowered his hood, revealing amber eyes that burned in the gathering dark.

The lead Ravager froze mid-lunge, a tremor running through its twisted spine. The others halted, as if yanked by an invisible leash. Samric moved among them, the crushed bone dust drifting from his palm. He pressed his hand gently to the brow of the first beast, its hide quivering at the touch. The creature shuddered, its body wracked with a strange ecstasy, then lowered its head in submission. The others followed.

He spoke to them, a promise and a command.

He called them kin. He spoke of birthrights reclaimed, of a world that had forgotten its true masters and would soon remember. He told them the gate was open, that they were the first of many, and that the old order was dead.

The Ravagers listened, awaiting the world promised to them.

1

Rain hammered the carriage roof hard enough to rattle its iron braces. Each strike carried the pitch like that of far-off drums, growing sharper as the wheels lurched through wet earth. Inside, the single passenger sat motionless, hands resting on his knees. Cords the color of midnight ribboned his wrists in three precise loops, each cinched with a domed seal of dark wax. Whenever the lantern swung, its yellow glow caught on the bindings and sent a ripple of violet light across the man's skin.

He watched the pulse without expression. Beneath the cords, shards of pale crystal showed through thin cuts in his sleeves, half-buried along the length of his forearms. The points shimmered like frost under glass. With every mile gained, they vibrated a shade harder, faint but impossible to ignore. Territory pushed back when it sensed Karthian stonecraft inside a living body.

He flexed his fingers once then twice. Pain stayed muted behind a wall of calm. Should have broken the courier's arm, he thought, Should have let someone else wear these cords. But Karth did not allow refusals. The towers had been silent for too long, and silence demanded an offering.

The carriage slowed, wooden brakes shrieked. The wheels met rough gravel, then mud, then nothing at all. Outside, voices traded curt orders, muffled by the rain. The lantern clipped to the cabin wall swayed again, and this time the shards in his arms thrummed loud enough for him to feel it in his teeth. He drew a breath that smelled of wet wool and old iron. Then the door cracked open.

Night air rushed in cold and metallic. Two figures in dark plate stood framed by the storm, helms turned into shadow. cloaks snapped around their shoulder, the folds stitched with a spreading raven in dull silver thread. Behind them, rows of sharpened stakes and razorwire fenced a shallow moat full of runoff. Beyond the barricade, the outline of a redoubt crouched against the sky, its parapet crowded with iron crows and rune lamps that guttered blue light.

One guard stepped forward, gauntlet closing on the man's upper arm. The other recoiled a fraction when his gaze landed on the crystal protrusions. Rain hissed on steel.

"Out," the first said, a young voice but certain. A nameplate on his pauldron read Verran.

The passenger obeyed, boots splashing into ankle-deep muck. The guard's leather grip tightened instinctively; the shards gave off a soft glassy clink. A visible shiver crossed Verran's shoulders. "Stone-rot," he muttered, low enough he might have hoped the prisoner didn't hear.

Not rot, the man thought, but said nothing. He kept his posture straight despite the mud, cloak hanging heavy with water. Only when another flash of lantern light struck did he speak carefully.

"My wrists," he said, tilting them for inspection. "Break the wax and the cord will cut deeper. Leave it, and I remain as I am. Your choice, Captain."

Verran frowned, eyes flicking to the seals. "Captains stand behind walls. I'm Sergeant." He nodded at one of the rear escorts. "Scroll."

A second soldier produced a tube of oiled leather, unrolled it beneath a lantern. Rain pearled on the parchment but refused to soak in, some invisible coating repelled the water. Verran traced the topmost sigil, a stylized mountain split by a spire, then read the heading:

By decree of House Trast, Karth. Liaison and Pledge of Good Faith.

His lips pressed thin. Lower on the sheet, another emblem, twin ravens bracing a sword glimmered faintly before settling into stillness. Ulzaan's mark. Even in the drizzle it carried weight.

Verran glanced up. "Name and function. Speak it plain."

The man inclined his head. "Idran of Karth, third son of Trast, initiated Stone-Channeler. I stand as pledge between your command and my homeland." His voice held the polished cadence of court tutoring, but underneath lay iron filings and smoke.

A gust drove rain sideways. One sentry cursed and raised his cloak collar. Verran lingered on the shard-studded arms, then jerked his chin toward the trench walk. "Search him. Not a single sliver past the boards."

Gloved hands patted Idran's torso, thighs, boots, efficient but impersonal. One guard brushed a shard and yanked back with a hiss. "Hot," he muttered, shaking his fingers.

Idran stared straight ahead at the black-wing banners, letting them do their work. When they finished, Verran snapped the scroll closed, melted a fresh stamp over the ribbon, and tucked it beneath one arm. "You walk in front. Try nothing. Those cords stay."

They crossed duckboards slick with algae toward the redoubt. Rune-lamps guttered where stormwater struck the charcoal sigils beneath. Every few yards, Idran noted a silver nail driven through a plank, simple warding to disrupt hostile casting. thorough and useless against what stirred in his bones.

Past the trench a tent city sprawled, all angles and lines, each canvas panel reinforced with iron stitching. Rain pooled on the seams, sliding off before it could soak through, spell-scars burned there long ago, now patched with metal. The smell of forge smoke drifted under the storm.

A doorway flap parted. Inside glowed a brazier half-full of coals, smoke curling toward a vent seam. Verran ushered Idran through, then paused to wedge a locking bar across the outer poles.

"This isn't a cell," the sergeant said, "but it won't be pleasant if you test the fabric. Sit and wait. Someone higher than me will decide if that scroll matters."

Idran knelt onto the woven mat. The mud on his boots bled into the straw, darkening it. He placed bound hands in his lap, palms up, as was custom when entering a warded space. "Understood."

Verran lingered, studying him a final time. Rain drummed harder, the brazier popped. "Never thought I'd see shard-filth walk in by choice," he said quietly in bemusement. "Whatever deal your masters brokered with mine, pray it's worth the risk." Then he stepped out, flap closing.

Silence settled, Idran inhaled. The cords tightened with the motion, and the shards beneath his skin sang a close, dissonant chord like glass that's about to shatter. He pictured the mines outside Kir-Harath where the fragments were harvested, columns of raw crystal rising through smoke, apprentices leaning over vats until their lungs burned. He had been twelve when a support pillar split under a surge of channelled power. The memory still smelled of scorched stone dust and someone screaming in the dark.

The brazier's coals glimmered dull red. Idran shifted to ease the pull on his arms. Hidden threads wove through the canvas walls, each knot cinched with a bead of cold iron. They thrummed faintly, wards shaped to muffle magic, not block it. Enough to reassure a nervous garrison.

Beyond the tent came muted calls: orders to tighten the perimeter, replace a torch, fetch a dry cloak for a lieutenant. Ordinary concerns that assumed the night's boundaries were fixed. Idran listened until the voices shrank into the rain.

The shards pulsed again, brighter this time in recognition. Something far away had moved, the way deep water shifts around a rising leviathan. He imagined lines stretching from every buried stonecraft vein in Karth toward a single vanishing point. Those lines were stretched now, singing across the miles.

He closed his eyes. Rain hammered canvas. From the brazier, a coal cracked, sending a ribbon of sparks upward. None of it touched the sensation gathering in his arms.

It begins. The thought arrived calmly. They will blame me first. Let them. A pledge only matters while there is ground to stand on.

He exhaled through his nose, slow as prayer. The cords darkened further, drinking lamp-glow. Somewhere beyond the trench, a raven screamed and took flight into a night no longer theirs alone.

LEONARD WOKE to the taste of iron in the back of his throat and the rattle of rain on canvas. Fourth bell, still a half-glass before dawn and the barracks smelled of damp wool, oiled leather, and men too tense to sweat. In the cramped aisle between bunks, warriors moved like wraiths, buckling greaves, checking straps, talking only when a murmured curse was unavoidable.

He sat on his cot, shoulders hunched, vambrace balanced across his knees. The lamp by his foot hissed, the wick guttering each time a draft slid under the tent flap. Across from him, Saran tightened the screws on her sword's crossguard, black hair pulled into a single braid that fell over one collarbone. Moonlit water beaded on the braid's edge, catching the lamp glow and scattering it across her cheekbones.

She didn't look up when she spoke. "How long since you slept, really?"

"Two hours. Maybe." Leonard bent the leather strap, listened for the faintest pop of a weak stitch, none came.

Saran rolled her shoulder, easing her harness into place. "Three towns in smoke now. One of the runners said you could taste it on the wind a league away."

Leonard slid the vambrace onto his arm. "I believe it."

"And the Karth line ruptured at Silver Pass while we were still cleaning out the cart trenches. Nobody told the cooks." She clicked her tongue. "Nothing like salted oats while half the frontier burns."

He grunted agreement, cinched the last buckle. Oil pooled at the lamp's lip, threatening to drown the flame. He reached to trim it, then paused, catching her eye for the first time. "We're full kits now. No more neophyte drills, no more clipped wings."

Saran gave him a crooked smile. "I'd brag, but promotion loses flavor when the world's cracking open the next day."

He allowed himself an answering smirk and tipped the spare oil back into the vial. Across the aisle, a pair of veterans argued over whether to drag extra bolts or just trust the supply runners to catch up. Beyond them, the flap parted, letting in a cold line of mist and the distant gleam of watch-fires on the trench edge.

Rain came down harder, the lamp hissed again.

Saran sheathed her sword, checked the tension one more time, then broke the silence that pressed every corner of the barracks. "And now this pulse."

Leonard exhaled through his nose. Every Ravenblood in the redoubt felt the first tremor five nights ago, a ripple that made bones sing. "Nobody's naming it yet."

She leaned forward, elbows on knees. "They don't have to. Tower flares, sky goes a wrong shade of bruise, scouts bring back stories of lights inside the stone. And Ulzaan still hasn't come down from the high trench. That never means good news."

Leonard's answer was a small nod, eyes fixed on the lamp. Flame... flame... a flicker too tall, then a shock lanced behind his eyes, pressure rolling from jaw hinge to crown as if someone pinched the world and twisted. The air around the lamp folded inward, the wick bent, pointed toward the canvas wall that faced the distant Black Tower. Leonard flinched, palm flying to his temple. He tasted blood. Not real but phantom copper, the flavor of resonance he'd never managed to name aloud.

Saran caught the movement. "Again?"

He forced his lungs open, fought the swirl in his head long enough to rasp, "Hush."

When the pressure eased a hair, he reached for the flattened mess-tin on his pack. With one shaky finger he traced a quick series of points and lines on the tin's dust-scummed surface: eight strokes, two curved, an angle he couldn't have explained under threat of swords. The pattern hung there in oily smear. He wiped it clean, drew it again. Same result.

Saran studied the marks, braid falling forward over her shoulder. "You heard the tower?"

He shook his head once, eyes watering. "No. Something under it. Like... numbers marching."

She pressed her hand to the tin. "Draw it again slower."

He did. She matched each line with a tap of her finger, committing it. No disbelief this time, only focus. Wind outside shifted, rattling the tent poles. The lamp's flame snapped straight again.

A horn blared, one long, two clipped the mark of a forward patrol returning. The aisle filled with motion: shields slapped onto backs, buckles yanked tight, blades drawn half an inch then seated again. The half-light bloomed with steel.

Saran rose, offered Leonard a hand. "Up."

He took it, pulling himself steady. The thrum in his skull hadn't faded, it burrowed behind his teeth like a living pulse. Together they fastened cloaks, tightened straps, and stepped into the trench-side dawn.

Fog clung to the duckboards like a second skin. Lanterns on posts shed thin halos that pushed maybe three yards before surrendering to dark mud. The forward redoubt's bulk lay beyond the wire, a squat silhouette, walls bristling with pike heads, banners limp in the wet wind.

Leonard tasted coal smoke, wet iron, and the faint copper whisper that rode the tower's distant heartbeat. Above the trench wall, the horizon bled from grey to leaden purple; the sun still hung below the ridge.

Near a sandbagged listening post, Darum stood with a clutch of officers, cloak hood back, the scar over his right brow catching weak lamplight. Even in half-armor he looked carved from the same stone as the barricades, scruff beard shot through with threads of silver. Rain turned to needles on his pauldrons. A raw-faced scout, couldn't be more than seventeen, stumbled through the muck toward them catching his breath.

"Sir," the scout said, voice cracking. "Movement inside the tower. Light like molten light ran the seams. We saw shapes past the doorline. Couldn't count them."

Darum's gaze hardened. "You got closer than last watch?"

"Fifty paces closer. Didn't dare more."

Leonard felt his stomach knot. Saran's hand touched his elbow, she felt it too. The scout's words matched the flare that still rang behind Leonard's ears. He opened his mouth to warn Darum.

Then the world fractured.

A line of black-violet light split the clouds over the valley, stabbing straight up from the tower's summit. The pulse ballooned, a corona of shimmering void that swallowed the upper sky and bled backward into dawn. Every lantern on the parapet spat sparks and died. The trench hissed as pitch lines guttered out.

Then came the wind like deep water surging through flesh, bending bones without breaking them. Leonard felt it crest three heartbeats before it arrived.

"DOWN!" he roared.

Saran obeyed without pause, shoulder-checking a bewildered pikeman behind her, dragging another warrior to the boards. Leonard threw himself to the ground.

The pressure washed over. Torches six yards away imploded, wood crackling inward instead of out. Warriors yelped, more from shock than pain. Vambraces sparked as incantation stones flared and snuffed. A canopy rope snapped, flinging soaked canvas across the trench like a flayed skin.

Sound vanished for a breath, replaced by a single note, the exact pattern Leonard had scrawled in tin, now vibrating through his fillings. Then the pressure broke, rain roaring back, men groaning.

Leonard lifted his head. Fog shredded across the trench line, revealing guards slumped against sandbags, hands pressing against their ears, some weeping silently. No bodies or blood. But a garrison struck dumb by an invisible choir.

Darum pushed upright near the listening post. He barked orders too quiet to hear over the ringing then spotted Leonard and Saran hauling the stunned warrior to his knees. A nod of grim approval crossed his scarred face.

The tower's light dwindled to ember, then nothing. But the silhouette looked wrong now, the edges softer, as though distance itself burned away.

Saran helped steady the warrior, then spat rainwater. "What in all storms was that?"

Leonard swallowed, throat raw. The note in his head faded, but residue lingered. "The pulse. Same shape as the numbers."

She wiped rain from her brow, braid dripping. "You yelled just in time. You're keeping that trick."

Darum strode over, mud sucking at his boots. "Report."

Leonard forced words through shock-stiff lips. "Signal before strike. I felt it, seconds only. Told those near me. Enough warning for them to drop."

Darum's eyes narrowed. He accepted the statement with a single curt nod. "Saved half a patrol from a concussive flash. Good."

Around them, officers dragged lantern boxes into new positions, tried to coax fire from damp tinder that hissed refuse. The fog drank lamp-glow quicker than before; color bled wrong where the tower still loomed.

A breeze pushed rain sideways, scraping glass. Not from the trench or from the tower.

Darum heard it too. "Orders will come from the wall," he muttered, almost to himself. "Until then we reinforce, get light back up, and stay ready."

Leonard stared at the distant black silhouette stabbing the sky, pulse spent but presence larger than ever. The silence afterwards made the air itself feel stretched.

Saran sheathed her damp sword, wiped her palm. "Think that was the start?"

Leonard answered without looking away. "No. I think that was the door opening."

He tasted iron again, stronger this time and the rain suddenly felt warmer on his skin. All along the parapet, people relit torches, blades bare and shaking. Somewhere behind the trench, a second horn called the redoubt to readiness.

The tower stood, mute guardian turned executioner, and every soul on the line understood dawn would rise on a different war.

2

The mist clung low on the berm, thick enough to choke a torch. Darum stood with one foot propped on a sunken sandbag, the ground beneath him saturated from the night's rain. The residue of the tower's pulse still rang in his bones, a thrum that lived just under the surface of hearing, neither pain nor comfort. He flexed his fingers, feeling the erratic spark in the incantation stone set into his palm. Light flickered in fitful pulses, bright one second, guttering the next.

The berm was barely more than a heap of dirt and tangled roots, but it marked the true edge of the forward line, past it, the ground dipped away to a ravine, and beyond that, only the Black Tower's silhouette stabbing through low clouds.

Behind Darum, Ravenblood archers worked fast in the half-light. Leather creaked, bowstrings were drawn and checked, fresh beeswax smeared along the lengths. The acolytes of the Stone Sages had lined up beneath a battered canvas tarp, their eyes hollow with exhaustion. Some whispered the litany of keeping, others pressed shaking hands to the small stones in their hands, willing them to stabilize. In the new silence, prayer and practicality ran together. No one wasted words or energy.

Ulzaan arrived without warning, his stride silent even across the mud. He was taller than Darum, with iron-gray at his temples and a face that rarely betrayed anything but tired calculation. He wore a battered half-cloak, the clasp engraved with the crest of the raven, and the faint glow of his incantation stone never dimmed. It was a steady inner lantern that set him apart from every other officer on the line.

Ulzaan paused beside Darum, gaze fixed on the distant tower. They stood in silence for a moment, listening to the hiss of rain against steel and the distant call of a watch-crow.

Finally, Ulzaan spoke, voice rough as worn leather. "How many stones failed?"

Darum glanced down the line, watched an acolyte fumble with a pendant until it sparked and died. "Half are dead. The rest flicker. Haven't seen that in my time, Fazrum stones aren't supposed to fail, not like this."

Ulzaan grunted, eyes tracking the flicker in Darum's gauntlet. "Yours too?"

"Mine's still alive, but it won't hold an edge. Surge, then nothing." Darum flexed his wrist. "Never seen one act like this. Heard old stories. Of cracked stones before Fazrum was even born. Never thought I'd see it myself."

Ulzaan's own stone glowed with a steady internal pulse, a heartbeat that never quite matched the rhythm of the world around it. "Old stories always talk about what comes after. Towers don't flare just to show themselves. They mark a border. When the light fades, something always comes through."

Darum glanced at the horizon. The Black Tower's corona had died back to a dull ember, but the sky still writhed, violet bleeding into ash, clouds shredded as if something huge had pressed through. "Any word from the high trench?"

Ulzaan shook his head. "Not yet. Signals stopped making sense after the flare. We're in the dark. Doesn't matter. We bind the flank now or never. Wait too long, and we won't have the stones or the men to do it."

Darum nodded, feeling the weight settle deeper in his chest. "You want the south end covered?"

"North, too. The Karthian vanguard's still moving, never seen them this quiet. Either they're hiding, or they're waiting for us to fall apart."

Darum smirked, the scar at his brow pulling taut. "I'd almost prefer them shouting. Quiet Karth means someone's already inside the wire."

Ulzaan's mouth twitched in something like agreement. "Set your line. No banners, no calls. I want shields up and bows drawn. If they test us, we bleed them, fast, quiet, and we hold. I'll pull the Sage Acolytes to the midline."

Darum turned to go, then paused. "Ulzaan, if the stones go completely, we're blind. No alarms, no wards. Nothing."

Ulzaan's eyes met his, hard as old iron. "If the stones go, we fight the old way. Metal and muscle. The kingdom didn't always have stones, Darum. We've got steel. Use it."

He left without another word, cloak snapping behind him, the glow of his stone painting fleeting shadows on the soaked earth.

Darum watched him disappear into the fog, then turned to the nearest archer, a broad-shouldered woman with a white streak in her braid and fresh mud caked to her boots. "Elin. Pass the word; bows up, shields up, quiet as the grave. No lights unless it's steel."

She nodded, eyes wide but steady. "Got it, sir."

The berm shifted as the rest of his squadron moved to cover the approach. Saran's voice floated up from behind a tangle of brambles, "Darum! Second team's up. They're covering the hollow. We've got maybe a handful with stones that'll still spark, but no one's sure how long."

Darum scanned the line. "Keep the archers close. Don't trust the wards, not tonight. If you see anything, anything at all, don't wait for a signal."

She gave a grim salute, black braid slick with rain. "Understood."

The wind shifted. Darum's incantation stone flickered, died, then pulsed once like a gasp. He flexed his hand, knuckles creaking. The frequency of the pulse still lived somewhere in the marrow of his bones. The air tasted of copper and broken wards.

He moved along the line, boots sinking into mud, offering a nod or a word to each small group. They didn't ask for speeches. The Ravenblood didn't do speeches. He watched the line form, bows half-drawn, swords slung loose, a half-dozen Sages pressing palms to flickering stones, sweat already slicking their foreheads. Nobody talked about fear, but nobody needed to. The pulse had shaken them all.

Near the end of the line, Darum paused, taking in the sight of the Black Tower looming in the east. The sky above it churned with purple clouds and the faint shimmer of wardlight dying out.

He rolled his shoulders, feeling the old aches resurface. The night wasn't done with them. Not by a long shot.

A distant sound, half-scream, half-bellow rippled through the fog from somewhere beyond the perimeter. Darum raised his blade, signaled for silence. Every archer froze, eyes wide, breath steaming in the cold.

Fog spilled over the berm, thick as wool and moving with a purpose that had nothing to do with the wind. It curled in off the hollow, obscuring the black earth and tangling around Darum's boots. The only clear things were the silhouettes of his own archers stiff with tension, arrows were drawn and held low, breaths measured in and out, barely fogging the air. Every heartbeat thumped louder, amplified by the pulse still humming beneath the skin.

A spotter's voice rang out from the battered wall at the far left. "Movement! North side! Fast, faster than horses—" The words cut off in a choked exhale.

Darum swept his gaze up, following the spotter's trembling finger. At first, there was only fog, denser than any natural mist. Then, an interruption. Not three shapes, not five, he lost count after the first dozen. Figures slipped and shuddered through the murk, bone-pale and thin, neither tall nor short, the kind of shape that looked wrong even in silhouette. They flickered with every stride, vanishing and reappearing feet ahead, as if the fog itself hid a break in the world's logic.

He narrowed his eyes. Even at this distance, he caught the first glint of color, eyes. An unnatural amber, set too wide in faces that seemed both human and not. They watched the line as if they could see straight through every man, every stone, every hidden fear.

A sergeant beside Darum, Meril, with the broken nose and an old wound running the length of his jaw breathed out, "Gods. Are those...?"

"No animals," Darum muttered. "Too organized. Not Karthian, either. Look at the way they move, don't even touch the ground half the time."

One of the Sage acolytes whispered something sharp and frantic, pressing his palm to the dim stone at his collar. "I can't feel them, not the way I should. They're not crossing the wards. They're inside already."

A wave of motion, one shape darted ahead, then another. They didn't charge or roar. They simply appeared, frame-skipping through the mist. Heads jerked at unnatural angles. Limbs, unfolded and retracted. A ripple, a stutter then another step closer.

The archers shifted, bows half-drawn. The leader, Elin, white streak flashing in her hair, called out, "Hold! Wait for my signal. Don't fire blind."

Darum's pulse ticked faster. He scanned for anything that looked like command, but the shapes seemed to operate as one mind, no voices or shouts. Only amber eyes in the dark, some small, some wide, all fixated on the living line.

In a pocket of denser fog, one shape flickered fully into view for half a breath. Its face was stretched, skull-like, mouth fixed in a fixed grin. Its torso twisted and realigned as if searching for a new axis.

A whisper moved down the line. "Those aren't men."

Darum braced, lifting his sword, and called quietly enough for his command to ripple but not echo, "Shields up! Hold until they break the wire!"

A single step then another flicker. The creatures never quite ran. They simply closed the gap. Amber eyes everywhere.

The fog thickened, swallowing the first ranks of razorwire, and the air filled with the faintest sound, a hum, not quite song, more like the frequency Leonard had described after the tower flare.

Darum gripped his sword tighter, knuckles white. This is what the pulse brought through. This is what we're for.

The first real contact was seconds away. The world shrank to the glint of amber eyes in the unnatural fog, and the waiting line of Ravenblood, silent but unbroken.

Darum moved before panic could set in. His voice, roughened by cold air and old command, cracked through the mist: "Spears forward! Anchor the left, Meril, on me! Hold the damn line!" His blade came up, catching the wavering light as the archers drew and steadied.

Ulzaan, cloak still slung over armor, strode to the edge of the berm with no hesitation. His left hand rose, palm out, stone embedded in the center of his palm burning suddenly with blinding white. The light cut through the fog like a blade, throwing monstrous shadows against the ground.

The creatures jerked back reflexively like a hive remembering an old pain. Their amber eyes flared wide. For a heartbeat, the world hung still.

Then they pressed in. Silent, fast, not breaking ranks but oozing through gaps, sliding between razorwire, their movement all wrong, as if the world itself didn't want them present.

"Brace!" Darum shouted, and the front line bent knees, spears leveled, shields locked. The first Ravager hit, a jolt of force, not a weight. Its body elongated in the lunge, mouth splitting wide. A spearhead punched through its ribcage. No blood, just a spasm. The thing's arm snapped backward, bone dislocating without pain, and it twisted around the shaft, tearing the spear from the Ravenblood's hands and using the leverage to launch itself at the next man in line.

Another Ravager followed, thinner this time, its face a blur of flickering angles. It took three spears to slow it, and still it writhed up the hafts, claws raking at shields, shrieking now in a way that vibrated more in the skull than the ear.

Steel cut, but didn't kill. A third, this one broader, jaw hanging loose swept an arm and sent two men flying, their armor ringing as they hit the ground. Darum surged forward, voice raw: "Hold!" He threw himself between the creature and his men, his own incantation-stone pulsing erratically.

He slammed his palm into the Ravager's chest. White fire seared the fog, the impact sending a sharp, nauseating jolt up Darum's arm. The creature convulsed its skin charring, the amber glow in its eyes flaring and then flickering out as it crashed to the mud, limbs still twitching.

Darum staggered, pain lancing through his arm, vision tunneling. He tasted copper, the price of channeling too hard, too fast. "Fazrum magic, on the forward!" he barked, not waiting for breath to return.

Ulzaan's light intensified, the fog boiling back with each pulse. The creatures recoiled, slower now, but not breaking merely adapting, their limbs resetting in grotesque patterns.

A chorus of steel and stone, chaos straining to become order. Behind him, the Sages shouted incantations in a desperate attempt to keep the wards active.

Darum sucked air, fighting the urge to collapse. If they breach, it's over. If we falter....

Another Ravager clawed at his armour, jaw wide enough to split a man's torso. Darum drove his blade up under the chin, wrenching it free as the head snapped backward, mouth still gaping.

For a moment, the line held, the dead and dying shifting shapes twitching at their feet. But the fog thickened again, more movement behind it.

He gritted his teeth, forcing his battered stone to flare again. Around him, Ravenblood warriors found new resolve not because of hope, but because the alternative was annihilation. Ulzaan shouted. "Form tight! Press them to the berm! Ravenblood on me!"

Light blazed, the creatures recoiled, and the ground beneath the fog became a killing floor, one that took as much from its defenders as it did from the enemy.

A Ravager, twice the size of the others and stitched with cables of bone, hurled itself over the trench wall. It landed amid the defenders with a hideous shriek, claws flaying in the air, and seized a Ravenblood archer by the chest. The man's scream cut short as he was flung, body tumbling end over end until it vanished behind the rampart.

"Reinforcements! On me!" Darum roared, already moving, eyes sweeping for a solution even as the line faltered. He locked eyes with a knot of guards further back who were hesitating, their faces half-formed in fear and doctrine. Behind them, a Karthian figure still in cuffs.

A sentry dragged Idran forward, shoving him through the melee's swirl. Idran's dark hair was slick with sweat, mud spattered up the hem of his grey cloak. He said nothing, just fixed his gaze on the flickering ward-torches, watching them gutter and spit.

Darum's blade came up, distrust plain in his clenched jaw. "Can you fix it?" He barked the words, voice slicing through the chaos.

Idran nodded, his eyes flat. "Yes. But I need a hand free."

Darum's hesitation lasted only a moment then he drew his knife and slashed the blacklink cord from Idran's right wrist. The cord hissed as it parted, the freed wrist mottled with the aftermath of its binding.

Idran flexed his hand once, winced, then pressed his thumb to a sliver of blue crystal set in the cuff. It broke with a sharp pop. He dragged the dust along the grooves in his forearm, humming a note low and broken, a triad of Karthian power, old and dissonant, forbidden on this side of the border.

The air snapped. The closest Ravager was still crouched, its jaw wide, seized mid-leap. Hairline cracks ran along its outer carapace, the lines glowing with cold fire. The monster's leap faltered, its shell splintering.

"Now, fire!" Darum yelled.

A hail of arrows followed, one, two, five, each shaft punching through the cracked armor. The creature convulsed, dropped, and did not rise.

A moment of stunned silence overtook the trench. Several Ravenblood warriors, spattered with muck and blood, took cautious steps away from Idran, muttering "shard-breaker" under their breath. Some with awe, more with suspicion.

Idran didn't react. He cleaned the dust from his palm and waited, eyes never leaving the fog.

Darum let the tension ride, pragmatism outweighing prejudice for now. "You stand by me until this is over," he growled. Idran nodded once, no argument in him.

But there was no respite.

A low rumble started beneath their boots, a subsonic vibration that set shields trembling on their racks. The fog thickened, turning leaden and close. Shapes emerged, more ravagers, larger and stranger, their silhouettes distorted by new mutations. One had a jaw fused entirely shut, the lower half split into two spine-like limbs that scraped against the earth as it moved.

Sentries at the rear cried out. The line buckled, men glancing over shoulders, courage stretched to breaking.

Ulzaan didn't hesitate. He strode into the thick of the fray, his incantation stone blazing at his palm, and drove his palm into the ground. A pulse of molten light ripped from his hand, forking across the trench like a living wave of light. Where it struck Ravagers, they simply ceased, bone and flesh vaporized in a flash, leaving only smoking heaps behind.

The trench lit up from fog-line to watchtower, the haze burned away in that radius. For a heartbeat, the earth itself seemed to scream.

When the brilliance faded, a wide swath of no man's land was scoured clear, only blackened marks and mounds of dissolving bone remained.

Ulzaan staggered, just for a moment, his hand shaking before he clamped it tight against his side. Darum's gaze flickered. He saw the cost. The uncertainty. For the first time, the Strategos had bled power, and it showed.

No one spoke it. But Darum felt the change. Ulzaan has limits?

The rest of the Ravagers didn't retreat in any ordinary way, half simply collapsed, twitching into piles of writhing limbs and bone splinters, their forms unfolding into the mud like bad dreams. The others melted back into the fog, vanishing before any volley could find them. The air was left ringing, warbled, the world a momentary echo chamber of pulse and death.

No one counted bodies, not yet. The dead were sprawled across both sides, limbs caught at unnatural angles, steel and bone mixed in the churned earth. The living were breathing hard, blood and fog thick in their lungs.

Darum's incantation stone pulsed at his wrist, still bright but unsteady, the inner glow flickering in sync with his heartbeat. He ignored the ache and turned sharply to Idran, who stood a few paces off, sleeves rolled back, fragments of blue stone dust still clinging to his forearm.

"What the hell did you just do?" Darum demanded, voice edged and hoarse.

Idran met his gaze, unreadable. "Your stones are out of phase. The tower's resonance distorts them, scrambles their channeling, makes them unstable. Karthian stonework is tuned for it. Yours is built for tradition, not adaptation."

Darum bristled, his jaw working. "So what? You're telling me Karth makes better weapons?"

Idran shrugged, face like granite. "Not weapons. Instruments. Ours listen better, that's all. Doesn't matter if you like it or not."

Before Darum could snap a reply, Ulzaan's shadow fell between them. The Strategos moved with the fatigue of spent magic, his eyes sharp and cold.

"Enough," Ulzaan cut in, his voice brooking no argument. "This is no time for border feuds or lectures. We hold the line, tend the wounded, and regroup. Whatever the hell just happened it's not over. And it's not to be explained away by doctrine."

He looked out at the battered trenchline, the battered soldiers, the fog creeping back toward the tower. "Move. All of you. We need answers. Now."

Officers peeled away, barking orders. Healers waded in with stretchers, gathering those still breathing. Archers scavenged arrows,

Sage acolytes drew old wards anew over the berm, hands trembling with exhaustion and fear.

Darum gave Idran a last look, not quite in trust. "Stay close," he said, voice low. "You're not done here."

Idran nodded once, lips pressed thin. "Wouldn't dream of it."

In the heavy, uncertain quiet, the fog thickened again. The Black Tower, distant and gleaming with a faint sickly light, seemed to pulse in time with every wound on the field. Whatever storm had begun, it was only just gathering force.

3

The last of the fighting had faded into mud and the scent of scorched bone, but the noise still clung to Leonard's ears. He stood outside the battered redoubt, boots planted in a churn of trampled grass and spent arrow shafts. The trench walls sagged in places, fresh stonework blackened and already pitted where Ravager blood had burned its way through. Smoke hung over the field, stubborn and bitter, refusing to lift. Through the haze, bodies were being dragged clear, some covered, some not.

Saran stood beside him, her black hair twisted into a tight braid, face streaked with fresh fatigue. She reached for her vambrace, flexing the leather where a new cut had marred its edge. "You're not the only one left out, you know," she said, her voice pitched low to blend with the wind. "Ulzaan kept back half his best, just in case the tower tried for a second round."

Leonard just stared at the horizon, jaw tight, fists balled at his sides. "It's not the same. I hear it first, but they won't let me do anything. What's the point of hearing it if I can't help?" His words bit sharper than he meant, the pressure of it all crawling up his spine.

She nudged him, shoulder against shoulder, not quite teasing. "You helped. Half the camp ducked because you shouted. They'll remember that. I'd take a pissed-off Leonard over a dead Saran any day."

He shook his head, not ready to let go. "Doesn't feel like it counts. Feels like I'm locked in the barracks while the world burns."

Saran's smile was thin, tired. "That's the job, sometimes. Survive, then do it again." She paused, nodding toward the redoubt's heavy door. "Come on. They'll want us inside before the next round hits."

The two of them stepped through the battered entryway, leaving the smoke and bitter air behind. Inside, the war-room glowed in the uncertain light of torch stubs, too many burned low, their scent fighting with the stench of blood, ink, and something sharp and chemical. Old maps were tacked to every board and table, black with troop marks and annotations layered thick enough to blur the lines.

Leonard paused at the threshold, letting his eyes adjust. The room was already crowded: officers hunched over ledgers, messengers pressed against walls, acolytes patching wounds and tending those who'd caught the worst of the blast. All of them looked hollowed out, faces drawn and eyes red at the rims. Fatigue echoed everywhere, barely suppressed arguments, slumped shoulders, hands trembling as they gripped mugs or weapons.

Ulzaan stood at the center, massive as ever, posture rigid except for the gauntleted hand that pressed down along the edge of the main war-map. Troop lines were scratched in ink and soot, the lines shivering as the surface shook with every movement. Leonard saw the tremor in Ulzaan's fist, a faint, rhythmic shudder. He said nothing. The room ran on the last dregs of order because Ulzaan was here. If he cracked, the whole command might shatter.

Near the door, half-shadowed by a pillar, Idran lingered. His wrists still looped with iron and black cord, one hand free, the other gloved and tense at his side. His gaze drifted from face to face, always wary. Leonard met his eyes, just for a second, and there was recognition, not quite kinship, but an understanding that ran deeper than banners or oaths.

Saran leaned closer, voice just above a whisper. "They look like hell."

Leonard nodded. "We all do."

They moved deeper into the flickering half-light, the war-room pulsing with the weight of what had just been survived, and what still waited outside.

A man in battered parade armor stepped to the front of the war-table, gold edging dulled by grime and fresh soot. His jaw was dark with stubble, his Fazrum uniform cut sharp even in defeat. He swept a hand over the mess of maps, knuckles white where they pressed down.

"Reports from the border," he began, voice trained for command but straining with exhaustion, "Mirevale, Trossin, and Harrowfield, all gone. Razed within hours. Our outriders never got a warning through. When they reached the smoke, there was nothing left but splinters and bodies. No resistance worth the name." His accent was old city, clipped. "Stones are acting wrong. Half our acolytes couldn't light a signal flare, the others nearly burned themselves out. I have no explanation."

He glanced around, eyes lingering on the Ravenblood, the Karthian, even the lesser field officers. "For those who haven't had the pleasure, Colonel Val Drast, Fazrum command." He tapped the edge of a broken ward-token for emphasis, then stepped back.

A second voice, rough and lower, cut in from near the fire gutter. "That matches what we saw north of Trossin. I led the advance myself, nothing left but scrap iron and bones, and a stink like old rot. Survivors didn't talk about men, or even beasts. They said 'things that weren't shaped right,' arms on backward, jaws splitting down the side. Tower pulsed right before it hit, and said they felt it in the ground."

The speaker was broad-shouldered, hair shorn to the scalp and old burn scars climbing his jaw. He wore the deep black of a Ravenblood field-commander, with the battered badge of a man who'd survived more than one border collapse. "Thane Ederic," he added. "We've posted a double watch on the trenches, but nothing's coming out now but smoke."

On the other side of the map, Eleseth, thin and spectral in her old sage robes, cleared her throat and gestured to a wax-sealed scroll. "It wasn't just the towns. Three wardstones cracked at the same hour. One at the southern bridge, two more along the old Karthian line. Whoever, or whatever sent the pulse didn't care about the border. They hit us everywhere at once."

A low murmur ran through the room. Ulzaan only grunted, the war-map trembling beneath his gauntlet. He did not argue. He didn't need to. With a curt nod, he turned his gaze to Darum, giving silent permission and burden to speak next.

Darum shifted his weight, boots ringing softly on stone. The fresh gash along his temple made his features harsher than usual, the greying scruff across his jaw accenting lines that hadn't been there a year ago. When he spoke, his voice was steady, but there was an edge to it, the kind that only came from losing more than you could name.

"We all know what started this," he said, meeting Ulzaan's gaze, then letting his eyes move to each officer in turn. "The tomb of the First King, desecrated, remains gone. No sign of resistance. That wasn't some Karthian raid or mercenary infiltration. Since then, it hasn't been a war. It's been a demolition. Fazrum towns first, but Karthian lines got hit next. None of it random. Someone's following a pattern we haven't caught up to yet."

He let the silence hang a moment, then looked toward the end of the table where a new court official stood, a slender man in a charcoal cloak, hair slicked back, eyes sharp behind wireframe lenses. The man tapped a sheaf of parchment, voice careful and too smooth by half.

"Darum speaks to the events as we have them," the official said. "But we must add: Samric, our late ritual secretary, vanished soon after the king's tomb was disturbed. Left behind only falsified orders, altered ritual permissions, and the mark of someone covering their tracks with skill. His last seal was used to open the sage archives, then nothing. No trail. No allies willing to claim him."

Idran, still cuffed but holding himself with the calm arrogance of someone used to being watched, spoke next. His accent was thicker now, more Karthian. "Our stonecraft in Karth, same pulses, same cracks. We felt it two nights after Fazrum did. The old stories said nothing about this scale, not with two towers active at once. Someone's done more than desecrate a tomb. They've reactivated a conduit."

Across the table, Leonard barely heard the words. His skull still thrummed with that same pressure, the note that had started with the first flare. Every so often, the war-table's iron rim would seem to vibrate with it, as if his own bones were caught in the resonance. He didn't speak, but the tension in his jaw made it clear, for him, the disaster hadn't stopped since the first signal.

General Orvek's uniform was streaked with blood at the cuff, his breastplate still marked from the trench hours before. He leaned over the war-table, voice carrying across the flickering torchlight.

"Let's not pretend," Orvek said, pointing a finger at Leonard from across the table. "You, Ravenblood. You felt the tower before it blew. Your eyes—" He gestured, not quite subtle, at the amber in Leonard's gaze, the color strange even in the dim hall. "I saw you drop before the rest. So I'll ask: What are you? What's in your blood that made the stones answer you before anyone else?"

The room went quiet. Leonard stared at the table, jaw working, trying to find words. He thought of the numbers he'd scrawled in the barracks, the diagram hidden deep in his kit. He didn't have a real answer. All he knew was the way the signal burned through his skull, familiar now, almost comforting in its wrongness.

He looked up, feeling every set of eyes, from Orvek to Ulzaan, burning holes through him. "I don't know," he said, voice lower than he meant. "I heard it. That's all. I always hear it before it happens. Not just the tone, the pattern. It's like it's waiting for me to listen."

There was a pause. Idran shifted, his cuffs rattling. "Fazrum doctrine doesn't like to admit it, but resonance matters. Some are tuned closer to the stones. In Karth, we teach that every stone has a frequency, sometimes a person lines up with it." He met Orvek's gaze, then flicked his eyes to Leonard. "He's not just sensitive. He resonates. That's why he heard the pulse before anyone else."

Darum slammed his palm against the map, the movement sharp

enough to make ink splash across the parchment. "Karthian idealism," he snapped. "You make it sound like a gift. In Fazrum, we know what happens to people who get too close to the old powers, they end up twisted, used, or dead. Don't turn this into a theory. He's not a tool, and he's not your damn test subject."

The table shivered with the sudden tension. Leonard just watched, the note humming in his teeth, feeling the argument wash over him like the world was talking about a body he wasn't quite in.

Idran's gaze was cold and precise. He shifted in his shackles, voice cutting through the rising squall of argument. "You're all fighting over the symptom, not the cause. The towers aren't just anchors, they're conduits. Someone has started sending signals through them, but it's incomplete. Distorted. Not meant for us, not at first. What comes through, it's fragments. Pieces that belong to something older than either kingdom dares to admit."

He looked to Leonard for a moment, then back at the crowd. "When the first pulse hit Karth, our stones responded not in defense, but in recognition. That's not invasion, that's resonance. Whoever did this, they're not opening a door, they're testing the wires."

Eleseth, hood low over pale eyes, didn't miss a beat. "No. The towers weren't built to open into the void. They were meant to open from it. We're not keeping the darkness out. We're inviting it to answer. The old pacts, the architecture, none of it was built for this kind of signal."

A heavy silence fell. Captain Vall, a Ravenblood field commander, spoke for the first time since entering, his voice worn raw by recent horror. "Then what accepted the invitation?"

The question lingered. No one offered an answer.

Tannis, the court official, broke the silence, his tone brittle. "The king will need more than testimony and theory. If we're to risk the capitol, we need proof. Orders won't be given on the word of a Karthian envoy and a stone-sensitive child."

Orvek nearly spat, palm slamming the table. "You want evidence? Look at the field outside this redoubt. I lost two patrols to creatures that weren't shaped right, wards cracked like eggs, and the tower's shadow crawls all the way over the horizon. If that's not evidence, then you deserve what's coming."

The voices rose, accusations traded like knives, reckless sorcery from Karth, cowardice and arrogance from Fazrum, both sides unwilling to cede the argument. Over it all, the pulse from the tower seemed to vibrate through the room itself, a quiet, unceasing pressure that made it clear: whatever was happening, they were already too late to keep it out.

Saran stepped forward, chin raised, voice steady despite the sting in the air. "If you're going to argue over proof, at least speak to someone who's actually seen it. I was there when the rift broke. I watched it burn through a squad in seconds. I carried two men out who'll never fight again."

Her words barely faded before a voice from the far side, Vall with a blood-stained sleeve, eyes hollowed by fatigue cut across. "You were a neophyte not too long ago. What gives you the right to attend this meeting?"

A ripple of low agreement, some muttered, some silent but evident in the eyes darting around the room. Saran didn't flinch. "I didn't come for a seat. I came because you keep asking who saw the truth. Leonard and I—" she gestured, the habit of partnership visible even now, "—were close enough to hear what the tower did, and survive it."

Ulzaan, who until now had watched the argument with cold restraint, let his hand drop to the table. The room stilled. "She's here because she's bled for both sides of this war," he said, voice iron. "And because Leonard trusts her judgment over any doctrine or rank."

Leonard, surprised at being put so squarely in the spotlight, nodded. His voice was quieter, but it carried. "Saran was there. She saw what happened when the rift opened, what it did to me. I wouldn't be here without her. You want a witness, you've got it."

That changed the temperature in the room, a handful of hard faces grudgingly looked her way now, seeing not just a survivor but a necessary witness. The debate lurched onward, but the shape of the table had shifted. Saran stayed standing, not needing a chair for her authority.

The Ravenblood field commander, Vall, spoke up first, his voice sharp with command. "We seal the southern borders, lock down the crossings, and pull the outliers back. Every day we wait, we lose more ground. If these things come again, I want a wall of iron between them and Fazrum."

General Orvek's fingers tapping against the hilt of his sword countered, "Recall every Pact operator from the frontier. Prepare for a full campaign. If this is war, we treat it as war. Half-measures brought us here."

The court official Tannis, thin-lipped, robes marked by the king's sigil lifted a hand. "This assembly oversteps. We await clarification from the king. To act rashly now, without the full authority of the crown, is to invite chaos."

Eleseth's voice, low but urgent, sliced through the growing noise. "The towers won't wait for your messages or your crown. Every minute the pulse spreads, it fractures more wards. You want to wait for orders, by the time they arrive, we'll be sifting bone from ash."

Idran, still at the periphery, stepped forward, his voice had the distant edge of Karth stone, precise and faintly mocking. "You argue doctrine while the signal warps. I've heard the resonance up close. Only by proximity can we decipher it. I volunteer to go, to the tower. Let those who understand stone handle what stone began. Let me guide the boy"

A stir, someone began to object, the start of a protest rising in the throat of an officer or a bureaucrat, but it faltered. Ulzaan, silent until now, stood straighter, presence radiating authority. The room turned.

All eyes landed on Leonard.

He felt the weight of a hundred eyes, the pressure of their fear and expectation as sudden as a punch to the ribs. The world shrank to the smear of lamplight on the war-map, the line of blood along Ulzaan's gauntlet, the pulse still echoing in his skull. He saw it again, the flare, the sky torn open, the void-wind flooding trenches and lungs, the sound only he had heard.

He swallowed, found his voice. "I can't explain it," he said. "Not in your words, not in anyone's. But I hear it. Not just the pulse or the tone, it's like... an intention. Like someone on the other side is waiting for an answer."

He glanced at Saran, at Darum, at Idran's bound hands. "I'll go. Not because I know what I'm doing. But because I'm tired of standing here while the world breaks open."

Ulzaan nodded, ironclad, the decision already in his eyes. "So be it. We are spread thin as we are so a small team will go. Leonard, Idran, Saran, Darum, you'll approach the tower quietly. No banners and no escorts. The rest is a distraction. I'll return to Fazrum and prepare the defense with Brent who is holding down our home in my absence. If they come for the capital, they'll find it ready.

A mutter of protest from Orvek and Tannis but in the end none dared challenge Ulzaan's word directly, not with the room poised on the edge of panic. One by one, voices died, faces turned down or away.

The decision was final. The night pressed in, heavy as the air before a storm.

Leonard stood, feeling the ground shift beneath him. His choice had become the axis of the war, and as he met Saran's eyes, her steady, unwavering nod, he knew there was no turning back.

The meeting dissolved in a scatter of orders and strained silences, boots clattering across stone and mud as commanders peeled off toward their duties. Leonard stepped out into the bitter air, letting the door thud shut behind him. The cold hit his cheeks, sharp and waking; campfires guttered along the lines, smoke drifting flat under the threat of another storm. The war-torn redoubt had gone quiet except for the distant grind of stretcher-bearers and the quiet murmur of sentries trading watch shifts.

He paused at the edge of the boardwalk, letting the cold settle into his bones. His eyes adjusted to the dark across the tangle of trenches, he caught a flicker, a solitary lantern bobbing along the wall haloed in the fog. For a moment, the light flared amber. His pulse spiked when he noticed a faint silhouette of a grey cloak, was it just a trick of the wind, or something else? It vanished behind a barricade.

Saran's boots sounded behind him, lighter than most. She pressed a battered canteen into his hand without a word, her braid dusted with rain, eyes shadowed but steady. "Drink," she said quietly, not quite an order. "You'll need it."

He took a long pull, the water cold, bracing. The night stretched in all directions, somewhere behind them, the camp pulsed with nervous life. Ahead, the trenchline and mud ran all the way to the horizon, and farther out, the black silhouette of the tower loomed, massive and indifferent, its broken peak lost in the clouds.

Saran stood with him a moment, silent, her presence a steady anchor. Neither spoke of what came next. The air between them carried the taste of iron and distant thunder.

Above, the tower's outline held. Whatever signal had started, it hadn't ended.

Leonard stared at it, the world shrinking to cold breath and waiting, and thought, not for the first time, that whatever answered out there, it was watching back.

4

Leonard's breath fogged in the still air as he crouched at the edge of the trench, boots sunk deep in the mud. He worked through his kit. Bedroll rolled too tight, ration bag fraying, the familiar ache of his vambrace straps chafing his wrist. Everything felt worn, as if this new war and the road had managed to grind down even the SkySteel. A lantern guttered behind him, its oil running low, the weak glow fighting the grey mist that clung to the lines.

Somewhere farther along the duckboards, Saran cursed softly at her pack. She shoved aside a sack of dried root and cheese, then muttered to herself in an irritable voice. "If I ever see another smoked beetroot, I'll throw it straight at the quartermaster." She gave up trying to coax a half-starved horse any closer. The animal danced sideways, its eyes white, nostrils flaring at the scent rolling off the fields to the north.

"Why do I even bother?" she called to Leonard, yanking her braid tighter. "They feel the tower before we do. Wouldn't drag the poor bastard two steps past the outer ward. We're walking."

Leonard straightened, slinging his pack over one shoulder. "It's just as well. We'd be on foot by noon anyway, the way that thing's burning through the ground."

Saran looked over, boots caked in the sludge that passed for earth here. Her features were drawn in the half-light, dark circles beneath her eyes, her jaw set like stone. "You sleep at all?" she asked, pretending to check the straps on her shoulder plate.

"Not really." He flexed his hand, feeling the ache in his knuckles. "Didn't want to. And if I did it wouldn't help anyway."

She pulled a battered flask from her belt and tossed it his way. "Here. Swear that's all the good drink left in the camp. If we're marching into whatever that was the last battle, might as well pretend we're alive."

He caught it, took a swallow, coughed at the bitterness. It was barely warm but better than nothing. "What's the word from the scouts?"

Saran shook her head. "No word worth a damn. Nobody wants to get close enough to see if the ground still moves out there. The last group sent their dog first, it howled once and bolted, broke its leash. They haven't seen it since."

Leonard looked north, where the sun tried to burn through the mist and failed. The tower's shadow didn't reach this far, but the air still felt different, like something old had crawled out and refused to be named. "Doesn't feel like the last time," he said quietly. "The first flare was just... light. Now it's like it's pressing back. Like it's waiting."

Saran tightened her chestplate and glanced at him, more serious than usual. "We don't have to play heroes, you know. There are ways to say no."

Leonard hesitated, then shook his head. "You'd do the same. Besides, it's not about being brave. It's about not letting the wrong person get there first."

For a moment, neither of them moved. The camp behind was starting to stir, officers shouting, stretchers moving, the hollow rhythm of boots and barked orders. But here, for just a breath, it was just the two of them and the mud, and the long road ahead.

Saran broke the silence. "You sure you're up for this?"

Leonard looked at her, really looked, at the fatigue behind her sharpness, the way she checked the world before checking herself.

"I'm not sure of anything," he admitted, voice raw. "But I'm going anyway."

She nodded, meeting his eyes without flinching. "That's the right answer."

He let out a breath, half a laugh, feeling the knot in his chest ease just a little. The mist shifted as the wind changed, and the weight of what waited beyond the trenches pressed in, heavy but not alone.

The fog thickened around the outer trenchline as a lone figure approached, boots squelching in mud, the heavy drag of travel layered over the more deliberate tension of someone who'd spent the morning waiting for a summons that didn't come.

Idran stepped into view with the rigid composure of a man who knew exactly how many eyes were on him. His cloak was deep blue, Karthian make, fastened with a stamped silver clasp. The rest of his gear looked ceremonial at first glance, a clean tunic, pressed collar, but there was mud up to his knees and the faint scrape of grit on his boots. He carried nothing in his hands, but every movement was careful. If he felt the cold, he ignored it.

Leonard straightened as he drew near, instinctively checking for weapons, an old habit, hard to break. Idran's gaze flicked between him and Saran, quick and analytic, but not hostile.

He offered a bow, just shallow enough to be formal. "Idran of Karth, third of Trast. Pledged envoy." His voice was smooth, almost mild, but something sharp lived in the undertone. "I am glad we may be formally introduced to each other, a war meeting is no place for pleasantries."

Leonard nodded, catching himself before glancing down at his hands. "Likewise"

Saran's arms stayed folded, her expression set somewhere between polite and skeptical. "You're early, for a man with a Karthian escort. Changed your mind about traveling with a bodyguard?"

Idran's mouth twitched at the edge, "I suspect they were as eager to see me gone as you are to see me here. Besides—" he dusted off the worst of the mud with a gloved hand, "—the job called for fewer banners."

Leonard studied the newcomer. Idran looked younger up close than Leonard expected, but there was something old in the set of his jaw, the careful way he let the conversation move around him. "Why'd you take this?" Leonard asked, words more direct than he'd planned. "It's not exactly a task most people would fight for."

Idran didn't flinch. He met Leonard's gaze head-on, that Karth steel under the surface. "Sometimes the job chooses you. My family's name got me the scroll. Karth needed someone visible, expendable, and easy to recall if it all goes wrong. That's the official story."

Saran cocked an eyebrow. "And the unofficial?"

He gave her a sideways look, less guarded now. "It's simple. I'm tired of being the weapon in someone else's hand. I'm tired of being proof that Karth can play diplomat when it's convenient. I wanted something that belonged to me." He shrugged, as if that admission cost nothing. "If I can prove I'm more than just a noble's placeholder, maybe the next time they ask for a volunteer, I get to say no."

Leonard heard the tone under the words, a worn kind of honesty. "Sounds familiar," he said quietly. "Having to play a part you never chose."

Idran looked at him, a hint of real recognition in his eyes. "I thought it might."

Saran's posture didn't loosen, but she nodded once, slowly. "We don't have to like it. Just have to get there in one piece."

"Agreed," Idran replied, still formal, but the sharp edge was dulled. "Let's not pretend we trust each other, but let's not sabotage ourselves either."

The three of them stood a moment in the shadow of the trench wall, the silence settling with the weight of what they'd just agreed to, uneasy, but real. The wind pulled at their cloaks, and somewhere behind them, the camp's morning routine pressed on. Out here, it felt like the road ahead had just shifted.

Darum approached from the rear of the encampment, cloak snapped tight against his battered armor, a coil of rope slung at his hip. The old, familiar scruff on his jaw looked a day rougher than usual, gray threading the black. His eyes cut immediately to Leonard and Saran, a nod for each, comfortable in the way of people who've bled together. When his gaze settled on Idran, there was no greeting, but a slow assessment you'd give a stranger who might be holding a knife behind his back.

"About time we got all the pieces on the board," Darum said, voice gravelly from too many nights in the cold. "No speeches. You know what this is."

He let his hand rest on the hilt at his belt, casual but not careless. "We're heading for the tower. Nobody's kidding themselves about why. The last time it pulsed, half our stones went dead and the trenches almost emptied. That won't happen again if I can help it."

He looked at Leonard, something steady and private in the way his gaze lingered. "Your job is to keep breathing and to listen. If the tower speaks to you, if you get even a tremor like before, you say so, no matter how small. This isn't the time to be a hero, or to keep secrets."

Saran shot Darum a dry look, but her shoulders eased a little as he spoke. "He knows," she said, backing him up without fuss.

Darum turned to Idran, the line of his mouth set. "You. I don't care about Karth's treaties or what they promised you in exchange for this little walk. You're here because you know things we don't, or so you say, and because Ulzaan thinks you're worth the risk. Don't make me regret it."

Idran met his stare, cool and unblinking. "My orders are the same as yours, Darum, is it? Get answers. Get out alive."

A short silence hummed between them, not yet hostility, but a test of intent.

"Good," Darum said at last, shifting the pack on his shoulder. "Then let's keep it simple. We scout the Black Tower, get eyes on whatever's rotting it from the inside, and if we're lucky bring back enough proof to justify this insanity. We do it quiet. We do it together. And above all—" he jerked his chin toward Leonard "—we keep him alive. Like it or not, the game's changed, and none of us are walking out if we lose our best piece."

He turned to the group, letting the words settle. "Questions? Ask them now. Once we cross that line, it's all mud and silence."

Idran grunted. "Let's have it out, then. Which path?"

Saran didn't wait. "The lower valley. We skirt the marsh, follow the old grain route. My old village sits halfway, if we need to hole up, there's shelter. I know the ground. It's not fast, but it's quiet, and there's a chance we'll find old stores or a dry barn."

Idran shook his head, arms crossed, boots still muddy from the night before. "Slower means more exposure. The old trade road's direct, we cut days off the march. Yes, there's rift-bleed, but it's mapped, and I have experience with unstable terrain, my homeland is full of it. We avoid the worst pockets and push straight through. Less time in the open."

Saran's jaw set, black braid twitching as she looked at Darum for backup. "You didn't see what happened last time that trade road twisted on itself. A whole patrol vanished, no trace, just static and blackened earth. My village may be abandoned, but it's real. The trade road isn't, not when the tower pulses."

Idran's reply was measured but sharp, each word weighed for effect. "Your village is familiar, yes, but it's on the Fazrum side. Anyone watching for us will check those roads. The riftfields are unpredictable, but so are patrols. If we're seen, we're as good as marked before we get close."

Darum snorted, a humorless edge in his tone. "Funny, hearing a Karthian argue for efficiency. Last war, you couldn't walk a mile in a straight line without losing half your scouts to mud and magic."

Idran met the jab with a cold smile. "Last war, we didn't lose half a country to tower-flare. We learned. I don't gamble with other people's lives."

For a beat, nobody spoke. The silence stretched, only the morning wind and the distant clang of the camp behind them.

Saran looked at Leonard, eyes searching his face. "You know I'm not just being sentimental. It's the safer way if things go wrong."

Idran watched Leonard as well. "We're running out of time, and the fewer steps between here and the tower, the better our chances."

Darum stayed out of it, arms folded, lips twitching as he watched Leonard. "Well? You've got both roads in front of you, lad. You make the call."

Leonard felt their eyes settle on him, the weight of the choice more real than any command he'd received before. The tower waited, either way, a shape in the mist, growing closer with every step, no matter which road they took.

He let the silence stretch just long enough to feel it in his bones. He looked down the line of battered gear, then out toward the haze where the valley path would wind away from the trenches, half-remembered from maps and Saran's stories. He tried to picture the trade road, straight, the rift-scarred hills pressing close on either side. The Karthian's route would get them there faster, maybe, but speed wasn't what lingered in his mind.

He thought about the last time they'd taken the fast way, how the landscape itself seemed to twist, time and distance stretching like old scars. He remembered Saran's tired voice, a note of longing beneath her insistence. An old home, even ruined, might mean food. Shelter. Or just a moment where they didn't have to keep running.

He drew a breath, glancing at each of them, Darum's weathered patience, Saran's stubborn hope, Idran's sharp reserve.

"We take the valley," Leonard said. "If something goes wrong, I'd rather have a roof, even if it's a broken one. And if the ground shifts under us, at least Saran knows where the cracks run."

Saran's relief was almost invisible, a softening at the corners of her eyes. "I'll get us there," she said. "Or as close as what's left allows."

Idran's nod was small, "Understood. You're in command, then." His tone was clipped, no argument, but a trace of cool assessment lingered beneath the words. He shouldered his pack with efficiency.

Darum just grunted approval and started moving, his usual stride a signal for the rest to fall in. "Let's not wait for the next pulse to decide for us," he said, already scanning the horizon.

As they set out, four figures carrying too many doubts and too little certainty, the group's energy shifted, wary but functional. No open harmony, but the gears meshed, at least for now.

Leonard fell in beside Saran, the first uncertain steps toward her past, and all their futures echoing in the damp grass behind them.

5

The wind carried a sullen grit as they moved along the broken road, clouds dragging their bellies low over the rolling hills. Birds didn't sing, just the slow shuffle of boots and the muted clatter of gear. The old valley road followed the spine of the land, a line of cracked stone slabs half-swallowed by wild grass and rain-carved tracks. Ruins rose at intervals on either side: the sagging remnants of farmsteads, a burnt barn leaning like a drunk, the collapsed arch of a bridge that no longer spanned anything but mud.

Leonard fell into step beside Idran, who walked with an upright, clipped stride. The Karthian's cloak snapped in the wind, catching the pale light, boots still caked in trench mud but laced with the fastidious care of a man raised on noble discipline and old pride.

They walked a hundred paces before Leonard spoke, voice low to avoid carrying back to the others. "You lived in the last war, didn't you? Not just drills, I mean. Real lines, real city walls?"

Idran's eyes flickered sideways, a short pause before answering. "I was there at the end. My family, House Trast, argued for peace before the blood ran too deep. But peace is a word in the mouth of the desperate, not the powerful."

Leonard frowned, uncertain. "In Fazrum they teach the war as a lesson. Say Karth bled itself dry with infighting. That we only pushed when the mines at Raal went dark."

Idran's jaw tightened, the lines in his cheeks more shadow than flesh. "Fazrum always needed a story that left them clean. The Raal skysteel mine... yes, that was the match. But your city—" He caught himself, correcting the tone. "Fazrum poured everything into the hills. Overextended. When the veins ran thin, war was the only way to cover the debts. Karth fractured along old family lines, Trast, Iln, Meridi. The Council broke trying to keep us from eating ourselves. The Pact... was meant to save us. In the end, it only split the pieces more cleanly."

He stopped talking for a beat, hands flexing at his sides as though checking for wounds that were still there, unseen. "My father chose the treaty, even when half our kin called him coward. We signed on to diplomacy. Some wanted the sword, some wanted to hide. You know what we got? A collection of city-states, arguing over the scraps."

Darum's footsteps caught up, heavy on the loose stones. He wore his cloak slung low, a battered satchel swinging at his hip, scruff beard bristling with sweat and the beginnings of grey. "You want to know how it ended, Leonard?" His voice was quiet, rough as old rope. "I was on the eastern ridge when the last ceasefire flares went up. We had orders to take the bridge, nothing left but cinders and bone by the time we crossed. My unit lost half its number before we even reached the other side. Found the survivors stacked in the root cellar, burned alive, because no one wanted prisoners. That's what peace meant, then."

He didn't look at Idran, but the words hung between them like a drawn blade.

Idran's lips thinned, color gone from his cheeks. "No one left that field clean, Darum. Not yours. Not mine."

The tension crackled, brittle and cold, each man's memories rubbing raw against the other.

Saran's voice cut through, sharp as glass. She was walking just ahead, black hair braided tight, the hilt of her sword peeking over one shoulder. "Are we doing this? Fighting over whose grave was dug deeper? Because I promise you, the land doesn't care. Not anymore." She turned, fixing them both with a stare that was older than her years. "We're all just walking on the bones now. I don't care who started it or whose story made it into the books. Nobody on this road is innocent, not after what we've seen, or what we're about to do."

For a moment, only the wind spoke. The hills rolled out ahead, marked with old scars, while behind them, the last remains of the ruined barn caught a gust and collapsed inward with a sigh of old ash.

Leonard let out a breath he didn't know he was holding, tension in his shoulders uncoiling. He looked at Idran and saw the set jaw, the glint of stubbornness that was almost pride. He glanced at Darum, the haunted set to his eyes, the way his knuckles whitened around the hilt of his sword.

He nodded once to Saran, grateful for the interruption, for the simple reminder that the world moved forward whether or not their stories ever got sorted.

They walked on in silence, each one retreating to his own shadows, the landscape around them feeling both vast and claustrophobic, haunted by a thousand wars that had never really ended.

The wind picked up as the road curved over an open ridge, dry grass bending flat, flecks of dirt swirling around their boots. A gull screamed somewhere far off, a coastal sound, lost this far inland. Leonard was staring at the way the clouds churned above the ruined valley when Darum's hand snapped up, palm rigid.

All four stopped in their tracks. Darum shifted, cloak flaring behind him, eyes narrowed toward the road's next bend. Saran let her hand hover near her sword hilt, braid tugged loose by the wind. Idran's head tilted slightly, always listening first, calculating threat and distance. Leonard just breathed and waited.

Then, hooves. Fast. The sound rolled up the hill like thunder, a detached rhythm of desperation. A shape appeared over the rise, silhouetted against the pale sky. Horse and rider, but neither moving right. The animal's flanks were slick with sweat, one foreleg dragging, head jerking in pain. The rider was barely in the saddle, slumped forward, clutching the reins with blood-slick hands.

He nearly tumbled from the saddle as the horse staggered to a halt, nostrils flaring, foam flecking its muzzle. The man's eyes were wide rolling whites, his mouth slack. Clothes torn, the collar of his shirt half-ripped, trousers spattered with mud and worse. He looked around blindly, jaw working, but no words came, only the ragged wet sound of breathing, like he'd run half the world and left his soul somewhere behind him.

Darum stepped forward, hands raised, voice calm but carrying over the wind. "Easy. You're safe enough for now. What happened?"

The rider stared at him, chest heaving. Blood trickled from a shallow cut above his brow, threading into the lines of his face. He tried to swallow but failed, voice coming out rough and stuttering. "They... they came out of nowhere. Not bandits, not, not anything I've ever seen. Teeth, arms too long, eyes like... like lanterns in the dark. Ruvar's gone. It's gone." His words broke on a sob, shoulders shaking.

Saran stepped in quickly, eyes locked on the man's face. "Which village? Was it Ruvar? Are you sure?"

He stared at her, pupils dilated, lips trembling. "Ruvar, yes. North side. I... I was on the hill, checking fences. When I heard screaming. I saw the barn fall." He squeezed his eyes shut, like he could force the memory out. "They tore through us without any warning. People started to run, some never made it to the road. I tried to—" He swallowed again, words catching.

Saran pressed closer, voice softer but urgent. "Kaelen? Uncle Kaelen, is that you?"

The man's eyes focused for the first time, blinking through shock. "Sarah...?" His mouth worked around the name, recognition finally breaking through the fog. "Gods, is that you?" He nearly fell from the saddle, reaching a hand down. Saran stepped forward, helping steady him as he slid awkwardly to the ground.

Leonard watched his chest tightend. Sarah?—no, Saran, he repeated in his mind—was all tension and disbelief, her face frozen between hope and terror. "My parents, my brother, were they...?" She couldn't finish.

Kaelen shook his head, tears streaking through the grime on his cheeks. "I don't know, Sarah. I saw the farmhouse, I heard shouting, something broke the window. I... I ran. I shouldn't have. I'm so sorry. I didn't see who made it out." He sagged against her, voice hollow. "Coward. Just ran."

Saran held his arm tight, her own hand trembling. "You did what you had to." The words were for him, but they sounded like a plea to herself.

Darum stepped forward, gentler than Leonard had ever seen him. "Listen to me, Kaelen. You're not safe here. Ride south, keep to the main road. Don't stop until you reach the Ravenblood forward camp. Show them your arm, tell them what happened. They'll take you in. Go, now. Don't look back."

Kaelen nodded, unsteady. Saran held his gaze for one last heartbeat, something passing between them, regret, forgiveness, all tangled up in the wind. Then she let him go, and he dragged himself back into the saddle, turning the horse with raw, shaking hands. He looked back just once, then kicked the animal on, spurring it into a limping canter down the road.

Saran stood frozen, staring after him, fists clenching and unclenching at her sides. Leonard moved to stand beside her. Idran gave her a curt nod, almost respectful.

Darum's voice came quiet but resolute. "We keep moving. Ruvar's not far. If anything's left to find, we'll find it."

Saran wiped at her eyes, once, then squared her shoulders. "Let's go."

They turned their backs to the wind and the last echoes of Kaelen's hoofbeats, pressing on toward Ruvar. Each step away from that meeting was heavier than the last, the road no longer just a path through ruined land, but a route straight into the heart of loss and memory.

They crossed into Ruvar at a cautious pace, boots sinking into mud churned by fleeing feet and the drag of heavy bodies. The fields were gone, only stubble and trampled furrows remained, a patchwork of blackened earth and pale, upturned roots. The sky pressed down, the color of old bone, wind slicing through the broken fences and scorched hedgerows. Even the crows were silent.

Leonard kept his hand close to his sword hilt, not for fear of ambush, there was nothing left alive here but to keep his fingers from shaking. He scanned the ground, hoofprints cut deep where a panicked herd stampeded, bloody tracks leading nowhere, the brittle glint of broken glass from a smashed lantern. A pig's carcass lay in the road, head torn nearly off, ribs cracked and splayed as if some force had ripped it apart out of pure spite.

Saran walked faster than the rest, shoulders drawn up, her breath sharp. Darum stopped beside a scorched wagon, jaw clenched, staring at the claw-marks raked across the sideboards. "Damn abominations," he spat. "Nothing natural leaves a trail like this. Nothing sane."

Idran moved in a slow, methodical arc, his boots tracing careful circles around the worst of the devastation. He knelt at a pile of torn-up sacks, studying the way the wheat was ground into the dirt, the arcs of blood on the nearby stones. "This isn't hunger," he muttered, almost to himself. "It's cruelty. Something ancient, made to hurt, not feed. It's not war, not as I know it."

Leonard didn't speak. He just watched. Every ruined doorway, every overturned cart, every lifeless patch of trampled garden. He took it all in and held it. He felt the wrongness under his skin, a silence so total it felt deliberate, like the world itself had flinched away from this place.

Then Saran broke into a run, boots pounding over the churned mud, braid streaming behind her. She veered off the main lane, cut between a pair of collapsed grain sheds, and sprinted toward the last intact house at the edge of the village, the one with a slant-roof, shutters still hanging, the faded blue paint of a child's handprint smudged on the door.

Leonard's pulse jumped. He went after her, the others close behind. He caught up as Saran threw herself onto the splintered porch, hands scrambling over the warped wood. She shoved the door open with a heave, the hinges shrieking. Inside was a cold, earthy hush.

He found her in the front room, on her knees in the dust. Before her, three bodies: a man, a woman, and a boy, her father, mother, and brother, Leonard assumed, limbs entwined as if they'd held each other until the very last. Blood had pooled beneath them, dried to a deep, sticky maroon, but there was no rot, no time for decay. The wounds were violent but quick, no sign of torture or lingering struggle. The blunt horror of an ending that came all at once.

Saran's hands hovered, then fell to her sides, fists clenched so tight her knuckles blanched. Her head dropped, breath shaking. She didn't make a sound—no scream, only a single breath that said everything.

Leonard lowered himself beside her, the floorboards creaking. He didn't touch her, not at first. He just sat, legs folded, letting her know she wasn't alone. He remembered too well the way silence could consume a room after the worst had happened, the feeling of a world snapped in half and left hanging, unfinished.

He stayed there for a time, watching her shoulders shake, listening to the ugly, wet sound of grief fighting to escape. When she finally leaned into him, shuddering, he let her. Leonard, who so often needed her to steady him, now found himself the anchor. He wrapped an arm around her, careful and solid, offering his presence.

Darum entered the house a minute later, boots scraping the threshold, face set like old stone. He stopped at the doorway, took in the scene, and let out a breath that sounded scraped from the bottom of his chest. He knelt opposite them, laying a scarred, callused hand on Saran's shoulder, gentle and steady, and so unlike his usual edge.

"I lost my home once," he said quietly. His voice didn't tremble, but there was something brittle underneath. "Not like this. Not blood and bodies. But I lost the place that made me. The name. The meaning." He paused, thumb rubbing a slow circle on her cloak. "You live through it. You carry it. But it never gets lighter. You just get stronger, or you break."

Saran didn't reply, but her breathing slowed, the jagged edges easing. Leonard held her tighter, feeling the weight of Darum's words settle over the room like dust.

Idran lingered in the doorway, a silhouette in the dim light. He didn't step closer, but he bowed his head, whether in respect, apology, or prayer, Leonard couldn't say.

The house was so quiet now, even the wind had left them. For a moment, it was just the four of them in a room full of memory, grief, and the cold certainty that nothing would ever be the same. And still, they endured, breathing together, alive in the ruin.

The sun dipped, staining the farmhouse walls a dirty gold as evening began to claw its way over the broken village. In the stillness, the inside air had grown thick, sorrow lingering, the world narrowing to grief and exhausted breaths.

Idran waited at the edge of the yard, arms crossed tight against the chill. He kept his eyes on the far fence line, where weeds tangled with the bones of ruined tools. The others lingered in the house, caught up in grief and memory, but Idran couldn't stay still. Something in the air had shifted, something off, a stutter in the silence that didn't belong.

He tensed, listening. There it was again, a wet, muffled tearing sound from the far side of the pigsty, just beyond the slumped barn. The hairs along his forearms prickled. "Outside. Now," he called, voice sharper than intended. "Something's here."

The group moved fast, Saran leading with her jaw set, sword already in hand, grief burning off into something feral. Leonard, blood cold, followed on her heels. Darum, armor buckled, eyes hard and narrow. Idran brought up the rear, scanning every shadow.

They rounded the barn to the acrid stink of rot and iron. At the edge of the yard, hunched over the ragged corpse of a pig, a single Ravager beast crouched, pale flesh peeled back in strips, limbs too long, back arched like a broken bow. Its jaw worked in slow, grinding motions, slurping greedily, eyes burning an unnatural amber in the gloom.

Saran didn't pause. The world shrank to a tunnel, her feet

pounding the churned mud, blade drawn in a two-handed grip, a scream of raw, ragged rage torn from her throat. "You bastard!" she howled, and charged.

"Saran!" Leonard shouted, his voice cracking against the wind. "Wait—!"

She didn't hear. Or didn't care.

The Ravager jerked up, head snapping toward her with a sound like gravel grinding. Its mouth stretched too wide, stained red-black, talons unfurling. Saran's momentum carried her in, a single heartbeat too close.

The beast swung, a blur of jagged bone, but Darum was already moving, shoulder low, incantation stone sparking to life in his palm. He slammed into the fight, sword swinging in a brutal, practiced arc. Steel flashed, and the creature's forelimb tumbled away in a gout of black ichor, landing with a wet thud at Saran's feet.

The Ravager shrieked, body spasming, half-turning to bring its second claw to bear. Saran staggered back, panting, blade up but off-balance.

Idran didn't hesitate. He darted forward, boots slipping in the blood-slick mud. His left hand swept through the pouch at his belt, crushing a pinch of powder over the stone fragments embedded in his arm. He pressed his hand flat against the Ravager's twitching spine and began to hum a low, dissonant Karthian resonance, the sound grinding like stone over gravel.

The effect was immediate: the Ravager convulsed its limbs seizing. Then, as Idran's hum deepened, the beast imploded from within, collapsing in on itself, bone and sinew turning to dry ash that blew away in the cold wind.

For a long second, no one spoke. Saran stood, chest heaving, sword shaking in her grip. Darum's blade dripped dark fluid, his face carved with lines of relief and fresh anger. Leonard backed up a pace, hand on Saran's shoulder. "You alright?"

Idran's voice interrupted, hard and sharp: "Are you out of your mind? You could have gotten yourself killed! Or all of us. There could be more. This isn't a place for heroics."

Saran turned on him, eyes wild with grief. "That thing was feeding on my family's land. What was I supposed to do, wait for it to finish?"

Idran shook his head, frustration twisting his features. "We're not here for vengeance. We're here to survive and reach the tower. Every time you let rage lead, you risk everything. For all of us."

Leonard stepped in, voice steady but fierce. "We're not machines. You can't ask us to be cold after what we saw. We're still human. She's still—" He cut himself off, meeting Idran's glare with one of his own. "She needed to act. I'd have done the same."

Darum shifted, stepping between the two, his sword flashing up at Idran. The steel was close, almost touching the Karthian's throat. "You forget where you are, envoy. This is our country, our pain. You don't dictate how we carry it."

For a moment, the threat hung, sharp and real. Idran's hands rose, palms open, a peace gesture, "I'm not your enemy," he said quietly. "But if we keep fracturing like this, we'll be dead before we even get close to the tower."

Darum didn't lower his blade at first. Only after a long, tense breath did he pull back, letting the moment settle. "Then start acting like you belong here," he muttered.

No one spoke for a while, tension still coiled in the ruin's shadow. Leonard kept his eyes fixed on the scorched earth, jaw clenched so tight it trembled. Idran lingered at the edge, watching the horizon. Overhead, the light was already thinning to gray.

Darum spat into the dirt, voice flat and decisive. "We're done for tonight. We're not pushing through darkness. We set camp here. Anyone who marches these roads after sundown deserves to die twice."

No one argued. They picked their way through the corpse-strewn yard to what was left of the old grain store, a collapsed skeleton of timber and stone, half-roofed but sheltered from the worst of the wind. Leonard kicked aside splintered boards, clearing a patch of earth. Saran dragged over an old trough, making a crude bench. Darum fetched scraps of dry timber and sparked a fire beneath the broken beams, coaxing a thin, blue flame into life. Idran busied himself with small, ritual motions, laying a circle of ward-dust around the camp's edge, hands working with silent efficiency.

As the fire burned low, a hush settled over the four of them, broken only by the distant call of nightbirds and the crackle of flame licking wet wood. Darum volunteered for the first watch, posting himself near the gap in the wall, incantation stone sputtering faintly as he surveyed the empty fields.

Idran crossed his legs in the dirt, eyes closed, hands folded in his lap. He slipped into meditation, humming so softly only the stones could hear, the sound more felt than heard.

Leonard and Saran sat side by side, backs against a scorched beam. For a while, they said nothing, shoulders pressed together in shared exhaustion. Then, quietly, Leonard broke the silence. "Back there, when he... your uncle, called you 'Sarah'... I've never heard anyone call you that."

Saran let out a breath, half-laugh, half-sigh. "Only my family. In Ruvar, I was Sarah. The dutiful daughter, the one who was always meant to stay, keep the house, follow the rules. When I left to join Ravenblood, I didn't want to carry that with me. 'Sarah' belonged to a life that ended the day I put on this armour." She looked down at her hands, the knuckles still white from the fight. "Saran became the one who survived. The one who killed, bled, didn't look back. Now I'm not sure which one fits anymore."

Leonard hesitated, then reached out, his fingers threading between hers. She let him. Their hands rested together, steady, warm in the dark.

"You don't have to choose," Leonard said quietly. "You're both. Or neither. You survived, that's all that matters."

Saran leaned her head on his shoulder, letting the last of her walls drop for a moment. The grief and anger in her chest softened, replaced by something simpler, the comfort of someone who understood what it meant to lose a name.

Darum returned to the fire, crouching beside them. He nodded to

Saran, his scruff catching orange firelight, a flicker of something proud in his eyes. "You're strong, Saran. Always have been. Doesn't matter what anyone calls you. Surviving this long takes more than just a hard name."

Saran managed a ghost of a smile, squeezed Leonard's hand. "Thanks, old man."

Idran stirred from his meditation, eyes open now and sharper than before. "I'll take next watch," he offered, the words plain, but there was something more in them, a quiet attempt to mend the crack from earlier, or maybe just a recognition that tonight, trust had to be earned one small act at a time.

Darum grunted, then looked back to Leonard and Saran. "Get what sleep you can. We're not done with hardship yet. Sun's barely half-set on what waits between here and that tower."

Leonard nodded, shifting closer to Saran as they settled on their bedrolls, using old cloaks and broken sacks for makeshift pillows. For a time, he watched the shadows play against the grain store's ruin, listening to the muttered prayer-forms of Idran and the steady, watchful breathing of Darum just outside.

Sleep did not come quickly, but when it finally did, it was deep and dreamless, anchored in the knowledge that, at least for tonight, they were together, and for the moment, safe. The fire burned low beneath the broken beams, and all around them, the ruined fields held their secrets close, waiting for dawn.

Interlude I

Ash drifted in the high wind, swirling in lazy patterns over the ridge, but none of it settled on the figure as he walked. He wore a grey cloak with its hood drawn low, though silver hair escaped the edges and gleamed whenever the faintest light touched it. Every step he took pressed no weight into the dust; the world parted for him in ways that defied sense.

At the ridge's edge, a black tower rose standing apart from the land like a thorn pressed into old scar tissue. No door or sentries at watch. The structure seemed to hum with its own gravity, shadows pooling at its base, daring the world to approach.

He did not hesitate. He moved as if this was always his destination. His hand pale, fingertips catching the chill, lifted to rest against the stone. Amber runes flickered to life beneath his touch, veins of ward-light pulsing outward, woven to keep out everything not born of this place.

He did not recite a word or move his lips. The light in the wards twisted, folding inward upon itself, turning from bright gold to dull iron to nothing at all. Not snuffed out, but drawn in, starved of purpose.

The wall in front of him parted. The stone slid aside, shadows folding back into a seam barely wide enough for a man.

He entered.

Inside, the tower was silent. The walls ran smooth and seamless, curving up and away to a roof lost in darkness. Every footfall was muffled, as if the air itself was thick with memory. The only light came from thin ribbons of amber, crawling over the stone in patterns.

He climbed the interior stairs in perfect calm, each step measured. At every turn, the architecture seemed to realign for him, corridors opening, then closing again, offering passage only as long as he wished it.

He climbed, the stairwell curling up and up with no handrail, no torch bracket, nothing to hold but his own composure. The tower swallowed him in cold, but it didn't resist; every step was permitted.

At the rooftop, the world opened wide above him. The sky was cloudless, deep blue, but cut through with stars that burned too bright and moved against the grain of ordinary constellations. Some winked in and out, like blinking eyes.

He stepped out onto bone-white stone, the wind dying as if in deference. Near the edge, a Ravager crouched, its jaw dark with blood, claws sunk into the stone, eyes a feral gold. It lifted its head, tense, ready to spring.

He only watched, hood slipping back to reveal hair the color of old silver. The creature tensed, a snarl curling in its chest, then, recognition or memory flattened it to the roof. Fear flickered in its gaze, an acknowledgment of something deeper than dominance. The Ravager turned and, with a scrape of claws, slunk past him, skittering down the stairs, desperate to be gone.

He didn't look back. The sky overhead pulsed once, like a heartbeat in the void.

At the center of the roof, a rift hung vertically, its edges shimmering, the seam of reality peeled back.

He stepped forward, stopping just at the brink. The rift's edge flared, a recognition, an answer to a question unspoken. The air pressed close, as if the whole world held its breath.

For a heartbeat, the wind was gone. The sky seemed to blink, stars and sun flickering, reality shifting its weight as something vast, unseen, gazed through the opening from the other side.

He offered no words. He simply stepped into the rift.

The rooftop was left empty: no scorch marks, no blood, no sign that anyone had passed this way at all.

6

Leonard woke with the heavy taste of ash in his mouth and the bite of the cold against his cheek. His body still ached as if he'd been running all night. The first light of dawn had crept through the gaps of the ruined grain store, smearing gray and blue across the splintered floor. Frost glimmered on the cracked stone where the fire had been, the last of the coals drowned beneath a spill of rainwater and blackened wheat.

He shifted, rolling stiff shoulders, the blanket stuck to his back by sweat and grit. A rotten draft curled through the gaps in the ruined walls, stirring the dust, prickling his skin. He tried to focus on the ordinar, boots, cloak, sword belt, but every movement echoed in his head like a bell struck out of time.

Across the dimness, Darum was already awake, hunched on an overturned crate, drawing a whetstone slow and methodical along the length of his battered blade. Each scrape set Leonard's nerves on edge. Darum's eyes were rimmed red from lack of sleep, but his hands were steady. The air around him was iron and resolve, the old soldier retreating behind the comfort of ritual.

Idran sat further off, cross-legged. The morning light caught the edge of the stones embedded in his forearms, each one glowing faintly as he hummed the last notes of a resonance chant. Idran's eyes opened, unfazed, too clear for someone who'd slept on broken earth. He nodded once, a silent greeting or maybe just an acknowledgment that the night was over.

Saran was awake too, just where she'd settled the night before, knees hugged to her chest, face turned away from the others. Her black hair had come loose from its braid, stray strands matted to her cheeks. She didn't speak, didn't move except to draw her cloak tighter around her shoulders. Leonard caught her eye for a moment. He pushed himself upright, Around them, the ruins of Ruvar were silent but not peaceful. Nobody asked if anyone slept. The question was pointless. All that mattered now was standing up, shouldering packs, and forcing themselves forward, one step at a time. The sun crawled higher, cold and uncaring, and they rose with it.

The work of breaking camp went on without a word. Each person moved through the motions as if sleepwalking, muscle memory driving them more than thought. Leonard rolled his blanket, shaking out the grit, and shoved it into his pack. The straps felt clumsy beneath his fingers, he yanked them tighter than he meant to, breath coming shallow with the effort.

Darum's voice cut through the brittle silence, low and gruff. "Light enough to march." His blade was already sheathed, pack slung across one shoulder, cloak knotted at the throat. He moved like a man who'd marched out of worse places and expected the rest of them to keep up or fall behind.

Saran finished lashing down her own gear. She glanced over as Leonard struggled with a tangled buckle, then stepped close and fixed it, fingers quick, gentle but unsparing. "Don't make it harder on yourself," she murmured, voice too quiet for the others to hear. There was no comfort in it, just a simple, practical mercy.

Idran was the last to join them, He knelt at the edge of their ruined shelter, brushing his palm over the half-buried symbols he'd etched in the dust the night before. The perimeter ward had held, faint as it was. Now he swept it away with one hard scrape of his boot, breaking the circle, erasing whatever faint protection it had offered. If it had offered any at all. He straightened, cloak settled about his shoulders, and looked back at the farmhouse just once, a frown creasing his lips.

No one lingered at the threshold. Leonard let his eyes drift to the battered door, the shadowed room where Saran's family lay. He thought about saying something, a prayer or a promise, anything but the words caught in his throat and never came.

They moved out in a line, boots crunching on frost-bitten stubble. Behind them, Ruvar's ruins sagged in the pale morning, bodies and memories left to the cold.

Darum took the lead, boots sinking into the churned mud as he set a pace that was steady, just enough momentum to keep the blood moving and the mind focused. The others fell in behind him, silent as a burial march, but none hesitated. Out here, hesitation got you killed.

His shoulders were squared beneath his battered cloak, the edge of steel at his hip swinging in time with every stride. The lines on his face were deeper this morning, stubble rough and flecked with gray, jaw locked against whatever words might have wanted to rise. He scanned the horizon with the same measured calculation as always, but there was something heavier in his gaze, a set to his brow that made it clear, today, he carried more than just his pack.

The air between them was thick with last night's grief and the knowledge that the world wasn't about to offer forgiveness.

When they reached the old village gate, a splintered arch still half-standing, the faded paint of some welcome long since worn away, Darum slowed. He paused there, just long enough to rest his hand on the wood. His eyes flicked up to the ragged sign, then down to the bloodstained dirt. The moment held, sharp and brittle, then he drew a breath and stepped through, never glancing back.

The others followed, the broken arch yawning behind them, swallowing the last of Ruvar as they left it to the crows and the coming sun.

They walked a long stretch before anyone found words worth breaking the morning hush. Frost clung to the grass along the ditch, melting slowly under the weak sun, their footsteps leaving ragged impressions behind them.

Leonard dropped back a pace, falling in beside Saran. Their boots squelched with every step, a rhythmic counterpoint to the soft crunch of gravel and the distant call of a crow.

"This road look familiar yet?"

Saran kept her gaze on the horizon, not slowing. "I used to walk it to market when I was younger. Before all this." Her tone was flat, "Fields were better then. Didn't have to watch the ditches for bones."

Leonard just grunted. "Guess it's still here. That's something."

She finally looked at him, lips twitching as if she might smile, but didn't. "Yeah. Still here."

Idran walked a few paces behind, his cloak fluttering in the wind. Occasionally he paused, gaze lifting beyond the tired stretch of field and ruin, head tilting as if he might catch a sound only he could hear. There was an edge to him this morning, more watchful. He bent once, scooping a clump of earth in his palm, sifting it with slender fingers. The dirt slipped through, brittle and gray, refusing to hold shape. He frowned, then straightened.

"The soil's changing," Idran said quietly, tone clinical but not detached. "Thinner than it should be. Look—" He crumbled another handful, letting it fall. "Even after fire, land keeps its scent. Here, it's just... spent. Like the blood's been drained out."

Darum shot a look back, boots crunching to a stop for a moment. "Must be worse near the tower line. Happened in the war too, fields dead for miles, even where the fighting never reached."

Saran wiped her hands on her trousers, jaw tight. "So we're walking into it, then? The place where nothing grows?"

"Worse than nothing," Idran murmured. "Sometimes you hear things. Like wind, but not wind."

Leonard watched the way Idran's eyes scanned the horizon, alert and wary, as if expecting something to answer back. He shivered, then kept moving, boots heavy with mud that didn't want to let go.

The land shifted as they went, almost without warning. Grass grew sparser, each blade dulled and brittle, patches of earth showing through like wounds. Insects vanished, not even the drone of a fly, just the hollow whisper of their own movement.

Up ahead, a line of skeletal trees clawed at the gray sky, bark bleached and peeling, branches stripped bare in the wrong season. Saran slowed, frowning as she swept her gaze along the treeline. "I don't think it should be like this," she muttered, more to herself than anyone else.

Then they saw it, a boundary post, half-sunken at an angle in the mud. An old lantern, its glass cloudy with dust, hung from a rusted iron hook. The flame inside had long since guttered out, but the lantern's base was stained with old amber resin, or something meant to mimic it. Around the post, footprints pressed into the soil, fresh, not more than a few days old leading away toward the tower.

The group halted, tension rippling through them. Leonard squinted, studying the footprints. "Someone made it out here. Scout party?"

Idran crouched, tracing a boot mark with his fingertip. "Not animals. Too regular. But no sign of a camp or fallback."

Darum's jaw tightened. "This marks the edge of the old survey zone." He nodded to the lantern. "After this, maps stop being useful." He didn't look at the tower, but the implication was clear. With a glance between them, they crossed the invisible line, boots crunching past the marker and into a country that no longer belonged to the living.

They crested a worn ridge, boots scraping over stone and brittle roots. The valley beyond dipped toward the Tower, no longer distant but close enough to dominate the world's order. It shouldn't have been possible, but the Tower seemed both far away and on top of them, as if every step only brought it more into focus, never nearer.

It rose impossibly tall, taller than the mind could hold, but its lines weren't clean. The surface warped in the air, shifting with a feverish shimmer like heat rippling above an oven. Its color wasn't just black, but an absence of light, darker than the shadow it cast, pulling in the outlines of everything around it, swallowing up the light, the sky, even the air. The world itself seemed to bend around its edges.

Nothing lived in its shadow. The sky directly over the Tower was a flat, bruised gray, starless even though the day was clear. Clouds skirted the horizon but never came close. It didn't look built. It looked imposed, like a wound cut open and never allowed to heal.

Each of them stared, letting the scene settle in. Saran wiped sweat from her brow, even though the air was cold. Leonard realized he'd been holding his breath. He let it out slowly, hands shaking.

Idran's voice was thin. "This is why nothing grows here."

Darum just grunted. "Not the worst thing I've seen. But it's close."

They moved on, no one eager to linger. But the Tower watched, a presence that made the ground feel unsteady beneath their boots.

The descent was gradual, but nothing about the land felt natural. The basin below the Tower was pocked with shallow craters, not made by war or weather but as if pieces of the earth had been scooped out, hollowed by something deeper. Some holes were filled with silty water, others with bone-white gravel, a few yawning open to darkness beneath.

As they walked, the earth changed beneath their feet. Veins of jagged black crystal pushed up through the soil, bursting through what remained of old stone walls and broken fence-posts. The crystals hummed, a vibration that Leonard felt more in his bones than his ears, a tension that prickled along his spine.

Saran skirted one of the larger veins, glancing at Idran. "You ever see this back in Karth?"

He crouched, careful not to touch the shard, studying the way it split an old boundary stone clean in two. "They're not natural," he said softly. "But they're the source. Where incantation stones come from, shard-growth, only wilder. Untamed. Most are cut and refined, not...this."

Darum knelt, running a knuckle along the edge of a smaller spike, not quite touching. "This is what's left when the land's been poisoned by the tower. Seen smaller veins in the deep mines, but nothing like this. Not above ground."

Leonard stared at the field of black crystal, the sense of infection spreading. veins running out from a rot in the world's heart.

He kept moving, the tower looming larger behind the haze, every footstep pressing further into the sick zone. Each step felt heavier. The closer they got, the more the world itself seemed to push back.

They stopped, every muscle, every sense on edge. The Tower's base, built broad and seamless as a tomb, now yawned open. Its door, a slab of stone twice as wide as a wagon, veined with black crystal, had been wrenched aside, opened, as if by invitation.

From the threshold, a figure stepped into the light. It was man-shaped, but only in the barest sense, too tall, limbs too long, the space around it blurred at the edges. Its "clothes" were more a shifting mass of shadow and glistening bone, glimmering in places like armor, vanishing in others. Where its face should be, the void pooled; only its eyes shone, burning amber, its pupils vertical.

The air behind it warped, half a pack of Ravagers melted into view, their claws scraping in eager silence. They paced just behind the Shade, held at bay by an unseen leash, watching the group with hungry calculation.

No one needed to say a word. Every instinct screamed to run or fight, but neither seemed possible.

Without plan or signal, the group tightened formation, Saran and Darum in front, blades half-drawn, Saran's jaw set in a grim line, Darum's stance wide and heavy. Idran hung slightly to one side, cloak parted, hands low, ready for the resonance he would need to wield. Leonard was pushed back, almost boxed in by the others like a living shield.

The Shade walked forward with no hurry, steps whispering against the brittle grass. It stopped a dozen paces away, the Ravagers fanning out in a ragged crescent behind.

Its voice didn't echo or threaten. It was cold and inhuman, resonant as if it spoke from somewhere beneath the earth.

"You are expected, Leonard. Step forward. The vessel is needed for what is to come."

The way it spoke his name made something crawl down

Leonard's spine, a familiarity that was personal, not just spoken by rote.

Saran hissed, "He's not going anywhere."

Darum said nothing, just squared his shoulders, eyes tracking every twitch of the Ravagers behind.

Idran kept his gaze on the Shade, searching for the trick, the plan, anything to exploit.

Leonard's voice came out sharper than he intended, snapping the silence. "What the hell are you? What do you want with me? Say something that actually means something for once."

The Shade turned its head, and for a breath the world felt thinner.

"I am a part of what your kind calls a 'Shade.' I am function, agent, warden, herald. There are others. Each has a purpose in the chain. The architect, you know him as Samric, laid the first stones. The ritual is not yet complete. You are required."

Saran spat into the mud. "Required for what? Killing more villages? Raising more monsters?"

The Shade ignored her, eyes fixed only on Leonard. "Come willingly. You will be treated as kin. Resist, and the outcome is decided already. No one else here must die."

Leonard felt rage boil up, hot, clear, desperate. "Every time someone wants to burn the world, it's my name on the altar. Why me? What's so damned special about me?"

The Shade's head tilted. "You are not the first vessel. But you are the only one left unbroken. Come now. There is no malice. Only the necessity of the design."

Darum stepped forward, sword bare, voice iron. "He's not going anywhere. Not on your terms. You want him, you go through us."

A shimmer rippled through the Ravagers, but the Shade raised a hand, holding them back.

"One last chance. This world can end quietly. Or not. Decide, Leonard."

The wind cut through the silence. Every heartbeat felt like the last before violence.

Leonard took a step back, pulse roaring in his ears, eyes never leaving the Shade. "No. I'm done running. You want me, you'll have to take me."

Saran drew first, a cold flash of steel, her voice guttural. "Over my dead body." Darum was right behind her, sword in hand, his whole frame blocking Leonard's path.

The Shade regarded them, almost with something like regret. "So be it."

It lifted one finger, just a breath, a wordless flicker. The Ravagers lunged, shrieking, claws lashing. The air split with sudden violence.

Darum met the first Ravager with a wide swing, shattering its jaw. Saran cut a second one down, blood streaking her cheek, eyes wild. Idran crushed a crystal and spread it in front of him, his voice rose in a harsh Karthian chord, resonance flaring as he sent another beast tumbling end over end. But for each one dropped, two more closed in, slashing, snapping, jaws dripping black ichor.

Leonard tried to stay behind them, trying to keep his feet. The mud slicked beneath him. He ducked a swiping claw, stumbled, brought up his blade in time to parry another. The world became chaos, shouts, metal ringing, bodies colliding, the ground chewed to black pulp beneath their boots.

Amid the battle, the Shade moved with an uncanny grace, gliding straight through the carnage. The Ravagers parted around it, never daring to close in.

Leonard saw it coming, tried to circle away, but the thing moved too fast. Its cloak swirled, arm rising, a blade in hand, jagged and black, the same impossible stone as the Tower. Light bent around it.

Leonard raised his sword to block, but the impact numbed his arm, sending his weapon spinning from his grasp. He staggered, desperate, swinging a fist. The Shade batted him aside with effortless precision, not cruel but inevitable.

Its hand closed around Leonard's shoulder.

Darkness flared, a cold pressure, a sound like the wind screaming through stone. The world slipped sideways. Leonard's sight twisted, shapes stretched, voices echoing. The ground fell away. He fought for breath, vision flickering between here and somewhere else, someplace where stars spun and shadows crawled.

He heard Saran scream his name, Darum shout something guttural, but their voices faded as the Shade's grip tightened.

Reality shuddered. Leonard's last image was the Shade's eyes, burning amber, filling his vision as the world went black.

Leonard felt himself slipping, his mind pulled down into cold depths, pressure building in his skull as the Shade's grip distorted the air and memory around him. A thousand distant voices filled his head.

And then, suddenly, a hand seized his cloak, rough and alive. Saran.

She tore him away, jaw clenched, every muscle straining. "Not today, you bastard!" she snarled, dragging Leonard bodily out of the Shade's grasp. For a moment the world wavered, then the darkness receded, reality snapping painfully back into place. Leonard gasped, lungs burning, vision swimming as the air righted itself. The ground was cold under his knees, and Saran was there, arms braced around him, keeping him rooted to the world.

The Shade recoiled, cloak flaring. It let out a guttural, inhuman roar, a sound of sheer, frustrated purpose. The tone was wrong, too intelligent, as if something was cursing a failed equation, not a lost kill.

"Back. Get back, both of you!" Darum's voice cut through the aftermath. Saran hauled Leonard up, half-carrying him as they staggered away. Idran joined, resonance flickering along his arms, eyes locked on the Shade.

Darum stood alone, battered but unbowed, blade angled low. "You want a vessel, take me instead. Leave the boy."

The Shade's eyes narrowed, something like amusement crossing its features. "You would offer yourself? You're not enough."

"Try me," Darum said.

Without warning, Darum lunged, all the force of a life spent in battle behind each strike. The Shade met him, blade whirling in a black arc, movements too precise, too smooth, almost inhumanly anticipatory. Steel rang against stone, sparks spitting. Every blow could have been fatal, each was turned aside by just a hair.

Darum ducked under a slash, pivoted, caught the Shade's wrist and yanked it forward, using its momentum to bring it off balance. The Shade slipped free like smoke, countering with a swipe that tore a notch from Darum's shoulder armor.

Still, Darum pressed on, never giving ground.

Locked blade to blade, Darum suddenly dropped his sword, seized the Shade in a brutal bear-hug. His palm stone embedded and flickering, pressed to the Shade's side.

The world stuttered. Both combatants went rigid, eyes wide. For a moment, nothing moved.

Darum's mind plunged into a roaring storm, a chasm filled with voices, memory, command. The Shade's presence was vast, almost endless, a cold dark sea filled with hunger. Darum gritted his teeth, forcing his will through the conduit, matching the Shade's pressure with his own: years of discipline, pain, memory, and loss.

He saw flashes, not his life, but foreign images: the first king, a throne of ash, the black tower rising. He felt the Shade's satisfaction, its anticipation, the joy of nearly completing a pattern.

Darum pushed back, channeling every ounce of will, every memory of every brother and sister lost on the field. The stone in his palm flared white, then blue, but the Shade surged, psychic pressure building, blackness pouring in through every weak point in Darum's mind. He felt himself slipping, the old wounds breaking open, strength draining away. The Shade's cold intellect pressed down, suffocating, relentless.

Darum's knees buckled. The stone dimmed. The Shade began to overpower him, inch by inch, will against will.

Leonard saw the instant Darum's knees dipped. Without thinking, he lunged, rushing into the psychic brawl, breaking every rule of training. "Get away from him!" he shouted, driving a shoulder into the Shade's side.

The contact, unexpected, broke the deadlock. The Shade's concentration fractured, its grip on Darum wavering. The psychic storm of will faltered. Reality flickered, snapping loose just enough for someone else to act.

Idran didn't hesitate. He surged forward, arms blazing with blue-white light. He drew a deep, vibrating breath, humming a broken Karthian triad, and unleashed the resonance straight at the Shade's heart. The note was raw, jagged, too much for a human throat.

The Shade tried to recover, to turn, but its shape rippled, edges coming apart.

The resonance hit like a hammer. The Shade convulsed, then imploded, folding in on itself with a soundless crunch. A cloud of black dust and amber sparks flared outward, then scattered into the wind. Its blade clattered to the earth, shattering into fragments of stone and nothingness.

Leonard and Saran scrambled to Darum, who was on one knee, hands braced in the dirt, breath coming in ragged gasps. Saran was the first to reach him, hauled him up by his arm, worry and anger wrestling on her face.

"You reckless old fool," she muttered, half-scolding, half-relieved. "You're not twenty anymore."

Leonard gripped Darum's other arm, hauling his mentor up. "You could have died."

Darum managed a dry, pained smile. "Wouldn't be the first time."

Idran dusted his palms off, face pale, breathing hard. "I'll admit it, Darum. That was... impressive. But you nearly killed yourself, and the rest of us. Next time, let's try something with less suicide baked in."

Darum just nodded, accepting the criticism with the faintest flicker of a grin. "If there's a next time."

Saran checked Leonard over with quick, practical hands. "You alright?"

He nodded. "I'm fine. You pulled me out."

Saran squeezed his shoulder.

The group gathered themselves. Darum straightened, still shaky but standing. Saran wiped a streak of dust from her cheek. Idran lingered at the edge, watching the tower with wary, clinical interest.

The echo of the Shade's last words hung over them, Samric's

name, the ritual, the sense that they were still only pieces in someone else's plan. Leonard felt the pressure of those words, but also the cold relief of surviving one more impossible fight.

There was little time for comfort or debate. The sky above the tower was a flat, bruised gray. The doors yawned wide, promising more answers, and more danger.

Saran glanced at Leonard. "Ready?"

He swallowed, nodded. "Yeah. Let's end this."

Darum rolled his shoulders, blade still in hand. "Stay close. No more solo heroics."

Idran moved to the threshold, eyes narrowing as he peered into the dark. "The real test starts now."

With only a shared glance and a collective breath, the four stepped forward, crossing from the scarred earth into the shadow of the tower.

7

The doorway swallowed them one by one, Saran leading, Leonard close behind, Darum and Idran at the rear, every sense stretched tight. The threshold felt like a border not just of stone but of air and intent. As soon as Leonard stepped in, the outside world died behind him. The light thinned. The temperature dropped by degrees, but it was not the chill of morning or shadow. It was colder than that, a cold that pressed against bone.

Their boots rang out against black tile, the sound sharp and clear, echoing up into heights hidden by gloom. Leonard looked around, half expecting filth or rot, signs of beasts, looters, decay. There was nothing. No broken furniture, no dust, no blood. The place was pristine, preserved as if nothing living had dared trespass in decades.

Saran moved to the wall, fingertips brushing ancient etchings, none of them glowing now. "This should be crawling with something," she whispered. Her voice barely carried.

Darum's beard twitched in a grimace. "Too clean," he muttered. "Old fortresses don't keep themselves."

Idran walked slower, boots light on the flawless stone. He paused at a carved pillar, running one hand across the inlaid amber veins.

"No growth of any kind, not even mold." He looked up, eyes narrowing. "Something wants this place untouched."

They shared a look, uneasy, but resolved. The entry hall opened into shadow ahead, the faintest suggestion of a spiral staircase curling upward, black as a vein in the world.

Leonard tightened his grip on his sword hilt, feeling every scuff and nick beneath his palm. He didn't want to say it aloud, but he felt it too, a pressure behind his eyes, as if he was being watched from above, below, every angle at once.

They advanced, boots ringing hollow, each footfall marked by the sound of their own breath. The spiral staircase began, a wide, shallow ascent around a central shaft that fell away into darkness below and rose higher than they could see.

As they climbed, side passages branched away, small antechambers, once perhaps storerooms or ritual spaces, their doorways sealed with smooth slabs of black stone or simply collapsed inward, nothing but silent promise behind. Leonard peeked into one, perfectly empty, dustless, a few old glyphs scored into the wall but no trace of violence or time.

"Like it's waiting," Idran said softly behind him.

Leonard nodded. "Or like something's already here and wants us to know it."

They pressed on, tension mounting, every step further into the unknown. The Tower's silence was not absence, but intention, a silence that watched and perhaps judged. Every shadow felt too thick.

The spiral ended without warning, a sudden emergence from the black coil of stairs into a wide open chamber. Overhead, the ceiling fractured into a rough-edged skylight, each stone slab split by old violence or impossible age. Through the gap, the sky pressed in. Not a single breeze reached them, but the air tasted metallic.

The group slowed as one, every instinct at war, curiosity pulling forward, survival screaming caution. The floor was smooth and dark, glassy in places, veined with hairline cracks that glowed faintly with a sick oil light. Nothing grew here. No moss, no dust, no sign of weather except for frost collecting around the room's single heart. The altar.

It wasn't truly an altar, not by the old rules. a slab of pale, bone-white stone in the center of the chamber, its edges warped and split. At its core, the rift bled upward, a gash about as wide as a sword, taller than any of them, but not huge. It shimmered in and out of focus, as if refusing to be looked at directly. Black-glow ether hung around it in sluggish, shifting strands, coiling upward toward the roof.

Leonard stopped on the threshold, unable to step closer just yet. The hum was in his chest again, a bone-deep vibration like an ache. It felt like a memory, but not his own.

Saran let out a slow, measured breath, hand never leaving her sword hilt. "That's it," she said quietly, jaw tight. "That's where they came from. The Ravagers, the ones in the fields. Came through here, I'd bet my oath on it."

Darum studied the edges of the rift, his expression grim, eyes flicking between the altar and the cracks in the floor. "Makes sense. There's no debris, no trace of battle, because they weren't here before. They bled in from somewhere else. This is the wound."

Idran moved with silent reverence, circling the rift, watching the shimmer of ether play across his outstretched hand.

"We can't leave it open," Idran said at last. "Whatever came through won't be the last. This... this is a breach, not a gateway. It'll keep bleeding until there's nothing left to bleed out."

Saran frowned. "So what's the plan, exactly? We don't know what started it, or what's waiting on the other side."

Idran gave a crooked, humorless smile. "You think I do? I'm improvising. The only thing Karth ever taught me was how to seal a wound, and this is a wound if I've ever seen one."

Leonard couldn't quite keep the skepticism out of his voice. "And if sealing it kills you?"

Idran met his gaze, something flinty there. "If it kills me, you'll know it didn't work. But it's worse if we walk away. The longer it's open, the more it eats through. I can feel it."

Darum limped forward, rubbing at the arm he'd half-dislocated in the last fight, jaw set like granite. He eyed the rift, then Idran. "You're a damn fool," he said, but there was no bite to it. Only a veteran's weariness. "But it's better than waiting for another horde to crawl through. What do you need?"

Idran exhaled slowly, flexing his fingers—blue veins of incantation stone under his skin catching the dim light. "I'll anchor the resonance, but I'll need you to brace it from the other side. Keep the pulse from rebounding and frying us both."

Darum grunted. "If we get vaporized, I'm blaming you in the next life."

Idran allowed himself a tight, brief smirk. "You won't be alone." He glanced at the others. "Get ready. If this goes wrong, run. If it works... you'll feel it."

Saran and Leonard exchanged a look, neither quite willing to say the thing they were both thinking: that nothing about this felt like salvation. But it was a plan, and for now, that was more than they'd had a moment ago.

Darum nodded once, jaw tight. "Let's close the wound."

Idran knelt, the powdered ward dust trailing in a careful circle around the altar and the rift. He worked with speed and precision, hands steady even as the ground beneath him seemed to thrum with some hungry, foreign pulse. Darum mirrored him on the opposite side, lowering himself to one knee with a grunt, his face drawn and pale under the torchlit gloom.

Leonard watched as Idran pressed his palm flat against the cold stone, fingers spread so the blue shards embedded in his forearm caught the sourceless, shifting light. Darum's hand joined his, Fazrum steel ringed with old scars and a faint, erratic glow leaking from his own incantation stone.

Then, the stone began to vibrate. The ward dust flared, lines of powder igniting in brilliant white, pushing back the darkness in sharp, jagged patterns. Idran's jaw clenched, sweat already beading at his hairline. Darum's breath came heavy, teeth gritted.

The rift responded, its edges flexed inward, the sickly black ether writhing as if caught in a closing fist. For one fragile moment, Leonard could almost believe it would work. The light tightened, the hum rose in pitch, space itself seemed to pull taut.

But then, like a snapped wire, everything recoiled.

The rift bulged and lashed out, a burst of force and sound that threw both Idran and Darum backward across the altar stone. The ward dust scattered in a smoking wave. Leonard staggered, Saran flung up an arm to shield her face. Idran landed hard on his shoulder, a hiss of pain escaping as the resonance in his arm flickered and dimmed.

The rift yawned wide, pulsing with triumphant black light.

From the heart of the rift, a shadow detached itself. A figure stepped from it as the void parted around him.

8

He was tall, his frame lean but strong beneath a grey cloak that hung untouched by the swirling chaos. The hood was drawn low, but as he stepped into the half-light, silver hair caught the glow, gleaming like moonlit steel. His face remained hidden, but there was nothing monstrous in his shape.

All four reacted instantly, steel flashed, incantation stones kindling, every muscle tensed. Leonard found himself just behind Saran, her sword at the ready, Darum already scrambling to regain his footing, Idran pressing a trembling palm to the altar stone, trying to draw strength from what little resonance remained.

The figure raised a single, gloved hand. His voice was low and absolutely even, unhurried, the words rippling across the fractured air.

"Stand down. I mean you no harm."

The words hung, too soft for command, too sure for a plea. The rift behind him pulsed once more, then narrowed, a clean seam in the world that refused to fully close.

"You have questions. I have answers. But you must listen, or all this"—a flick of his hand to the rift, the ruined ward circle,—"will be for nothing."

Saran's blade remained leveled at his heart, Darum's fists curled at his sides, Idran's face a mask of pain and calculation. Leonard, heart pounding, felt the old pulse in his head, the same song from before, now harmonizing with this newcomer's presence.

Saran's blade was still up, but Darum, shaking off the worst of the backlash edged forward with a growl, sword held at a defensive angle. Idran watched in wary silence, the blue fragments in his arms guttering with aftershock. Leonard tried to find breath; the song in his bones felt tangled and strange.

The figure turned directly to Leonard, and in the unnatural hush, the words landed with the weight of inevitability.

"I've been watching you for a long time, Leonard. Before the tower flared. Before the Pact. Before even Ulzaan guessed what was coming."

Darum's knuckles whitened on his hilt. "Who the hell are you?"

The stranger smiled faintly. "You can call me Alistair. I walk between what is and what must not be." He spoke it as if it was fact. "Ulzaan warned you once. After the Ninearts fell on your barracks. Do you remember what he said?"

Leonard's mouth went dry. Memory stabbed through the haze of battle, the night in his chamber, the copper stink of old blood.

'Alistair".

Leonard blinked, cold sweat trickling down his spine. "That was you."

Alistair nodded, gaze never wavering from Leonard's. "It was always me."

Leonard's hand clenched at his side, jaw set. "How could you possibly know that? You weren't there. No one but us, no one outside Fazrum even heard it."

Alistair regarded him for a moment, as if weighing how much truth the room could bear. He reached up, unhurried, and pulled back his hood.

The half-light caught his features: high cheekbones, sharp jaw, silver hair falling in clean lines around his face. But it was his eyes that caught them all, amber, clear and piercing, the same hue that haunted the records, the same uncanny shade as Leonard's own.

A breath seemed to leave the room.

Saran glanced at Leonard, then at Alistair, understanding flickering behind suspicion.

Darum's blade dropped another inch, eyes narrowed, reading the shape of a threat he didn't understand.

Alistair's lips curled in a quiet, humorless smile. "The world thinks this is about bloodlines or fate. It isn't. It's about resonance. The same song plays in both our bones."

He looked each of them in turn, but when his gaze landed on Leonard, it held. "You're not alone in this, Leonard. Not anymore. You never truly were."

Leonard couldn't pull his gaze from Alistair's eyes. Not just the color, but the weight behind them.

He found his voice, hoarse and thin. "What are you?"

Alistair didn't answer right away. He stepped forward, cloak whispering against stone, the rift's dark glow flickering over the scars in the floor. "That isn't the question that matters," he said, his words measured, almost gentle. "You want to know why I'm here. Why this rift exists. Why the world feels thinner every time you close your eyes."

Darum's jaw flexed. Saran hovered close, blade still in hand, though her posture had shifted, less threat, more bracing against a tide.

There once was a single being, a Creator, vast and solitary. From his longing, divine children were born. They grew proud, and in their pride, they coveted the power that shaped them."

Leonard felt the story coil through the bones of the tower, a myth with the iron taste of truth.

"There was war among them. A shattering. The Creator broken. The children scattered. The fragments of that first god fell through the world like burning stars."

Alistair's gaze flicked to Idran, to the blue stones still glowing faintly in his arms. "From those fragments, the first Eosians arose.

Not men, not gods, but something in between. Star-born. Amber-eyed. Builders of towers. They were meant to bridge what was broken, between this world and the place beyond the stars."

"The Towers were never prisons. Or relics. They are antennas. Through them, the Eosians sang to the void, called it close, sought answers from what came before. And the rifts above them—" He gestured to the wound in the air, bleeding black light. "—were not mistakes. They are doors. Offerings to what made us."

Idran scoffed, low and sharp. "Myths and children's tales."

Alistair's amber eyes narrowed, "And yet you speak to stone, shape the world with resonance. Would you call that science, son of Karth? Or something older, dressed in new names?"

Darum grunted, arms crossed. "Keep going."

Alistair nodded once, a concession and a warning. "You want answers. You deserve them. But every answer comes at a price."

He glanced up. The sky through the rift was wrong, stars sliding in unfamiliar patterns.

"All of this began with jealousy, and it ends in longing. The world isn't haunted by monsters. It's haunted by what it used to be, and by those who want it back."

His gaze landed again on Leonard, amber to amber.

"And some of us," he said softly, "carry the pattern inside us still."

Alistair's gaze drifted across the group, lingering on Darum's weathered brow, on Saran's white-knuckled grip, on Idran's stony defiance, and, last, on Leonard. There was something mournful in that final glance.

"Two of us survived the end of Eosian civilization," he said, voice threaded with memory. "I will not name the cause, for it's irrelevant now. What matters is that the pattern broke. Only two of us, myself, and the one you know as Samric."

He let that hang. Even the rift seemed to still.

"Samric, he who became your Enemy, the architect of purity. He believed in returning to the old ways, no matter the cost. Divine order. Genocidal ideals. A cleansing that would leave only those marked as worthy. His kin became his instruments, monsters now, but once they were children of the same shattered line."

Darum spat on the stone. Idran's lips pressed tight. Saran stared into the rift, refusing to flinch.

"And I—" Alistair's shoulders squared, silver hair shifting with the wind. "I watched. I learned. I refused to repeat the cycle. Exile was the price I paid. Waiting was the punishment I gave myself. Watching for a moment when the pattern might be broken, instead of repeated."

His eyes flicked upward, as if he saw that distant past play out among the unnatural stars. "The First Great War was not between gods and men. It was survival, humanity's last gasp before annihilation."

He paused, then spoke with deliberate clarity. "A desperate human warlord made a bargain. He sacrificed his own son to a raven-shaped god. In return, he received power enough to end the Enemy's war. This act became legend: the tale of the First King, of divine blessing and heroic death."

Alistair's voice hardened. "But the official story was written to bind a kingdom, not to free its people. The king was not blessed, he was condemned. The son was not martyred, he was spent."

Leonard's breath caught. The wind in the tower seemed to howl with accusation.

"A kingdom was born on that pact, Fazrum, your home. A lie at its root. You built your house on a foundation of blood and shadow, and called it triumph."

Saran shook her head, her voice barely above a whisper. "Then what are we fighting for?"

Alistair met her gaze. "For the truth. For the hope that history does not always have to become prophecy."

He looked at Leonard, apology in every line of his face. "You fight with blades forged from a lie. But you're not to blame for wielding them."

The silence following Alistair's confession was nearly suffocating. Wind pressed against the broken stones, whistling through cracks, scraping across the scarred altar at the tower's heart. Leonard's eyes fixed on Alistair, in the kind of hatred born from a lifetime of wounds given purpose.

"So what does any of this have to do with me? Why not choose anyone else, why build this around my life?"

Alistair's gaze didn't falter. His eyes are the same amber as Leonard's, filled with starfire. "Everything, Leonard. All of this. The towers. The rifts. Samric's war. You."

He moved forward, advancing on a patient who needed to hear the diagnosis. "I did not find you through prophecy, nor by accident. The world is made of threads, lives, choices, blood. Most pass and vanish, but a few leave marks on the pattern, scars in the fabric. I learned to read those scars, the way the stars shift, the way fate recoils from certain names."

Leonard shook his head, fists clenched. Alistair continued, voice quiet but merciless: "You weren't bred for this. You were born into it. One or both of your parents carried what remains of the Eosian blood, a faint, barely visible residue, but present enough to matter. Enough to make you a vessel. A flaw. A break in the cycle. I could not let that thread fray or disappear. They had to die."

A sound escaped Saran, a quiet, breathless cry of shock. Leonard's mouth twisted, pain flickering across his features, but Alistair did not soften.

"I did not kill them myself," he said, almost clinically. "That would have been an act of war, a god killing those with divine trace. But I ensured it happened. I moved pieces. I sent messages. I made sure the right doors were left open, the right people arrived too late or too soon. And when the blood settled, I was there to clean up, to erase the signs that would have given you away too quickly. I left you alone."

Saran's whisper cut the air. "You used him."

Alistair's face remained inscrutable. "I prepared him. I shaped the world so that when the pattern bent toward crisis, you, Leonard, would be its hinge. Its point of failure or of breaking free."

Leonard's hands tremble. "All this time, you made me this? Just another damn tool."

Darum's face was stone, but his eyes are glassy with anger. Idran, silent until now, spoke up, his voice hard. "So you're telling me... this boy is your weapon?"

Alistair's reply was immediate. "He is the only one who can break the cycle. Because he is not divine enough to perpetuate it, and not human enough to ignore it. I made sure of it. Samric's war cannot be won by gods or monsters. It can only be ended by someone broken enough to choose differently."

He let the words land, heavy as iron. "You are not a saviour, Leonard. You are the flaw. The thing they never planned for. The only hope this world has to refuse its inheritance."

Around them, the rift pulsed in slow, sick rhythm. The group was silent, caught between outrage and revelation, all eyes on Leonard, because at last, for good or ill, the pattern was clear.

Leonard's head felt packed with static. The wind clawing across the exposed stones at the tower's summit, rift pulsing at his back. The world, the war, his own memories, they were all just scaffolding now, bracing him against the truth as Alistair continues.

Leonard ground out the question, "And Samric? Where does he fit? What the hell is he planning?"

Alistair looks at him for a long moment. "Samric is The One. Not by fate, but by his own choosing. He is the last fragment of what the Eosians were meant to become, a vessel for divine reclamation. Now he intends to use the Black Tower in Fazrum as his altar, his engine, and his throne."

He gestures east, as if the tower were visible through the broken stone. "The tower is the kingdom's symbol. The place your first king made the sacrifice. That's why Samric chose it. When he completes his ritual, he will tether himself to the tower's heart. He becomes Fazrum. Fazrum becomes his prison. Or, if left unchecked, his gate."

Leonard's jaw clenches. "So what, you want us to just let him do it? Let him finish?"

Alistair's voice didn't rise, but there was weight behind it now.

"That's exactly what I want. You can't stop the ritual from starting. If you fight it, you only strengthen the bind. With you in his hands, he would finish it perfectly. Without you, the ritual will be desperate and fractured, Samric knows this, but he will still try. The divine blood must reclaim the earth, he cannot allow the cycle to fail, not now."

Darum snapped, fists bunched at his sides. "So we let him win? We stand by and watch him burn everything down?"

Alistair's expression hardened, for the first time a glint of something like resolve flickered in those alien eyes. "We let him finish. And then you, Leonard, refuse what he wants from you. You break the chain. You seal the rift from the inside. It will unbind Samric, weaken him enough to kill him. End the line for good. The cycle breaks not because we stopped the ritual, but because you refused to be used by it. That's the difference."

A long silence settles over the group. Even the rift's pulsing feels muted, as if waiting for their answer.

Saran's hand found Leonard's, steadying both of them. "So it's on us. On you."

As the final threads of Alistair's explanation settled, Darum's posture changed. He took one slow step forward, gaze fixed on the man by the rift. No hand to sword yet, but violence hung ready, knuckles bloodless on the hilt.

"I know you," Darum said. The words came out like something bitter dredged up.

Darum's voice was rough as gravel. "Years back. A letter, delivered by hand. No seal, just a time and a place. I was told to come to a house. And there you were. Cloaked, hood pulled low. Told me to go inside, right then, no matter what I saw." His breath hitched. "That was you. All that time."

Alistair inclined his head, the smallest nod. "And you found the boy."

Recognition hit Leonard with a physical force. That first night, the cold, the voices, Darum's arms scooping him from the wreckage. The memory flashed, half-lost in trauma.

Leonard: "That was you?"

Alistair, almost gently: "You don't remember me. That is the point."

Darum's fists closed, cords standing out on the backs of his hands. For a moment, it looked like he'd close the distance and punch the old man straight through the stone.

Saran was already moving. She stepped between them, shoulders square, not stopping Darum but intercepting the worst of his anger. "He wasn't the enemy. Not then."

Alistair stood still, perfectly balanced, observing Darum as a smith studied a flawed blade. Waiting to see if it would break.

Leonard couldn't stand still. He started to pace constrained circles near the rift, each step scraping the floor harder than the last. The rift's pulse throbbed louder, picking up his agitation.

"All of this," Leonard muttered, voice growing rough. "Every moment since that night. Every damn choice. You set it all up. None of it was ever really mine."

He halted, staring at Alistair, fists balled.

"What happened if I just walked into that rift and didn't come back? What then?"

Alistair answered evenly: "Then the cycle breaks. Just not in the way I hoped."

Leonard closed the distance in two angry strides, just shy of shoving Alistair, face to face. Darum's blade came out halfway with a hiss of steel. Idran's hand twitched toward his stones, not sure who to defend.

Leonard: "You killed my parents. You made me. You were no better than Samric."

Alistair met his fury with something utterly calm. "Correct."

"But I didn't make you choose to keep going."

Darum lowered his sword, jaw working. His voice was thick. "It was just like the Pact. We turned children into blades and called it duty. Called it peace."

Saran's hand found Leonard's shoulder. "You didn't have to decide everything right then. Not all of it."

Leonard looked at her, then back at the rift. The pulse slowed, drawn by something in him.

Alistair stepped away, moving toward the edge of the rooftop, cloak trailing. "You were a weapon. Now you were the one holding the fuse."

"And if I just walk away? If I refuse?"

Alistair's reply was soft, but final: "Then the divine falls to silence. And maybe, finally, something else will have a chance to speak."

A chill wind swept the tower, and for a moment it felt like all of history was balanced on the edge of Leonard's answer.

9

Leonard stood at the heart of the tower, feeling the echo of every choice that had brought him here. Cold wind curled around his ankles, pulling at his cloak, but the chill inside him ran deeper than stone or sky. The rift's black light bled into the chamber, and the weight of expectation pressed in from all sides.

Saran's hand caught Leonard's wrist before he could step forward. "Don't let him rush you," she whispered, voice filled with fear she barely bothered to hide. "We don't know what's on the other side."

Darum just shook his head, fists clenched. "It's a trick. There's always a cost, Leonard. Don't buy into his riddles. We came here to close this, not get lost in whatever hell that thing leads to."

Leonard met their eyes, heart pounding. "What choice do we have? If this is how we end it, we end it."

He turned to Alistair. "Then tell me. What has to be done?"

Alistair gave a small nod, like a teacher at a test's threshold. "You must learn to close it, Leonard. Not just seal the wound, but unmake the channel. That's why you're here."

Leonard eyed the altar, the dusting of crystal around the rift. "So I just... perform a ritual? Like Idran and Darum tried?"

Alistair shook his head. "No. The rift isn't a wound you stitch shut from the outside. It's a gate. You have to enter it. I'll guide you through. Only those with eosian blood can pass the threshold safely.."

The words seemed to ring louder than any pulse of void-magic. Saran's face went pale, and she stepped between Leonard and the scar in the world. "Absolutely not. We don't even know if that's true, what if you're wrong? What if you're lying?"

Alistair met her stare evenly. "You saw what happened when you tried to close it by force. This is the only way. If you want to keep your world, let the boy decide."

Darum spat onto the stone, jaw tight with barely-suppressed rage. "You just want a key. You're using him like the rest of them."

Leonard shook his head. "No. This time, I'm choosing."

He broke away from Saran's grasp, every step feeling heavier than the last. "If I don't come back, close the door behind me. Whatever happens, don't let anything else through."

Idran watched him with narrowed eyes, but said nothing. There was an understanding there, sharp and unspoken.

Leonard stepped to the edge of the rift, darkness licking up like a living tongue. Alistair moved to his side, hand hovering just behind Leonard's shoulder.

Saran called his name one last time, voice shaking. "Leo—"

He turned, caught her eyes, and nodded. "Trust me. Please."

She didn't answer, but she didn't move to stop him again.

Alistair gestured to the rift, the unending void shimmering just out of reach. "Breathe. Let it in. And walk forward. I'll be with you, every step."

Leonard took a breath so deep it threatened to shatter him. The rift pulsed. He stepped forward. The world flickered, then broke apart.

Leonard's first step into the rift was like plunging face-first into a memory too raw to hold. There was no sense of any floor, no wind on his skin, no resistance, only an immediate unraveling of everything that defined his place in the world. His feet found no ground, but somehow he moved, tumbling and floating at once, lost between breaths.

Sound and color exploded across his vision. He glimpsed bands of blue and gold, heard the shuddering clang of bells and a dozen voices singing at once, none of it in a language he recognized. For an endless heartbeat, his body forgot itself. His skin was a membrane, his mind, a tide. Everything else,the tower, the others, his own voice, vanished.

Then something steadied him. Alistair's hand, impossibly solid, gripped Leonard's forearm. "Steady. It passes."

Leonard tried to focus. Shapes pulsed around him: a thousand motes of light swimming in a vast, horizonless dark, like a sea without gravity or anchor. Some flared and winked out, others pulsed with an oily, slow illumination. The ground, if it was ground, shivered underfoot. Above, or maybe below, a storm of void and starlight brewed.

A sensation swept over him, falling, but upward, stomach lurching, vertigo without descent. He tried to orient himself, but the effort left him dizzy and weak. "What is this place?" he managed, voice nearly lost in the hollow echo.

Alistair, gliding forward with unnatural ease, turned and beckoned. "This is the space between spaces. The tissue the divine once walked to bind worlds together." He gestured, and the plane seemed to widen: as Leonard's vision cleared, he saw nodes of bright, crystalline light hanging at impossible distances, each like a lantern behind thick glass. "Here, we are neither alive nor dead, neither present nor past. Here, what we bring is what we become."

The song of the towers, so faint in Leonard's waking world, now screamed through him. He clutched his head, staggering. The harmonics were endless, a chorus of commands, warnings, prayers, all at once. Each note twisted, distorted, undercut by a grinding undertone he knew, somehow, was not natural.

Alistair steadied him with a hand on his shoulder. "You hear it more clearly than most. Don't fight it. Listen."

Leonard tried. In the cacophony, a pattern flickered, a code, something like memory and warning braided into one.

They moved through the liminal plane, weightless. Each step brought them closer to those shining nodes. Leonard realized what they were: the rifts, each beacon the mouth of an active Black Tower bleeding into this realm, each one a door into the mortal world.

Alistair's gaze flicked between them. "These are the wounds. Samric opened them, each one an invitation. And our kin, those who remain on this side, have begun to answer. Some twist into forms that should never have been, Ravagers, Shades, and worse. Others simply listen, hoping for the cycle to be broken, or continued."

For a moment, Leonard let the weight of the place settle around him, cold and vast. The towers' song pulsed again, and he realized he could feel the others far away, Darum, Saran, Idran, just faintly, their lives tethered to his own.

He moved forward, following Alistair, into the sea of suspended light and gathering dark. The path ahead waited, wide and wild. And somewhere in the song, he heard his own name called, as if by voices that had never been human.

The light of the liminal space warped as if it were a thin sheet drawn over a vast, restless sea. Leonard felt it first as a shifting at the edges of vision, nodes of rift-light shivering, their glow no longer steady. The whole place dimmed and brightened in irregular pulses, shadows twisting in directions that had no correspondence to the world he knew.

Alistair stopped so abruptly that Leonard almost floated past him. His shoulders squared, silver hair haloed in unnatural radiance, gaze suddenly very far away. Even his calm fractured for an instant.

"We do not belong here long," Alistair said, voice clipped, wary. "There are things in the void that are not blind. The longer we remain, the more we risk being seen."

Leonard's nerves shrieked with a new kind of pressure, a spiritual weight that dragged at his bones and heart. He tried to breathe, but the act felt borrowed. The light grew colder. Somewhere in the unfathomable distance, the shadows twisted tighter, a ripple in the ether revealing a presence watching back.

He couldn't see its form only that the void itself recoiled around it, shapes collapsing into a brief, jagged outline. An impression of limbs, too many and too long, like a trick of vision caught between one blink and the next. The song of the towers warped, every harmony souring for a heartbeat.

"Focus, Leonard," Alistair said, stepping closer, drawing his attention away from the yawning dark. "We are here for the gate, not the abyss. Whatever stirs beyond, it is not yet awake. But it will be, if we linger."

Leonard forced himself to meet Alistair's eyes, trying to shut out the sense of being noticed, picked out of a crowd by something that had never learned to blink. The pressure faded a notch, but the memory of that shadow's outline stuck in his vision like afterimage.

"Move with me," Alistair urged, his voice low. "We have little time. The longer the rift is open, the louder its song, and the more attention it draws. If the wrong eyes turn here, no door you close will hold them out."

Leonard nodded. He gritted his teeth, bracing himself against the weight of everything unseen, and followed Alistair onward, deeper into the light and toward the waiting gate, the threat of the void dogging every step.

Alistair led Leonard through the rippling dark, guiding him to the edge of the chosen rift, a swirling wound in this non-place, black at its core but rimmed with amber fractures, as if the scar itself were burning from within. Leonard could sense, not see, that this was a quieter gate. The song here was softer, the pressure less keen. Even so, the air, if it could be called that, trembled with the threat of collapse.

"Here," Alistair said, his hand steady on Leonard's shoulder. "I mapped this rift before. If we can close one without alerting Samric, it's this. Once we're done, we return to our entry. We mustn't linger."

Leonard nodded, every nerve tight. Alistair did not produce symbols or relics,no incantation in the physical sense. The ritual, if it was one, began inside: Leonard closed his eyes and tried to find the center of himself, the place where memory and pain met something older.

"Feel the thread," Alistair said, voice a deep chord beneath the endless music. "Not the tower, not the song, yourself. The echo the world left in you. The thread I marked but never owned."

It was agony, dredging up the shape of who he was. Grief, stuttered through him: his mother's voice, his father's smile, the cold night Darum found him, the years of forging purpose in the Pact. Every injury, every scar. For a moment, the rift sang back, offering to pull him apart, split him into all the things he might have been.

Leonard refused. He locked his jaw, focused on the names and faces that tethered him, Saran, Darum, even Idran and Ulzaan. He willed himself to remain whole.

Alistair's presence was there too, harmonizing with him, a resonance, amber and sharp, not quite comfort but not abandonment. For a beat, their lights flared together, two amber flames against the void.

The rift writhed, trying to catch and duplicate Leonard's essence, searching for a crack. He gripped tighter to his own identity, forcing it back, clinging to the idea that he was still himself.

Then, everything inverted. Light collapsed inward, folding on itself in a silent, implosive twist. The rift contracted to a burning point, then winked out, leaving nothing but chill silence and the memory of its hunger.

Leonard staggered, gasping, sweat on his brow though he wasn't sure he still had a body here. Alistair caught him with a hand, urgent. "Quickly. The gate we came through, move. Before anything else answers the call."

Together, they wove through the liminal dark, the warning pressure from earlier rising behind them. Leonard didn't look back. When they reached the rift that led home, Alistair didn't hesitate. He pulled Leonard with him, stepping through the threshold and out of the void, back into the mortal world.

Leonard hit the tower stones with a rattling, bone-deep thud. He coughed, gasped air and time slamming back into his chest in a rush. His senses sputtered, the sky overhead was sharp and colorless, the rift now only a faint scar of light where he and Alistair had emerged.

Saran was there first, hands firm on his shoulders. "Leo! Are you—?"

He nodded, unable to get words out at first. Darum knelt on his other side, already checking for broken bones or worse, one steady hand at Leonard's wrist to find his pulse.

"Give him room," Darum muttered, but he looked relieved. Even Idran hovered close, wary but attentive.

Alistair stood over them. The calm he wore was real, but his cloak was torn at the hem, and his silver hair was tangled, wet with sweat. His left hand trembled, the first visible sign of strain Leonard had seen in him.

Leonard forced himself to sit up. The world spun, but he swallowed it down. "Is it... always going to feel like that?" His voice was hoarse.

Alistair's answer was blunt but not unkind: "That was your first. The last must be yours alone." He looked down. A simple truth, as old as the towers themselves.

Saran squeezed Leonard's shoulder, not letting go even when he tried to stand. "You did it," she murmured, half in awe, half in terror.

Darum, still kneeling, wiped blood from Leonard's cheek, just a scrape. "Next time, warn us before you go walking through the sky,"

Leonard tried to laugh. It came out as a ragged exhale.

The group gathered themselves, exhaustion a mantle they all wore. The wind across the roof was cold, and the closed rift still pulsed faintly under Leonard's skin.

Alistair pulled his cloak tight, meeting the group's eyes one by one. "We're not finished. Samric will move soon. We must reach Fazrum, the capital. Ulzaan must hear the whole of it."

Darum nodded, jaw set. "We can make it in three days, if the roads hold."

Saran looked at Alistair, then Leonard. "You're coming with us. No more shadows. No more secrets."

Alistair inclined his head, a wry glint in his tired eyes. “As you wish. For now, we walk together.”

Idran spoke quietly from the side. “Let’s move before the tower decides to wake something else.”

No one argued. They gathered their things in silence, battered but alive, and made for the stairs, five shadows cast long across the stones, leaving the tower and a wound in the world behind them.

Ahead, the road to Fazrum waited. And with it, whatever choice would come at the end.

10

Ulzaan walked the broad stone parapet, boots scraping along grooves worn by centuries of sentries and storm. The citadel crowned Fazrum's heart, its towers catching the city's first gold, dawn or dusk, it barely mattered anymore. Every day was shadowed, every night too thin. Below, the city churned in a slow, uneasy rhythm.

Civilians queued beneath market awnings, their lines patient but stretched thin, hands clutching ration tokens and hollow hope. Overhead, the banners hung flat and colorless, black on silver, no wind to stir them. Drills echoed in the lower yards, watchmen running through sword forms and shield drills with grim efficiency. Hammers struck against wood and iron, the clangs ringing out through streets that should have been filled with the raucous noise of festival or trade.

No fear in the faces below, only exhaustion and resignation. Ulzaan watched it all with the dispassion of a man who'd spent decades preparing for a war no one wanted and everyone expected. There was order, yes, but order was a blade, sharpest just before it broke.

He paused near the bastion's edge, hands folded behind his back, eyes scanning the city's arteries. He could see the outer walls, lines of soldiers stationed every hundred paces, faces obscured by helm and distance. Further on, the refugee camps pressed up against the stone, shanties and tents braced for a siege that hadn't yet come but lived in every rumor.

The king's banners still flew above the keep, but the king himself had not been seen in days. The ministers were nervous and divided, some were quietly missing, others too vocal, ran the business of the city with trembling hands. Ulzaan's authority had grown in the vacuum, but he wore it like a wound, not a crown.

He looked up as a courier hurried across the walk, nodding a silent report, nothing new, not yet. From the east, thunder rolled, but it was only the gates opening, a squad in Ravenblood black approaching, travel-stained and battered, but alive.

Even at this distance, Ulzaan felt the hairs on his arms rise, a memory of old prophecy and recent warnings flickering to life. He exhaled through his nose, cold and steady.

He left the wind and gold behind, descending into the bones of the citadel. The stone corridors felt colder, chiseled with the history of every siege and every failed peace. His footsteps fell in time with the muted march of the city above, never rushed, but never slow enough for doubt to settle in.

He passed Ravenblood officers in close conference, their faces hard and sleepless, voices pitched low. One relayed a report of breaches in the west quarter, only rats, not spies. Another handed out new patrol orders, the ink still drying. No one wasted words. Walls were being shored up with scrap wood and battered barricades. In one corner, a scribe fed documents into a brazier with ink-stained fingers, eyes red, watching as secrets curled into ash.

A few of his men spotted him and gave the nod, a subtle tilt of the chin, a brief touch to the hilt. Not for ceremony. For certainty. Habit that ran deeper than the blood-stained flags above their heads.

He crossed a landing where an old shield hung askew, its raven crest blackened and split. On the flagstones below, a skysteel resonance token, once meant to carry spells and hope, lay shattered, kicked to the side and forgotten.

Ulzaan paused, studied the fracture lines, then kept walking. This was the way of it, things breaking quietly before the loudness came. He walked on, shoulders squared, bearing the silent cost.

Ulzaan stepped inside the cramped war room, ducking through the narrow arch and letting the door thud behind him. The space was smaller than the grand council chamber, deliberately close, lit by a battered lamp and thick with the smell of wax and old parchment. Here, decisions were made without the trappings of the throne, just enough room for a handful of the right people, and never quite enough air.

Brent looked up first, posture snapping to something near parade-ready, though exhaustion carved deep under his eyes. "Ulzaan." The word carried a relief he didn't bother to hide. "Lines are holding. Just. Most garrisons are at half-strength, some less. We're burning through rations faster than command will admit. If the next push comes before the outer wards reset, we'll be choosing which street to lose."

Eleseth barely moved, hunched over a table heavy with open scrolls, candle stubs melting onto the map beneath her elbows. Her hair was streaked with new grey since Ulzaan had seen her last, her robes patched at the cuffs. She didn't bother looking up as she spoke. "We're no closer to a pattern. The tower pulses don't match the old concordances. Everything's fragmentary, deliberately so, I suspect. Even the wards are singing out of key."

At the far side of the table, Tannis lingered near the wall, back straight as a pike, hands folded over a slim satchel. The court official's sash was wrinkled at the collar, and a hint of nervous sweat had gathered beneath his powdered hair. "His Majesty's office expects a full report within the hour." He tried to sound brisk, but the words tripped at the end, strained. "I'm to reiterate the need for restraint, no escalations unless provoked. And strict adherence to the council's protocol regarding—" his gaze flicked to Eleseth and quickly away "—arcane intervention."

Brent rolled a shoulder, glanced at Ulzaan. "That's the long and short of it. What we need is more time than the enemy's willing to give. What we have is a wall of tired men and a ledger that won't balance."

Eleseth snorted softly. "If the enemy is what I think it is, I doubt the king's protocols will buy us much."

Ulzaan held the center of the room, listening. The air pressed in, full of words left unsaid and the gnawing sense that the next decision would matter more than any order from the throne. There was no comfort here, only the cold arithmetic of survival. And in the city below, dawn was shifting to day, the weight of every cracked shield and broken token echoing in the stone.

The war room had been stripped of pretense by the time Ulzaan finally spoke. Candle stubs leaned into puddles, their light guttering under the weight of stale air and clashing words. He'd let the bickering play out until silence became a dare, until the tension left even the stone beneath their boots thrumming.

Brent's voice was a cracked blade, every edge dulled by repetition but still willing to cut. "We can't keep waiting. Last time they hesitated, we lost the east bank and two squads with it. You want to watch the same thing happen here because the king's seal isn't warm enough?"

Eleseth's hands hovered above the parchment marking invisible connections. "I've cross-checked every record, every prophecy, every wild-eyed warning the Sages kept buried. The only constant is chaos. The signs, the cycles, some say we're past the time of reckoning. Others claim we're still early. I've heard of convergence before, but this, this isn't in any doctrine."

Tannis bristled, rolling his cuffs as if the fabric might give him backbone. "The king's command stands. His seal remains unbroken. Unless the council convenes or His Majesty issues new orders, our hands are tied. The protocols—"

Brent cut him off with a look that would have felled a lesser man. "Protocol's going to get us killed. Or worse, it'll keep us here, comfortable and blind, until the city's nothing but banners and bodies."

Ulzaan let the silence build, absorbing every flicker of accusation. His gaze drifted from the tired lines in Brent's brow to the grey spiderwebbing at Eleseth's temples, to Tannis's eyes darting like a trapped animal's. Only then did he speak.

"If we wait for the next order, the city will be lost by the time it's written."

The table stilled. The sentence landed like iron.

Tannis dabbed at his hairline, blinking. "His Majesty is occupied. In spiritual preparation. The rites require his full attention. The burden of sovereignty—"

Brent laughed, the sound brittle and cold. "Burden? I've seen kings lead from the front. I've seen them die in mud and worse. Don't tell me a private rite is more important than the city choking on its own fear."

Eleseth's voice was colder. "Every hour we delay, more are lost. The enemy isn't waiting for the king to finish his prayers."

Tannis's reply came fast, desperate. "He is aware. He knows the city's condition. He receives daily reports. You—" He faltered, hands trembling as he gripped the edge of the table. "Your responsibility is to maintain order until the council convenes."

Ulzaan fixed Tannis with a stare that didn't blink. "Order." He tasted the word, found it wanting. "We have order, Tannis. It's what's left when everything else is already gone. You want more banners, more decrees? I want enough men to hold the line through another night."

A silence hung, the kind that carried all the wrong questions. Somewhere in the distance, another bell rang, a signal, or maybe just time dragging its feet.

Eleseth leaned back, shadows hollowing her cheeks. "You're either lying, or you're being lied to."

Brent's eyes didn't leave Tannis. "Tell us, councilor. When did you last see His Majesty with your own eyes?"

Tannis's mouth worked, then set into a pale, uncertain line. "His Majesty is conducting a personal rite. No one is permitted to disturb him."

A lie, or something close enough that it made no difference.

Ulzaan didn't move. The room had already chosen its center of gravity, and it wasn't protocol. Not anymore.

The air in the war room was close, heavy with old smoke and the taste of coming storms. Outside, the city creaked on, brittle and sleepless, the next hour promising nothing but harder decisions.

Ulzaan's hand rested on the table, fingers splayed on cold wood, steady as stone. The arguments had nowhere left to run. They would either break here, or in the streets above.

Tannis's lips had just begun to tremble, some last excuse dying on his tongue, when the heavy door shuddered open. The noise broke the air like a dropped shield.

A Ravenblood runner skidded to a halt just inside the threshold, tunic askew, breath punching out of his lungs. "Lord, visitors at the inner gate. Blade Veteran Darum is among them. Others, too." His voice tried for steadiness, failed, but no one seemed to notice.

Every face in the room turned, tension splintering into raw attention. Ulzaan was already rising. "Bring them here," he said, not loud but enough to fill the space.

Brent's brows jumped, then settled into a frown, surprise, calculation, relief, all tangled in a moment. Eleseth watched, something like recognition flickered beneath her fatigue. Tannis pressed one hand flat to the table, the other gripping the sash at his waist, clinging to order by a single thread.

The runner vanished, boots echoing down the hall, and for a breath nobody moved.

It wasn't long before the door swung open again, this time more deliberate. The first figure to cross the threshold was Darum, cloak heavy with dust, the old veteran's face carved deeper than when he'd last stood in this room. He didn't bother with ceremony, just a curt nod.

Saran followed, eyes flicking between faces, her stance loose but her gaze already mapping exits and threats. Idran, entered after, offering a formal bow but no words.

And last, Leonard. He looked older, the soft edges burnt away, jaw set, shoulders straight. The torchlight caught in his eyes, a molten amber that seemed almost to hum. It was the kind of gaze you didn't meet by accident. Ulzaan felt something old and prophetic coil in his gut. He didn't look away.

A single heartbeat hung between them, thick with everything they'd carried to this room.

Then the air shifted. From behind Leonard, a figure slipped through, a cloak the color of grey ash, hood drawn low over his face. His footsteps were quiet, almost soundless against the flagstones, the weight of his arrival more felt than heard.

The room seemed to pull tighter, as if his presence bent gravity itself. Even Eleseth sat up straighter, wariness chasing exhaustion from her eyes.

Ulzaan watched as Alistair lifted his head, just enough for their gazes to meet. The faintest glimmer of amber in his eyes, more memory than reflection. For a moment, the world shrank to the space between those two men, history older than the city, burdens that could not be named.

Ulzaan's hand hovered above the map, then dropped to his side. He spoke with the weight of command and the hunger of a man who knew he'd waited long enough.

"Bring them forward," Ulzaan said. "All of them."

11

The war room held its breath. Leonard felt the charge roll through every body present, tension arcing from floor to ceiling, dust swirling in the lamp-lit hush. The last words had barely settled, but the myth was real now, Alistair stood before them, hood thrown back.

Eleseth broke the silence, not with fear but a sharpness born of desperation. "If we're to believe any of this, we need proof." Her hand hovered over the rune-etched table, fingers twitching for certainty, for anything solid. "Let me test him with the stone."

Ulzaan stepped in. " No, I'll see to the test." He didn't wait for assent. His gaze swept the room. "No one interferes."

Brent's jaw clenched. "But Ulzaan, if he isn't what he claims—"

"Then we'll know," Ulzaan said. He turned his palm over, the faint glow of his incantation stone flickering to life, casting hard shadows up his wrist.

Darum grunted, low. "Let him do it. He's the only one here with the will to see this through." Still, Leonard caught the twitch in Darum's stance, the barest signal, ready to move if anything went wrong.

Idran, arms crossed, offered a half-smirk. "Only in Fazrum do they test gods with stones made for men. Try not to burn down your own council chamber."

Saran didn't speak, but her eyes traced every breath, her stance ready, reading the smallest shifts, every heartbeat a signal.

Alistair didn't flinch. He raised his own hand, pale, old scars ribboning the palm. For a moment, Leonard thought he saw something move beneath Alistair's skin, a flicker, a constellation just below the surface.

Ulzaan placed his hand atop Alistair's, palms pressed together. The room went still. The air tightened, thick as blood.

Light bled out, first soft, then searing. Leonard felt his stomach clench, sweat prickle down his back. The temperature climbed, a roaring, silent fire pressing in from everywhere. Saran edged a step closer to Leonard, as if she could shield him from what came next.

The flare peaked, then snapped. The world jerked back into focus. Ulzaan's jaw was set, eyes wild for half a second before cooling again. Alistair staggered, breath hitching. The room exhaled, but no one moved. Leonard felt the weight of what they'd just witnessed settling over them. Eleseth's hand still hovered over the table, slightly trembling. Brent's knuckles were white where he gripped his sword hilt, as if expecting Alistair to explode into violence at any second.

Darum shifted, just barely, but Leonard caught it, the way his gaze swept the room, cataloging exits, measuring distances. Old habits. Soldier's instinct. Even now in the face of the divine.

Idran broke the silence with a low whistle. "Well. That was either proof or the most elaborate suicide attempt I've ever seen."

Saran shot him a look. "Shut up."

Alistair wiped the blood from his thumb, as if giving them time to process. His breathing steadied, the pain already fading from his expression.

"He is what he says he is," Ulzaan said.

Eleseth exhaled, shoulders dropping as if a noose had loosened. "I saw it too. The resonance, no normal mortal could have survived that. Especially not coming from the strategos"

Brent stepped back, knuckles white. Darum eased, just a hair, giving Ulzaan the smallest nod, trust reaffirmed, at least for now.

Idran let out a laugh, sharp, with a Karthian edge. "Fazrum, trying to make gods bleed to feel safe in their faith."

Saran shot him a look, but kept her thoughts close, scanning the corners of the room, cataloguing the way every person shifted now that the impossible had a name.

Darum stood just behind Leonard, a silent wall. He had one eye on Brent, one on the assembled outsiders, his presence a quiet promise: nothing comes for you unless it goes through me.

Leonard tried to steady his own pulse, amber gaze darting between faces. The world had just changed. He wondered if anyone in the city would ever know how close they'd just come to disaster, or what they'd unleashed by letting a living myth bleed onto their council floor.

The room's heat drained away, replaced by something heavier like acceptance, or maybe the edge of panic held in check. Leonard watched Ulzaan, and saw the moment the Strategos' patience turned to iron. Whatever argument was left in the room was dead now, smothered by the myth bleeding quietly at the heart of Fazrum's war council.

Ulzaan squared his shoulders, voice flat as stone. "No more debate. We go to the throne room. We speak to the king, or to whatever is left of him." His eyes never left Tannis, whose lips moved but found no sound.

Tannis tried to rally, fingers clinging to council orders like a child to a drowning plank. "We are not authorized...protocol and council procedure—"

Ulzaan didn't so much raise his voice as step closer, a living wall blotting out the bureaucracy. "There's no council left. Only the city, and those willing to stand for it. Out of my way, Tannis. Or you can explain to the people why you waited for a dead seal while the walls fell."

Brent's armor groaned as he shifted his weight, jaw clenched, eyes darting from Ulzaan to the stunned courtier. Eleseth rolled up her scroll, hands shaking just a little, but her mouth was set.

Darum moved to the rear, a silent anchor, making it clear with a look and the threat of his bulk that no one would slip away unnoticed.

They left the war room in a procession that felt more like a verdict than an order. Down the corridors, the pace brisk, Ulzaan's stride dictating urgency, Darum herding stragglers with a glance. Servants scattered at their approach, some ducking behind columns, others fumbling with messages they'd never deliver. A pair of guards blocked the hall, then stood aside without a word, uncertain whether to salute or bar the path. The group swept past, a wedge of purpose cutting through the drifting fog of palace routine.

Leonard felt every eye of confusion and awe, the budding panic of people who sense that history is shifting and no one's steering anymore.

The doors to the throne room loomed ahead, taller than any man, banded in black iron and battered wood. For a heartbeat, the party hesitated, then Ulzaan pushed through, doors groaning open on their ancient hinges.

Inside, the grandeur was wasted. Light slanted through high windows, catching dust motes dancing in stagnant air. The banners, once black and silver, proud and heavy, hung limp, the color leeched from them. At the throne, the king's chair sat vacant. Near it, a trunk gaped open, garments and seals scattered, a wax signet crushed underfoot. One chair lay on its side, legs splintered. An inkwell had spilled, the stain dried and crusted, a little map of abandonment. It was a room that had been left in a hurry.

Leonard took a step forward, boots scraping against something. He looked down, a child's toy, carved wood, a horse with one leg missing. His stomach twisted. The royal family had children. They'd fled so fast they'd left pieces of their lives scattered like refuse.

Brent made a sound, half-choked, and turned away. His shoulders shook once, then went rigid.

Eleseth moved to the throne, ran her fingers along the armrest.

"The cushion's gone," she said quietly. "They took it. For comfort on the road, maybe. Or to sell." Her voice was hollow. "They left the throne but took the cushion."

Darum's hands curled into fists. Leonard heard his breathing change, sharp and controlled, the kind of anger that didn't explode but burned deep.

Saran didn't move, but her gaze swept the room methodically, looking for threats that weren't there anymore. Looking for anything to focus on besides the enormity of the betrayal.

Tannis, sagging, let out a sound between a sob and a gasp. “They're gone. The royal family, all of them. Fled days ago. I stayed, I thought they'd return. I thought...” He couldn't finish. He wilted, shame pouring off him in waves.

Brent closed his eyes, lips pressed flat, fury and grief battling for purchase. Eleseth's gaze was faraway, lost in the dust. Saran shifted, always between Leonard and disaster, eyes darting over the room as if waiting for the walls to fall next.

Darum stepped forward, voice a low grind. “You let us fight, let people die, for a crown that already ran. You coward.”

Tannis broke, crumpling to his knees amid spilled ink and scattered seals. He had nothing left.

Alistair stood at the edge, cloak like stormcloud, posture untouched by the wreckage of protocol or faith. He studied the empty throne, then spoke, not loud, but it carried.

“Your kings built this city with blood and stone. The first of them, brutal as he was, stood for his people when the sky darkened and the earth split. This one? He ran before the bell even rang.”

Leonard watched, pulse racing, the amber in his vision burning bright. There was no myth left to hide behind. Only themselves, and what they would do next.

~

THEY REGROUPED in a chamber stripped of ceremony, a council room, once polished for visiting dignitaries, now raw-boned and honest.

The torches guttered low, casting everyone in flickering relief, the air thick with the iron tang of disappointment and the faint smell of old ink.

Ulzaan stood at the head of the battered table, hands braced on scarred wood, voice cutting through the stunned hush. “We move now. We cannot let the city see a vacuum, not for an hour. Ravenblood does not defend shadows, we break them. We strike at the nearest black tower before Samric or his little spies realize the king is gone, Samric cannot know what Alistair told us, so we keep him in the dark as much as possible.”

The weight of what Ulzaan was proposing settled over the room, a battle, but a gamble with lives they couldn't afford to lose.

Leonard felt it in his chest, the tightness of knowing this was the only move left. Not the smart move. Not the safe move. But the only one.

Darum's gaze met Ulzaan's across the table, and something passed between them, the grim recognition of men who'd run out of good options a long time ago.

Eleseth's fingers stilled on the map. She didn't look up when she spoke. "If we fail, the city won't have time to mourn us. Samric will be through the gates before the bodies are cold."

"Then we don't fail," Ulzaan said.

Brent shook his head, already pacing. “That’s madness. You could get good men killed before we even breach the perimeter. The city’s half-starved, morale’s in the gutter. You want to bleed our best for a show?”

Ulzaan’s gaze never wavered. “A show is exactly what we need. The Pact was never made for safe victories. We were made for this, for the impossible, for the walls everyone else says can’t be held. If we sit and wait, the city falls apart before the enemy even touches the stones.”

Darum, hands folded behind his back, nodded, weariness layered over conviction. “It’s not about glory, Brent. It never was. We fight because we’re all that’s left. The moment we let them smell fear, it’s over. We’ve survived worse. Most of us shouldn’t have lived to see this day. But we did. We're still standing. That's the reason to fight, not the banners or the old king's crown."

Eleseth, hunched over a half-rolled map, tapped the surface for silence. "If we want the bluff to work, we need the appearance of overwhelming strength. Reinforcements, real or not, must be visible on the walls. Sages in plain sight. If the city looks vulnerable, Samric will see through the ruse in a heartbeat. The city must look defended."

Saran, quiet until now, drew a sharp breath. "Leonard doesn't go alone this time. Not again." Her tone was calm, but there was steel in it. "I failed once and couldn't protect him. I won't stand aside and watch it happen again."

Idran, eyes narrowed, arms folded, muttered, "If I'm to help, I'll have to call in favors I thought were spent. My family in Karth, if I promise them safety, maybe troops will come. But you know how far that trust runs."

Saran turned to Idran, "I'm going with you to Karth"

Idran's eyebrows rose. "You sure about that? Karth isn't Fazrum. My family's court makes this place look like a monastery."

"I've been through worse," Saran said, though her tone suggested she wasn't entirely convinced.

Leonard opened his mouth, then closed it. He wanted to argue, to say she shouldn't go, that splitting up was madness. But he knew that look on her face, the one that said the decision was already made, and arguing would only waste time they didn't have.

Ulzaan nodded once, accepting it. "You'll need papers. Credentials. Something to get you past the border patrols without starting a conflict."

"I'll handle it," Idran said. "My family seal still carries weight. For now."

Darum turned to Saran, voice low and meant only for her. "You're right to go. But Karth politics is a nest of blades. Don't get caught thinking it's just another campaign. I've seen alliances turn on a phrase."

Saran nodded once

Ulzaan swept the room with a final look. “This isn’t unanimous. It doesn’t have to be. Brent, you stay here. Organize the defense, keep the streets full and the lies believable. If Samric suspects for a moment that the city’s hollow, we’re finished. Darum and Leonard, you’re with me. Saran, Idran, make your calls, move now. Eleseth, I need you and every Sage you can muster on the ramparts, set up as many ward stones and runes as you can.

The plan was a patchwork of desperation and old legend, but the only option left. The group broke, some with certainty, most with only the necessity of motion.

Brent looked gutted, lips pressed white, but nodded once. “I’ll make it work. I always do.”

Through it all, Alistair moved quietly along the room’s far edge, hands clasped behind his back, head bowed as if listening for something only he could hear.

Leonard felt his gaze first, a silent weight, neither burden nor blessing, just recognition. No advice passed between them. Except the silent confirmation that, whatever else might come, Alistair would not be there to intervene.

Eleseth noticed, cutting through the haze of orders and stratagems. “Will you stay?” she asked, her tone not quite pleading,

Alistair offered the faintest smile, weathered and almost gentle. “My part here is finished. This is for you now.” He dipped his head in a gesture that held both farewell and absolution.

Darum caught the movement, eyes narrowing just enough to mark the departure. He didn’t call Alistair back, there was nothing left to demand.

A moment later, when Leonard looked again, the space by the door was empty. No footsteps or echoes were heard.

Leonard stared at the empty space, something cold settling in his chest. He'd expected, what? A warning? A blessing? Something to justify the weight Alistair's presence had carried.

But there was nothing.

Darum moved to his side."He gave you what he could. The rest is on us."

Leonard nodded, he wanted to believe that. Wanted to believe any of this was enough.

Eleseth broke the moment. "If we're moving, we need to move now. Every minute we delay, the city slips further into chaos."

Ulzaan was already heading for the door. "Then let's not waste them."

The room emptied quickly after that, each person carrying their piece of the plan into the uncertain night.

THE CITY beyond the walls was a mosaic of torches and scattered shouts, the old stone echoing with unrest that wouldn't settle. Up on the parapet, Saran rolled her shoulder, testing the ache that lingered beneath the fresh linen of her chest. She'd never let it slow her, she'd never let anyone see if it did.

Leonard leaned beside her, knuckles pale on the weathered stone, posture just a little too stiff. Neither spoke at first. Far below, someone barked orders. Someone else cursed the cold.

Saran broke the quiet with a familiar snort, jabbing an elbow at him. "If you'd learned to strap your armor straight, maybe you wouldn't walk like the world's about to trip you up."

Leonard managed a thin smile. "Coming from the woman who once put her breastplate on backward and called it fashion." He tried to keep the beat alive, but the words died off, swallowed by the night.

The silence that followed was heavier, the kind that knew what was coming.

Saran turned, study in her gaze, all the shielded humor falling away. "I hate leaving you behind, you know." She didn't soften it. "Doesn't matter that you've got Ulzaan, Darum, a war host and every damn legend to hide behind. It doesn't feel right. But... I have to do something. And I trust you'll make it through."

Leonard looked for words, anything steady, and came up short.

"Didn't think it'd be you walking away first. Figured I'd be the one marching out, not the one left watching."

She smiled, but it was all pain and pride. "We both know you're safer here than with me running point into Karth. But I'm tired of standing still." Her voice dropped, raw. "Just...remember what matters. Not the Pact, not banners, not what they want you to be. The only thing worth it is the people still standing with you. That's it."

He wanted to say something that mattered. Something about not wanting to lose her. About how she'd been his line in every fight since the first day. But all that came out was a nod, too sharp.

She caught it, gave him a look that said she knew, that he didn't have to force it. She'd seen him worse, and she'd never held it against him.

Saran's last words came as she picked up her helmet, voice dry but edged with something fragile. "Stay upright, Leo. Save something for me to come back to."

He huffed a crooked half-smile, reached out and squeezed her arm. "Only if you hurry."

The embrace that followed wasn't for show. Arms locked, just a little too long, breath caught between them, neither wanted to be first to let go. Saran's hair brushed his chin, and for a moment, the noise of the city faded.

When they finally stepped back, she gave him a last look, one part challenge, one part goodbye, and turned, heading down the steps with purpose that didn't quite hide the tremor in her stride.

Leonard watched her go, loss gnawing at the inside of his ribs. They were moving forward now, all of them. If they came back, it wouldn't be to the world they'd left behind.

12

Saran had never liked mornings on the road, there was too much space, too much time to think, and nowhere to put her hands but on a sword she half-hoped wouldn't be needed. The grasslands behind them were brown scars and blackened husks, borderland outposts hunched like old teeth on the horizon. She tugged her cloak tighter to her armour, tasting old smoke in the wind.

Idran walked beside her, wrapped in his own thoughts, boots crunching loose gravel. The first slivers of Karth's glass towers shimmered in the distance, rising from a tangle of stone and smog. Saran let the silence stretch until it started to itch, then spoke..

"So, is it as wild as they say? Karth." She kept her tone easy, a little lazy, the way you'd talk about bad weather.

Idran didn't answer right away. He shrugged and forced a half-smile. "Depends who's telling the stories. Some say Kir-harath's all glass bridges and clever thieves. My father used to say you could buy a soul for less than the price of a lantern, if you didn't mind it coming cracked."

Saran snorted. "That sounds like a yes."

He laughed, but it didn't last. His gaze went distant, picking over the ruin-strewn fields. "It's... different. The tales talk about honor. But the city I left had more hunger than pride. Too many people, too few miracles."

The towers on the horizon caught the late sun and splintered it in fifty directions. Saran squinted, uncertain if it was beautiful or just broken.

"People back home used to call it a city of glass. My grandmother called it a city of traitors. So which is it?"

Idran's jaw tightened. He looked away, boots scuffing a charred patch of earth. "Depends who you are when you get there."

The conversation hit a wall, and he was quick to turn it. "What about you? Fazrum isn't exactly a city of open arms. How'd a farmer's daughter end up escorting nobles and relics?"

Saran shrugged, used to the question. "Same way anyone does. I kept my head down until someone tried to take it off." She smiled, rough and wry. "Didn't work. Now here I am,one foot in the mud.

They walked on. The smoke from the city mixed with dusk, a line of old song echoing in the back of Saran's mind. Keep your back to the wind, and your knife in your boot.

They crested the last ridge as afternoon bled out behind them, and Kir-Harath snapped into view, a crown of glass towers catching fractured sunlight, every window throwing broken rainbows into the low-hanging smoke. The city looked half-sculpted, half-shattered, beauty and ruin welded together, spires reaching skyward while scarred stone huddled below.

Saran whistled low. "I'll give them this, didn't think anything called 'city of traitors' could look like that." She nodded at the light-show, but her eyes narrowed on the smoke drifting from a wound along the city's southern edge, and the black streaks crawling up old walls. "Was it always like this, Idran?"

Idran stared at the city, some old calculation flickering in his eyes. "Not really. There was a time, before the wars, when the glass was for hope. Every new bridge, every tower, it meant things might get better. Now..." He shrugged, voice thinning. "Now it's just armor. The city glitters so you won't look too close at the cracks."

Saran let out a dry laugh. "Armor, huh? No one warned me I'd need to polish my boots before showing up." She looked down at her dusty cloak and battered boots, scuffing one heel. "I'm going to look like I crawled out of a ditch compared to these people."

That got a real smile from Idran, quick, almost shy, but it cut through the old tension. "Believe me, half the city is just as battered. They just hide it under more glass and silk."

They started down the ridge, the city growing taller with every step.

"Back home," Saran said, "market day was as wild as things got. Maybe a hedge-witch with a love charm, maybe a cow in the council square. No bridges of light or anything of the sort.

Idran chuckled. "In Kir-Harath, that's just a quiet afternoon. The mages can't resist showing off, and the markets, well, you could buy anything if you don't mind the price. Even a little luck, if you trust the vendor."

Saran grinned, shaking her head. "Sounds exhausting. In Fazrum, ritual is something you mumble at dawn and hope the ancestors aren't listening."

"Here?" Idran gestured toward the glowing skyline. "Every ritual is a performance. Every day is a gamble."

The city waited, all fractured beauty and desperate shine. Saran squared her shoulders. "Well. Here's hoping we don't break before the glass does."

Together, they stepped off the ridge and headed for the gates, the shadows of towers stretching long before them.

The approach to Kir-Harath's main gate felt like walking into a dare. Saran took in the guards posted there, too many for comfort, none matching, half of them in battered house colors, the other half patched together from whatever survived the last street fight. They watched every stranger with the patience of men who'd seen too much and trusted nothing.

Saran nudged Idran, her voice pitched low. "Are we expecting trouble? Or does your family name still open doors?"

Idran shrugged, never quite meeting her eye. "Depends who's on watch. Some of these men would sell their own boots for a grudge, and the rest probably bought theirs that way."

She let her fingers brush the hilt of her sword, more for the look than any real threat. "If it comes to it, I can always try talking with this. Not much for small talk, but it gets the point across."

Idran flashed a smile. "In Karth, showing steel might win you a duel, but cleverness will keep you alive after. Try not to get us invited to both."

As they neared the gate, a pair of guards stepped forward, spears crossed. Suspicion cut through their expressions, not just at Saran but at Idran, too, like they couldn't decide if they should salute or spit.

Idran lifted his sleeve, exposing the shards of incantation stones embedded in his forearm. The stones caught the evening light, flaring in sharp colors, unmistakable as a House crest.

He spoke with careful formality. "Idran of House Trast. We seek passage."

Recognition flickered in the guards' eyes. One muttered something to the other, too low to catch. After a moment, the spears parted. The older guard gave a shallow bow "Welcome, Lord Idran. Mind your step, the city bites deeper these days."

Saran followed Idran through the gate, jaw tight, heart pounding in her ears. She shot him a sidelong glance. "Cleverness and a little light show, huh? I'll have to remember that trick."

The city swallowed them in noise and fractured color. Shardlight lanterns flickered above the markets, painting the crowd in wild, shifting bands of green and blue. Vendors bellowed charms from beneath hanging curtains of glass beads. A pair of children, skin traced with faint crystal veins, raced through a pack of livestock, with a rooster trailing behind, feathers dyed violet for luck. Saran nearly collided with a merchant balancing three cages of glowing moths.

She blinked, fighting the urge to duck behind Idran's shoulder. "You ever get used to this?" she muttered, eyes wide as a man with a face etched in runes set off a spray of sparks, sending the crowd scattering and laughing all at once.

Idran kept close, but his eyes roamed the city's heights, always checking windows and alleys. "You adapt, or you get left behind. The shardlight's more than show, it's warning, marker, sometimes a weapon. We use what we have, even if it burns us. And it does burn, sometimes."

Saran watched a young woman with glass splinters woven through her braid trade coins with a bent old mage for a whisper of luck. "First time I saw real magic, it wasn't so pretty. Stone Sage in Fazrum, collapsed in the square, tried to push too much will through a stone. They keep it so strict there. Doctrine for every spark, and three more rules for how not to embarrass the city." She shook her head, voice caught between memory and new awe. "Here, it feels like anything goes. Makes me wonder how you all aren't at each other's throats every hour."

Idran's smile was small and crooked. "We are. But we're used to the mess. Fazrum's got its order, stone sages and rulebooks. Karth's all loose wires and wild growth. It means a little more freedom, and a lot more ways to get hurt. Neither side's perfect. We just find different ways to break."

Saran nodded, letting the crowd press past. Glass towers loomed above, every surface cracked and beautiful, reflecting a city that looked alive even in its wounds. For a moment, she wondered if anyone here had time to heal, or if they all just learned to live with the pain.

Idran caught her eye, the old tiredness back. "If you stay long enough, you'll see it, Karth's alive, but it's never really whole. That's how it survives. The trick is not letting it swallow you before you figure out how to stand."

The market pressed in, all noise and glass-draped shadows, when the trouble started, three men in battered house colors, a fourth with a crimson sash and a knife too clean for honest work. They blocked the alley exit with that slow confidence particular to idiots and men with friends watching.

Idran barely slowed, but Saran felt the way his shoulders tightened. The leader spat, "Trast blood shouldn't walk here, not without tribute." He flicked a glance at Saran. "Or is that why you brought muscle, Idran? You know Ravenblood isn't welcome here."

Saran rolled her neck, one hand at her sword. "I charge extra for ugly clients."

The tension crackled, until a new voice cut through, sharp as broken glass. "If you want to make trouble for House Trast, you'll have to grow taller or get smarter. Preferably both."

She strode into the alley, cloak thrown back, dark hair bound in a messy knot, shardlight pendant glinting at her throat. She looked like Idran, but if Idran had been carved down to nerves and cleverness, same sharp eyes, same bearing, but built for the gameboard instead of a council chamber.

The would-be thugs wilted instantly, muttering curses and slinking away.

She turned on Idran, eyes narrowed. "You're supposed to be in Fazrum. What, they run out of cowards there? Or did father finally throw you a leash?"

Idran's smile was all old wounds. "Nice to see you too, Risa. Keeping the family name out of the gutter?"

"Someone has to," she snapped, then caught sight of Saran, really saw her, taking in the scars, the battered gear, the way she stood. "And who's this? You bring home stray ravenblood now, brother? Or is she here to keep you from running off again?"

Saran squared up, unruffled. "If I'm a stray, I bite. Idran needed a guide with less tendency to bleed on the carpets."

Risa snorted, grudging approval in the sound. "At least you don't flatter easy. That's new for him."

Idran rolled his eyes. "Are you done? We're here for help, not any family judgment."

Risa cocked her head, the familiar worry sharpening her sarcasm. "You picked a good time to come home, if you're looking for a city ready to eat itself. Every gang is flexing, councilors are sniffing for blood, and father's gotten even less reasonable. I hope you brought more than travel stories, because Kir-Harath is just waiting for a match."

She flicked a glance between the two of them, "If you're going to survive, you'll need more than family ties. Let's move before someone decides to test how much you're worth in ransom."

She turned, leading them deeper into the shifting crowd.

Risa moved through Kir-Harath like someone who knew where every shadow fell and which ones bit back. She led Idran and Saran down alleys where the light fractured into shards, past doorways marked with sigils, warnings or invitations, impossible to tell.

"House Mirthin's got half their banners in storage and the other half buried with last week's dead. Lady Harl's been 'missing' for a month, her cousins say she's meditating, but that's just code for plotting murder. And if you see anyone wearing black pearls at the wrong time of day, look away. Means they're carrying messages, or usually a grudge."

Saran tried to map the politics in her head, but it all sounded like blood feuds tied off with a ribbon. "And the council, still pretending to run things?"

Risa laughed, bitter. "No one trusts a council that changes by the week. Especially not a Glass one. Every decision's a gamble, every alliance good for about two meals. Father says it keeps us sharp. I say it just keeps us bleeding."

Idran snorted. "Some of us left because we got tired of the same old games."

Risa shot him a glare over her shoulder. "Some of us stayed because someone had to keep the house from turning to dust. Or are you here to finally claim the high ground, Idran? Little late for that."

He set his jaw, picking his way past a broken mosaic. "I'm here for help. Even if you think I don't belong anymore."

"Belonging's for people who think the city remembers. The city forgets everyone, eventually." Her words were brisk, but Saran caught the hurt beneath.

They skirted a broken fountain, water leaking through cracks, shards of old glass winking up at them. Saran glanced between the siblings.

Risa's stride faltered just a moment, her tone careful. "Father's not what he was. Too many losses, not enough years left. You'll see soon enough."

Idran's face hardened, old pain briefly naked. "I didn't come back for him."

Risa scoffed, voice low. "Doesn't matter. In this city, everything circles back to him. To all of us."

The street narrowed, giving way to the threshold of the Trast estate, a riot of mirrored walls that twisted torchlight into a hundred suspicious eyes. Mosaic floors caught the color of the sky, fracturing it beneath their boots. The guards, draped in glass-and-mail armor, stood at rigid attention, gaze sharp and posture sharper. Saran couldn't tell if they were meant to be a welcome or a warning.

Risa paused at the gate, mask slipping into something more regal, spine straightening, chin high. "This is where the real knives come out. Eyes everywhere, tongues sharper than steel. If you want to keep yours, stay close to Idran. Everyone here's hunting for something, sometimes it's just a reason."

Saran gave her a half-smile. "I'm used to places where you only have to watch your back. This seems... overachieving."

Risa's lips twitched, "Don't say I didn't warn you."

Saran kept her gaze moving, noting the subtle hand signals between guards, the house crest on the arch, the way even the sunlight seemed to hesitate before touching the glass.

"What about your father?" Saran asked quietly as they stepped inside. "What am I meant to expect?"

Risa's mouth tightened. "Admire him from a distance. He's still the Lord of Glass, but he's, old now. Slipping, maybe. Doesn't mean he isn't dangerous. He built this house out of grit and spite, but the cracks show more every year."

Idran offered Saran a steady look as they crossed the first hall. "Nothing here is ever just business. Not with family. Every gesture means something, usually two or three things. Best advice? Watch, don't talk. And if someone offers you wine, count the sips."

The doors to the estate loomed ahead, mirrored and tall enough to make a grown woman feel like a child. Saran drew a slow breath and followed the Trast siblings in.

13

Dawn crept over the war host, all gray mist and cold that bit through wool and armor both. Leonard stood at the edge of the assembly yard, watching warriors check straps, sharpen blades, and trade the kind of silence that came when words felt too expensive to waste.

He flexed his fingers inside worn gloves, feeling the ache settle deeper into his knuckles. The gear checked the same as always: sword loose in its sheath, vambraces buckled tight, the small knife at his belt. Everything in its place and ready. He just wished his head felt the same.

Darum's voice cut through the hush, rough as gravel. "Rations up. Two days' worth, no more. If you're still chewing after that, you've lived longer than expected."

A scatter of dry laughs followed. Darum moved through the ranks, handing out hard bread and strips of dried meat with the efficiency of a man who'd done this a thousand times and expected to do it a thousand more. He caught Leonard's eye, gave a single nod of acknowledgement.

Leonard took his share, tucked it into his pack. Nearby, a young sage-acolyte fumbled with his incantation stone, the glow sputtering like a candle in wind. His hands shook just enough to notice. He saw Leonard watching and forced his shoulders back, Trying not to look afraid.

"First march?" Leonard asked.

The acolyte swallowed. "Second. First one, we didn't see combat."

"We will today."

The kid nodded, eyes fixed somewhere past Leonard's shoulder. Smart enough not to ask questions he didn't want answered.

Colonel Val Drast shouldered past, armor clanking, a map tube slung across his back. He stopped long enough to scan the ranks, face carved from old leather and bad sleep. "Mount up in five. Anyone not ready rides rear guard and eats dust the whole way."

No one argued. The column began to form, horses stamping, men adjusting saddles. Leonard swung up onto his mount, feeling the animal's warmth seep through his legs. The beast snorted, ears flicking toward the road. It knew. They all knew.

Somewhere up ahead, Ulzaan sat motionless on his horse, cloak settling around him like smoke. He didn't shout orders or rally spirits. He was a fixed point in the chaos. The war host moved because he did. That was enough.

The gates creaked open. The column lurched forward, hooves clattering on stone, then muffled as they hit dirt road. Leonard glanced back once at the capitol's walls, already fading into mist. Then he turned his gaze forward and rode.

The land bled out the farther they went. Fields that should have been green or gold were scorched black, stubble poking through ash like broken teeth. Farmsteads sagged into themselves, roofs caved in, walls stained with soot and worse. Scavenger birds circled overhead, too lazy to scatter, their patience rewarded by bodies no one had time to bury.

Leonard rode in silence, jaw tight. Around him, the host moved in a long, uneven line, dust rising in their wake. The road was wide enough for three mounts, but no one crowded. Space meant reaction time. Reaction time meant living another hour.

They passed a marker stone half-toppled into a ditch, the carved sigil too weathered to read. Someone had tied a scrap of cloth to it, faded red, fluttering in the breeze. A grave, maybe. Or just a wish that someone would remember.

Ahead, Darum raised a fist. The column slowed. Leonard's horse tossed its head, nostrils flaring. He scanned the tree line, saw nothing but shadow and shifting leaves. Darum gestured to a pair of scouts, who peeled off without a word, vanishing into the brush.

They waited. The wind carried smoke and something sharper, rotting meat, old blood. Leonard's hand drifted to his sword hilt. Behind him, the sage-acolyte muttered a prayer under his breath, fingers white-knuckled on his reins.

The scouts returned at a trot, faces grim. One leaned close to Darum, spoke too low for Leonard to catch. Darum's jaw worked, then he nodded once and waved the column forward.

Leonard urged his horse alongside. "What'd they see?"

Darum didn't look at him. "Movement. Could be ravagers. Could be survivors. Either way, it's trouble."

"How close?"

"Close enough." Darum spat into the dirt. "We keep moving. Eyes open, mouths shut."

They rode on. The land didn't improve. If anything, it got worse. Burned-out wagons littered the roadside, some still half-loaded with possessions no one would ever claim. A child's doll lay face-down in the mud, one arm missing. Leonard looked away.

Then a straggling column appeared, maybe forty strong, moving south with the slow, dreamlike shuffle of the broken. Old men leaning on staves, women with hollow eyes and children clinging to their skirts. A few had bandages, rust-brown with old blood. Most just looked tired. Too tired to be afraid anymore.

The war host slowed. Some of the soldiers called out, asking where they'd come from, what they'd seen. The refugees barely answered. One woman pointed north, her hand trembling. "Don't go that way," she said, "There's nothing left."

Darum nodded to her, but the column didn't stop. They passed the refugees like ships in fog, close enough to see faces but not close enough to help. Leonard felt their eyes on him, not accusing, just watching. Witnessing.

He looked at Darum, who stared straight ahead. "We can't take them with us."

"I know."

Leonard looked back at the crowd. "They won't make it to the capitol."

"I know."

The silence stretched. Leonard glanced back once more, saw the refugees fading into the mist, He faced forward and rode.

A WALLED TOWN rose out of the haze like a broken tooth. What had been a garrison town, neat rows of barracks and supply sheds, was now a smear of rubble and scorched timber. The outer wall still stood in places, jagged gaps where stone had been torn away by force or fire or something worse. Smoke curled from a dozen fires, some still burning, others long dead.

Ulzaan raised a hand. The column halted. He sat for a moment, surveying the ruin with that cold focus that made even seasoned warriors uneasy. Then he turned his horse and rode back along the line, stopping in front of Darum.

"Scouts report movement inside. Could be kin. Could be holdouts." His voice was matter-of-fact. "We clear it street by street. No heroics. No strays. You see something, you call it. Understood?"

Darum nodded. "Understood."

Ulzaan's gaze swept the war host. "Vask is a staging point. The horses won't go closer to the tower. We secure it, we hold it, then we move on foot.

He didn't wait for acknowledgement. He rode to the front, dismounted, and drew his blade, the column followed.

Leonard swung down from his horse, boots hitting mud. Around him, soldiers did the same, forming up in loose ranks. Drast barked orders, sending a squad to cover the flank, another to scout the perimeter. The sage-acolyte hovered near the center, stone flickering in his palm, eyes darting everywhere.

Darum clapped Leonard on the shoulder. "Stay close. If it moves and it's not us, put it down."

Leonard nodded, drawing his sword. The weight felt good in his hand. Familiar. The only thing that made sense.

The streets were a labyrinth of collapse. Buildings leaned into each other, walls cracked open, glass dust glittering in the gutters like frost. Blood dried on stone, black and thick. Somewhere a door swung on broken hinges, creaking with each gust of wind.

Leonard moved with the lead group, Darum to his left, a cluster of archers spread behind. They cleared the first few buildings without incident, empty shells with nothing left but shattered furniture and the smell of rot.

Then the first one came.

It lunged from a doorway, limbs bent at angles that shouldn't work, jaw unhinged, eyes clouded amber. It shrieked, a sound that scraped the inside of Leonard's skull.

He didn't think, only moved. His blade caught it across the throat, black ichor spraying. The thing collapsed, twitching.

"Contact!" Darum roared. "Tighten up!"

More of them poured from the shadows. Not many, five, maybe six, but in the narrow street it felt like a flood. Leonard parried a clawed swipe, drove his boot into a knee that bent backward with a wet crack. Something grabbed his cloak. He spun, slashed, felt resistance give way.

An arrow hissed past his ear, punched through a ravager's skull. It dropped. Darum was everywhere, blade flashing, voice cutting through the chaos. "Left flank, cover! Acolyte, ward the rear!"

The sage-acolyte stumbled, then dragged his palm to the ground. Light flared, a jagged line of runes crackling to life across the cobbles. One of the ravagers hit it and convulsed, smoke rising from its skin. The acolyte nearly collapsed from the sheer effort of will.

Leonard caught a glimpse of a young warrior, barely out of training, backing up too fast. A ravager closed the gap. Leonard lunged, drove his sword through its spine, yanked it free. The warrior stared at him.

"Move!" Leonard shoved him toward the archers. The kid scrambled back, still alive. For now.

The skirmish broke as fast as it started. The last ravager went down under a hail of arrows, pinned to a wall, still twitching. Silence crashed back in, broken only by ragged breathing and the creak of settling rubble.

Darum wiped his blade on a corpse's rags. "Anyone bleeding?"

A few raised hands. Minor cuts, nothing fatal. The acolyte was on his knees, gasping, stone still glowing faintly in his palm. Drast moved through the ranks, checking wounds, barking orders to regroup.

Leonard stood in the middle of the street, blood drying on his sword, heart pounding in his ears. He looked down at the writhing masses. Darum stepped beside him. "First blood's done. You good?"

Leonard nodded. He wasn't, but good enough didn't exist anymore.

The rest of the clearing went faster. The host fanned out, sweeping buildings, dragging out anything that moved and putting it down. By midday, the streets were quiet again, the air thick with smoke and the stink of burnt flesh.

Leonard drifted away from the main force, boots crunching over broken glass. He didn't have a destination. Just needed to move, to shake off the weight pressing into his chest.

He turned a corner and stopped.

Two bodies, laid out against a shattered wall. Not ravagers. Men. Ravenblood, by the scraps of black still clinging to their armor. Their faces were wrong, torn, but Leonard knew them anyway.

Tomas. Marel.

His breath caught. He'd trained with them. Eaten with them. Laughed at Tomas's awful jokes and listened to Marel talk about the farm he'd never get back to. They'd been posted here, holding Vask while the rest of the Pact mobilized.

Now they were just meat.

Leonard's knees hit the ground before he knew he was falling. His hands shook as he reached out, tried to close what was left of Tomas's eyes. The throat burned, vision blurred. He wanted to scream, to tear the world apart, but all that came out was a ragged breath that tasted like ash.

Footsteps behind him.

Darum stopped at the mouth of the alley. For a long moment, he just stood there, looking at the bodies. Then he moved forward, slow, like every step cost him something.

He crouched beside Leonard, stared at Tomas and Marel. His face didn't change, but something in his shoulders bent. "Theran's boys," he said, voice scraped raw.

Leonard nodded, couldn't trust his voice.

Darum reached out, fingers brushing Marel's torn cloak. "Theran would've been proud. They died fighting. That's more than most get."

"Doesn't make it right." Leonard said.

"No." Darum's hand curled into a fist. "It doesn't."

Leonard wiped his face, came away with blood and ash. "How many more, Darum? How many do we bury before it's just us?"

Darum was quiet, staring at the bodies like he could will them back to life through sheer stubborn refusal. When he finally spoke, his voice cracked at the edges. "Theran and I fought the last war together. Bled together. I once promised him I'd look after his students if he ever fell." He exhaled through his nose, sharp. "Now I get to break that promise twice in one day."

He stood, knees creaking, and turned away, gathering himself.

Leonard stayed kneeling, hands hovering over Tomas's chest. He remembered the sparring yard, Tomas laughing after getting his ass kicked, saying next time like it was a promise he'd get to keep. Marel, quieter, always checking his gear twice, the kind of careful that should've kept him alive.

Drast appeared at the mouth of the alley, took one look at the scene, and went still. His gaze flicked between Darum and the bodies, something old and heavy settling over his features. "Theran's?" he asked quietly.

Darum nodded once.

Drast swore under his breath, long and inventive. Then, softer: "We're gathering the dead. Got a spot cleared near the square." He hesitated. "I'll help carry them."

"No." Darum's voice was iron. "We'll do it."

Leonard looked up, saw the grief carved into Darum's face, buried under discipline and old scars. He stood, legs unsteady, and moved to Tomas's shoulders. Darum took the feet. They lifted together, moved in silence through the ruined streets.

Drast followed with Marel, his usual gruffness stripped away. When they reached the square, fourteen others were already laid out. Fourteen who'd held the line and lost.

Darum set Tomas down with a care that didn't match his hands, scarred and blunt as they were. He knelt between the two bodies, one hand on each. "Theran," he muttered, almost a prayer. "I'm sorry"

Leonard grabbed a shovel, started digging. The blisters came fast, burning through old calluses. He didn't stop. Darum joined him, working in grim silence, each strike of the blade into earth a punctuation mark on grief.

When the graves were ready, they laid Tomas and Marel side by side. Brothers in all but blood. Trained by the same hand, dead in the same ruin.

Darum stood at the edge, staring down. For a long time, he said nothing. Then: "You were Theran's. That made you mine in a way. You fought like he taught you. You died like Ravenblood." His voice cracked. "Rest now. Both of you. Tell Theran we're still standing. For now."

Leonard stood between the graves, fists clenched so hard his nails drew blood. Tomas's laugh. Marel's quiet competence. Theran's legacy, buried twice over. He wanted to rage, to break something, but all he had was dirt and silence.

He wiped his hands on his cloak, turned away. The war host was forming up again, faces drawn, eyes hard. No time for mourning. No time for anything but survival.

Darum caught his arm. "Holding on?"

Leonard met his eyes. Saw the same grief mirrored there, the weight of every promise broken, every life lost. "No," he said quietly. "But I'll keep moving."

Darum's grip tightened, then released. "That's all we can do."

The sun sank, bleeding rust across the broken skyline. The war host settled into wary rest, fires guttering in the cold. Sentries moved along the perimeter, Ulzaan walked the line, presence like iron, holding the frayed edges together through sheer refusal to break.

Leonard sat with his back to a wall, sword across his knees, still stained. He should clean it. He didn't. The exhaustion pulled at him, but sleep felt like surrender.

Darum dropped down beside him, handed over a waterskin. Leonard drank, tasted metal and ash.

They sat in silence. Then Darum spoke, voice low and tired. "Theran saved my life in the last war. Karthian ambush, outnumbered three to one. I was pinned, bleeding out. He dragged me clear, held the line until reinforcements came." He stared at his hands. "I told him I owed him. He said I could pay it forward by lasting longer than him."

Leonard looked at the graves in the distance. "You did."

"I did" Darum's laugh was bitter. "They chose this. Same as we did."

"Doesn't make it easier."

Leonard thought about Tomas's grin, Marel's careful hands. "No. It doesn't."

They sat in the gathering dark, the weight of the dead pressing down. Finally, Darum broke the silence. "Tomorrow we move on the tower. Ulzaan's got a plan, I can feel it.

Leonard looked past the graves, past the smoke, toward the black silhouette on the horizon. "You think we can win this?"

Darum was quiet for a long moment. When he spoke, his voice

carried the weight of every loss, every broken promise, every grave he'd dug. "I think we keep fighting until we can't. That's the only winning left. Theran knew that. So did his boys. Now it's our turn."

Leonard closed his eyes, let the exhaustion pull at him. Somewhere in the dark, a raven called.

14

The estate's walls loomed up from the street like the side of a jeweled tomb, glittering reflections, and twice as cold. Saran could feel her skin crawl as they passed beneath the iron arch, glass splinters catching the late sun, the guards at the gate eyeing every move with the kind of boredom that could snap to violence in a heartbeat.

Servants lined the path, their uniforms immaculate, their eyes not so much dull as... unfocused. They bowed just a second late, movements too precise to feel human. Saran glanced at Idran, whose jaw clenched; Risa just muttered under her breath, "Loyalty's cheap in these halls, cheaper if you can buy it with spellwork or threat. Don't let the glass fool you."

They crossed into a courtyard floored in mirrored tile, the reflections dizzying. Above, on marble balconies and behind latticed windows, minor lords and cousins watched the procession, their faces half-shrouded by veils of shards of colored glass.

One guard's hand rested a little too comfortably on the pommel of a sword as they passed. From behind a half-open mirrored door, a child's voice drifted: "...said he wouldn't come back this time, but here he is..." The door clicked softly shut.

Saran caught a glimpse of a woman in elaborate mourning black, she tracked Risa's every step. On another balcony, two young men leaned close, heads together, eyes bright with either gossip or ambition.

The very air felt thick, full of old secrets, new rumors, and the weight of too many grudges left to rot behind glass. Saran kept her hand close to her side and her back a little straighter, grateful for every hour she'd spent learning to read a room full of knives.

The hall was a cathedral to ambition, and it didn't pretend otherwise. Mosaic floors glittered beneath Saran's boots, patterns shifting with each step as if the stone itself were watching. Colored sunlight streamed through glass cut high in the walls, staining mirrored columns with bleeding reds and bruised violets. Along the periphery, glass artifacts sat on pedestals, some elegant, others clearly meant to warn off sticky fingers. More than one looked like it might explode if you breathed wrong.

Servants hurried past, faces pinched and distant, some with gem-studded brands winking at their throats, others with tiny crystal shards set like teardrops into skin. They moved with a kind of desperate precision, eyes darting away from Saran and Idran as if too much curiosity might get them sent to some even colder wing of the estate.

Risa was in her element now, guiding them through the shifting light and glancing off invisible currents. "See those portraits?" She nodded to a gallery hung with a rogue's row of grim-faced ancestors. "Never turn your back on Lady Renet, legend says her ghost throws fits if someone with weak blood comes too close." She grinned. "The far wing is all old vaults and broken spells. Don't go unless you want to end up half glass yourself."

Saran cocked a brow, unimpressed. "Is that a real threat, or just family tradition?"

Idran's voice was a mutter as he eyed the columns. "In this house, it's both. Honestly, safest to assume every portrait here is cursed. Some more than others."

Risa flashed a crooked smile at Saran, clearly enjoying the brief flash of normalcy in all the paranoia. “If you get lost, scream twice. First time’s for help, second’s for luck. Both are in short supply these days.”

Saran let the rhythm of glass and rumor settle over her. Every reflection was a potential enemy. She realized, with a small chill, that the hall didn’t just look warped. It felt it, like something inside was always bending, never breaking, and watching to see who would snap first.

The heart of the Glass Court was a theater built for judgment. Saran felt it as soon as she stepped through the last set of mirrored doors, the light fractured, the air suddenly turned cold and sharp, the sense that every movement echoed in a thousand hidden eyes. The seat at the center drew her gaze, a monstrous spire of woven glass and black steel, part throne, part cage. On it sat the lord of glass.

He looked nothing like Saran imagined, no glittering tyrant or unbreakable patriarch. He was gaunt, skin almost translucent, veins spidering up his throat and temples, his hands twisted around the arms of the throne. But his eyes, when they found Idran, still had bite, sharp as broken quartz, hard and bright and utterly impossible to read.

A hush fell as they crossed the floor, Saran could feel other eyes on her, courtiers and would-be lords, allies and enemies circling at the edges of the light, every glance calculating, waiting for the first drop of blood.

“Idran.” The name was a blade. The lord didn’t rise, but the air in the hall shifted with his voice. “You return to my hall with your pledge in Fazrum unfinished. Has exile grown so tiresome, or do you think your old bargains no longer bind?”

Saran saw Idran tense, his careful composure slipping for just a breath as he took in the shrunken form of the man he’d left behind. He dipped his head in a courtly bow that was all muscle memory. “Thacien. The times have changed. I’m here at urgent request,for the good of both our house and the city.”

Thacien’s lip curled, exposing the ghost of a smile. “The city is always someone else’s concern until it comes to collect, isn’t it?” He leaned forward, his voice carrying a hint of iron beneath the frailty. "And who is your shadow, Idran? She wears black for war, but carries herself like one of Fazrum's ravens."

His eyes turned on Saran, measuring, dissecting, already suspicious. Saran straightened, meeting the old man's gaze. There was a flicker of something feral in him, something that made her feel like she'd wandered too close to a wild dog.

"I don't know your face," He continued, "but I know your colors. Ravenblood. What is your business in my court? Or have you come to collect what was never yours?"

There it was. Saran didn't flinch, but she could feel the political predators circling, their whispers building in the edges of the chamber. "I am Saran. I serve as Idran's companion for the time being.. I am not here to take anything from Karth."

Thacien's eyes narrowed, searching her face for cracks. "You expect me to believe the Ravenblood came all this way to deliver courtesies? The last time your kind walked these lands, my house lost its legacy." His fingers dug into the throne's glass, and for a moment, Saran thought she saw the faintest tremor in his grip.

Idran stepped forward, but Thacien's attention didn't waver. "You stand with her now, Idran? After all I've built? Was it not enough that the relic vanished from my care? You bring a thief's company into my own hall and expect me to call you kin?"

Saran kept her voice calm, refusing to betray the truth. "If your relic was lost, I had nothing to do with it, Fazrum never sent us to steal from Karth. If your legacy is so fragile it can be carried away by travelers, maybe it's not worth as much as you think."

That got a few sharp glances from the gallery, but Thacien only glared, his breathing harsh now. "Watch your words. I built this house with my own will, and I can break it with the same." He looked to be tiring, the anger burning through his strength. His lips pressed thin, color draining further from his cheeks.

Risa shifted uncomfortably, glancing at Saran with something like concern. Idran's fists were clenched at his sides, eyes flicking between his father and the gathering rivals, knowing that any sign of weakness here would be blood in the water.

Thacien straightened with effort, pulling the remnants of dignity around himself like a battered cloak. “Enough. My health does not permit more tonight. We will meet at council tomorrow. Then, perhaps, I’ll have answers, and so will you.”

He dismissed them with a flick of his wrist, a gesture that seemed both imperious and desperate. As the courtiers closed in, hungry for scraps of rumor and power, Saran felt a chill settle over the room, a sense that the ground beneath them was shifting, and no one knew whose feet would slip first. A couple of servants rushed to Idran shepherding him away.

Risa found Saran the moment the doors closed behind the council’s exit, caught her by the elbow, guiding her through a maze of mirrored corridors until the sounds of the hall faded behind a thick glass door. They emerged onto a small balcony overlooking the city, the glass catching the last sickly colors of dusk.

Risa leaned on the rail, arms folded, her voice pitched for privacy but sharpened by the weight of old habit. “Don’t bother pretending you just wandered into Karth for the scenery. You were there when the relic disappeared, weren’t you? I see it in your eyes, we received reports of ravenblood near the old mine the week it went missing”

Saran didn’t bristle, she was too tired for pretense, “I was there,” she admitted, watching the city lights splinter on the towers below. “But nobody in Fazrum knew what it really was. We thought it was just another cursed heirloom or artifact, bad luck, maybe. I didn’t even touch the damn thing, not after what it did to the last one who tried.”

Risa studied her, gaze flicking between Saran’s hands and her face. “You’re not lying. I can tell. But you’re not telling everything, either.”

Saran let out a rough breath. “You think I’d be standing here if I’d known what your father was using it for? I don’t care about relics. I care about people getting ground up for things they can’t even name.”

Risa’s face closed off, then cracked. She tapped the glass rail, eyes distant. "He was always a hard man, proud and paranoid. But the relic... he used it to hold back death. For years. Fed it everything, our family's best sorcerers, his own body, whatever it took to keep breathing and ruling. That's why he clings so hard to power, he thinks if he lets go, the city will shatter. Or maybe he just doesn't want to watch someone else sit in his chair."

Saran felt the confession hit like cold rain. The city sprawled beneath them, restless and beautiful and haunted by secrets none of its people chose.

Risa's voice softened, a strange edge of relief and regret. "Now that it's gone, the magic's fading. So is he. Some part of me hates that you were there when it vanished. But another part—" She shrugged. "Maybe it's for the best."

Saran said nothing. She looked out over Kir Harath, wondering how many others would pay the price for the end of one man's reign. In this city, nobody got out clean.

Idran found them still on the balcony, shadows long and faces pinched. He looked gutted, the lines around his eyes deeper, the old certainty stripped away by the throne room's ghost-show. He didn't speak right away, just stood with the city at his back, shoulders hunched like a man who'd taken a punch he should've seen coming.

Risa met his look with a sharp tilt of her chin, equal parts concern and "I told you so." Saran watched the siblings, the glass court looming behind. "I've seen crypts warmer than your family estate."

That drew a brittle laugh from Risa. "Give it a week, and it'll feel like home. If you're still breathing."

The three of them let the hush stretch, the night air sharp with secrets. Inside, the estate murmured, servants passing, glass chimes tinkling with every shift in the wind.

Risa cut through the noise. "Tomorrow's council is a pack of wolves. Watch Lady Pyrrel, she'd poison the soup and call it tradition. Cousin Elt is sniffing for scandal, he'll dig up every old wound he can.

Someone will try to block your appeal outright. Or worse, use you as a pawn in their own grudge match."

Saran eyed the door, half-joking. "So what's the trick to winning them over? Threats, favors, or just surviving until the vote?"

Risa's smile was thin. "All three, if you're lucky. Around here, luck means you're only bleeding a little."

Idran's hands curled tight at his sides. "Father's already made up his mind. To him, I'll always be the boy who broke his word and ran. The council's just a stage. None of them care what happens to the city, not unless they can profit from it."

Risa's glare was flint. "So why are you here, Idran? You want to save Kir-Harath, or just prove something to the old man?"

He looked away, jaw working. "I'm here because someone has to be. I just don't know if I can stomach playing their games again."

Saran stepped between them, her voice low, practical. "Doesn't matter why. We don't have the luxury of picking at old wounds. Everybody in that council chamber's out for themselves. If we want to get through this alive, never mind with any reinforcements, we're going to need each other. No one else is coming."

The word "relic" hung unspoken, until Risa shot Idran a pointed look. "You know Saran was there when the relic vanished, right?"

Idran didn't look surprised. "I suspected. Some strange astrologer mentioned it a while ago. Doesn't matter now. What's gone is gone."

Risa frowned, but let it drop. "Just as well. Maybe the city's ready for power that isn't stolen from the dead."

Idran's voice was quiet, haunted. "Or maybe it's time we stop trying to rule at all. Just... hold the line for a while. See what's left when the dust settles."

Saran ran a hand along the glass rail, studying the sprawl of the city below. "Do either of you actually want to rule this place? Or are we just trying to walk away with enough soldiers to keep Fazrum standing?"

For once, Risa didn't have a clever answer. She watched the lights dance on the towers, her face lost in thought. "I don't know what future's left. For any of us."

The chimes behind them stirred, sharp and strange, as Risa straightened and jerked her head toward the hallway. “Come on. I’ll show you to your rooms. Try not to talk too loudly. They followed her back inside, words trailing off as the glass doors shut behind them. The hallways shimmered with reflection, every step echoing with the weight of old stories and everything they’d already paid to get here.

SARAN WOKE BEFORE DAWN, the city’s sounds already in her bones, glass bells rattling in the wind, somewhere below a vendor calling for bread and luck, the faintest echo of last night’s arguments lingering in the stone. The room was grand by Fazrum standards, vaulted glass, colored light spilling across her black armor and worn boots but it felt less like comfort and more like being displayed in a trophy case.

She drifted to the window, arms folded tight, watching Kir Harath peel itself awake. Markets setting up beneath cracked bridges, a plume of smoke rising where it shouldn’t, banners from a dozen feuding houses already catching the first sun. Nothing about it looked settled.

A soft knock, then Idran’s head appeared around the door. He looked like he hadn’t slept at all, his shirt half-buttoned, eyes ringed with that old Karthian hunger. “You up?” he asked, already knowing the answer.

She nodded, shouldering her cloak. “Couldn’t sleep if I tried.’

He offered a half-hearted smile. “Walk with me? I need to remember if the city still feels like something worth fighting for.” He glanced down at his hands, flexing them as if expecting old scars to split open.

The estate’s corridors were mostly empty, only a servant or two, heads bowed, echoing their steps with nervous precision. Saran waited until they were clear of listening ears.“You barely looked at home last night. Ever feel like this place was more than just another battlefield?”

Idran led her down a spiral stair, boots ringing against glass and steel. He didn't answer at first.

"Maybe once," he said finally. "When I was a boy, I thought the towers were magic, the mosaics were stories that belonged to us. By the time I was old enough to know better, there was always a siege, or a riot, or someone else dying for the promise of something new." He shook his head, jaw clenched. "Now it just feels... brittle. Like one more blow and the whole place will come down."

Saran eyed him, not unkindly. "You think it can change?"

Idran's eyes flicked up. "I don't know. I'm not even sure what'll be left after the old powers die. Maybe nothing. Maybe that's the point."

Saran followed Idran through a crush of morning markets where the chaos felt less like danger and more like survival. An old woman brushed glass dust from her apron, bartering it to a jeweler who tasted every pinch as if it might be laced with gold. Spell-junkies huddled in the shade, hawking charms and pocket curses, their hands twitching around stubs of broken crystal.

Kids darted between booths, some with ink-smudged fingers, others bare-armed and quick. Saran watched as a pair of them lobbed pebbles at a faded wall painting of Thacien, a caricature of the Lord of Glass with monster horns and a crown sliding off his head. Nobody scolded them; a few adults even smiled, though only when the children couldn't see.

She nudged Idran, nodding to a line of beggars near a shrine. Most had the distinctive gleam of embedded shards, some fresh and bleeding, others dulled with time. "Your city's got range. You could rule a kingdom or rob it blind just by picking the wrong street."

Idran's lips twitched, but the humor didn't reach his eyes. He steered her into a quieter alley, away from the clamor, and gestured to a ruined corner where sunlight bounced through a collapsed roof. "Used to hide there when I was small. Thought it was a fortress. Now..." He shrugged, letting the rest hang.

She studied him, his shoulders were set tight, hands working at his sides. "If the Glass Court were just handed to you, would you take it?"

He didn't answer, at least not directly. His gaze went distant. He changed the subject, pointing out a nearby mural, where an artist had painted the council as glass puppets, strings trailing into the shadows. Saran read the message in the tension of his stance more clearly than any words: he wanted no crown, but neither could he walk away.

She let it go, scanning the crowd. "What happens if your father dies before the council meets?"

Idran's jaw locked, and he stepped in closer, voice low and flat. "That's not something you say aloud here. People have vanished for less."

Saran gave a slow, knowing nod. The city's music, its shouts, the jangle of charms, the crackle of burning glass, swelled around them.

They rounded a corner into a plaza cracked wide by sun and old grudges. Shardlight flickered overhead. Gray sashes and polished staves, backs tense as rival house enforcers circled in matching glass-laced armor. Blood stained the cobbles near a shattered cart, drying fast in the heat. The crowd pressed in close but careful, every face holding back more than curiosity.

Idran's jaw tightened. "This is where debt gets paid in daylight," he said quietly, eyes flicking over the banners, weighing allegiances like he was counting knives. "Best keep your hands clear and your voice lower."

Saran scanned the edge of the crowd, reading posture as much as words, here and there, a hand hovered close to a hidden blade, or a shimmer at the cuff . "I've seen crowds turn ugly before," she muttered, "but never where everyone's packing magic and three different knives. This city's healers must have their hands full."

As they moved to skirt the worst of it, a sharp-eyed woman in House Mirthin blue called out, voice slicing through the tension: "Idran Trast, back from exile?" That was all it took, the ripple of recognition and suspicion sharpening as heads turned.

And then someone pointed at Saran's black armor, and a murmur grew. Ravenblood, whispered and spat like a warning. She felt the shift, the way the air thickened, every old wound and rumor stirred by their presence.

Idran stepped slightly in front of her, but Saran stayed where she was.

The plaza tension snapped with all the subtlety of shattering glass. Someone shoved, a curse went up, and suddenly a knife flashed in the sunlight. Saran barely sidestepped the first wild swing, planting her boot into the attacker's shin and sending him sprawling across broken tile. The crowd surged and split, rival enforcers drawing glass-edged blades that caught the light like fangs.

Saran kept her stance tight. She dodged a clumsy hook, slammed the heel of her hand into a chin, twisted a knife from another's grip and sent it skittering into a gutter. Each movement was precise.

Idran fought beside her, less graceful but dangerous in a way that made Saran's stomach knot. He fought like the city itself. grabbing whatever came to hand. He smashed an attacker's wrist against a wall, then elbowed another in the gut. There was nothing noble in his style.

The chaos spun around them, glass blades, shouts, the smell of blood and burning spell-oil. Saran ducked a fist, landed a hard kick to a knee, and caught sight of Idran as he pinned a rival to the ground, fist full of the man's collar. A sliver of broken glass hovered inches from the thug's throat, Idran's eyes cold and far away, too far, Saran realized.

"Idran!" Her voice was sharp, dragging him back. He hesitated, then dropped the glass and pushed the man away, panting hard. For a split second, something old and ruthless flickered in his gaze, something Saran hadn't seen before, and hoped wouldn't come back.

The fight broke as quickly as it began. The enforcers forced a wedge, driving off the worst of the brawlers. Survivors spat curses and limped away, a few trailing blood, most with nothing to show for it but bruises and old grudges. The plaza's air rang with the aftermath.

Saran wiped a trickle of blood from her mouth, watching Idran out of the corner of her eye. He was hunched, jaw tight, hands trembling as he stared at the ground. Quietly furious with himself.

The brawl sputtered out as the enforcers forced order back into the plaza, boots crunching over blood and broken glass. Shardlight flickered overhead, coloring the chaos in sickly greens and bruised blues. A woman wrapped in Mirthin blue spat at Idran's feet as she was herded off, voice dripping venom. "Glass-blood traitor. City'd be better if you'd stayed gone."

Idran didn't rise to it. He just stood there, chest heaving, eyes shadowed, hands slow to unclench. Saran pressed a strip of cloth to a slice on her forearm, nothing deep, but it stung all the same. She glanced sidelong at him, quiet for a breath.

"Funny," she said, dry. "Sometimes it feels like everything could be solved if we just broke enough heads. But then you look around —" She swept a hand at the wounded, the snarling survivors, the uneasy crowd—"and nothing's any different. Just new bruises on top of the old ones."

Idran wiped blood from his jaw, jaw set hard. "It's what this city understands. Power, violence, threats. Sometimes it's the only way to get through the noise." He hesitated, as if the words were a confession.

Saran let the silence hang, weighing his answer. She was impressed, in spite of herself, at how far he'd gone without flinching, but she was worried too. Karth made monsters, or brought out what was already hiding.

She tucked away the rag and started walking, nodding for Idran to follow. "Maybe. But if that's all it takes, I hope you've got enough left for the rest of us."

15

The council hall in Vask had seen better days. Hell, it had seen better hours. The roof was mostly canvas now, stretched over charred beams and held down with scavenged timber. Rain dripped through gaps, pooling on the cracked stone floor. Torches guttered in brackets, throwing shadows that jumped and twisted with every gust of wind.

Leonard stood near the back, his arms were folded, watching the war host's command argue over a table that listed hard to one side. Maps weighed down with stones, a few rusted daggers, and someone's empty cup. The kind of setup that screamed we're making this work because we have to, not because it's good.

Ulzaan sat at the head, cloak draped over his shoulders like something carved from iron. He didn't speak much, just listened, eyes tracking every face. Beside him, Darum leaned against the wall. Drast paced near the door, armor clinking with every step, looking like a man who'd lost too many arguments and expected to lose this one too.

A handful of others filled out the room. Captain Rennik, gaunt and hollow-eyed, the one who'd seen the first wave hit the outer settlements. A logistics officer whose name Leonard never caught, fingers stained with ink. A few squad leaders waiting for orders they already knew would cost lives.

Drast stopped pacing, slapped a hand on the table. "We're bleeding supplies. Rations'll last three days, maybe four if we stretch it. Half the acolytes can't hold a flicker, and the other half are burning themselves out trying." He looked at Ulzaan. "We need to pull back, regroup at the capitol. This push is suicide."

Ulzaan's gaze didn't shift. "And let Samric consolidate? Give him time to fortify whatever hell he's building in that tower?" His voice dropped "We move forward."

Rennik spoke up, "I've seen what happens when we hesitate. Watched three towns burn because we waited for orders. The ravagers don't slow down. They don't negotiate. Every day we sit here, they get closer to the capitol."

"And every day we march closer to that tower, we lose more men," Drast shot back. "You saw what happened to the scouts we sent north. None came back. Not one. You want to feed the whole host into the same grinder?"

Darum pushed off the wall, boots scraping stone. "We've been fighting for ruins since this started. Every town we 'save' is already ash. Every stand we make, we leave more bones behind." His eyes swept the room. "So what's different this time? Nothing, this is what we do, what we always did.

The logistics officer shifted, uncomfortable. "There are a handful of refugees. They want to stay, fortify what's left. Some are begging to come with us." He hesitated. "We can't take them.

Ulzaan leaned forward, hands flat on the table. "Here's what's different. This time, we're not defending. We're attacking. Samric thinks we're scrambling, thinks we're in the dark to his plan.. We let him keep thinking that." He tapped the map, finger landing on the tower's crude outline. "We move before dawn. Split the host into three squads, one hits the main approach, loud and obvious. The other two flank from the east and west, regroup at the tower's base for a full assault."

Drast's jaw tightened. "That's not a plan. That's bait."

"It's bait that works," Ulzaan said. "Samric expects us to come at him head-on, desperate and stupid. We give him that. Then we hit him from three sides before he realizes the first wave's a feint."

Leonard stepped forward, voice cutting through the murmur. "What are we really buying with this? How many men do we lose before we even get close?" He met Ulzaan's gaze. "What if Samric's already waiting? What if this whole thing's a trap and we're just walking in because we're out of options?"

Ulzaan's expression didn't change. "Then we spring it. Better to die fighting than starve in the ruins waiting for someone else to save us."

Darum grunted. "And if the 'mock' battle gets real? If we're bleeding out before we even reach the tower?"

"Then we bleed," Ulzaan said. "But we bleed forward."

Rennik looked at the map, then at the others. "I've seen what the ravagers do. They don't leave survivors. They don't leave anything." His voice dropped. "If we're going to die, I'd rather it be with a sword in my hand, not cowering behind walls that won't hold."

The logistics officer rubbed his face, exhausted. "What about the refugees? What do we tell them?"

Ulzaan stood, the room going quiet. "Tell them the truth. We can't save them. They stay or they run, but they do it without us." He looked at each face in turn. "We move at first light. Prepare your squads. Anyone not ready rides rear guard and prays."

He left, cloak sweeping behind him. The room emptied slowly, officers drifting out into the cold, muttering orders or curses under their breath.

Leonard stayed, staring at the map. Darum lingered near the door, watching him.

"You think he's right?" Leonard asked.

Darum was quiet for a moment. "Doesn't matter. Right or wrong, it's all we've got."

Leonard nodded, the weight settling deeper. "Yeah. That's what I'm afraid of."

NIGHT PRESSED down on Vask like a hand over a mouth. The perimeter was quiet, too quiet, broken only by the shuffle of boots and the distant creak of settling rubble. Leonard walked the line, sword at his hip, eyes scanning shadows that moved just a little too much.

Darum fell in beside him, uninvited but expected. "Couldn't sleep?"

"Didn't try."

They moved, passing sentries who nodded without speaking. The air was cold, sharp enough to sting, carrying the smell of smoke and old blood. Leonard flexed his fingers inside his gloves, trying to shake the stiffness.

Darum broke the quiet. "You ever forget their faces?"

Leonard glanced at him. "Who?"

"The ones you lose. Friends, brothers, whoever."

Darum's gaze was distant. "I used to remember all of them. Every name, every scar. Now..." He shrugged. "Some blur. Some just... disappear."

Leonard thought about Tomas's laugh, Marel's careful hands. "I remember them."

"For now." Darum's tone wasn't cruel, just tired. "Give it time. You'll forget, or you'll go mad holding on. Either way, it doesn't stop."

Leonard's jaw tightened. "Maybe I want to hold on. Maybe that's the only thing keeping me standing."

Darum looked at him, something almost like sympathy flickering in his eyes. "Careful with that. Clinging too hard to the past just makes it harder to see what's in front of you."

They walked on, boots crunching frost. Leonard thought about Saran, wondered where she was, if she'd made it to Karth, if she was still breathing. The not-knowing gnawed at him, worse than any wound.

"You think they're alright?" he asked. "Saran and Idran?"

Darum snorted. "Saran's tougher than half the men in this host.

She'll be fine. Idran... who knows. Karth's a pit of knives. If he's smart, he'll get what he needs and get out."

"And if he's not?"

"Then we'll hear about it won't we." Darum's tone was dry, but there was worry underneath. "I miss her too, if that's what you're asking. She's got a knack for keeping things together when they're falling apart."

Leonard nodded, the ache settling deeper. "Yeah. She does."

Darum stopped, hand raised. Leonard froze, following his gaze. Movement at the edge of the firelight, low to the ground, quick. Could've been a dog. Could've been a shadow. Could've been something worse.

Darum's hand drifted to his sword. "You see it?"

"Yeah."

They watched, breath misting in the cold. The movement stopped, then started again, circling. Too deliberate for an animal. Too patient.

"Could be a scout," Leonard said quietly.

"Could be bait." Darum didn't take his eyes off the darkness. "Either way, we're being watched."

A sentry nearby shifted, spear raised. Darum waved him down, then stepped forward, boots loud on frozen ground. "Show yourself, or I'll assume you're dinner and act accordingly." Then the movement stopped

Leonard exhaled, shoulders loosening. "Think it was one of theirs?"

"Don't know" Darum turned back toward the camp. "But we're not alone out here. That's enough."

They walked the rest of the perimeter in silence, the cold settling deeper, the sense of eyes on their backs never quite fading. When they returned to the fire, Leonard sat, staring into the flames.

Darum dropped down beside him, handed over a waterskin.

"You really believe in this?" Darum asked. "This mission, this fight, all of it?"

Leonard looked at the fire, watched sparks spiral into the dark. "I don't know. Maybe I'm just following orders because it's easier than thinking."

Darum grunted. "That's honest, at least." He stretched his legs, wincing. "You asked earlier what we're buying. The answer's simple. Time. Maybe a chance. Probably just more graves."

"That doesn't sound like enough."

"It never is." Darum's voice was rough. "But it's what we've got. And out here, that's the only thing that matters."

Leonard nodded, the weight pressing down. Somewhere in the dark, something moved. He didn't look up.

DRAST FOUND Leonard near the makeshift HQ, sitting on a pile of salvaged timber, near a fire, cleaning his sword for the third time. The blade didn't need it, but his hands needed something to do.

Drast dropped down beside him, armor clinking. "You're Darum's protégé, aren't you?" Drast finally said.

Leonard didn't look up. "I'm not sure 'protégé' is the right word."

"Close enough." Drast leaned back, arms crossed. "I don't know the full story. Don't need to. But I trust Ulzaan. He doesn't gamble on people without a reason." He paused. "So whatever's going on with you, whatever weight you're carrying, just know, you're not carrying it alone."

Leonard stopped, blade resting across his knees. "You ever wonder if we're just delaying the inevitable?"

Drast snorted. "Every damn day. But delaying's what we do best. We hold the line until someone smarter figures out how to win." He looked at Leonard, something almost kind in his eyes. "You're young. You've got time to doubt. But when the fighting starts, you do what you've been trained to do. You stand. You swing. You survive. That's the job."

Leonard nodded, throat tight. "What if I can't?"

"Then you fall. Same as the rest of us." Drast stood, clapped a hand on Leonard's shoulder. "But until then, you keep your blade sharp and your head down. That's all anyone can ask."

He left, boots echoing on stone. Leonard sat alone, staring at the blade, seeing his reflection warped in the steel.

Later, alone by a guttering fire, Leonard pulled out a scrap of parchment and a piece of charcoal. He stared at it for a long time, trying to find words that didn't feel like lies.

"To the family of Tomas,"

He stopped. What could he say? That their son died brave? That it mattered? That Leonard had been there and done nothing to stop it?

He crumpled the parchment, tossed it into the fire. Watched it curl and blacken.

Maybe some things didn't need to be said. Maybe the dead didn't need his apologies.

The sage-acolyte found Leonard near the fire, fumbling with a bowl of something that might've been stew in a previous life. The kid looked worse than before, his hands still shaking.

"Mind if I sit?" the acolyte asked. "I'm Briar, by the way."

Leonard gestured to the ground. Briar dropped down, too hard, like his legs gave out. The stew was awful, thick and tasteless, but it was hot. That counted for something.

"You ever study at the temple? In the capitol?"

Leonard shook his head. "No. Joined the Pact young. Never had the patience for doctrine."

"Lucky you." Briar snorted, almost a laugh. "I spent two years there. Sage Pelin ran the trials. Strict as hell, but..." He hesitated, stirring his bowl. "He wasn't cruel. Just... rigid. Believed in the order more than anything."

Leonard's jaw tightened. He remembered Pelin. Remembered the testing chamber, the stone burning through his palm, the way Pelin watched with that cold, clinical focus.

"He tested me once," Leonard said quietly. "Nearly killed me doing it."

Briar winced. "Yeah. He had a reputation. But he died believing he was protecting the city. Samric killed him in the temple. Didn't even give him a chance to fight back."

Leonard stared into the fire. "Good."

Briar blinked. "What?"

"I said good." Leonard's voice rose up. "Pelin cared more about doctrine than people. He'd break you to prove a point, call it discipline, call it faith. Maybe Samric did the city a favor."

Briar shifted, uncomfortable. "That's... harsh."

"Maybe." Leonard shrugged. "But I'm not going to mourn a man who thought testing kids to the edge of death was holy work."

Silence stretched between them, awkward and sharp. Briar looked down at his bowl, then back at Leonard. "You really think that? That he deserved it?"

Leonard exhaled, some of the anger bleeding out. "No. Maybe not. I don't know." He rubbed his face. "I'm just tired of pretending everyone who dies was a saint. Pelin was a bastard in his own way. Doesn't mean I'm glad he's dead. Only that I'm not crying over it."

Briar nodded slowly, processing. "He used to say the stones don't lie. That if you couldn't hold the power, you didn't deserve it." He looked at his own stone, doubt creeping in. "I used to believe that. Now I'm not sure what I believe."

Leonard glanced at him. "You hold a stone. You're still breathing. That's more than most can say."

"Barely." Briar's laugh was bitter. "Half the time I feel like it's holding me."

"Then let it." Leonard picked up his bowl again. "You're not supposed to wrestle the damn thing into submission. That's Pelin's way. Just... stop fighting so hard."

Briar frowned. "That's not what they taught us."

"Yeah, well, look where their teaching got Pelin." Leonard took another bite, chewed thoughtfully. "You ever meet any Karthian mages?"

Briar shook his head.

"They don't bend the stone. They let it bend them. Looks ugly as hell, but it works." Leonard shrugged. "Maybe there's something in between. Or maybe we're all just making it up as we go."

Briar smiled, small and tentative. "That's... not very reassuring."

"Wasn't trying to be."

Briar spoke again, lighter this time. "You know what I miss? Bread. Real bread. The kind the temple bakers made in the morning, still warm, with butter melting into it."

Leonard snorted. "You're reminiscing about bread?"

"It was really good bread." Briar's grin was genuine now. "Better than this slop, anyway."

Leonard allowed himself a crooked smile. "Fair point."

Briar stood, a little steadier now, bowl empty. "Thanks. For... not pretending everything's fine, I guess."

Leonard nodded. "Don't die stupid out there."

"Wasn't planning on it." Briar hesitated, then added, "And for what it's worth, I think Pelin would've hated you. But maybe that's a good thing."

Leonard watched him go, then turned back to the fire. The coals glowed faint and stubborn.

He thought about Pelin. About doctrine. About all the ways people convinced themselves suffering was sacred.

The fire burned down. Leonard stayed.

DAWN CREPT IN LIKE A THIEF, all gray light and cold wind. The camp stirred, warriors hauling gear, sharpening blades, checking stones. The air smelled like smoke and sweat.

Leonard stood near the center, watching the host form up. Ulzaan walked the line, boots ringing on stone, presence cutting through the noise.

Darum appeared at Leonard's side, armor buckled tight, blade ready. "Last chance to run."

Leonard managed a crooked smile. "Where would I go?"

"Nowhere good." Darum clapped him on the shoulder. "Let's get this done."

Ulzaan's voice cut through the murmur. He swept his gaze over the assembled warriors. "We move"

The host tightened, shifting into formation. Leonard checked his sword, his straps, his breathing. Everything in place.

He thought about Tomas and Marel. About Saran, wherever she was. About the tower waiting in the distance.

He drew his sword, felt the weight settle in his hand. Darum grinned, all teeth and old scars. "Let's show them what Ravenblood does."

The host moved. Leonard moved with them.

16

Dusk came with a fever in the air, no one in Kir-Harath walked easy, not with the council set to meet by nightfall. Saran drifted from window to window, watching the city lean toward the edge. Glass chimes sounded everywhere, strung in archways and doorways, clattering out rumors with every breeze. The markets teemed with bodies, the smell of spiced bread and smoke clung to everything. At every corner, someone hawked news, real or invent-ed,about who would stand, who would fall, and who might not see tomorrow.

Taverns overflowed, bets called out over clinking glasses and hunched shoulders. Some gambled with coin, others with glass shards, each piece worth a promise or a threat. At one stall, Saran saw a clutch of women exchange a silver ring for whispered odds on Thacien's survival. The whole city was gambling on outcomes, everyone picking a side or pretending they had none.

Nobles' guards moved in packs, crests flashing, weapons visible. Servants and hired runners darted between estates with sealed notes, some clutching tokens that glittered in the dawn light. The sigil of an ally, the broken wing of a dead bird for a warning, a bloodied glass chip for a promise of trouble. Even in daylight, back-alley deals happened in the open, men and women meeting in the shadow of ruined arches.

At the Trast estate, Idran was a storm bottled up, fielding messages from every quarter, face drawn with sleepless tension. He passed Saran a folded scrap that reeked of perfumed oil and old bitterness; she unfolded it and found only a line of poetry and the half-mark of a council rival. He handed her another token, a jagged shard, stained red. "Subtle, isn't it?" he muttered. "A little reminder from the cousins."

For every warning, there was an offer, a trinket from someone who wanted to trade favors, a message couched in flattery, promises of safety if only they would back the right house. Saran watched Idran accept, decline, or ignore each one, his jaw set harder each hour.

She moved through the city with her own wariness. Every glance lasted a breath too long, every greeting weighed for hidden intent. She saw old men trading stories about what would happen if the council split, young women whispering about assassins and traitors hiding in the Glass Court's walls. The weight of the day pressed close, Saran's own nerves uncertain how the council would see her, or what price she might be asked to pay. Even among supposed allies, trust felt as thin as spun glass.

By sunset, the city was humming at a pitch that promised either triumph or catastrophe. Saran stood on a balcony, watching the lights flare in the streets, the glass towers reflecting more shadows than sun, and wondered, if the council broke, would any of them survive the night?

Risa cornered them in the long gallery. Sunlight fractured through stained glass, slicing the corridor into shifting bars of color. "New faces on the council tonight," she warned, ticking names off on her fingers. "Lady Pyrrel's brought two of her bastard cousins, both with more debts than sense. Elt's gathered a block of younger lords, and rumor has it someone's backing him with coin from the guilds. Don't count on the usual splits, they'll turn faster than you think."

Before Saran could ask how bad things might get, a minor

servant, one of the estate's retainers, his hands jittering with leftover spell-burn glanced up at her. "Word is you're not the only outsider with a stake tonight," he whispered, palm out for coin or promise. "Heard a certain councilor's been meeting in secret with your rivals. Some talk of a formal challenge to your claim, Lord Idran. And..." He smirked at Saran, "they say the Lord of Glass won't last the night. Maybe someone's planning to hurry that along." Saran slipped him a silver, earning a hasty bow and another tidbit. "Watch the west balconies during the vote. That's where the knives will be."

Risa's jaw tightened as the servant slunk away. Idran, meanwhile, looked ready to crack his knuckles straight through the glass floor. He started pacing. "We lead with the threat to Fazrum, show them the city's at risk, that we need troops or the whole border collapses. They can't ignore it."

Saran shook her head. "They can, and they will if it serves them. Play up Karth's danger. Remind them if Fazrum falls, it's Karth next. Fear is the only thing they respect more than profit."

Idran bristled. "If you admit your part in the relic, they'll use it to bleed you dry, leverage for a hundred years. Better to let them guess."

Saran's gaze was steely. "If I don't, someone else will, secrets pour out as fast as blood. If we act first, maybe we control the story."

They stood close, shoulders tense, the arguments trailing off into exhausted silence. Trust was a luxury neither could afford, not with every corridor echoing with threats, every ally poised for betrayal. Saran glanced down at her hands, then up at Idran. "We keep our eyes open. We stick together. And if it comes to knives, I'll make sure you're not the first to eat some glass."

Idran gave a grim, crooked smile. "Not planning on being anyone's martyr."

Saran and Idran moved through the outer hall, tension in their shoulders matched by every servant they passed, all of them running with quiet purpose.

At the foot of a stair, an older looking councilor intercepted them, eyes rimmed red with too many sleepless nights and too few allies left. He didn't bother with pleasantries. "Lose tonight and the city fractures for good. Every rival you've ever known will carve off a piece and call it survival. There'll be no house Trast left to rebuild, only scavengers.." His gaze lingered on Idran, then Saran, as if memorizing the faces of the last ones likely to care. "Choose your fights, but don't leave this room hoping mercy will find you." With a grunt, he limped off toward the council chamber, the weight of too many failed bargains trailing behind him.

In the corridor, Risa pressed a small token into Idran's palm, a piece of river glass, blue and cloudy, strung on an old cord. "For luck, or whatever's left of it. Don't forget who you're fighting for, Idran. Not tonight." To Saran, her tone softened. "They'll try to box you in, turn the room against you, make you feel small. Don't let them. It's just noise."

Upstairs, the estate bristled with preparation. Servants fussed with formal sashes, pressed coats, and kept a careful eye on weapons, some collected and locked away, others left where they'd do the most intimidation. Guards posted at every entry, no one in the house trusted that tonight would stay inside council walls.

In a rare pocket of privacy, a small anteroom with glass doors closed, Saran found Idran checking the edges of a ceremonial dagger, hands too steady to be anything but anxious. He looked up, and for a moment the weight dropped from his face, leaving only the question that kept him awake.

"If this goes wrong," he murmured, "I don't know what I'll be. Walk away, try to start over somewhere they don't know my name... or stay and fight dirtier, even if it means becoming something I hate."

Saran, for once, let her own guard down. She leaned against the wall, voice gentle but firm. "Doesn't matter who wins tonight, not really. The only thing that'll kill you is letting this place eat you alive the way it did your father. That's all Karth is good at, making monsters out of men who thought they'd be the last to fall."

Idran nodded, closing his fist around the river glass, as if it could anchor him. "I don't want to be him, Saran."

"Then don't be." She held his gaze, steady as iron. "Whatever happens in there, remember who you were before this city tried to shape you into a weapon. I'll remember too."

A servant called from the hall, time to go. Saran straightened her back, adjusted the blade hidden under her bracers, and offered Idran a crooked smile. "Let's show them you're still your own man, council or not."

The halls buzzed with tension as Saran and Idran made their way toward the council chamber. Familiar faces, some from childhood, others from the earlier brawl, watched them pass. A few nobles gave stiff, formal nods, masking their wariness in brittle politeness. Others didn't bother, letting sneers or whispered curses slip free. Saran met each look without flinching, Every face was a reminder of how many knives were in the room, how many waited for the right moment to slip between ribs.

At the threshold, the city's noise fell away as if the air itself were holding its breath. The great doors loomed ahead, carved with the sigils of every major house, old glory layered over centuries of fresh betrayal. Two guards in mirrored breastplates stepped forward, their hands raised.

"Council regulations," one intoned, holding out a palm. Saran surrendered her obvious sword but kept the hidden one just in case. The guard patted her down a little too thoroughly, pausing when fingers brushed the Ravenblood sigil etched into the shoulder. His stare lingered. "We'll be watching you closely."

"Good," Saran said. "Wouldn't want to disappoint."

Idran passed through with only a brief check, though the herald's eyes lingered on the token of river glass at his throat, as if daring him to wear a family's memory into the pit.

At the last moment, Saran and Idran paused, just outside the glare and hush beyond the door. They met each other's eyes, the city's weight and everything unsaid tightening between them. Resolve, dread, and a flicker of something that felt almost like hope. Or maybe just the grim knowledge that, whatever came next, they'd face it together.

The herald swung the doors open. Light flooded out, spilling over the waiting council.

The council chamber was a crucible, mirrored walls rising high and cold, catching every face and secret. A great circle of glass thrones formed the heart of the room, each one different, a webwork of obsidian, a sunburst of fractured color, a jagged monolith of green shot through with veins of old blood. Every seat was filled, and every occupant wore their ambition like a blade.

The nobles and councilors sat rigid or sprawled with studied indifference, flanked by retainers in finery or lacquered armor, house crests stitched or hammered into every visible inch. Saran could see the lines of alliance and hatred in the subtle glances, the way a hand tightened on an armrest or a shoulder leaned forward when a rival entered. Here, even a yawn could be a threat.

Servants lined the edges, armed guards stood at every arch. The steel and magic on display was enough to turn any argument bloody before it reached the council floor.

Saran took in the thrones, the finery, the waiting violence, the air that seemed heavier than the city's own hunger. It was dazzling in the worst way, beauty layered thick over rot, power disguised as tradition.

She glanced at Idran and felt the eyes of a dozen lords and rivals sweep over them.

At the head of the chamber, Thacien sat on his throne of black-green glass, his frame sunken but his presence undiminished. His voice, when it rang out, had lost some strength but none of its acid. The ritual opening began, hands raised, words of unity were recited by repetition, every face in the room practiced in pretending belief. The performance was for show, and everyone in the chamber knew it.

A council spokesman named each house in turn, Lady Pyrrel, draped in dove-grey silk, leaned forward to offer a backhanded greeting, her smile tight as wire. "We're honored by such rare visitors, Lord Idran. Does your return signal a new era, or simply the final one?" The ripple of polite laughter that followed sounded more like sharpening knives.

Cousin Elt, lounging in his glass-and-bronze chair, shot Saran a lazy, appraising look. "And the Ravenblood, we've all heard the stories. Some good, some very bad. Should we be expecting a lesson, or a warning, from our neighbours?"

A military Captain, scarred and tired-eyed, pushed his ringed fingers together, his tone clipped. "Reports from the market say the unrest's growing. Fights, spells, riots. Outsiders seem to multiply every hour, and the city's nerves are frayed thin. The Glass family's grip, it's said, isn't what it once was."

Thacien's voice cut through the mutters. "Order will be restored. This council was built to weather worse than a few squabbles."

Elt flicked his gaze to Idran, voice honeyed with malice. "But are all our guests here to help... or simply to see who falls first?"

All eyes swung to Saran. She met each stare without flinching,

Saran spoke,"Outsider or not, I've bled in your streets and seen what's coming. Blame who you want, but you can't blame the world outside for every crack in your glass. The real threat is what happens if you stand divided, while your enemies watch."

A pause fell, thick with grudges and curiosity. No one welcomed her, but no one dared look away.

The ritual, already brittle, was shattered when Thacien's voice rose over the bickering. "Enough of formalities. Karth is not a stage for empty speeches. There is a matter more pressing, one the council cannot ignore."

His gaze pinned Saran, then swept the chamber. "A relic. Stolen from my hand, vanished in the hands of outsiders and traitors. And now you come, Fazrum's hound—asking for troops, for trust, for anything?" He let the word curdle, savored the power. "I say, nothing leaves these gates until what was taken is returned."

The air thickened. Pyrrel, quick to seize an opening, chimed in. "If Fazrum seeks our aid, let them make amends. Bring back what you stole, or bring something greater." Her faction nodded along, eyes bright with appetite.

Cousin Elt grinned, relishing the turn. "We've bent for the Glasses long enough. Perhaps it's time someone else named the price."

Other voices joined, some pressing for restitution, others hungry to see the family's grip break. The chamber became a tidepool of old feuds and new ambitions.

Idran bristled, "Karth is days from disaster and you all want to pick bones over the past? The threat outside these walls won't wait for your pride to catch up. If we don't stand together—"

Thacien cut him off with a rasping laugh, cruel and public. "You think to lecture this council on unity? You, who ran at the first taste of burden, who brings a thief and a beggar to my table and calls it a homecoming?" He leaned forward, every line in his body radiating spite. "The city is fragile enough without your failures paraded in front of the world. Perhaps it is better we let it break, than trust its pieces to hands already stained."

Lady Pyrrel's voice cut through the clamor. "Perhaps it's time the Glass family steps aside, let those with less tarnished histories guide Karth through the storm. New blood, new vision. We cannot cling to the old wounds forever, not when the city itself cracks." She smiled thin as a razor, her retinue nodding behind her, noting the shift.

Cousin Elt was bolder, rising from his chair with a theatrical bow that mocked its own formality. "Idran, did you come home to patch the roof or just to see what scraps were left for the prodigal? You broke your oath, and now you return with a foreigner on your arm and expect our trust? This is not a council for redemption stories. It's power, plain and simple."

The tension tightened, but another voice broke in, Sennak, the old warhound with fresh scars, his uniform still marked by last night's unrest. "Every minute we waste here, the threat outside the walls grows. Fazrum is not our only problem. There are worse things coming, and this infighting is an invitation." He looked around, eyes hard. "The city won't survive if we tear it apart for pride."

But Sennak's warning barely rippled the water. Another rival, Lord Harth, turned his attention on Saran, the accent thick with Karthian contempt. "Should we trust a Ravenblood, when all we've heard are rumors of their meddling? Fazrum's shadow has always been long in Karth. Why should we risk our sons and stones on an outsider's word?"

Saran rose, black armor catching every glint of hostile light. She let the silence gather, feeling every eye in the chamber fix on her. Her voice was even, iron underneath the exhaustion. "I was there when the relic vanished. Not as a thief, but I was there. If you want to blame me, do it to my face. If you want to waste this city's last chance settling grudges, do it openly. But understand, the world outside these walls won't care who wins your little feud."

The chamber spun into chaos, old men shouting, younger lords flashing rings heavy with crystal. A vein of purple light flickered up the mirrored walls as Pyrrel and Elt's factions closed ranks, voices rising, overlapping, sharpened with insults and centuries of resentment. Someone hurled a threat in Karthian dialect, another countered with a curse half-whispered, half-sung. Magic prickled in the air, the taste of ozone and old wards rising as tension spiked.

Councilors leaned forward as if ready to leap from their glass thrones, retainers slid hands to hilts or crystal-tipped rods. Sennak tried again. "Enough! The city won't survive another war if—" But he was drowned out.

Then Thacien struck the arm of his throne, a hollow, ringing blow that silenced the worst of the noise.. He looked skeletal, sweat beading his pale brow, voice jagged with a fury that almost sounded like fear. "This is my city! By ancient law, my word binds this council. I name Idran traitor, for oath-breaking and collusion with our enemies. Let him be held until his loyalty is proven, or until he rots."

He turned on Saran, eyes wild, the mask of command slipping for all to see. "And you, Ravenblood, by the rights of this chamber, I strip you of guest protection. Let Fazrum claim your bones if it has the strength."

For a heartbeat, even the glass seemed to shudder. The room teetered on the edge of violence, half the council eager for blood, half caught between fear and disbelief, every hand close to a weapon.

The words "let him rot" were still hanging in the chamber when

Idran stepped forward, all the pretense burned away. His voice hit the glass walls like a hammer, the desperation and rage barely reined in.

"You want to know why Karth is dying?" His eyes swept the council, not missing a face. "It's not the relic. It's not outsiders. It's all of you, hoarding power, making fear your gospel, letting one man's rot infect every stone in this city. You built this council as a shield, and you turned it into a cage. Every house in here has bled for your secrets. How much more do you want?"

He pointed at Pyrrel, at Elt, at each lord and captain in turn. "You cling to old wounds and call it legacy. You let children starve in the shadows so you can count who bows first. You let a dying man rule you because you're too afraid to face what comes next."

His voice shook, but only from anger. "It ends here. Break the cycle or let the city choke on your cowardice. I'm done watching you feed on our future for another generation of empty crowns."

Thacien, white-knuckled on his throne, spat back. "This is my council. My city. You are nothing without—"

Idran's fury surged, stones in his flesh burning suddenly bright. "No, Father. That's the lie you fed yourself to keep breathing another day."

In a blink, the air went electric. Thacien lurched as if reaching for a weapon, his pride refusing to die quiet. But Idran was faster, his arm flared with the cold blue light of the family stones, power resonating through his veins. He reached out, touched Thacien's chest, and for a heartbeat the chamber sang with the sound of breaking glass and memory.

It was quick. The light died as fast as it sparked. Thacien's body slumped, eyes wide, mouth frozen in a last, unfinished order.

Saran moved to Idran's side, standing tall as the silence hit, "Unity, or ruin," he said. "That's the choice now. The old ways are dead. What will you do with the city that got left behind?"

For a single, shuddering moment, the council chamber hung frozen, every hand a hair from violence. Then the aftershock hit. Pyrrel shrieked for justice, Elt launched himself half out of his throne, red-faced and howling, "Murder! Traitor! Blood for blood!"

Others rose, some to demand Idran's head, some, with cold calculation, to stake their claim on the ashes.

The chamber exploded into motion. Magic flared in jagged bursts: a sigil blossomed on a captain's arm, a noble's retainer barked a curse that cracked a mirror. Guards forced themselves between feuding lords and weeping old women. A glass rod shattered at Saran's feet, she stepped over it, drawing her hidden blade, placing herself squarely at Idran's back.

She saw the line in the sand, saw it redrawn every second as old rivals shifted, recalculated, measured the odds of vengeance versus survival. "Step closer," she warned a would-be avenger. "And I'll show you what loyalty looks like on this side of the sea."

Sennak bellowed from the floor, his authority battered but not broken. "Enough! You think Karth survives another day if you tear each other apart now? The city needs allies, not more orphans and broken glass!"

It was the ugly, necessary truth. No one here loved Idran for what he'd done, some hated him more for breaking the rules that kept their own power safe. But the fear was real, the threat outside the city too pressing to ignore. One by one, grudgingly, the voices for open revenge faded. The lords and captains drew in, circling around a new, uneasy order.

The council gave way, Kir-Harath would send aid to Fazrum, if only to keep the world outside from finishing what Thacien started.

When it was over, the room was littered with shards and blood, the ghosts of the old city swept aside by a tide of necessity. Saran kept her place at Idran's shoulder, both of them knowing this wasn't a victory.

17

Saran's boots squelched with every step, the ground churned to slop by the column ahead, Karthian soldiers from Kir-Harath, a couple hundred strong, armor gleaming dull in the gray light. Behind them some refugees walked. Maybe fifty, maybe more. Hard to count when they kept their heads down, wrapped in whatever rags they'd salvaged from Karth's chaos.

Saran walked near the middle of the column, close enough to Sekkan's command group to hear orders but far enough back to see the whole mess. Idran was a few paces ahead, shoulders hunched, the shards in his arm pulsing faintly beneath his sleeve. He'd been quiet since they left Karth. Like he was carrying something too heavy to share.

The refugees trailed behind the soldiers, keeping pace but never quite closing the gap. Some were loyal to Karth, families of soldiers, craftsmen who'd supported Idran's gamble. Others were just fleeing, desperate to put distance between themselves and the city's knives. And some glared at the column's back, resentment simmering in their eyes. They blamed Karth for the chaos.

Saran's jaw tightened. Ravenblood doctrine was clear, civilians weren't combatants, they were the reason you fought in the first place. You kept them safe, even if it cost you.

But the Karthians didn't see it that way.

She'd watched Sekkan's officers organize the refugees like cargo, who could walk, who could carry, who was too old or too sick to be worth the rations. The refugees who could work got food and a spot in the wagons when they faltered. The rest got what was left.

Ahead, Sekkan rode at the column's head, his posture straight despite days in the saddle. He trusted his officers to handle it and kept moving. Competence, not sentiment. Orders given once and expected to be followed.

Saran had trained under Darum, who barked orders and checked every soldier twice to make sure they weren't bleeding out quietly in a corner. Ulzaan, who'd walk the line before every march, meeting eyes, saying nothing but making sure everyone knew he saw them.

Sekkan didn't do that. And somehow, his troops still moved like a machine.

Idran drifted back, falling into step beside her. His face was pale, shadows under his eyes, but his voice was steady. "You're thinking too loud."

Saran snorted. "Am I?"

"Loud enough." Idran glanced at the refugees, then at the Karthian rear guard. "It's different here. I know."

"Different, that's what we're calling it?"

Idran's jaw tightened. "They're not being cruel. They're being efficient. In Karth, if you can't contribute, you're a liability. That's just—" He stopped, searching for the word. "—how it is."

"Doesn't make it right."

"No." Idran's voice was quiet. "But it keeps people alive. More than sentiment does, anyway."

Saran looked at him, saw the exhaustion there, the weight of choices he'd made and couldn't take back. She wanted to argue, wanted to say there was a better way, but the words stuck in her throat.

They walked for a while, the column grinding forward. Somewhere behind them, a child cried, with a mother's voice soothing. The sound faded into the trudge of boots.

Sekkan's voice cut through the noise, sharp and commanding. "Halt! Five minutes. Water, check your feet, then we move."

The column stopped, soldiers dropping packs, refugees collapsing where they stood. Saran grabbed her waterskin, took a long pull, tasted metal and grit. She wiped her mouth and looked around.

The refugees huddled in clusters, eyeing the soldiers with suspicion or exhaustion. One man limped forward, asking a Karthian officer for more water. The officer shook his head, pointed to the wagon where rations were kept. "You get your share. Same as everyone."

The man's face twisted, but he turned away.

Saran's stomach churned. She looked at Idran, who was sharing his water with an old woman too proud to ask. He didn't make a show of it, he handed it over, waited for her to finish, then took it back.

Sekkan approached, boots squelching in the mud. He stopped beside Saran, gaze sweeping the column, checking everything without seeming to. "You look troubled."

Saran met his eyes. "It's nothing, just tired."

"Mm." Sekkan's tone was dry. "Tired, or conflicted?"

Saran scoffed. "Does it matter?"

"Not to me." Sekkan's gaze didn't shift. "But it will to you, eventually. Fazrum trains you to protect everyone. Karth trains you to protect what matters. Different wars, different lessons." He paused. "You'll figure out which one keeps you alive."

He walked away before she could answer, already barking orders to the officers, getting the column ready to move again.

Saran stood there, fists clenched, the weight pressing down. She thought about Darum, about Ulzaan, about the Ravenblood that said every life mattered, even the ones that slowed you down.

Idran appeared beside her again, quiet. "He's not wrong."

Saran looked at him. "Doesn't mean he's right."

"No." Idran's voice was tired. "But it means he's survived."

The column started moving again. Saran fell in, boots sinking into the mud, the weight settling deeper.

The terrain shifted as they crested a low rise. Below, a village spread across the road like a corpse, buildings collapsed into themselves, walls cracked open, rubble spilling into the streets. The main road cut straight through the center, narrow and choked with debris.

Saran's stomach dropped. She scanned the ruins, saw too many shadows, too many places to hide. Her hand drifted to her sword, instinct screaming at her to stop, to send scouts, to find another way.

She moved up beside Sekkan, keeping her voice low. "Commander. That village—"

"I see it." His gaze swept the ruins then dismissed. "We're behind schedule. We go through."

Saran's jaw tightened. "It's a chokepoint. If there's anyone waiting—"

"Then we deal with it." Sekkan's tone was final. "Detours cost time. Time costs lives. We move."

Saran opened her mouth to argue, then stopped. Sekkan was the commander. She was the liaison. This wasn't Fazrum. This wasn't a ravenblood war host where everyone had a voice.

This was Karth. And Sekkan's word was law.

She glanced at Idran, saw the worry flicker across his face, but he said nothing. He tightened the straps on his gear and kept walking. Trusting the man who'd survived years of border skirmishes and worse.

The column tightened as they entered the village. Karthian soldiers shifted formation, weapons up, eyes scanning rooftops and alleys. The refugees bunched together, a nervous energy rippling through them. A few whispered prayers. Others walked faster, their heads down, desperate to be through and gone.

Saran's hand stayed on her sword. She scanned the ruins and saw some movement in a window, maybe just wind catching a torn curtain, she hoped.

The column pushed deeper. Halfway through now, the road

narrowing, rubble pressing in from both sides. Sekkan was at the front, posture calm, but his hand rested on his blade.

Then a pack of ravagers poured out of the ruins. They came from everywhere, rooftops, alleys, collapsed buildings, a wave of twisted limbs and amber eyes, shrieking as they hit the column's flanks.

The refugees screamed. Some ran back the way they came, trampling each other in the chaos. Others froze, too terrified to move, and the ravagers tore into them.

Sekkan's voice boomed through the noise, "Form squads! Protect the wounded! Abandon the flanks!"

The Karthians responded instantly, shields locking, spears angling out. They pulled back in tight formation, dragging their wounded with them, ignoring the refugees scattering around them.

Saran's instinct screamed. "Form a perimeter! Regroup! Defend—"

But the Karthians didn't respond. They followed Sekkan, not her. The line buckled, soldiers fighting to hold ground while refugees ran in all directions, some straight into the ravagers' claws.

Saran drew her sword, lunged into the gap. A ravager swung at a refugee, an old man and too slow. Saran's blade caught it across the throat. Black ichor sprayed. The man stumbled and kept running.

Another ravager lunged. Saran blocked, kicked it back, drove her sword through its chest. It collapsed, twitching.

The chaos escalated. A knot of refugees was pinned down near a collapsed wall, ravagers circling. Saran saw Karthian soldiers move past without stopping, their orders clear. Protect the formation, leave the rest.

Her breath caught. The gap was widening. If she didn't act, the whole column would collapse.

Then she saw her, a woman, maybe Saran's age, pinned under a collapsed wall. The stone had her from the waist down, her face streaked with blood. A child couldn't be more than four clung to her, sobbing, trying to pull her free.

"Help me!" The woman's voice cracked, desperate. "Please! My daughter—"

Saran's hand tightened on her sword. Ten seconds. Maybe fifteen. She could pull the woman free, get her moving, save them both.

But the line was buckling. Ravagers were closing in from three sides. If she stopped, if she broke formation to save one—

Sekkan's voice roared through the chaos. "Hold formation or we all die!"

Saran looked at the woman. The woman looked back with pleading eyes.

She couldn't turn away.

Her boots hit the ground before she'd made the choice consciously, sprinting toward the woman. The chaos blurred around her, screams, the wet sound of bodies hitting stone but all she saw was the woman's face. She dropped to her knees, grabbed the edge of the rubble, and pulled.

The stone shifted, grinding against itself, but wouldn't budge. The woman was pinned by weight.

Her hands slipped, blood smearing the stone. She screamed over her shoulder, voice cracking. "Help me! Just two of you! We can move this!"

A pair of Karthian soldiers fought nearby, close enough to hear. One glanced her way and hesitated, then turned back to the line. The other didn't even look.

She pulled harder, muscles screaming, hands tearing on the rough stone. The woman gasped, reaching for her daughter, trying to push the child away. "Take her! Just take her!"

"I'm not leaving you!" Saran's voice was desperate. She braced her feet, hauled again. The rubble shifted an inch but it wasn't enough.

Then Idran was there, he crashed into the space beside her, shoved her back with one hand. "Move!"

His arm came up, shards flaring blue-white, so bright it hurt to look at. His face twisted with concentration, sweat and blood streaming down his temple.

"Idran, don't—"

The blast hit.

Stone shrapnel sprayed outward in a wave of dust and debris.

Saran threw herself over the child, felt fragments slam into her back, her shoulders. The woman screamed.

Saran looked up, her vision blurry for a moment. The woman was free, gasping, blood streaming from fresh cuts across her face and arms, but alive. The child clung to her, sobbing but whole.

Then Saran saw the others, two refugees who'd been sheltering behind the same wall. One lay motionless, head caved in by a chunk of stone. The other clutched a shredded arm, mouth open in a silent scream, then slumped sideways.

Idran staggered back, hand pressed to his face, blood was pouring from his nose. The shards in his arm pulsed violently, glowing veins spreading up past his elbow, crawling toward his shoulder. He stared at his hand, horror carving lines into his face.

Saran couldn't move, she stared at the two bodies, then at the woman and child she'd saved.

The woman looked at her, eyes wide, gratitude and horror tangled together, neither one winning. "Thank you," she whispered. "I'm sorry."

Saran couldn't speak, she knelt there, blood on her hands,

Idran approached her. "We need to move."

Saran nodded and pulled the woman to her feet, grabbed the child, shoved them both toward the Karthian line. "Go. Now."

Saran stood in the rubble, staring at the dead. Idran stood beside her, breathing hard, shards still glowing beneath his skin.

The battle raged around them. Ravagers shrieked. Soldiers shouted. The world kept moving. Saran forced herself to turn away, to keep fighting, to keep moving. But the image stayed. The woman's face., the child's tears. The two bodies she couldn't save because she'd tried to save the two she could.

The ravagers broke, it happened all at once, one moment they were swarming, and the next they scattered like smoke, fleeing back into the ruins. A few Karthian soldiers pursued, spears flashing, but Sekkan's voice roared through the chaos. "Regroup! Let them run!"

The soldiers pulled back, forming up around the survivors. The column was battered, bloodied, but intact. Mostly.

Soldiers moved through the aftermath mechanically, checking gear, binding wounds, wiping blood from blades. Their faces were carved from exhaustion and the kind of numbness that came from doing this too many times.

The refugees huddled together in tight clusters, staring at the dead. Some wept, others were too numb to cry, and sat with hollow eyes, clutching children or each other or nothing at all.

Saran stood in the middle of it, breathing hard, blood drying on her hands. She looked at the woman and child she'd saved, then she looked at the two bodies beside the shattered wall.

Idran sat on a chunk of rubble nearby, staring at his arms. The shards glowed faintly, pulsing beneath his skin, then flickered and went dark. Blood dripping from his nose onto his lap. He didn't move to wipe it away.

Saran walked to him, boots crunching over broken stone. "You saved them."

Idran didn't look up. "I killed them too."

Saran opened her mouth, trying to find words that would make it better, that would undo what had happened. But there weren't any.

She sat beside him, shoulder to shoulder, and said nothing. What was there to say?

The man came out of nowhere.

Older and covered in dust and blood. He stumbled toward Saran and Idran, stopped a few paces away, and pointed at the two bodies beside the shattered wall.

"You did that." His voice filled with grief and rage. "You saved her, but what about them? What about them?"

Saran looked at him, saw the accusation in his eyes, the pain. She wanted to explain, to say she'd tried, that Idran had tried, that it had been an accident, a mistake, a desperate gamble that went wrong.

But none of that mattered. The bodies were still there. The man's grief was still real.

She had no answer.

The man stared at her, hoping for something, an apology, a justification, anything. When Saran said nothing, he spat into the dirt and turned away Saran watched him go

Sekkan appeared a moment later, wiping blood from his blade with a rag. He glanced at the woman and child, then at the two dead

"You broke formation," he said

Saran didn't answer, instead looked away, not wanting to acknowledge his presence.

Sekkan continued, "You saved two but lost two. Could've been worse. Could've been better." He paused, finally meeting her eyes. "You did what you thought was right. That's not nothing. But next time, you might not have the luxury."

He walked away, already barking orders to regroup, to count the wounded, to get the column moving again.

Saran sat there, fists clenched, the weight settling deeper.

Idran's voice cut through the silence. "I was trying to help."

"And I killed them," he finished.

Saran's throat tightened. "I asked for help, you gave it but they died anyway."

Idran spoke again. "There's no right choice out here. Only the choice you can live with."

Saran nodded."Yeah. I'm learning that".

She looked at the woman and child one more time, then she looked at the two bodies, already being dragged aside by Karthian soldiers who didn't have time to bury them.

The column was already forming up. Sekkan's voice rang out. "Move out! We're behind schedule!"

Saran stood, offered Idran a hand. He took it, pulled himself up, swaying slightly.

They walked back to the column in silence, the weight of what they'd done pressing down with every step. The road to Fazrum stretched ahead, long and unforgiving.

18

The war host gathered in clusters, checking straps, testing blades, saying nothing that needed saying.

Leonard stood near the center with Darum and Ulzaan, surrounded by squad leaders who looked like they'd aged a decade overnight. Maps were spread across salvaged crates, marked with routes that looked more like scars than strategy.

Ulzaan's finger traced the tower's outline, then swept outward. "Three prongs. North, east, west. You hit them from every side, force them to spread thin." His voice bore no theatrics or false hope. "The objective is simple: break through, reach the tower and climb. Don't stop for the wounded. Don't stop for glory. Just move."

One of the captains, a woman with a broken nose and mud-caked armor, spoke up. "What about casualties? We're already stretched."

"Accept them." Ulzaan didn't blink. "We're not here to win clean. We're here to reach the top. Everything else is noise."

Darum grunted. "And if the noise gets too loud? If we lose half the host before we even touch the tower?"

Ulzaan met his gaze. "Then the other half better run faster."

The captains exchanged looks, grim but unsurprised. This was the math they'd all done in their heads already. No one argued.

Ulzaan turned to Leonard. "You stay with us. Darum, you too. We push straight through the center once the flanks engage. No detours."

Leonard nodded, throat tight. "What if Samric's waiting?"

"Then we deal with him." Ulzaan's tone didn't shift. "But we don't reveal what we know. Not yet. Let him think we're desperate. Let him think we're stupid." He looked at each of them in turn. "We get to the top. We confront him. Everything else is just surviving long enough to do it."

Darum cracked his knuckles. "Simple enough."

"Simple doesn't mean easy." Ulzaan rolled up the map, handed it to a runner. "Squads move in ten. Say your goodbyes now."

The captains dispersed, Leonard watched them go, each one carrying the weight of lives they'd lose before sunset.

He spotted Briar near a cluster of acolytes, hands shaking as he checked his stone. The kid looked up, caught Leonard's eye, and managed a weak nod. Leonard nodded back.

Darum clapped Leonard on the shoulder. "You ready?"

Leonard looked at the tower in the distance, black against the gray sky. "No. But I'm going anyway."

"Good enough." Darum's grin was all teeth. "Let's not die stupid."

The squads fanned out like fingers spreading across scorched earth. Leonard moved with Ulzaan and Darum, their group slipping through burnt woods and shattered outbuildings, boots crunching over glass and bone. The air tasted metallic, like a storm that refused to break.

Around them, the forest warped. Trees bent at angles that hurt to look at, their bark slick with something that wasn't sap. The ground shimmered in places, heat rising from cracks that glowed faint amber. Magic bled into the world here.

Leonard heard voices carried on the wind, words in languages he didn't know, screams that might've been his imagination. He kept his hand on his sword, eyes scanning shadows that moved too deliberately.

The rest of the squad followed in tight formation, archers with arrows nocked, acolytes clutching stones that flickered like dying stars.

They passed a clearing where a Ravenblood banner hung from a broken tree, tattered and stained. No bodies nearby. Just the banner, swaying in wind that didn't exist.

Leonard's stomach twisted. "Where are they?"

"Gone." Ulzaan didn't slow. "Don't stop to wonder."

A shout cracked through the trees ahead. Steel on steel, screams, the wet sound of bodies hitting dirt. Ulzaan raised a fist. The squad halted.

One of the other groups, ambushed. Leonard could see them through the gaps in the trees. Ravenblood warriors backed against a collapsed wall, ravagers pouring in from three sides.

"Move!" Ulzaan barked.

They broke into a run, crashing through underbrush. Leonard's blade was out before he thought about it, Darum beside him, roaring orders. The squad hit the ravagers from the flank, a wedge of black armor and flashing steel.

Leonard drove his sword through a ravager's back, yanked it free, spun into another. The world narrowed to motion, block, strike, move. Darum was everywhere, blade carving arcs through the chaos, voice cutting through the noise. "Tighten up! Archers, cover left!"

An arrow hissed past Leonard's ear, punched through a ravager's skull. It dropped. Another lunged, claws raking Leonard's vambrace. He kicked it back, drove his sword through its chest. Black ichor sprayed.

Ulzaan moved like something built for this. No wasted motion, no hesitation. His blade flashed, ravagers fell, and where his stone flared, the air itself seemed to crack. A pulse of light, a ravager convulsed and collapsed, smoke rising from its skin.

The ambush broke. The ravagers scattered, melting back into shadow. The Ravenblood squad regrouped.

One of the survivors, a grizzled sergeant with a gash across his temple, nodded to Ulzaan. "Appreciated, lord."

Ulzaan wiped his blade. "Fall in. We move together now."

The combined squads pushed forward, numbers bolstered but nerves frayed. Leonard checked his sword, saw his reflection in the steel. It was pale, streaked with black ichor and blood.

Darum caught his eye. "First blood's done. You good?"

Leonard nodded, not trusting his voice.

They broke through the tree line and the tower loomed, close enough to touch the sky. Its base was ringed with ravagers, hundreds of them, maybe more. A seething mass of twisted limbs and glowing eyes, packed so tight they looked like a single organism.

The black tower itself pulsed, slow and rhythmic, like a heartbeat dragged up from the void. Light bled from cracks in the stone, violet and sickly, casting shadows that moved against the grain of reality.

Leonard's breath caught. This was a slaughter waiting to happen.

Ulzaan surveyed the field, an expression carved from stone. Around them, the other squads emerged from their routes, forming up in ragged lines. Archers in the back, warriors in front, acolytes scattered through the ranks like sparks in a fire.

No grand speech. No rallying cry. Ulzaan just raised his blade, held it high for a breath, then brought it down.

The Ravenblood charged.

The world exploded into noise. Steel clashed, screams tore through the air, arrows hissed overhead in black waves. Leonard ran, boots pounding dirt, the mass of ravagers rushing to meet them.

The lines collided.

Leonard's sword caught a ravager mid-leap, threw it sideways into another. Darum was beside him, roaring, blade carving through bone and sinew. The formation held, barely, warriors locked shield-to-shield, pushing into the horde.

Ulzaan cut a path through the center, his stone blazing white-hot. Where he moved, ravagers died. The air around him crackled, reality bending under the weight of his will.

An acolyte screamed, his stone shattering in his palm. He went down, ravagers tearing into him before Leonard could reach him. Another warrior took his place, stepped over the body, kept fighting.

Leonard blocked a clawed strike, drove his elbow into a ravager's jaw, felt bone crack. Something slammed into his side, threw him off balance. Darum's blade flashed, the ravager's head tumbled.

"Watch your flank!" Darum snapped.

Leonard nodded, gasping, lungs burning. The chaos was overwhelming, bodies everywhere, blood slicking the ground.

Briar appeared in the chaos, stone flickering, face pale but set. He threw out a hand, light flaring, a ward crackling to life. Ravagers hit it and convulsed, falling back. The line held, just barely.

Then a massive ravager, twice the size of the others, tore through the ranks. It scattered warriors like straw, claws raking armor, jaws snapping shut on a soldier's arm. The man screamed and went down.

Drast charged, sword high, and drove the blade through the thing's spine. It roared, twisted, hurled Drast backward. He hit the ground hard, armor clanging, blood streaming from a gash across his ribs.

"Drast!" Leonard lunged forward, but the tide pushed him back. Warriors swarmed the massive ravager, hacking at it until it finally collapsed, twitching.

Drast hauled himself up, one hand pressed to his side, blade still in the other. "I'm fine! Hold the line!"

The Ravenblood pushed. Inch by inch, step by step, bodies piling up on both sides. Leonard's arms burned, his vision blurred with sweat and blood. He killed, and killed, and killed, and it didn't stop.

Then Ulzaan's voice cut through the chaos, sharp as a blade. "NOW!"

Leonard looked up. The path to the tower was open, carved through the horde by Ulzaan's relentless advance. Bodies littered the ground, smoke rising from scorched earth.

Ulzaan gestured. Leonard and Darum broke from the melee, boots pounding dirt, the tower looming ahead.

Behind them, the battle raged on. Screams, steel, the crackle of dying stones. Leonard didn't look back.

The tower's entrance yawned open, black and alien. Leonard stepped through, sword ready, and the world shifted.

The air inside was cold, too cold, biting through armor and skin.

The walls pulsed faintly, veins of light crawling through the stone like living things. The stairwell spiraled upward, steep and narrow, shadows pooling in every corner.

Ulzaan led, blade in one hand, stone blazing in the other. Darum followed, Leonard at the rear, every step echoing too loud.

They climbed. The tower fought them. Doors slammed shut, forcing Ulzaan to blast them open with bursts of light that left scorch marks on the stone. Ravagers appeared from alcoves, lunging with claws and teeth. Leonard cut them down, Darum covering his back, the climb a blur of violence and exhaustion.

The stairs buckled underfoot, stone cracking, gaps opening into darkness. Leonard jumped, landed hard, kept moving. His lungs burned, legs screaming, but he didn't stop.

Near the summit, a cluster of ravagers blocked the way. Ulzaan didn't slow. He raised his hand, light flared, and the ravagers were torn apart by raw force. The stairs were slick with ichor.

Leonard stumbled, vision swimming. Darum grabbed his arm, hauled him up. "You're not quitting now."

Leonard nodded, found his feet, kept climbing.

The final door loomed ahead, massive and black, veins of amber light crawling across its surface. The battle below still raged, the tower shaking with magical backlash, but the noise felt distant now.

Ulzaan stopped, turned to look at Leonard and Darum. His face was carved from exhaustion and resolve. "This is it. Whatever's up there, we end it. No retreating. No second chances."

Darum grinned, bloodstained and grim. "Wouldn't dream of it."

Leonard drew a breath and steadied himself.

Ulzaan raised his blade, drove it into the door's center. Light erupted, cracks spiderwebbing outward. The door groaned, then split, swinging open.

19

The summit was a wound in the world.

Leonard stepped through the shattered door and stopped, lungs seizing. The rift hung overhead, vertical and vast, a gash in reality that bled violet-white light across the rooftop. It pulsed, slow and rhythmic, and with each pulse came a sound, whispers, screams, voices muttering in languages that hurt to hear.

Shadows crawled across the stone, moving against the light, bending in directions that shouldn't exist.

At the center, before the rift, stood Samric.

He was tall, draped in gray that shifted like smoke, silver hair catching the sickly glow. His back was to them, gaze fixed on the battle below, the distant screams, the flash of steel, the dying. He didn't turn. Didn't acknowledge them.

Leonard's hand tightened on his sword. Beside him, Darum shifted, boots scraping stone, breathing hard. Ulzaan moved forward, blade steady, eyes locked on Samric's back.

Then Samric spoke.

"You made it. I'm impressed." He turned, slow, amber eyes cutting through the gloom. His smile was thin, amused. "Most wouldn't have lasted the climb. But then, you're not most, are you?"

Ulzaan didn't answer, just spread his stance, blade angled low.

Samric's gaze swept over them, Darum, bleeding from a dozen cuts; Leonard, trembling with exhaustion. Ulzaan, stone-faced and ready. "Three mortals. One very old grudge. And so much ignorance." He sighed, almost fond. "You think you understand what's happening here. You don't. You can't. But that's the tragedy of humanity, isn't it? Always grasping at shadows, mistaking them for truth."

Darum spat blood. "You done monologuing, or should we wait for the choir?"

Samric's smile widened. "Still defiant. I like that. It makes the futility sweeter." He gestured to the rift, light flickering across his palm. "Do you know what this is? Not a weapon. Not a door. A correction. The world was never meant to belong to you. It was taken. Stolen by a desperate warlord who murdered his own son for a scrap of divine power." His tone turned cold. "The First King built his throne on blood and lies. I'm simply reclaiming what was always ours."

“You lie.” Darum growled.

Leonard's jaw clenched. "Ours? You mean the twisted things you dragged out of the void? The ravagers tearing through villages, killing everything they touch?"

Samric shrugged, unbothered. "Corruption was inevitable. They spent millennia in the dark, exiled by their own kind. What did you expect? Mercy?" He looked at Leonard, something almost kind flickering in his gaze. "But you, Leonard. You're different. You carry the old blood. The last echo of what we were before humanity crawled out of the wreckage." He stepped closer, voice softening. "I tried to bring you to me. The Ninearts, crude as they were, should have been enough. I should have come myself. That was my mistake."

Leonard didn't move, didn't breathe. "What do you want from me?"

Samric tilted his head. "To give you a choice. Join me. Embrace what you are. Help me restore the world to its rightful masters. Or stay with them—" He gestured dismissively at Darum and Ulzaan. "—and die pretending you're one of them."

Leonard's voice was steady, colder than the air. "I'm not one of you. I was raised by them. Trained by them. They're my people. Whatever blood I carry doesn't change that."

Samric's smile faded. "How disappointing."

His gaze snapped to Ulzaan, and for the first time, something like genuine hatred flickered in those amber eyes. "You." The word dripped venom. "Do you know how many times you've ruined me? How many plans, how many carefully laid threads, shattered because you wouldn't break?" He stepped forward, cloak billowing. "I've toppled kingdoms. I've outlived empires. And yet, a mortal, a human has been my greatest obstacle. Not because you're strong. Not because you're clever. But because you refuse to know your place."

Ulzaan's expression didn't shift. "If my place is in your way, I'll stay there."

Samric's jaw tightened. "I'm done with posturing."

He drew his blade.

It was black as the rift, obsidian and pulsing with the same corrupt light. The air around it shimmered, reality bending, and when it moved, it left afterimages burned into Leonard's vision.

Ulzaan raised a hand, sharp and final. "Stay back. Both of you."

Darum hesitated, then stepped aside, pulling Leonard with him. "He's not asking."

Leonard wanted to argue, wanted to help, but one look at Ulzaan's face, stone-cold, focused, burning, and he knew better. This wasn't his fight. Not yet.

Samric lunged.

The first clash was thunder. Steel met obsidian, light flared, and the rooftop shook. Leonard staggered, Darum bracing him, as the two blades locked, then broke apart in a spray of sparks.

Ulzaan moved like something built for war. No wasted motion, every strike precise, brutal. His blade carved arcs through the air, skysteel singing, and where Samric's darkness pressed, Ulzaan's light pushed back.

Samric was faster, older, every movement fluid,, like he existed half a second ahead of the world. He parried, twisted, struck, his blade slicing through stone like flesh. Ulzaan blocked, barely, the impact driving him back a step.

They circled, breathing hard, eyes locked.

Leonard watched, heart pounding. Every clash sent feedback rippling through the rift, light flickering, shadows deepening, two forces tearing at the fabric of the world just by existing in the same space.

Samric feinted left, lunged right, blade aimed at Leonard.

Ulzaan threw himself between them, shoulder catching the blow. Armor screamed and blood spraying. Ulzaan grunted, didn't fall, just drove his blade up in a savage arc that forced Samric back.

"Stay sharp!" Darum barked at Leonard, blade ready, eyes tracking every movement.

Ulzaan pressed the attack relentlessly. His incantation stone flared, white-hot, and with every swing, light erupted from the blade. Intent, focus, will, strength, the old mantra made manifest. Each strike burned brighter, faster, hotter, until the rooftop was ablaze with it.

Samric snarled, blocking, parrying, losing ground. His composure cracked, amber eyes wild. "You should be ash! You're nothing! Just meat and bone and stubborn refusal!"

Ulzaan didn't answer. He kept moving, kept striking, kept pushing.

Samric stumbled, blade raised too late. Ulzaan's sword carved across his ribs, black blood spraying. Samric gasped, staggered, then threw himself backward, toward the rift.

The void swallowed him whole like he'd never been there at all.

Ulzaan surged forward, blade raised, momentum carrying him toward the rift's edge.

"Don't!" Leonard's voice cracked through the air. "Ulzaan, stop!"

Ulzaan halted, boots scraping stone, inches from the threshold. His chest heaved, sweat and blood streaming down his face. He stared into the rift, jaw working, every muscle coiled to move.

"Don't follow him," Leonard said, stepping closer, voice steadier now. "I've been inside. You don't know what it's like in there. The way it pulls at you, the way reality just—" He stopped, swallowed. "You go in, you might not come back."

Ulzaan's hand tightened on his sword, knuckles white. He stared into the void, breathing hard, weighing the choice. Then, slowly, he stepped back.

Darum moved to Ulzaan's side, blade ready, eyes scanning the rooftop. "He's not done. He'll come back."

"I know." Ulzaan wiped blood from his face, gaze never leaving the rift. His voice was hoarse, edged with exhaustion and something harder. "We wait. He wants this fight. He'll finish it."

Leonard stood between them and the void, sword in hand, heart pounding. The rift hummed, voices muttering just beyond hearing, light flickering across the stone.

The rift screamed.

Light erupted from its core, white-violet and amber, crackling like a storm trapped in glass. The rooftop shook, stone cracking beneath their boots. A low howl tore through the air, ancient and furious, the sound of something vast and wounded clawing its way back into the world.

Then Samric burst through.

He staggered, one hand pressed to his ribs, black blood staining his cloak. His face was pale, twisted with rage and pain. But he wasn't alone.

Shadows peeled from the rift behind him, twelve of them, maybe more. Shades. Humanoid, taller than men, their forms flickering like smoke given shape. Amber eyes burned in hollow sockets, and each one held a blade identical to Samric's: obsidian, pulsing with void-light, in a way that made Leonard's vision swim.

Leonard's sword trembled in his hand. Darum swore, low and vicious, backing up a step.

Samric straightened, grin sharp and hateful. "Did you think I'd come alone? Did you think I'd need to?" He gestured, and the shades fanned out, encircling the rooftop, cutting off the stairs. "You made me bleed. I'll give you that. But now you die."

Ulzaan stood between them and the stairwell, the only way out.

His breathing was ragged, armor dented and slick with blood, but his gaze was steady. He looked at Samric, at the shades, at the impossible odds.

Then he looked at Leonard and Darum.

"Go," he said, voice hoarse but absolute. "Now."

Leonard's stomach dropped. "No. We can—"

"Go!" Ulzaan's roar cut through the noise, sharp as a blade. "That's an order!"

Darum grabbed Leonard's arm, hauling him backward. Leonard fought, twisting, trying to break free. "We can't leave him! Darum, we—"

"Trust him!" Darum's voice cracked, eyes wide and desperate. But Leonard saw the lie in his eyes.

The first shade lunged, blade flashing. Ulzaan's sword met it, sparks erupting, and he shoved it back with a snarl. His incantation stone flared, brighter than Leonard had ever seen, white-hot and burning.

"Move!" Ulzaan roared.

Darum yanked Leonard toward the stairs. The world tilted, chaos pressing in from all sides. Leonard's boots hit the first step, then the second, Darum dragging him down.

Behind them, Ulzaan's stone blazed.

Light exploded across the rooftop, a blinding white flash that burned through Leonard's eyelids, seared into his skull. He stumbled, vision swimming, Darum's grip the only thing keeping him upright. The sound was everywhere, a wail that vibrated in his bones, in his teeth, in the marrow of his ribs.

Then they were falling, tumbling down the stairs, the light fading, the world snapping back into focus.

Leonard hit the landing hard, gasping, ears ringing. Darum was beside him, panting.

Leonard crawled to the edge of the stairs and looked up.

Ulzaan stood at the threshold, alone. The shades were frozen at the edge of the rooftop, snarling, clawing at empty air. Between them and Ulzaan, a line of light burned across the stone, a rune circle, jagged and incomplete, glowing white-hot.

Ulzaan's hand was pressed to the center, palm flat against the stone, fingers spread. His whole body shook, muscles tensed, veins standing out like cords beneath his skin. Sweat and blood streamed down his face, dripping onto the rune, feeding it.

The ward held.

Samric stepped forward, eyes blazing. "You're doing this? For them?" He laughed, sharp and cruel. "You're not even divine. You're just meat pretending to be more. And you think you can wield our power?" He sneered. "Intent requires focus. Focus requires will. Will requires strength. Is that the best you've learned from false gods?"

Ulzaan's head lifted, eyes burning white, brighter than the stone in his palm. His voice was a low growl, scraped raw. "No."

He pressed harder, the ward flaring, light crawling up his arm like fire. His flesh blackened where it touched, armor fusing to char, the smell of burning meat filling the air.

"Strength requires sacrifice."

The ward roared.

Light engulfed Ulzaan, white fire consuming him from the inside out. His body cracked, skin splitting, blood boiling away in steam. The shades recoiled, Samric threw up an arm, shielding his eyes.

Leonard watched, frozen, as Ulzaan burned.

The man who'd stood at the front. The man who'd carried the weight when no one else could. The wall that never broke.

Breaking now.

Ulzaan's form blackened, collapsing inward, armor melting into slag. His hand stayed pressed to the rune, the only thing still moving. The light pulsed once, twice, brighter than the sun.

Then it guttered out and Ulzaan fell.

What was left wasn't a man anymore. Only blackened bone, scorched armor fused to charred flesh, barely recognizable. The ward flickered, then died, runes fading to ash.

Silence crashed down.

Leonard couldn't breathe. Couldn't move. His chest felt hollow, scooped out, nothing left but the taste of smoke and copper.

Darum's hand was on his shoulder, gripping too hard, shaking. "Come on," he whispered, voice broken. "We have to go. Leonard. We have to go."

Samric stepped forward, He crouched beside Ulzaan's remains, reached down, and pried something from the ruined hand.

The incantation stone.

It was dim now, the light gone, just a dull piece of crystal. Samric held it up, studying it with disgust, then tucked it into his cloak. "A fitting end," he muttered. "Burning himself out for nothing."

He looked down the stairwell, amber eyes finding Leonard. "Run while you can. It won't save you."

Darum yanked Leonard back, down the stairs, into the dark. Leonard stumbled, boots slipping on blood-slick stone, vision blurred with tears he didn't remember shedding.

Behind them, the rooftop burned with dying light.

THE STAIRS BLURRED beneath Leonard's boots, the world tilting with every step, stone slick with blood and worse. Darum led, shoulders hunched, breath coming in ragged gasps. Leonard followed, numb, his sword still in his hand though he didn't remember drawing it.

Behind them, the rooftop burned with dying light. Ulzaan's light. Gone now. Only ash and smoke and the empty space where a man used to stand.

Leonard's chest ached, hollow, like something vital had been scooped out and left to bleed.

A shadow moved ahead. Darum stopped, blade up. A ravager lunged from an alcove, claws raking stone, jaws wide. Darum met it head-on, sword carving through its forearm. The limb tumbled, black ichor spraying. The thing shrieked, twisted, and Darum slammed his palm against its chest.

Light flared, weak and sputtering. The ravager convulsed,

collapsing into smoke and char. Darum staggered, nearly went down. Leonard caught him, hauled him upright.

"I'm fine," Darum rasped, but his hand shook, stone dim in his palm. "Keep moving."

They pushed on. The tower groaned around them, walls cracking, the rift's power bleeding through stone. Shadows crawled at the edges of Leonard's vision, voices muttering just out of reach. He didn't look. Couldn't afford to.

Another landing. Another turn. Then steel rang out ahead, shouts, the wet sound of bodies hitting stone.

Darum cursed, broke into a stumbling run. Leonard followed, legs burning, lungs screaming.

They hit the ambush head-on. Three ravagers, maybe four, swarming a knot of Ravenblood warriors backed against a collapsed wall. Blood everywhere, armor dented, faces pale with exhaustion and fear.

Drast was there, limping, one arm hanging limp, but his blade was still up. He drove it through a ravager's throat, yanked it free, spun into another.

"About damn time!" he roared, spotting Darum and Leonard.

Darum didn't answer, just charged. His blade flashed, cutting through the chaos, and the warriors rallied, pressing the attack. Leonard moved on instinct, sword heavy in his hand. He blocked a clawed swipe, drove his boot into a knee, felt bone crack. The ravager fell. He didn't stop to see if it got back up.

The fight broke fast. The last ravager went down under a hail of blades, twitching in the dark. Silence crashed back in, broken only by ragged breathing.

One of the warriors, a young woman with a gash across her temple, stared at Darum. "Where's the strategos? Is he—"

"Still up there." Darum's voice bore no room for argument. "His last order was full retreat. Anyone who goes back up doesn't come back down."

The words landed like stones. Faces went pale, jaws clenched. The woman's eyes filled with tears she didn't let fall.

Drast stepped forward, jaw tight, something raw flickering in his gaze. "You're sure?"

Darum met his eyes. "There's no time for this, we need to move, now!"

Drast's hand tightened on his sword, knuckles white. For a moment, Leonard thought he'd turn, charge back up the stairs, throw himself into the same fire. But he didn't. He just nodded, once.

"Then we move," Drast said, "Now. Before they regroup."

The group formed up, battered but moving. Darum led, Drast covering the rear. Leonard walked in the middle, numb, legs carrying him without thought.

They smashed through the last resistance; ravagers scattered, disorganized, more fleeing than fighting. The tower's base loomed ahead, the doorway yawning open, spilling gray light.

They stumbled through, into the open air.

The battlefield was chaos.

Ravenblood banners fell back in ragged lines, warriors dragging wounded, limping, bleeding. The enemy howled from the tower's shadow, but they didn't pursue. Just watched, amber eyes glowing in the dark.

Horns blared, retreat signals cutting through the noise. Drast's voice joined them, hoarse and commanding. "Form up! Vask! Move to Vask!"

Darum grabbed Leonard's arm, hauled him forward. Leonard stumbled, boots sinking into mud and blood, the world tilting. Everything was muffled, distant, like he was underwater. Sounds came in fragments; screams, steel, the wet crunch of bodies hitting dirt.

He saw faces. Briar, stone flickering in his palm. A warrior he didn't know, eyes wide, mouth moving but no sound reaching Leonard's ears. Another, collapsed in the mud, staring at nothing.

Tomas. Marel. Ulzaan.

Gone.

All of them, gone.

Leonard's vision narrowed, the edges darkening. His heartbeat thundered in his skull, drowning everything else. The world slowed, each step stretching into eternity. Mud splashed, armor clanked, someone screamed his name.

He didn't answer.

Then, in the silence, he saw it.

Black wings.

Not real. Not there. A flicker at the edge of his vision, a shadow that moved wrong. But it was enough.

The world snapped back.

Sound crashed in, Darum shouting his name, Drast barking orders, the roar of the retreating host. Leonard gasped, stumbled, Darum's hand gripping his shoulder, keeping him upright.

"Stay with me!" Darum's voice was raw. "Leonard! Stay with me!"

Leonard nodded, found his feet. The enemy wasn't following. They stood at the tower's base, content to let them go.

For now.

The host ran. Leonard ran with them.

Vask rose out of the haze, broken and familiar. The war host staggered through its gates, bloodied, diminished, barely holding together. Leonard and Darum were among the first through, boots dragging on stone, armor caked with mud and worse.

They stopped just inside, chests heaving, and for a moment, neither moved.

Then Darum turned, pulled Leonard into an embrace. the weight of grief, gratitude, and the brutal fact of survival. Leonard's hands gripped Darum's armor, shaking, and something in his chest finally cracked.

He didn't cry. Couldn't. He held on, breath hitching, the world narrowing to this single moment.

Darum's voice was rough in his ear. "You're still standing. That's enough."

Leonard nodded, throat too tight to speak.

Drast found them, limping, one arm bound in a blood-soaked rag. His face was carved from exhaustion and something harder. He grabbed Darum's shoulder, eyes wild. "What happened up there? Where's Ulzaan?"

Darum pulled back from Leonard, met Drast's gaze. His voice was barely a whisper. "He's dead. He bought us time. That's why any of us are breathing. You're in command now"

Drast recoiled, jaw clenching. A muscle ticked in his cheek. For a heartbeat, he looked ready to deny it, to argue, to demand proof. But the blood, the bodies, the silence where Ulzaan's presence should've been, it all told the truth.

He nodded, once. A jerk of the head. "Then we keep moving. There's nothing left for us here."

His voice cracked at the edges, but he turned away, barking orders to the nearest warriors, organizing a perimeter, filling the void left behind.

Leonard watched him go, then looked at Darum. The old warrior's face was streaked with blood and grime, eyes red-rimmed. He wiped them with the back of his hand, squared his shoulders, and looked at Leonard.

"We need to get back to the capitol," Darum said, voice hoarse. "We did what we came to do. Kept Samric in the dark. But the cost—" He stopped, swallowed. "The cost was high."

Leonard nodded. "War's not done yet."

Drast returned, face set. "We'll need a new strategos. Ulzaan's gone. Someone has to step up. War or no war"

The words hung, unspoken implications dragging at them. Leonard looked at the battered warriors gathering in the square, carrying their dead, tending their wounded.

"Not tonight," Darum said quietly. "Tonight, we remember our dead and rest. Tomorrow, we figure out what's left."

Drast grunted agreement, limped off to check the perimeter.

Leonard stood apart for a moment, staring at the distant tower, black against the dying light. The weight of what had been lost pressed down. Ulzaan. Tomas. Marel. All the names he couldn't remember, the faces blurred by exhaustion and grief.

He turned back to the host, saw Darum watching him, steady and patient. Saw the warriors looking to them, not for hope, but for orders. For someone to tell them what to do next.

Leonard drew a breath, felt the cold air bite his lungs.

"We march at first light," he said, voice carrying. "Back to the capitol. We tell them what happened. We regroup. And we finish this."

Darum nodded, something like pride flickering in his eyes.

Night fell over Vask, Leonard sat against a broken wall, sword across his knees, staring at nothing. Somewhere in the dark, a raven called. But he didn't look up.

20

The capitol rose from the haze like something out of a half-remembered dream. Towers Leonard had known his whole life, stone he'd walked past a thousand times, walls that should've felt safe. They didn't. They looked smaller than he remembered, worn down by time and siege and the weight of too many people trying to fit inside something that was never meant to hold them all.

The war host slowed as they crested the final ridge, boots dragging, armor clanking with every step, they stared at the city sprawled below, taking in the changes.

Refugees packed the outer gates, a sea of bodies pressed against barricades that hadn't been there when Leonard left. Makeshift camps spread like rot along the approach roads, canvas shelters and scavenged timber, cook-fires smoking in the cold. Faces turned toward the host, their eyes suspicious, too tired for hope.

Leonard scanned the defenses. New earthworks ringed the outer wall, stakes driven into the ground at sharp angles, trenches dug deep enough to slow a charge. Fazrum soldiers manned the paraposts, crossbows ready, carrying the knowledge that the assault was coming whether they were ready or not.

He spotted something else. Uniforms that didn't match. Different cuts, darker colors, the glint of shardwork on armor instead of skysteel. Karthian troops, scattered along the line, standing shoulder-to-shoulder with Fazrum defenders but never quite mixing.

A shout went up from the gate. Not a welcome, but acknowledgment. The Ravenblood host was back. What was left of it.

They marched closer. The crowd shifted, muttering rising. Leonard caught fragments, where were they, did they run, why'd they come back now, cowards. Someone spat into the dirt as they passed. Another turned away, their face twisted with contempt.

Leonard's jaw tightened. No one had told them. No one had explained what the host had fought through, what they'd lost. To the refugees, the Ravenblood were just soldiers who'd left and come back beaten.

Darum's voice cut through the noise, "Eyes forward. Don't give them a reason."

Leonard nodded, kept walking. The gate loomed ahead, iron-banded wood scarred by fire and patched with fresh timber. Guards flanked it, hands on weapons, watching the host like they might turn feral any second.

The gate creaked open, slowly. Like the city wasn't sure it wanted to let them in.

Leonard stepped through first, Darum beside him, Drast limping a few paces back. The noise hit, shouts from the market district, the clang of a smithy still working despite the hour, prayers being chanted from the temple steps. All of it laced with tension, the brittle edge of a city holding its breath.

The Karthian troops watched from the walls. Leonard met one's gaze, saw no warmth there.The man's hand rested on a blade inlaid with shardwork, the faint glow visible even in daylight. A Ravenblood warrior nearby noticed, shifted his stance, fingers drifting toward his own sword.

Darum stopped just inside the gate, turned to Leonard. His face was carved from exhaustion, scruff beard shot through with more gray than Leonard remembered. "We need to split up."

Leonard blinked. "What?"

"Command needs me. Reports, strategy, whatever the hell Brent's going to ask for." Darum's tone was practical. "You need to not be around all that. Not yet."

Leonard wanted to argue, felt the pull to stay close, but he knew Darum was right. The thought of walking into another war room, another set of orders, another crisis, his chest tightened just thinking about it.

"If Karth's here, Saran made it," Leonard said quietly.

Darum nodded. "Or she's dead and they sent troops anyway. Either way, we'll know soon enough." He clapped Leonard on the shoulder, grip firm. "Go find somewhere quiet. Breathe. I'll find you when I know more."

Leonard swallowed, throat tight. "Yeah. Alright."

Darum held his gaze for a moment longer, something unspoken passing between them, gratitude, grief, the exhaustion of men who'd survived when they shouldn't have. Then he turned and walked toward the inner citadel, Drast falling in beside him.

Leonard stood alone in the crowded street, noise pressing in from all sides. He needed to move, needed to find somewhere that didn't feel like it was closing in on him.

He turned away from the citadel, boots crunching over cobblestones, and headed for the only place left that might still feel like home.

The barracks were quieter than they should've been. Half-empty, most of the bunks stripped bare, gear missing from the racks. Too many dead. Too many still out on the walls.

Leonard's boots echoed on stone as he climbed the stairs, each step heavier than the last. He stopped at the door, his door, their door and stared at the iron handle for a long moment before pushing it open.

The room was exactly as they'd left it.

Two cots, one on each side. A narrow window letting in gray light. A cupboard leaning slightly to the left, same as always. Saran's sword-cleaning kit still sat on the small table between the beds, oil-stained rag folded beside it. His own pack hung from a peg on the wall, half-unpacked from the last time he'd bothered.

Leonard stepped inside, closed the door behind him. The latch clicked, too loud in the hush. He stood there, breathing, trying to make the space feel familiar again. It didn't work.

His hand drifted along the edge of the table, fingers tracing the grain of the wood. Saran had carved her initials into the corner once, bored during a long night watch. He could still see the faint S, half-hidden under layers of oil and grime.

He moved to his cot and sat down hard. The frame creaked, familiar and foreign all at once. His armor felt too tight, straps cutting into his shoulders, the weight pressing him down. He started unbuckling, methodical at first, vambrace, pauldron, chest plate. Each piece came off slowly, his hands shaking just enough to notice.

Then the frustration hit.

He yanked the last strap free, ripped the greave off his leg, and hurled it across the room. It crashed into the cupboard, the door swinging open, wood splintering at the corner. The sound echoed, sharp and final.

Leonard sat there, chest heaving, staring at the damage. The cupboard tilted further, threatening to collapse. He cursed under his breath, stood, and crossed the room to right it.

As he grabbed the frame, something fell from the open door, a small bundle of letters, tied with a frayed piece of string. They scattered across the floor, old parchment yellowed at the edges.

He knew those letters. Saran had mentioned them before. Letters from her parents. Before Ruvar burned. Before everything fell apart.

He knelt, fingers hovering over the nearest one. The handwriting was careful, practiced, the kind taught in village schools where parchment was expensive and mistakes weren't forgiven. The ink had faded, but he could still make out the first line: My dearest Sarah—

His throat tightened.

He picked up the letter, turned it over in his hands. The paper was soft, worn from being read too many times. He could open it.

Could read the words her mother had written, the life she'd had before the Pact, before the war. Before Leonard.

But he didn't.

He stared at the letter, guilt twisting in his chest. This wasn't his. It was hers. The last piece of a world she'd lost, carried with her through blood and everything after.

Leonard set the letter down, gathered the rest, tied them back with the string. His hands were careful, making sure they were exactly as she'd left them. He placed the bundle back in the cupboard and tucked it into the corner where it wouldn't fall again.

Then he straightened the cupboard, checked the hinges, made sure it wouldn't collapse.

The room was quiet again. Just the sound of his breathing, the faint creak of the building settling.

The door opened.

Leonard's head snapped up, heart lurching. For a second, he didn't recognize her, he saw a figure backlit by the hallway, cloak hanging crooked, mud caked to her boots.

Then she stepped inside, and the world settled.

She looked like she'd been dragged through every bad road between here and Karth. Hair pulled back in a braid that had come half-undone, strands falling loose around her face. Travel cloak stained with dust and worse, hanging lopsided where the clasp had broken.

She paused in the doorway, taking in the room. Taking in Leonard.

Her gaze swept over him, battered, armor scattered on the floor, face pale and hollow. She didn't say anything but stood there, bracing like she was waiting for the floor to drop out.

Saran stepped inside, let the door close behind her. She dropped her pack with a grunt, rolled her shoulders like she was shaking off weight she'd carried too long. Leonard stood by his cot, watching her, fingers fidgeting with a loose strap on his vambrace.

They looked at each other.

Seconds stretched. Saran's mouth twitched, almost a smile. “You made it too, huh?”

Leonard exhaled, a sound somewhere between a laugh and a sigh.

Saran crossed the room, stopped in front of him. For a moment, they stood there, close enough to touch but not quite moving. Then she reached out, pulled him into an embrace.

Leonard's arms came up, wrapped around her, and something in his chest finally cracked, a breath he'd been holding since Vask, since the tower, since Ulzaan burned and the world tilted sideways.

Saran held him, solid and warm, her chin resting on his shoulder.

After a moment, she pulled back, sat on the edge of his cot. Elbows on her knees, hands loose, gaze fixed somewhere past the window. Leonard sat down too.

Leonard spoke first. "How did it go? In Karth?"

Saran stared at her hands, jaw working. "Messy." She paused, choosing words carefully. "Idran killed his father. In front of the whole council. It was—" She stopped, shook her head. "It wasn't clean. The council fractured. Some wanted him executed, others saw an opportunity. We got troops because they were too busy fighting each other to say no."

Leonard blinked. "He killed—"

"Yeah." Saran's tone was flat. "Old bastard was dying anyway. Using that relic to hold off death, bleeding the family dry. Idran ended it, the council called it murder." She rubbed her face. "We left before they could process what really happened."

Leonard swallowed. "Is he—"

"Alive. For now." Saran's smile was bitter. "Risa, his sister stayed behind to keep the city from eating itself. We came back with the troops. Don't know if that makes us brave or stupid."

She looked at him, gaze sharp despite the exhaustion. "And you?"

Leonard's throat tightened. He tried to find the words, tried to piece together the chaos of the tower, the rift, the climb. "We made it to the tower. Ulzaan, Darum, and me. Samric was there. Waiting, like he knew we would come."

Saran's hand drifted to his, fingers brushing his knuckles. He didn't pull away.

"Ulzaan fought him. One-on-one." Leonard's voice cracked. "He was winning. Drove Samric into the rift, forced him back. But then—" He stopped, breath hitching. "Samric came back with shades, the same kind Darum fought. A dozen of them, maybe more. Ulzaan told us to run. Ordered us."

Saran's grip tightened.

"He stayed." Leonard's eyes burned, but the tears didn't come. Only the ache, the hollow space where something vital used to be. "Drew a ward line. Held them off while we escaped. He burned himself out. Just—" He gestured, helpless. "—ash and light and nothing left."

Saran went very still like she was holding something fragile that might shatter if she moved too fast. Her hand stayed on his.

"Darum?" she asked, voice barely above a whisper.

"He's fine." Leonard nodded. " At least, he'll tell you he's fine.

Saran exhaled, slow and controlled. "And you?"

Leonard looked at her, saw the worry, the grief mirrored in her eyes. "I don't know."

She nodded, didn't push and sat with him, shoulder to shoulder, the weight of everything pressing down on both of them.

Outside, the city murmured. Boots on stone, distant shouts, the clang of a forge still working despite the hour. The war waited. It always waited.

But for now, they had this. The quiet. The room. Each other.

Saran's thumb traced the back of his hand, slow and deliberate. "We'll figure it out," she said quietly. "One step at a time."

Leonard closed his eyes, leaned into her. "Yeah, always"

The silence stretched, comfortable but fragile. Leonard shifted, glancing at Saran. "Where's Idran now?"

Saran snorted, a ghost of her old humor surfacing. "Went to see Eleseth. Something about magic, resonance, I stopped listening after he started comparing Karthian stonecraft to Fazrum doctrine." She rolled her eyes. "Never thought I'd see a Karthian mage and an ex-

Stone Sage having a civil conversation. Strangest council I've ever heard of."

Leonard's chest loosened, just a little. Eleseth. A friendly face that wasn't covered in blood or barking orders. Someone who might talk about something other than strategy and death counts.

"I'd like to see her," he said quietly. "Just—" He stopped, searching for words. "Just to see someone normal. For a minute."

Saran looked at him, something soft flickering in her gaze. "Yeah. I get that." She stood, joints creaking, and gestured to the basin in the corner. "But first, we wash up. You smell like death and burnt stone, and I'm not much better."

Leonard glanced down at himself, mud-caked, blood-stained, armor scattered like a battlefield. "Fair point."

Saran grabbed a rag, tossed it to him. "Clean yourself up. I'll do the same. Then we'll find Eleseth"

Leonard caught the rag, felt the weight of mundane routine settle over him like armor. Washing. Changing. These were small, ordinary tasks that had nothing to do with war or dying.

It felt like a lifeline.

He stood, moved to the basin, and started scrubbing the worst of the grime from his hands. The water turned black almost immediately. Saran did the same.

Saran finished first, wrung out the rag, and reached for a clean shirt from her pack. "You ready?"

Leonard nodded, drying his hands. "Yeah. Let's go."

They left the room together, boots echoing in the empty hall.

The streets Leonard had known his whole life were packed with bodies, refugees huddled in doorways, Fazrum soldiers on patrol, Karthian troops clustered near supply depots. Everyone moved with purpose, but the tension was palpable.

Leonard and Saran walked in silence, weaving through the crowd.

No one looked at them twice. Two more battered warriors in a city full of them.

They turned onto the old temple road, and the noise began to fade. Fewer people here. The stone underfoot was worn smooth by centuries of pilgrims, seekers, the desperate and the faithful. The temple rose ahead.

Leonard slowed as they approached the entrance. Above the door, carved into the lintel in mirrored script, was the mantra. He'd seen it numerous times, memorized it before he even understood what it meant.

Intent requires focus. Focus requires will. Will requires strength.

His lips moved, murmuring the words. Then, quieter, he added, "Strength requires sacrifice."

Saran stopped beside him, following his gaze.

"Ulzaan's line." Leonard said. "He said it at the end. Right before —" He stopped, couldn't finish.

Saran studied the carving, jaw set. "It's what they left out. What everyone in this city pretended wasn't true." Her tone was bitter. "They wanted the power. The glory. But they didn't want to name the cost."

Leonard looked at her, saw the anger simmering beneath the exhaustion. "Yeah. That's why it mattered. Why he added it."

Saran exhaled, sharp and final. "Then let's make sure it wasn't for nothing."

They stepped through the door.

The air inside was thick, incense, dust, and something else. Old regret, maybe. The kind that settled into stone and refused to leave.

The temple's interior was exactly as Leonard remembered. High ceilings lost in shadow, columns carved with sigils he'd never learned to read, alcoves filled with artifacts no one touched anymore. The light came from narrow windows, slanting in pale and cold, catching motes of dust.

Leonard's chest tightened. He'd been tested here. Pushed to the edge of what he could endure, then pushed further. Pelin's voice still echoed in his memory. He remembered the archives, row after row of scrolls and tomes, locked behind doctrine. Dead knowledge, hoarded like treasure but never shared. Wisdom turned to dust because no one was allowed to use it unless they proved themselves first. And the tests, always the tests. Pain as proof. Suffering as devotion.

It had felt wrong then. It felt worse now.

Saran's hand brushed his arm, grounding him. "You alright?"

Leonard nodded, not trusting his voice. He looked around, half-expecting to see Pelin's ghost standing by the altar, judging him. But there was only silence.

"Come on," Saran said quietly. "Eleseth's probably in the back."

They moved deeper into the temple, boots echoing on polished stone. Leonard kept his eyes forward, trying not to look at the alcoves.

The inner chamber was quieter than the main hall, tucked away behind a narrow archway that Leonard had never noticed before. The air was cooler here, less oppressive, though the incense still clung to everything.

Eleseth stood near a stone table, her gray robes dusty at the hem, hair pulled back in a loose knot. Beside her, Idran leaned over something laid out on the table, a relic, bone-pale and faintly glowing, wrapped in old velvet that had seen better days.

Idran looked up as they entered, nodded once. "Leonard. Saran."

Eleseth turned, and her expression softened immediately. She crossed the room in quick strides, stopping just in front of Leonard. "You're back." Her voice was gentle, careful. "I heard what happened. At the tower."

Leonard met her gaze, saw the concern there, the worry she wasn't quite hiding. "Yeah. We made it."

"And Ulzaan didn't." Eleseth's tone wasn't accusing. "I wish I could help you more, Leonard. I truly do. But I don't know how."

Leonard swallowed, throat tight. "You being here helps."

Eleseth's hand found his shoulder, squeezed once. "Then I'll stay."

Saran stepped forward, eyeing the relic on the table. "What are you doing here, Eleseth? Thought you'd left the Sages behind."

Eleseth let out a bitter laugh, stepped back toward the table. "I did. After I helped Leonard get into the archives, after what happened with Pelin—" She shook her head. "The rift between me and the order is too wide to cross. But I still have a duty to Fazrum. One I can't ignore, even if the Sages don't want me."

Leonard frowned. "Are you a full Sage again?"

"No." Eleseth's voice was firm. "And I won't be. Not after everything. But that doesn't mean I can't work." She gestured to the relic. "Idran needed help understanding this. I had some knowledge. So here we are."

Saran glanced around the chamber. "Where are the others? Veyra? Orin?"

Eleseth's expression darkened. "Veyra's isolated herself. After Pelin's death, after the tower flared and the stones started failing, she's buried herself in her study. Scrolls, old texts, anything to avoid facing what's happening outside. She rarely comes out."

"And Orin?" Leonard asked.

"Preparing for the Trial of the Raven." Eleseth's tone was measured. "It has to happen quickly. A new Strategos must be chosen. Orin will preside, as is tradition. Pelin would have, if he were still alive."

She paused, gaze settling on Leonard. "Orin regrets what he did to you. During your testing. He was complicit, followed Pelin's lead without question. He's trying to make amends, in his own way."

Leonard didn't know what to say to that. He just nodded.

Saran crossed her arms. "Thought the Sage order and Ravenblood didn't interfere with each other's business."

"They don't. Usually." Eleseth's smile was faint. "But both orders trace their origins back to the founding of Fazrum. The Trial of the Raven is one of the few traditions where doctrine and duty intersect. A Sage must witness. It's always been that way."

Saran grunted. "Of course it has."

Leonard's gaze drifted back to the relic. "What about this? Why are you studying it now?"

Idran straightened, wiping dust from his hands. "Because it's a mirror. What my father did with this relic, what Samric's doing with the towers, they're connected." He looked at Leonard, then Saran. "I knew. Not the full extent, but I suspected. My father was using it to stave off death. I wasn't allowed to interfere. Family politics, tradition, all the usual excuses."

He leaned closer to the relic, fingers hovering just above its surface. "One piece of stone. That's all it took to destroy so much. My father's mind, my family, the council—" He stopped, gaze dropping to the shards embedded in his forearm. The faint blue glow pulsed beneath his skin. "I look at these and wonder if they were worth it. If any of it was."

Eleseth's voice was quiet. "You can't undo what's already done. But you can choose what comes next."

Idran nodded, jaw tight. "Yeah. I know."

Leonard looked at each of them, Eleseth, still carrying the weight of her exile, Idran, haunted by the choices he'd made, Saran, standing steady despite everything she'd lost. They were all broken in their own ways. But they were still standing.

"When does the trial start?" Leonard asked.

Eleseth glanced toward the door. "Soon. Maybe a day, maybe less. Orin's finalizing the preparations. You'll be summoned when it's time."

Leonard exhaled, the weight settling back over him. "Then we wait."

"And prepare," Saran added, voice hard. "Whatever comes next, we need to be ready."

Eleseth nodded. "Agreed."

Idran wrapped the relic back in its velvet, careful not to touch it. "I'll keep working on this. See if there's anything we can use when the time comes."

Leonard turned toward the door, Saran following. "We'll be ready," he said quietly. "We have to be."

They left the inner chamber, stepping back into the temple's main hall. The weight pressed down, familiar and heavy, but Leonard kept walking

21

The chamber was older than most of the men in it. Stone walls carved with sigils Leonard didn't recognize, worn smooth by centuries of hands running over them in moments of doubt or prayer. The air smelled like cold iron and old incense, the kind that clung to your throat and settled heavy in the chest.

Leonard stood near the back, his shoulder pressed to the wall, trying to make himself small. Around him, the Ravenblood leadership filled the room, Blade Veterans with scars older than Leonard, senior officers who'd held the line when others broke, a handful of Stone Sages in their gray robes standing like granite pillars. Faces he knew, faces he didn't. All of them looked hollowed out, like the march back from Vask had scraped something vital away and left only shell.

Darum was near the front, his arms crossed. Drast leaned against a pillar, one arm still bandaged, exhaustion carved into every line of his face. He'd refused a sling, but the way he held himself said the wound was deeper than he'd admit.

Brent stood beside the empty chair at the room's center, hands folded behind his back, posture parade-ready despite the weight pressing down on him. His armour was immaculate but his eyes were red-rimmed. He hadn't slept in some time.

Saran slipped in beside Leonard, quiet as a ghost. Her hair was still braided tight, but dust and travel clung to her cloak, and her boots left faint prints of Karthian mud on the stone. She didn't say anything, just stood close enough that their shoulders touched. Leonard exhaled, some of the tension bleeding out.

The empty chair loomed.

High-backed, carved from black wood so dark it drank the torchlight. A raven's wings spread across the headrest, each feather etched with painstaking detail, the edges worn smooth. No decoration beyond the wings.

Leonard stared at it, the empty space louder than any speech. He could almost see Ulzaan there, eyes burning white, voice cutting through chaos. Could still hear him. “Do the job. Don't die stupid.”

The murmur of conversation died as Brent cleared his throat. He didn't raise his voice. "Ulzaan is dead." His voice was steady, but there was something brittle underneath, like glass held together by will alone. "The Strategos seat is empty. By tradition, we convene to choose his successor through the Trial of the Raven."

The words landed heavy. No one moved. Leonard felt the weight of it, the grief everyone was holding back because there was no time to fall apart. Not yet. Maybe not ever.

One of the Sages stepped forward, Orin, Leonard realized. Older, with a beard gone white and eyes that carried the kind of weariness that came from watching too many suffer for doctrine. He'd been at the temple when Pelin ran the place, back when Leonard was tested and nearly broken.

Orin's gaze swept the room, lingering on faces, counting the absent. "The trial requires three components," he said, voice carrying the weight of centuries. "The Vigil. The Testimony. The Stone's Judgment." He paused, letting the words settle. "Since the death of Sage Pelin, I have taken his place in these proceedings. And I must inform you—" His jaw tightened. "—the Strategos Stone was taken. Samric has it. Without the stone, the ritual cannot be completed."

The murmur started again, low and tense, a wave building. Someone cursed, sharp and vicious. Another voice rose from the back, a younger officer Leonard didn't know: "Then we recover it first. We don't bastardize tradition because it's inconvenient."

Drast pushed off the pillar, grimacing as his wounded arm pulled. "We're at war. We can't wait. The enemy won't give us three weeks to hold hands and pray for guidance." His tone pragmatic, the voice of a man who'd seen too many delays turn into graves.

"Then you appoint someone by acclaim and call it done," a grizzled Blade Veteran said, voice rough as old rope. He was ancient, the kind of man who'd outlived his generation through sheer stubbornness. "Darum takes the seat. He's earned it. End of discussion."

The room shifted. All eyes turned to Darum.

He didn't move, and met the gaze of every man who looked at him. When he spoke, his voice was final. "No."

The Veteran frowned, confusion flickering across his weathered face. "Darum—"

"I said no." Darum's voice was iron, no room for argument. "I'm not Strategos. I won't pretend to be. Find someone else."

The silence stretched, uncomfortable. A few exchanged glances, some nodding slowly, others looking like they wanted to argue but didn't dare.

Brent stepped forward, hands raised in a placating gesture. "There's a compromise." His voice was measured, careful. "We conduct the Vigil and Testimony. Let candidates prove themselves. When the stone is recovered, and it will be, the final judgment can happen. Until then, whoever survives the trial best serves as acting Strategos. The authority, not the title."

Orin's jaw tightened, the lines deepening around his mouth. He looked at the empty chair, then at Brent, then at the assembly. For a long moment, he said nothing. Then, slowly, he nodded. "Unprecedented. But acceptable. For now."

The words carried weight, permission granted by doctrine even as doctrine bent. The room exhaled, tension easing just enough to breathe.

Leonard watched the shift, felt it ripple through the assembly.

Saran leaned close, voice low enough that only he could hear. "This is going to get ugly."

"Yeah," Leonard muttered, eyes still on the empty chair. "It already is."

The call went out. Any who wished to stand as candidate could do so. Just step forward and accept the trial.

For a long moment, no one moved. The room held its breath, every warrior weighing the cost of ambition against the weight of the empty chair.

Brent was first. He moved to the center with parade-ground precision, stood before the empty chair, and said nothing. His face was pale, jaw set like he was bracing for a blow, but he didn't look away. The room watched, some nodding approval, others exchanging glances that said traitor louder than words. The shadow of the forged summons hung over him, unspoken but present.

Drast was next. He limped forward, wincing as his wounded arm pulled, and stopped beside Brent. For a moment, he just stood there, breathing hard, then spoke. "I'm here because someone has to be." His voice was rough, scraped raw. "Not because I want this. Because the Pact needs leadership and I'm not dead yet." He glanced at Brent, then at the assembly. "I don't believe in half the spiritual mess you all cling to. Maybe that disqualifies me. But I know how to keep men alive when everything's falling apart. That's all I've got."

A murmur rippled through the room. Some nodded. Others frowned. Drast's honesty was brutal, but it was honest.

Then a woman stepped forward from the back, and the room went still.

She was older, late fifties maybe, with iron-gray hair pulled into a tight knot and a scar running from her temple to her jaw, jagged and deep. Her armor was worn, practical, the kind earned through decades of holding the line, not standing at ceremony. Skysteel plate, battered but functional, with the raven sigil barely visible beneath layers of repair and grime. Leonard didn't recognize her.

She stopped in front of the chair, studied it like it owed her money, then looked at Brent. Her eyes were flat, unimpressed.

"Verath. Blade Veteran. Been holding the Karth border for years while you lot played politics in the capitol." Her tone was dry, almost bored, but there was an edge underneath, old bitterness, worn smooth by time but never quite gone. "Ulzaan and I disagreed on how to handle the last war. He thought we could bleed Karth into submission. I said we'd bleed ourselves dry first." She shrugged. "He won. I took a different path. Now he's dead and you need someone who knows how to run a garrison when everything's on fire."

She tilted her head, gaze sweeping the assembly. "I'll stand. Don't expect me to be nice about it."

A ripple of shock moved through the room. Whispers started, low and urgent. Someone muttered, "Didn't know she was still alive."

Verath's smile was sharp, all teeth. "Disappointed?"

Darum snorted, almost a laugh. The tension cracked, just a little. A few of the older Blade Veterans exchanged glances, recognition, respect, maybe a little fear. She'd been a legend once, before she'd been exiled. Now she was a ghost come back to haunt them.

Then a voice from the side, young and earnest: "What about Darum? We need him."

Darum's glare could've cut stone. "I already said no."

"You're the only one Ulzaan trusted completely," the voice pressed. It was one of the younger captains, barely out of training, desperate for certainty in a world that had none left. "If you won't stand, who will?"

"Anyone but me." Darum's voice was final, the kind of tone that ended arguments. "I'm a soldier. I follow orders. I don't give them to the whole damn Pact. Find someone else."

The captain opened his mouth to argue, but Verath cut him off, voice sharp. "He said no. Move on."

Then, from near the door, someone spoke. An older Blade Veteran, gray-bearded and scarred. "What about the boy?"

Leonard's stomach dropped. Every eye in the room turned to him.

Orin stepped forward, gaze sweeping from Leonard to the assembly. "He touched the relic without harm. Ulzaan protected him specifically." His tone was neutral, but the weight of the words was undeniable. "Some say he's marked by old powers."

"He's a child," someone snapped from the back, voice thick with disgust.

"He's Ravenblood," another countered, a woman Leonard vaguely recognized from the march. "That's all that matters."

Leonard felt Saran tense beside him, her hand drifting toward her sword. Darum's gaze found his across the room, steady and questioning, giving him the choice.

Leonard stepped forward, not to the chair, but to the center where everyone could see him. His boots echoed too loud on the stone. His voice came out rough, louder than he meant, cracking at the edges. "I'm not Ravenblood because I wanted to lead. I'm Ravenblood because Darum pulled me out of blood and gave me something to do with my hands besides shake."

He looked at each of them in turn, Brent, pale and brittle, Drast, exhausted and pragmatic, Verath, sharp and unbothered. "I'll fight. I'll die if it comes to that. But I'm not standing for Strategos. Find someone who actually knows what they're doing."

He turned and walked out. The door slammed behind him, the sound echoing through the chamber.

Saran followed, boots echoing in the silence. Darum watched him go, something like relief and something like pride flickering in his eyes. He didn't call him back.

The room was silent for a beat. Then Verath spoke, dry as dust. "Well. That settles that."

Leonard didn't stop until he hit the outer courtyard. The cold air bit at his face, sharp and bracing, and he sucked it in, trying to slow his pulse. His hands shook, adrenaline still surging through him.

Saran caught up, quieter than her boots should've been. She didn't say anything at first, but stood beside him, shoulder to shoulder, letting him breathe.

"You know they're going to ask again," she said finally.

Leonard shook his head."Let them."

She studied him, eyes sharp. "You did the right thing."

"Doesn't feel like it."

"Never does." She leaned against the wall, arms crossed. "But you're not ready. And pretending you are would get people killed."

Leonard looked at her, saw the exhaustion in her eyes, the weight she carried too. "You think any of them are ready?"

"No," she said quietly. "But someone has to be."

They stood in silence, the cold pressing in. Somewhere inside, the trial continued. Somewhere, men and women prepared to suffer for the right to lead.

Leonard closed his eyes, felt the weight of expectations still pressing down. The burden wasn't done with him. He knew that. But for now, he'd refused it.

THE VIGIL BEGAN AT SUNSET.

The chamber was stripped bare for it, torches extinguished, save for a single lantern placed at the foot of the empty chair. The four candidates, Brent, Drast, Verath, and two others who'd stepped forward after Leonard left and stood in a circle around it. No food. No water. No sleep. Three days and nights. The trial wasn't meant to test strength. It was meant to break anyone who wanted the position for the wrong reasons.

Before they began, Verath turned to Darum. He stood near the door, arms crossed, watching the candidates with the detached focus of a man who'd survived too many of these rituals.

"Darum," she said, voice low enough that only he could hear.

He looked at her, gaze steady. "Verath."

For a moment, neither spoke. Then she stepped closer, boots scraping stone. "You were a Blade Veteran under Ulzaan. That means you stood beside him, like myself." Her tone wasn't quite accusatory, but there was an edge. "And you're refusing this. Why?"

Darum's jaw worked. "Because I know what it costs. I watched him carry it for years. Watched it hollow him out piece by piece until there was nothing left but duty." He met her eyes. "I'm not built for that. I follow. I don't lead."

Verath studied him, something unreadable flickering in her gaze. "You underestimate yourself. Always did." She paused, then added, quieter, "But I respect it. Takes more courage to say no than to step up when you're not ready."

Darum's expression softened, just a fraction. "You served with him too. Back when he was young. Before the wars ground him down."

"I did." Verath's smile was faint, nostalgic. "He was insufferable. Thought he could solve every problem with enough will and sharp steel. Took him years to figure out leadership wasn't about being the strongest in the room." She looked at the empty chair. "I disagreed with him on Karth. Told him we were bleeding the Pact dry for nothing. He wouldn't listen. So I left."

Darum frowned. "He didn't exile you."

"No." Verath's tone was firm. "He offered me a choice. Stay and follow orders I didn't believe in, or take the Karth border garrison and do things my way. I chose the border." She shrugged. "A decade holding that line. Lost good people. But I did it on my terms."

Darum nodded slowly. "And now you're back."

"Now I'm back." Verath glanced at the other candidates, then back at Darum. "Because someone has to be. And because I'm tired of watching from the margins while the Pact tears itself apart." Her voice dropped. "He was a good man, Darum. A hard man, but a good one. I won't let his death be wasted on politics and cowardice."

Darum's hand found her shoulder, gripped it once. "Then don't fall in the Vigil. We need you standing at the end."

Verath's smile was sharp. "I've held worse than three days without sleep. I'll be here."

She turned back to the circle, taking her place among the candidates. Darum watched her go.

Leonard didn't watch. He sat in the barracks with Saran, staring at nothing, the weight of the room's expectations still pressing down. The space was quiet, most of the warriors out on patrol or tending wounds. Just the two of them, a dying fire, and the knowledge that somewhere inside the Pact's sanctum, people were suffering for a crown no one wanted.

They sat in silence, listening to the distant sounds of the city beyond the walls, boots on stone, the clang of a smithy still working despite the hour, the low murmur of voices carrying orders. Somewhere, the Vigil continued. Somewhere, men and women stood in the dark, pushing themselves past exhaustion, past doubt, toward something they might not survive.

Saran shifted, glancing at him. "Verath's tougher than she looks. If anyone makes it through, it's her."

Leonard grunted. "You know her?"

"No. But I know the type. Border garrison commander for years? She's seen worse than this." Saran's tone was dry. "Besides, Brent's going to collapse from guilt before the second day's out, and Drast's still bleeding from that wound. She's the only one with a real shot."

Leonard looked at her, saw the exhaustion in her eyes, the weight she carried. "You ever think about it? Leading?"

Saran snorted. "Hell no. I'm good at keeping people alive, not telling them what to die for." She paused, then added, quieter, "That's the difference. Leadership isn't about being the strongest or the smartest. It's about being willing to carry the weight when everyone else breaks."

Leonard nodded, throat tight. "Yeah. That's what scares me."

They sat in silence until the fire burned low and the cold crept in.

THE FIRST CANDIDATE withdrew on the second day. Collapsed mid-morning, couldn't stand, was carried out by his brothers. The second lasted until the third morning, then walked away without a word, face pale, hands shaking.

Brent, Drast, and Verath remained.

By the time the Vigil ended, all three looked like ghosts. Pale, trembling, eyes sunken into skull. Brent's uniform hung loose, soaked through with sweat. Drast's wound had reopened, blood seeping through the bandage, but he didn't fall. Verath stood straighter than the others, but only barely, her jaw was clenched so tight it looked ready to shatter, and her hands trembled where they rested at her sides.

But they stood.

The Testimony came next.

The chamber filled again, this time with the full assembly. Warriors lined the walls, Sages at the front, everyone watching in silence as the candidates stepped forward one by one. The air was thick, suffocating with anticipation and dread.

Brent went first. He stood before the empty chair, hands clasped, voice steady despite the exhaustion. "My greatest failure." He swallowed, throat working. "I suspected the summons that pulled Ulzaan away were wrong. I felt it. The timing, the wording, something didn't sit right. But I followed protocol anyway because questioning them felt like treason." His voice cracked. "I delivered the letter. I let the NineArts get close. I failed the pact and so I failed Ulzaan."

The room was silent, heavy with judgment. Brent's gaze swept the assembly, landing on Darum. "The one I couldn't save was Ulzaan. And I'll carry that until the day I die."

He stepped back. No one spoke. A few exchanged glances, some nodding slowly, others shaking their heads.

Drast limped forward next, wincing as his wounded arm pulled. He stood before the chair, breathing hard, then spoke. "My greatest failure is believing competence is enough. I've spent my whole life thinking if I was good at my job, that was all that mattered." He looked at the chair, then at the assembly. "But the Pact isn't just military. It's faith. Brotherhood. Spirit. I've never believed in that. Maybe that's the problem." He paused, jaw tight. "The one I couldn't save was a squad under my command in the last war. Sent them into an ambush because I trusted bad intel. Twelve men and I still see their faces."

He stepped back, shoulders hunched. The room stayed silent, but the weight of his words lingered.

Verath was last. She stepped forward, studied the chair like it was an opponent she'd already beaten, then spoke. Her voice was rough, scraped raw by three days without water. "My greatest failure was thinking I could do it alone. A long time ago, I told Ulzaan the war with Karth was pointless, that we were bleeding for pride, not necessity. He disagreed. I pushed back." She smiled, bitter. "So I took the border garrison and did it my way. Held that line, lost good people, and convinced myself I was right because we survived."

She looked at the assembly, gaze hard. "Turns out we were both wrong. The war happened anyway, and it didn't matter who was right. What mattered was that I left. That I let pride keep me from bending when it counted." Her voice dropped. "The ones I couldn't save were the soldiers I commanded at the border. Every one of them who died because I was too proud to ask for help, too stubborn to admit I didn't have all the answers." She paused. "I won't make that mistake again."

She stepped back. The room was heavy, suffocating with honesty and the weight of confessions that couldn't be taken back.

The vote came at dawn. Men and women raising hands, choosing a leader because someone had to be chosen.

The chamber was packed, every Blade Veteran, every officer, every Sage who could stand crowding in to witness. The air was thick with exhaustion and doubt or the knowledge that whatever they chose here would have consequences none of them could predict.

Orin conducted the count, his voice steady and formal. Hands rose, were tallied, lowered. The process was mechanical, stripped of ceremony.

The count was close. Brent had support, those who believed in redemption, or at least in second chances. But the shadow over him was too heavy. The forged summons, the NineArts breach, Ulzaan's death. Too many couldn't look past it.

Drast had respect. His pragmatism, his competence, his willingness to admit he didn't believe in half of what the Pact stood for, that honesty earned him votes. But no one trusted him to hold the spiritual weight, to stand as the Pact's symbol when faith was all that kept them together.

Verath won by a narrow margin, she was the least broken of the three, and pragmatism was all they had left.

Orin announced the result, voice carrying across the chamber. "Verath. Acting Strategos, pending the recovery of the stone."

Verath stood, walked to the empty chair, and stopped before it. She didn't sit but placed one hand on the armrest, fingers tracing the worn wood where Ulzaan's hand had rested for decades.

Her voice was cold, stripped of anything but resolve. "When Samric comes for the capitol, I want to be the one standing between him and this city. And when we take him down, I want to be the one who rips that stone from his corpse."

The assembly murmured agreement.

Verath turned to face them, gaze sweeping the room. "Samric's target is here. The Black Tower in Fazrum. The last one standing. He'll come for it, and he'll bring everything he has left." She paused, letting the weight settle. "We don't march. We don't run. We hold this city. And when he arrives, we make him bleed for every step."

Her voice hardened. "This war ends here. One way or another. Prepare yourselves."

The room was silent for a beat, then slowly began to empty. Warriors drifted out into the cold morning light, shoulders heavy, faces set. No one lingered. There was too much to do.

Leonard stayed, rooted near the back, staring at the empty chair. Saran stood beside him, quiet, her hand resting on the hilt of her sword. Darum was near the front, watching Verath with approval, maybe, or the grim satisfaction of seeing someone else carry the weight for once.

Leonard felt the ghost of Ulzaan pressing down. The man who'd stood at the front. The man who'd burned himself out so the rest of them could survive. Gone now. Only ash and memory remained.

Saran touched his arm, gentle. "Come on. Let's get out of here."

Leonard nodded, throat too tight to speak. He followed her toward the door, boots echoing on stone.

Behind them, Verath turned away from the chair, already barking orders to the officers who remained.

The sun was rising over Fazrum, cold and pale, casting long shadows across the city. Leonard stepped into the courtyard, breath misting in the air. The capitol sprawled below, walls reinforced, barricades raised, warriors moving through the streets in tight formation.

Saran stood beside him, arms crossed, gaze distant. "You think we can hold?"

Leonard looked at the Black Tower rising in the distance, dark against the dawn. "We have to."

She nodded, jaw set. "Then let's make sure we do."

They turned back toward the barracks, the weight of what was coming settling over them like a shroud. The Pact had a leader. The city had a plan.

All that was left was to see if it was enough.

22

Leonard couldn't stay in the barracks.

The walls pressed too close and the silence too loud. After the Trial, after watching Verath take the empty chair and the assembly disperse into cold morning light, the weight settled over him. Ulzaan's absence, the enemy that was coming, the certainty that time was running out and there was nothing he could do to stop it.

So he left.

The city swallowed him whole. Noise everywhere, shouts from the walls, the clang of hammers on iron, boots marching in tight formation. The capitol was transforming, shedding its peacetime skin. Barricades reinforced with salvaged timber and scrap metal. Soldiers drilling in the squares, movements crisp despite the exhaustion carved into every face. Refugees being herded toward the inner wards, clutching what little they had left, eyes wide with fear or dull with resignation.

Leonard moved through it all, aimless but unable to stop. His legs carried him past market stalls being dismantled, past taverns now serving as makeshift infirmaries, past the temple where Sage acolytes stood at every entrance, hands pressed to stone, runes flickering to life as they locked the doors with ward-runes.

He passed a cluster of Fazrum soldiers working beside Karthian troops, hauling crates of arrows up to the ramparts. The Fazrum soldiers moved with the efficiency of men who'd done this a hundred times. The Karthians were sharper, faster, their armor gleaming with embedded shardwork that pulsed faint blue in the dim light. They didn't speak to each other, but they worked in parallel, the tension visible in the way they kept space between them, hands never far from weapons.

Leonard kept walking. The city felt like a coiled spring, wound so tight that the slightest touch would send it snapping. He could feel it in the air, taste it on his tongue.

He turned a corner, found himself near the outer wall. Above, archers lined the battlements, eyes scanning the horizon. Below, engineers worked on siege defenses, oil pots ready to be heated, stones piled in neat rows, ballistae being winched into position. A captain barked orders, his face streaked with grime.

Leonard stopped, stared up at the wall. Solid stone, thick enough to withstand a battering ram, tall enough to make scaling a nightmare. It should've felt safe. It didn't.

He thought about Vask. Thought about the outer settlements, the towns they'd passed on the march. All of them had walls. None of them had held.

His hands clenched, nails digging into his palms. He couldn't stop moving. Couldn't shake the feeling that every second spent standing still was a second wasted, a second closer to the moment when everything collapsed and there'd be nothing left but ash and screaming.

So he walked. And the city kept transforming around him, preparing for a war it couldn't win but refused to surrender to.

Leonard found Darum near the outer wall, overseeing a section of defenses that looked half-finished and twice as desperate. Soldiers hauled sandbags into place, stacking them against the base of the wall where the stone had cracked during some forgotten siege. Others ran drills, formation shifts, shield walls, the kind of repetitive muscle memory that kept men alive when thinking got you killed.

Darum stood in the middle of it, barking corrections when someone's footwork slipped or a spear angle dropped too low. His voice was rough, scraped raw from shouting orders all morning, but steady, like if he just kept moving the exhaustion wouldn't catch up.

Leonard stopped a few paces away, Darum spotted him, nodded once, and turned back to the drill.

"Tighten that line! You're not dancing, you're holding ground!" He gestured sharply at a young soldier whose shield wobbled. "If you can't hold it now, you won't hold it when something's trying to tear your throat out."

The soldier adjusted, and the line reformed. Darum grunted approval, then stepped aside, wiping sweat from his face with the back of his hand.

Leonard moved closer. "You ever sleep?"

Darum snorted. "When I'm dead." He glanced at the wall, then back at Leonard. "What're you doing out here? Thought you'd be resting."

"I couldn't." Leonard shoved his hands into his pockets, watching the soldiers drill. "Needed to move."

Darum nodded, understanding without needing it spelled out. "I understand."

They stood in silence for a moment, the noise of the city filling the gap. Then Leonard spoke, quieter. "Verath's first orders, they sound?"

"Sound enough." Darum's tone was pragmatic, no false hope. "She's not sending men to die for glory. She's buying time, making Samric work for every inch. Won't save the city, but it'll slow him down."

"Long enough?"

Darum's jaw worked. "Long enough for what?"

Leonard didn't answer. Darum didn't push.

Leonard scanned the defenses, the soldiers, the barricades that looked too thin against what was coming. "Where's Saran?"

"Eastern gate." Darum's tone shifted, just slightly. "Verath's got her coordinating with the Karthians. Bridge the gap between our troops and theirs. Unusual, but necessary. Needed someone who wouldn't start a fight just by existing."

Leonard almost smiled. "She's good at that."

"She is." Darum glanced at him, "She'll keep them working together. That's more than most could do."

Leonard nodded, the knot in his chest loosening just a fraction. Saran was still alive, doing what she did best.

The weight of Ulzaan's absence settled between them, unspoken but undeniable. Leonard felt it pressing down, the space where the old man's presence should've been. Darum felt it too, Leonard could see it in the set of his shoulders, the way his gaze drifted toward the inner citadel before snapping back to the work at hand.

Leonard finally asked the question he'd been avoiding. "You think we can actually do this?"

Darum didn't answer right away. He stared at the wall, at the soldiers drilling, at the barricades and the oil pots and the desperate hope that any of it would matter. When he spoke, his voice was honest. "No. Not the way you mean."

Leonard's stomach dropped.

"But we'll make him bleed for every step to that tower." Darum's gaze was steel. "He wants the Tower? He can have it. But he'll crawl through our dead to get there."

Leonard swallowed. "And if we die?"

Darum looked at him, something hard and final in his eyes. "Then we die making sure he remembers us."

The words landed heavy. Leonard nodded, throat too tight to speak.

Darum clapped him on the shoulder, grip firm. "Go. Keep moving if you need to. But don't get lost in your head. We need you sharp when it starts."

Leonard nodded again, stepped back. Darum turned back to the soldiers, already barking another order, falling back into the rhythm of preparation.

Leonard walked away, boots crunching over gravel, the noise of the city swallowing him whole. Darum's words echoed in his head.

We'll make him bleed for every step.

It wasn't hope. But it was something.

He headed toward the eastern gate, weaving through alleys clogged with supply carts and soldiers hauling gear. The noise shifted as he got closer, sharper commands, different cadences, the clang of armor that didn't quite match Fazrum's standard issue.

He rounded a corner and found Saran standing in the middle of controlled chaos.

Two groups of soldiers faced each other across a narrow courtyard. Fazrum on one side, black armor and skysteel blades, disciplined and rigid. Karthian on the other, lighter gear studded with shardwork, their movements more fluid, but edged with impatience. Between them, Saran stood, translating orders from a Fazrum captain to a Karthian commander and back again.

The Karthian commander was older, maybe fifty, with gray streaking through his close-cropped beard and scars crisscrossing his forearms. His armor was functional but battered, the kind earned through decades of holding lines that shouldn't have held. Shardwork ran along his pauldrons in clean, efficient lines.

"—not asking you to abandon your formations," Saran was saying, voice clipped. "I'm asking you to coordinate with ours. When the ramparts signal a breach, we need both forces converging, not fighting over who gets there first."

The Fazrum captain, a stocky man with a broken nose, grunted. "Their signals don't match ours. Horn calls, flag positions, none of it lines up. We'll be tripping over each other."

The Karthian commander spoke, "Your signals are archaic. Horns echo, flags get obscured. Shardwork flares are instant, visible from any angle."

"And drain power," the Fazrum captain shot back. "What happens when your stones fail mid-battle?"

Sekkan's smile was thin. "Then we adapt. Unlike some, we don't cling to tradition when it gets us killed."

The tension spiked. Saran stepped between them, hand raised. "Enough. We're not debating doctrine. You both report to Verath now, and she wants cooperation, not a pissing contest." Her gaze swept both men. "Figure out a hybrid signal system by sunset, or I'll tell her you're both too busy being stubborn to do your jobs."

The Fazrum captain glared, but nodded. The commander's smile sharpened, almost amused, but he inclined his head. "As you say."

Saran exhaled, tension bleeding out of her shoulders. Then she spotted Leonard.

Her expression shifted, She crossed the courtyard, boots crunching over gravel. "Didn't expect to see you here."

Leonard managed a faint smile. "Couldn't sit still."

"Yeah." Saran glanced back at the two groups, already bickering again in lower tones. "I know the feeling."

Sekkan approached, gaze assessing as he looked Leonard up and down.

"Leo, this is commander Sekkan of Karth."

"You're the one Verath mentioned. The boy Ulzaan took an interest in." Sekkan said.

Leonard stiffened, met Sekkan's eyes. "I am."

Sekkan nodded slowly. "It's a shame about Ulzaan. I would've liked to meet the man who made such a name for himself in the old war." His tone was respectful, almost wistful. "He was a thorn in my side from a planning standpoint. Every strategy I devised, he found the weak point and exploited it. Frustrating, but... admirable."

Leonard didn't know what to say to that. "He was good at what he did."

"Better than good." Sekkan's gaze drifted toward the inner citadel, where the Black Tower loomed. "But your new Strategos seems to have a clear head on her shoulders. That's more than most can claim in times like these."

Saran cleared her throat. "Verath assigned me to keep Fazrum and Karth from killing each other before Samric does the job for us." Her tone was dry, but there was weight underneath. "I've been to Karth, got a feel for the place. Figured I could bridge the gap."

Leonard glanced at the two groups still arguing in the background. "How's that going?"

"About as well as you'd expect." Saran's smile was crooked, tired. "Karthians don't trust Fazrum doctrine, too rigid and too slow. Fazrum doesn't trust Karthian shardwork, too unstable, or whatever they like to say. I'm stuck in the middle, convincing them they're both idiots if they don't work together."

Leonard almost laughed. "Sounds like you."

"Yeah, well." Saran's gaze softened, searched his face. "You holding up?"

Leonard shrugged, the weight pressing down again. "Moving. That's all I've got."

Saran nodded, understood without needing more. "Stay sharp, I need you alive."

"I know." Leonard met her eyes. "You too."

Sekkan called out, voice sharp. "Saran. We need you."

Saran sighed, rolled her shoulders. "Duty calls." She touched Leonard's arm, just once,

"Don't get lost out there."

"I won't."

She turned back to the courtyard, already slipping into the role. Leonard watched her go, saw the Fazrum captain and Sekkan both turn to her, waiting for her to make it work.

She did. She always did.

His path bent without him choosing it.

He'd been walking the outer wards, watching soldiers reinforce gates, checking barricades, keeping his mind occupied with anything that wasn't the weight pressing down on him. But his feet carried him inward, away from the walls, away from the noise, until the alleys narrowed and the air grew colder.

The Black Tower loomed ahead.

He stopped at the edge, staring up at it. Taller than anything else in the city, all sharp angles and black stone that drank the light. The same tower he'd seen his whole life, familiar and distant all at once. But now it felt different.

The pull was stronger here. Like a hand pressing between his shoulder blades, urging him forward. He'd felt it before, faint echoes when he'd touched the relic, when he'd stood too close to the rift before. But this was deeper, resonating in his chest like a second heartbeat.

The tower's base was empty, cordoned off by Ravenblood guards who watched him approach but didn't stop him. They knew his face. Knew Ulzaan had protected him.

Idran was there, crouched near the tower's foundation, a notebook balanced on his knee, charcoal scratching across the page in quick, precise strokes. His sleeves were rolled up, and the shards embedded in his forearm pulsed faintly, blue light flickering in rhythm with something Leonard couldn't see.

Idran didn't look up. "You feel it too."

Leonard stopped a few paces away, staring at the tower. "Yeah."

Idran set the charcoal down, closed the notebook, and stood. His face was pale, shadows under his eyes like he hadn't slept in days. "It's building. Energy, resonance, whatever you want to call it." He gestured at the tower, frustration bleeding into his tone. "It’s as if the world itself knows what's about to happen. Maybe even the gods have finally taken an interest, if they're still paying attention at all."

Idran looked down at his arm, at the shards pulsing beneath his skin. "These are reacting. They've never done this before, not this strongly." His voice dropped, almost bitter. "I'm connected to it somehow. The tower, the rift, all of it. I don't like it."

Leonard stepped closer, following Idran's gaze to the shards. The light flickered, steady and rhythmic, like a pulse. "Does it hurt?"

"Not yet." Idran flexed his fingers, the shards brightening for a heartbeat before dimming. "But it will. When the ritual completes, when the rift opens fully—" He stopped, shook his head. "I don't know what happens then."

Leonard looked back at the tower, the pull stronger now, almost magnetic. "I feel it too," he admitted quietly. "Like something's calling. Not words, just—" He struggled to name it. "A song. Playing in my head."

Idran's gaze sharpened. "A song?"

"Yeah." Leonard's hand drifted toward the tower's base, drawn without thinking. "It's been there since the first rift even opened. Faint at first, but it's louder now."

"Don't—" Idran started, but Leonard's palm was already pressed against the stone.

The hum hit him instantly, thrumming under his skin like a living thing. The world tilted, edges blurring, and for a heartbeat Leonard wasn't standing in the plaza anymore, he was inside the tower, or the tower was inside him, the boundaries between them dissolving.

His eyes flickered. Amber light flared, bright and sharp, then faded back to their normal color.

Leonard yanked his hand away, stumbling backward, breath catching. The world snapped back into focus, but the hum lingered in his chest.

Idran grabbed his arm. "You alright?"

Leonard nodded, throat tight. "Yeah. I think."

Idran studied him, concern flickering across his face. "Your eyes. They—"

"I know." Leonard swallowed, rubbed his face. "It's the blood. The Eosian line. It reacts to—" He gestured helplessly at the tower. "—this."

Idran's grip tightened, then released. "Be careful. Whatever's waking up in there, it knows you. And it wants something."

Leonard looked at the tower, the black stone looming overhead, silent and patient. "Yeah. I know."

Idran stepped back, picked up his notebook. "I'm heading to the temple. Eleseth's helping settle refugees, and I need to compare notes on the relic. See if there's anything we missed."

Leonard nodded. "I'll keep moving."

Idran paused, glanced back. "Leonard. When it starts, when the tower opens, don't let it pull you in alone. You hear me?"

Leonard met his gaze, saw the worry there, the weight of knowledge Idran carried but couldn't share. "I hear you."

Idran nodded, turned, and walked toward the temple, his silhouette shrinking against the city's noise.

Leonard stood alone, staring up at the tower. Then the sky changed.

Leonard felt it before he saw it, a shift in the air, pressure dropping, he looked up, and the clouds were rolling in from the north, black and thick, roiling like they were alive. Violet light crackled through them.

The horns sounded.

Three long blasts, then silence. The enemy had been spotted.

Too soon. They weren't ready. No one was ready.

The city snapped into motion. Soldiers broke into runs, boots pounding stone, voices shouting orders that blurred together into chaos. Gates slammed shut, the heavy iron bars dropping into place with a sound like thunder. Reinforcements scrambled up the walls, archers taking positions, engineers hauling oil pots and stones into place.

Leonard ran, the pull of the tower faded behind him, replaced by the immediate need to move. He cut through alleys, dodged supply carts, pushed past civilians being herded toward the inner wards. Their faces were pale, eyes wide with fear, but there was something else underneath, grim determination. This was their city. Their last stand.

The ramparts loomed ahead, crowded with bodies, warriors in black armor, Karthian troops with shardwork gleaming faintly, archers nocking arrows, captains barking final orders. Leonard shoved through, found a gap in the line, and climbed.

The wind hit him as he reached the top carrying the smell of ozone and rot. He looked out over the wall, and his breath caught.

The enemy host stretched to the horizon.

Ravagers, thousands of them, a seething mass of twisted limbs and amber eyes. Shades flickered at the edges, half-real, their forms bending light and shadow. And behind them, towering above the horde, the corrupted kin, massive, hulking things that shouldn't exist, their bodies warped by the void into something monstrous.

Leonard's hand found his sword and drew it without thinking and ran unto the nearest wall.

Saran was already there.

She stood a few paces down the wall with her mixed squad,Fazrum and Karthian side by side, tension still visible in the way they held themselves.

Leonard moved to her side, checked his straps, his sword, his breathing. Everything in place.

Darum was further down the line, sword already drawn, voice cutting through the chaos. "Tighten that formation! Bows up, spears forward! First wave hits hard, don't let it scatter you!"

The soldiers around him responded, muscle memory overriding fear. The line firmed, arrows drawn.

Footsteps behind. Leonard turned, saw Verath moving along the wall, checking positions, her armor battered but functional, her gaze sharp. She stopped near Leonard, met his eyes.

"You're still here," she said, tone neutral.

"Where else would I be?"

Verath's mouth twitched, almost a smile. "The tower. It's calling, isn't it?"

Leonard's jaw tightened. "Yeah."

"When it's time, you go." Her voice was final. "Until then, you fight here with the rest of us. I don't need you to be a hero. I just need you to live long enough to finish this."

Leonard nodded. "I will."

Verath held his gaze for a heartbeat longer, then turned, moved down the line, already barking orders to the next section.

Saran leaned close, "She seems to be on top of things."

"Yeah," Leonard muttered. "She is."

The horizon darkened. The horde surged closer, the ground trembling under the weight of their charge.

Verath's voice rang out, cutting through the noise, carrying over the walls. "Ravenblood!"

The soldiers turned, eyes on her. She stood at the center of the rampart, sword raised, silhouette sharp against the storm.

"We were made for this," she shouted, voice hard and clear. "Not for glory. Not for conquest. For this. To stand against the old enemy when the world forgot they existed. We forgot too. All of us. But today —" She paused, gaze sweeping the line. "—today we remember. Today we fulfill our duty."

A roar went up from the Ravenblood warriors, fists slamming against armour, swords ringing against stone. The Karthians didn't roar, but stood straighter, shardwork flaring brighter.

Verath lowered her blade, pointed it at the horde. "Make them bleed for every step!"

The roar swelled, louder, angrier.

Leonard drew his sword, felt the weight settle in his hand. Beside him, Saran did the same, her blade catching the violet light. Down the line, Darum raised his sword, eyes locked on the approaching flood.

The storm hit.

The horde crashed into the outer defenses, a wave of bodies and claws and screaming. Arrows hissed overhead, oil poured down from the ramparts, fire blooming across the field. The siege had begun.

Leonard planted his feet, gripped his sword, and waited for the first ravager to reach the wall.

The world narrowed to steel and blood and the sound of his own breath.

23

Leonard stood on the ramparts, sword drawn, the steel cold in his grip despite the sweat slicking his palms. The wall stretched to either side, packed shoulder-to-shoulder with Fazrum soldiers, Ravenblood warriors in black armor, archers with arrows nocked, engineers crouched beside ballistae, oil pots simmering over open flames. Everyone watching the horizon.

The storm pressed down, violet light crackling through black clouds.

Then the horde hit.

It wasn't a gradual approach. No warning. But a sudden, overwhelming roar of thousands of bodies surging forward, a tide of twisted limbs and amber eyes and screams that scraped the inside of Leonard's skull. Louder than anything he'd imagined. They moved faster. The ground trembled under their charge, dust rising in a choking cloud.

"LOOSE!" someone roared.

The first volley went up, a wall of arrows darkening the sky, hissing through the air like a swarm. They fell into the horde, punching through flesh and bone, ravagers collapsing mid-stride. But the tide didn't slow. More poured over the fallen, trampling them, a flood that swallowed its own dead.

The ballistae fired. Heavy bolts the size of spears tore through the air, slamming into the horde with wet, crunching impacts. Bodies exploded, limbs scattering. Still they came.

Leonard's breath came short and fast. His hands tightened on his sword, knuckles white. Beside him, a young warrior muttered a prayer under his breath, eyes wide.

The horde reached the base of the wall.

"OIL!" Drast's voice cut through the chaos.

Engineers tipped the pots, flaming oil cascading down the stone in a burning waterfall. It splashed across the ravagers below, igniting instantly. Screams tore through the air. The smell of burning flesh thick and choking. The front ranks collapsed, writhing, but the ones behind climbed over them, using the burning bodies as ladders.

"BRACE!" Darum roared from further down the line. "They're coming up!"

The first ravager crested the wall in front of Leonard.

It lunged, claws outstretched, jaw unhinged, eyes blazing amber. Leonard didn't think. Just moved. His blade came up, caught the thing across the throat, black ichor spraying hot across his face. The ravager collapsed, twitching, and Leonard kicked it off the wall.

Another appeared. Then another.

The line erupted into chaos.

Steel clashed, screams mixed with roars, Leonard blocked a clawed swipe, drove his sword through a ravager's chest, yanked it free. Something clawed his armour and dragged him backward. He twisted, slashed, felt resistance give way.

Around him, the line held, barely. Soldiers fought back-to-back, blades flashing, shields locked. Archers fired down into the mass below, arrows punching through skulls and spines. A warrior to Leonard's left went down, throat torn open, blood pooling across stone. Another stepped over him, filled the gap, kept fighting.

"HOLD THE LINE!" Darum's voice, hoarse but steady. "Make them bleed for it!"

Leonard's arms burned, lungs screaming, vision narrowing to the immediate, block, strike, move. A ravager lunged, he parried, drove his boot into its twisted knee. Bone cracked. It fell. He stabbed down into the mass.

The ballistae fired again, the heavy thrum of the cords followed by the wet crunch of bodies obliterated. Oil kept pouring, flames climbing the wall, heat washing over the defenders. The air was smoke and copper and the stench of burning meat.

Leonard glanced down the line, saw the outer defenses holding, for now. But the horde was endless, a tide that didn't stop, didn't slow, just kept coming.

Leonard killed another ravager, yanked his blade free. The line was holding, the rhythm settling into something brutal but manageable, block, strike, move, repeat. He could do this. They could do this.

Then the world tilted.

A section of the wall twenty paces down erupted. The air shimmered, twisted, and shades poured through the stone itself, flickering forms that bent light and shadow, phasing through debris and defenders alike. They just appeared, materializing inside the line, behind the shields, in the gaps where soldiers stood unprepared.

Screams tore through the air. Different from the battle noise.

The line buckled.

Leonard watched it happen in slow motion, a warrior swinging at a shade, blade passing through empty air, then the shade solidifying, claws raking across the man's throat. He went down. Another soldier turned to help, exposing his flank. A ravager took him. The gap widened. More shades poured through.

The flank was collapsing.

Leonard's chest seized. If that section fell, the ravagers would pour through the breach, flank the entire wall. The outer defenses would fold. Everyone on this section would be surrounded, cut off.

His post was here. Orders were to hold the wall, don't abandon position, maintain the line. Darum's voice echoed in his head: Stay where you're assigned. Don't be a hero.

But the flank was breaking. Right now. And no one else was moving to plug it.

Leonard's jaw clenched. His feet were already moving before he made the choice.

"With me!" he roared, grabbing the nearest warrior, a woman with blood-slicked armor. She was startled.

"Now!"

He didn't wait for acknowledgment. He ran, boots pounding stone, sword in hand. Two more soldiers peeled off, following on instinct, trusting the urgency in his voice even if they didn't know him.

The breach loomed ahead, chaos incarnate. Shades flickered in and out of reality, soldiers swinging at ghosts, ravagers pouring through the gaps. Bodies everywhere, the line dissolving into scattered pockets of desperate fighting.

Leonard hit the edge of the breach, A shade materialized in front of him, claws raised. He slashed through it, blade passing through smoke then it solidified, caught his vambrace. He twisted, drove his elbow into where its face should be. It recoiled and vanished when they met eyes.

"Form up!" Leonard shouted at the surviving soldiers, voice cracking. "Shield wall! Now!"

A soldier with a broken nose moved beside him, shield raised, spear leveled. Two others fell in, creating a ragged line across the breach. It wasn't much. But it was something.

A ravager charged. Leonard's blade met it, steel carving through bone. Another lunged from the side. The woman's spear caught it mid-leap, drove it back.

The gap was a nightmare.

Shades flickered in and out of reality, untouchable one second, solid the next. Leonard swung at empty air, felt his blade bite flesh, then the thing dissolved into smoke and reformed behind him. A soldier to his left screamed as claws raked across his back, tearing through armor like parchment.

"Tighten up!" Leonard roared, voice raw. "Watch each other's backs!"

The ragged line shifted, warriors pressing closer, trying to cover the angles the shades exploited. It wasn't working. They were too fast, too unpredictable. Every time Leonard thought he'd found a rhythm, another shade phased through the line, struck from behind, vanished before anyone could retaliate.

A ravager charged through the chaos, claws outstretched. The woman beside Leonard, her name was Kerra, he'd heard someone shout it, drove her spear through its chest. It collapsed, twitching. Two more took its place.

Then, in the chaos, Leonard spotted Briar.

The young acolyte was pressed against the wall, stone clutched in his trembling hand, face pale as death. His lips moved, murmuring the words of some incantation, but the stone barely flickered, just a weak, sputtering glow that died before it could catch.

A shade materialized in front of him, claws raised.

Leonard lunged, blade sweeping up. The shade recoiled, flickered, but didn't disperse. It turned on Leonard instead, shrieking. He blocked the strike, felt the impact jar his bones, kicked it back. The thing vanished.

"Briar!" Leonard grabbed the kid's shoulder, shook him. "Fall back! Your stone's dead!"

Briar's eyes were wild, unfocused. "I can—I can do it. Just need—"

"Fall back!" Leonard shoved him toward the rear. "Now!"

But Briar didn't move. That same stubborn terror Leonard had seen before, the fear of failing, of being useless, of surviving when others died because he couldn't pull his weight.

"One more," Briar gasped. "Just—give me one more—"

The shade reformed, lunged at Leonard's exposed flank. Briar's stone flared, white-hot, blinding. He charged forward, tackled the shade. Light erupted from his palm, a jagged bolt that caught the shade mid-strike. The thing convulsed, shrieked, and burned, collapsing into ash.

Briar stumbled, stone going dark, his hand shaking. Blood dripped from his nose. But the shade was gone.

Leonard grabbed him, hauled him upright. "Good. Now get behind the line before you kill yourself."

Briar nodded, dazed, and stumbled back. Another warrior caught him, dragged him clear.

The breach was holding. Barely. Leonard's arms burned, grinding pain of muscles pushed past their limit. His sword felt heavier with every breath, the grip slick with blood, his blood, theirs, he didn't know anymore. The air was thick with smoke and the stench of torn bodies. He couldn't tell if the ringing in his ears was from the battle or just exhaustion clawing at the edges of his mind.

He scanned the gap, bodies everywhere, soldiers gasping, leaning on spears and shields, faces streaked with blood and soot. Kerra was still standing, somehow, spear broken but sword drawn. A grizzled veteran Leonard didn't know held the left flank, armor shredded, bleeding from a dozen cuts but refusing to fall.

The shades had pulled back, circling at the edges, wary now. The ravagers were regrouping, snarling, preparing another push.

Footsteps, heavy and deliberate, cut through the chaos. Leonard turned, saw Verath moving along the wall, armor dented and blood-streaked but her stride steady. Her gaze swept the ramparts, taking in the breach, the bodies, the exhausted survivors clinging to their positions.

She stopped at the gap, looked at Leonard, then at the ragged line holding it. "You plugged it."

Leonard nodded, too tired to speak.

Verath's gaze drifted past him, down the wall to the sections beyond. Leonard followed her eyes and felt his stomach drop. The outer defenses were crumbling. Smoke rose from three different breaches, flames crawling up the stone where oil had ignited and spread. Soldiers were falling back in scattered clusters, some in formation, others just running. The horde pressed everywhere, relentlessly, pouring through every gap.

Verath's jaw tightened. She turned back to Leonard, to Kerra, to the handful of survivors still standing. "We're pulling back.".

One of the soldiers, the grizzled veteran holding the left flank spoke, "We hold here. That's the order."

"The order's changed." Verath's tone was flat, final. "Fall back to the secondary line. Now."

The veteran didn't move. "We leave, they pour through. The whole wall collapses."

"The wall's already collapsing." Verath gestured at the carnage around them. "You stay here, you die for nothing. You fall back, you buy time. Those are your choices."

The veteran's jaw worked, his hand tightening on his sword. He looked at Leonard, searching for something, confirmation, defiance, anything. Leonard met his gaze, saw the exhaustion, the desperation to believe holding mattered.

Leonard's voice came out hoarse. "She's right. Staying here doesn't save the city. It just gets us killed faster."

The veteran's shoulders sagged. He nodded, once. "Alright."

But not all of them moved. A few stayed rooted, staring at the wall like abandoning it meant betraying every brother who'd died holding it. One muttered something under his breath, a prayer, maybe, or a curse. Another just shook his head, jaw clenched so hard Leonard thought his teeth might crack.

Verath didn't wait for them to process it. "You want to die with honor? Fine. Die buying time for the people behind you. Now move."

Verath's gaze swept the breach. "All of you. Secondary line. Move."

The soldiers hesitated, some already shifting, others frozen, staring at the wall like abandoning it was treason. Leonard understood. Leaving felt like surrender. Felt like everything they'd bled for was wasted.

But staying meant dying. And dying here wouldn't stop what was coming.

"Move!" Verath's voice cracked like a whip.

The line broke. Soldiers turned, started retreating, some running, others backing up slowly, weapons still raised, eyes scanning for the next attack. Kerra grabbed a wounded warrior, hauled him to his feet, dragged him toward the stairs.

Leonard saw one soldier, a young man, barely older than Briar still standing at the edge, staring down at the horde below, sword gripped so tight his knuckles were white.

"Let's go," Leonard said, moving to him.

The soldier didn't respond. Just stared.

Leonard grabbed his arm, pulled. "We're leaving. Now."

The soldier resisted, voice cracking. "I can't—they're right there—if we leave—"

"If we stay, we die." Leonard's grip tightened. "And dying here doesn't save anyone. Move."

The soldier's face crumpled, but he nodded, let Leonard pull him away from the edge. They stumbled toward the stairs, boots crunching over broken stone and blood-slick rubble.

The retreat was chaos. Warriors pouring down the stairs, archers firing covering volleys, engineers abandoning their ballistae and oil pots. Behind them, the horde surged over the wall, flooding the ramparts, a tide that couldn't be stopped.

Leonard reached the base of the wall, turned back once, a soldier, couldn't have been more than twenty stumbled at the top of the stairs, an arrow punching through his shoulder. He tried to keep moving, but a ravager caught him from behind, dragged him back over the edge. His scream cut short. Leonard's hand tightened on his sword, but there was nothing to do. The kid was already gone.

The outer defenses were gone. Ravagers swarmed the stone, shades flickered through the ruins, and above it all, the storm pressed down, violet light crackling through black clouds.

The Black Tower loomed in the distance, humming louder now, vibrating in Leonard's chest like a second heartbeat. He could feel it pulling.

He shook his head, forced himself to turn away.

Leonard broke into a run, following the retreating line, the horde's roar pressing at his back.

The barricade rose ahead, a desperate patchwork of sandbags and sharpened stakes, debris scavenged from collapsed buildings wedged into gaps. It looked fragile, like it might collapse under the weight of a strong wind. But it was all they had.

Leonard stumbled through the gap, boots catching on rubble, chest heaving. Around him, soldiers collapsed against the barricade, gasping, armor streaked with blood and soot. Some sat hard, heads in their hands, trembling. Others just stared at nothing, eyes hollow.

A few didn't get up.

Leonard scanned the survivors, counting faces. Kerra was there, leaning against a sandbag, spear gone, sword in one hand. The grizzled veteran from the breach sat with his back to the barricade, pressing a rag to a gash across his ribs. Briar stumbled in last, pale and shaking, stone clutched to his chest like a talisman. He caught Leonard's eye, nodded once, exhausted but alive.

Others were missing. Faces Leonard had seen on the wall, fought beside, pulled back from the edge. Gone now. Dead or scattered or left behind in the chaos.

He wiped his blade on his vambrace, the steel smeared with black ichor and rust-red blood. His hands shook, just a little, barely visible, but he felt it. He flexed his fingers, tried to steady them. It didn't work.

He checked his straps, his vambraces, the buckles on his armor. Everything still in place. Everything functional. But it didn't feel like enough.

The horde pressed forward, a black tide surging toward the secondary line.

24

Saran stood at the eastern gate, watching two armies pretend to be one.

A mix of Fazrum soldiers and Ravenblood warriors lined the left side of the courtyard, black armor gleaming dully in the storm's violet light, locked in tight formation, spears angled forward. Every movement precise, drilled into muscle memory through decades of training. They moved like a single organism, no wasted motion.

The Karthian troops held the right side, lighter armor studded with shardwork that pulsed faint blue, blades curved and ready, formations looser, more fluid. They shifted on their feet, eyes scanning the approaches, hands never far from weapons, fast and Adaptable. Built for mobility, not endurance.

Between them, a gap. Ten paces wide, but it might as well have been a chasm.

Saran stood in the middle, watching both sides watch each other instead of the horizon.

Sekkan moved along the Karthian line, checking gear, murmuring orders in clipped Karthian. He was older, gray streaking his close-cropped beard, scars crisscrossing his forearms where his sleeves were rolled back. His armor was functional, battered, the kind earned through holding lines that shouldn't have held. Shardwork ran along his pauldrons in clean, efficient lines.

He stopped beside Saran, gaze flicking to the Fazrum line, then back to his own troops. "They're too slow," he said, voice low. "By the time their horns sound, half my squad will be dead from standing around waiting."

Saran didn't look at him. "And your shardwork flares are too unpredictable. Half their line won't know if it's a signal or just another stone failing."

Sekkan's jaw tightened, but he didn't argue. "This is going to get messy."

"Yeah," Saran muttered. "It is."

On the Fazrum side, Captain Myran, the kind of man who'd been a sergeant too long before they made him an officer, barked orders at his troops. "Tighten that line! Shields up, spears forward! When the horns sound, you hold. You don't break, you don't scatter, you hold!"

The soldiers responded, shields locking, the line firming into something solid. Myran turned, caught Saran's eye, "Your Karthians ready, or are they still deciding if they want to fight today?"

Saran's hand drifted to her sword, "They're ready. You worry about your side."

Rennik snorted. "My side knows how to follow orders. Yours looks like they're about to bolt the second something scary shows up."

Sekkan's voice cut across the courtyard, sharp. "We fight faster than you bleed, Captain. Maybe that's why you need so many shields."

Mayran's hand tightened on his spear. "Maybe that's why half your sages burn out before the enemy even arrives."

Saran stepped forward, voice loud enough to carry. "Enough."

Both men turned to her, tension crackling in the air.

"We're not fighting each other today," Saran said, gaze sweeping both lines. "Save it for the horde. They'll be here soon enough."

Mayran's jaw worked, but he nodded, turned back to his line. Sekkan held Saran's gaze for a moment longer, something almost like approval flickering in his eyes, then he moved back to his troops.

Saran exhaled, shoulders tight.

The storm pressed down, violet light crackling through the clouds. The air tasted like copper and ozone, thick enough to choke on. In the distance, the horde's roar grew louder, a low, grinding sound like the world tearing itself apart.

Myran raised his hand, ready to signal. Sekkan's troops shifted, shardwork beginning to glow.

Saran drew her sword, the steel cold in her grip.

The horde appeared on the horizon, a black tide surging toward the gate.

"Brace!" Rennik roared.

Sekkan's hand flared, shardwork blazing. "Hold formation!"

The two signals went out at once, horn blast and light flare overlapping A few Fazrum soldiers glanced at the Karthian line, hesitating. A Karthian warrior shifted, unsure if the horn meant advance or hold.

Saran cursed under her breath.

The impact was thunder.

Ravagers crashed into the gate, bodies slamming against iron-banded wood, claws raking stone, the structure groaning under the weight. The sound was deafening, screams, snarls, the splintering crack of wood beginning to give.

"Shields!" Myran roared.

The Fazrum line locked tight, shields overlapping, spears bristling forward like a wall of steel. The formation didn't waver, waiting for the enemy to break themselves against it.

The ravagers surged around the gate's flanks, trying to find gaps, claw their way up the walls. Arrows hissed from the ramparts above, punching through skulls and spines, bodies tumbling back into the horde. But more kept coming, an endless tide pressing forward.

On the Karthian side, Sekkan's troops moved differently. No shield wall. They spread out, lighter on their feet, shardwork flaring in their bodies. Blue light crackled, arcing through the air, striking ravagers before they reached the gate. The creatures convulsed, collapsed, smoke rising from charred flesh.

Saran watched a Karthian warrior, young, maybe twenty, step forward, hand raised, shard glowing bright in his knuckles. He muttered some words, focused, the light building—

The shard exploded.

The sound was sharp, a wet crack followed by a scream that cut through the chaos. The warrior's hand burst open, blood and shattered crystal spraying. He collapsed, clutching the ruined mess, shrieking, his voice raw and broken.

Two Karthians grabbed him, dragged him back, but the damage was done. The gap he'd left opened, ravagers pouring through, claws and teeth and amber eyes.

Myran's voice cut across the courtyard, sharp and venomous. "This is what we're trusting our lives to?"

Sekkan's head snapped toward him, jaw tight. "Your stone magic fails too, Captain. Or have you forgotten how many of your acolytes burn out?"

"Our doctrine doesn't explode in our soldiers' hands," Myran shot back, voice rising. "Your shardwork is unstable. Reckless. You're as dangerous to us as the enemy."

"And your formations are slow," Sekkan snarled. "By the time you move, half the horde's already inside. Maybe if you fought instead of hiding behind shields—"

"Enough!"

Saran's voice cracked like a whip. She stepped between them, blade still in hand, gaze hard enough to cut stone. "We're not fighting each other today."

Myran's jaw worked, hand tightening on his spear. "Tell that to him. His people are getting us killed."

"My people are keeping your line from being overrun," Sekkan shot back.

Saran turned on him, eyes blazing. "And your shardwork just opened a gap that let a dozen ravagers through. So maybe both of you shut up and do your jobs before I decide you're both liabilities."

Silence crashed down. Both men stared at her, tension thick enough to choke on.

Saran's voice dropped. "You want to fight each other? Fine. Do it after we survive this. Until then, you follow orders, you hold your positions, and you stop wasting my time with your egos."

She didn't wait for a response. Turned back to the gate, raised her blade. "Plug that gap! Now!"

Fazrum soldiers moved, shields shifting, spears driving forward into the breach. Karthian warriors circled the flanks, shardwork flaring, cutting down ravagers before they could exploit the opening.

The gap closed. The line held.

Myran and Sekkan exchanged one last glare, then turned back to their troops, barking orders, pulling focus back to the immediate threat.

The second wave hit like a hammer.

An overwhelming surge of bodies slamming into the gate, harder, faster, the wood groaning under the impact. Cracks spiderwebbed across the iron bands, splinters flying. The structure shuddered, tilted inward, threatening to give.

Then the shades came.

They appeared, flickering forms phasing through the gate itself, bypassing stone and iron like they weren't there. One moment the courtyard was clear, the next it was full of them—amber eyes burning in hollow sockets, claws raking through air that bent wrong around them.

"Shades!" someone screamed.

The Fazrum line tried to hold, shields locking, spears thrusting forward. But the shades were too fast, too unpredictable. They flickered in and out of reality, dodging strikes, reappearing behind the line, claws raking across exposed backs. A soldier went down, throat torn open. Another swung at empty air, then collapsed as a shade solidified behind him, drove claws through his spine.

The formation buckled.

Sekkan's troops reacted faster. No shield wall to anchor them, no rigid discipline to slow them down. They scattered, breaking into pairs, moving fast, engaging the shades on their terms. Shardwork flared, blue light crackling through the courtyard, striking at the shades when they solidified. Some burned, collapsing into ash. Others flickered away, untouched.

But the scatter left gaps. Ravagers poured through, exploiting the chaos, clawing at anyone who stood still too long.

"Tighten up!" Myran roared, trying to pull his line back together. "Reform! Don't break!"

But it was too late. The formation was fracturing, soldiers turning to face threats from three directions at once, the disciplined wall dissolving into scattered pockets of desperate fighting.

The gate groaned again, louder this time. Saran's head snapped toward it, saw the wood splintering, the iron bands bending, bolts tearing free from stone. The whole structure was coming apart.

"It's going to fail!" one of the engineers shouted, backing away from the gate.

Saran's mind raced. If the gate collapsed on its own, the horde would flood through, uncontrolled, overwhelming. The courtyard would turn into a slaughter, both sides caught in the chaos with no way to funnel or contain the enemy.

But if they held, tried to brace it or shore it up, they'd be pinned in place, fighting a losing battle against a tide that wouldn't stop. The gate would fall anyway, and they'd die for nothing.

Sekkan appeared beside her, breathing hard. "We can't hold this."

Myran shoved through the line, face streaked with blood. "We hold the gate. That's the order."

"The gate's failing," Sekkan snapped. "You hold it, you die. We all die."

"Then we die doing our job!" Myran's voice was raw. "We don't abandon the gate. That's not how this works."

Sekkan's jaw tightened. "Your doctrine's going to get us killed."

"Your tactics already are."

Saran stepped between them, voice cutting through the noise. "Both of you, shut up."

They turned to her, mouths opening to argue.

"Now!" Saran said.

She stared at the gate, the wood groaning, the horde pressing, the shades flickering through the courtyard, the line dissolving into chaos. Her chest tightened, the weight of the choice pressing down.

Hold the gate. Follow doctrine. Die in place, maybe buy a few more minutes before it collapses anyway and the horde pours through uncontrolled.

Or collapse it. Deliberately. Control the flow, funnel the enemy into a kill zone, give them a chance to hold what came after.

The Fazrum way: Stand your ground, no matter the cost.

The Karthian way: Adapt, control, survive.

Saran's hand tightened on her sword. She made the call.

"We collapse it."

Myran's face went pale. "What?"

"We collapse the gate," Saran said again, louder, voice carrying over the chaos. "Rig the supports. Bring it down inward. Funnel them into a choke point."

"That's insane," Myran hissed. "We lose the gate, we lose the approach—"

"We're already losing the gate!" Saran snapped. "It's failing. Right now. We collapse it on our terms, or it collapses on theirs. Choose."

Sekkan nodded, sharp and immediate. "She's right. We control the fall, we control the fight. We let it break, we're dead."

Myran stared at the gate, jaw working, the weight of the decision landing. Around them, soldiers fought and died, the horde pressing closer, the shades flickering through the line.

Finally, Myran exhaled, sharp and bitter. "Fine. Do it."

Saran turned to the engineers huddled near the wall, terrified and frozen. "Rig the supports! Collapse it inward! You've got thirty seconds!"

They hesitated, staring at her like she'd lost her mind.

"Move!" Sekkan roared.

The engineers broke, scrambling toward the gate, pulling tools from belts, hacking at the weakened supports. Karthian warriors moved to cover them, shardwork flaring, cutting down ravagers that got too close. Fazrum soldiers formed a shield wall in front, blocking the approach, buying seconds.

The gate groaned, tilted further. Wood splintered, iron screamed.

"Everyone back!" Saran shouted. "Clear the approach!"

The line pulled back, soldiers stumbling over each other, shields raised, eyes on the gate. The horde pressed forward, sensing the weakness, surging harder.

The engineers ran, one of them shouted, "It's going!"

The gate collapsed.

It didn't fall clean. It twisted, groaned, then slammed inward with a sound like the world breaking, wood and iron crashing down in a cloud of dust and splinters. The impact shook the courtyard, debris flying, soldiers thrown back by the shockwave.

When the dust cleared, the gate was gone. In its place, a jagged corridor of rubble and shattered wood, the horde funneled into a narrow choke point barely wide enough for three ravagers abreast.

Saran raised her blade. "Kill zone! Now!"

The Fazrum line reformed at the corridor's mouth, shields locking, spears leveled. The Karthians spread along the flanks, shardwork flaring, raining down into the packed mass.

The ravagers charged into the corridor. And died.

Spears drove through chests, shields bashed aside claws, shardwork burned through flesh. The narrow space turned into a killing ground, bodies piling up, the horde unable to spread, unable to flank, forced to push through the chokepoint one wave at a time.

It was working.

But the cost was immediate.

Saran saw a Fazrum soldier crushed under the falling gate, pinned beneath debris, screaming until he wasn't. Saw a Karthian warrior caught in the open when the gate collapsed, torn apart by ravagers before anyone could reach him. Saw the faces of the engineers who'd rigged the supports, pale and shaking, staring at what they'd done.

Saran stepped into the line, blade flashing, cutting down a ravager as it tried to claw through the shields. Beside her, Myran fought in grim silence, spear driving forward, again and again. Sekkan moved along the flanks, shardwork crackling.

The kill zone held. Barely.

Bodies piled at the corridor's mouth, ravagers trampling their own dead, pressing forward with mindless hunger. The Fazrum line stood firm, shields locked, spears thrusting in rhythm. The Karthian flanks rained shardwork into the mass.

Saran stood in the center, blade slick with ichor, breath coming hard. Her arms ached, shoulders screaming from the constant motion, block, strike, kill, repeat. But the line was holding.

A young acolyte in grey, barely out of training, stumbled into the courtyard, gasping, gray robes torn and bloodstained. "Reinforcements!" he shouted, voice cracking. "The temple district, they're under attack! The refugees are trapped inside, the enemy broke through the wards!"

Saran's stomach dropped. She turned to the gate, the line holding but fragile, ravagers still pressing, the corridor choked with bodies. If she pulled troops, the balance would shift. The Fazrum line might buckle. The Karthians might scatter. The kill zone could collapse.

But the temple, hundreds of civilians huddled in the sanctum, had nowhere to run.

Myran stepped beside her, breathing hard, spear dripping. "We can't spare anyone. We pull troops, this line folds."

Saran's jaw tightened. She knew he was right. The gate was holding by a thread. One wrong move and it would all come apart.

Sekkan appeared on her other side. He looked at the runner, then at Saran, then at his own troops spread along the flanks.

"Take my squad," he said.

Saran blinked. "What?"

"We're faster." Sekkan's voice was calm, matter-of-fact. "Mobile. Built for this. Your Fazrum line holds position better than we do anyway." He gestured at Myran's shield wall, still locked tight despite the chaos. "They can manage the gate. We go to the temple."

Myran stared at him, something flickering in his eyes, surprise, maybe, or grudging respect. He looked at the gate, at his own line, then back at Sekkan.

Finally, he nodded. "Go. We'll manage."

Saran met Myran's eyes, saw the exhaustion there, the weight of holding the line alone. "You sure?"

Myran's mouth twitched, almost a smile. "No. But we'll do it anyway." He turned back to his troops, already barking orders, pulling the line tighter to cover the gaps.

Sekkan raised his hand, his Karthian squad responded immediately, peeling off from the flanks, forming up around him. A dozen warriors, light armor, shardwork glowing faint blue,

Saran looked at the gate one last time. The Fazrum line held firm, shields locked, spears driving forward. Myran stood at the center, voice hoarse but steady. The kill zone still worked.

She turned to Sekkan. "Let's move."

They ran.

Boots pounding stone, armor clanking, breath coming fast. Saran led, Sekkan beside her, the Karthian squad spread out behind in loose formation, scanning alleys and rooftops for threats.

The city was chaos. Smoke rose from a dozen fires, ash falling like snow. Civilians fled in every direction, some toward the inner wards, others just running, terror-driven, nowhere to go. Soldiers shouted orders, tried to maintain formation, but the lines were fracturing, scattered pockets of resistance barely holding.

Saran didn't look back. The eastern gate was behind her now, Myran's line holding without her. She had to trust it. Had to trust him.

The black tower loomed ahead, closer now, its silhouette cutting through the smoke like a blade. The hum was audible even over the chaos, vibrating in Saran's chest like a second heartbeat. It pressed down, pulling at something deep inside her.

She shook it off, focused on the path ahead. The temple district was close. Smoke thicker here, the air tasting like burnt incense and charred flesh.

Sekkan ran beside her, breathing steady despite the pace. "You made the right call," he said. "At the gate."

Saran didn't answer. The faces of the soldiers crushed under the collapsing gate flashed through her mind. The engineer who'd hesitated. The Karthian warrior torn apart in the rubble.

"It cost lives," she said finally.

"Saved more." Sekkan's tone was pragmatic, no false comfort. "That's the job."

They rounded a corner and the temple district opened before them.

Thick smoke, rising from the temple's shattered peaks. The outer walls were scorched, stone cracked and bleeding violet light. Bodies littered the approach, refugees, soldiers, sage acolytes in gray robes, all of them torn apart, sprawled in the rubble.

Screams echoed from inside, fire crackled, stone groaned, the sound of something massive collapsing deep within the sanctum.

Saran's chest seized. She could see the temple's entrance, the doors blown open, shades flickering in and out of the smoke, ravagers prowling the courtyard, feeding.

"Too late," one of the Karthian warriors muttered.

Sekkan's hand found Saran's shoulder, grip firm. "Maybe not."

Saran drew her blade, the steel catching the firelight. She checked her squad and looked at the temple, the smoke, the bodies.

"Move!" Saran broke into a sprint, boots pounding stone, blade raised.

Sekkan and the squad followed, shardwork blazing, voices rising in a Karthian war cry that cut through the smoke.

25

The temple had become a tomb waiting to happen.

Idran stood near the inner sanctum's entrance, watching refugees pack the stone floor, families huddled together, children pressed against their mothers' sides, old men clutching walking staves like weapons. The air was thick with incense and fear, the scent of burning sage mixing with sweat and the stench of blood from those who'd arrived wounded.

Whispered prayers filled the silence, fragmented and desperate. Some called to the old gods, names Idran barely recognized from Fazrum doctrine. Others just murmured nonsense, words meant to fill the void, to keep the terror at bay.

Eleseth moved through the crowd, gray robes sweeping across stone, her presence calm and authoritative despite the chaos pressing in from outside. She knelt beside a woman clutching a crying infant, spoke quietly, placed a hand on her shoulder. The woman nodded, tears streaking her face, and pulled the child closer.

Idran watched her work, felt the weight of his own uselessness pressing down. He was Karthian, trained in shardwork, a noble who'd killed his father and left his city with blood on his hands. Surrounded now by Fazrum's dying stones, their ancient relics, their doctrine that felt foreign and rigid compared to the fluid pragmatism of Karth.

The shards in his arm pulsed, faint but insistent, a rhythmic throb that matched the distant hum of the black tower. He flexed his fingers, felt the embedded crystal shift beneath his skin, the blue glow flickering like a heartbeat trying to sync with something vast and terrible.

He didn't like it.

Eleseth appeared beside him, her gaze sharp despite the exhaustion carved into her face. "You're restless."

Idran glanced at her, then back at the crowd. "I don't know what I'm doing here."

"You're standing between them and what's coming." Eleseth's tone was matter-of-fact. "That's enough."

"Is it?" Idran's voice came out bitter. "I'm not a soldier. I'm not even from Fazrum. I'm just—" He stopped, jaw tight. "I'm just here because I have nowhere else to go."

Eleseth studied him, something almost like sympathy flickering in her eyes. "You're here because you chose to be. That's more than most can say."

Idran didn't answer. The shards pulsed again, stronger this time, and he pressed his palm against his forearm, trying to dull the sensation. It didn't work.

A distant crash shook the temple. Dust rained from the ceiling, stone groaning. The refugees gasped, pulled their children closer, eyes wide and terrified.

Eleseth's head snapped toward the outer halls, her calm cracking just slightly. "They're here."

Idran's stomach dropped. He moved toward the entrance, peered through the archway into the temple's outer corridors. The wards were still holding, faint lines of light etched into the stone, Fazrum incantations layered over centuries of tradition. But they were flickering, the glow unsteady, like candles in a storm.

"How long?" Idran asked.

Eleseth joined him, her gaze fixed on the wards. "Not long.

Minutes, maybe. The wards are old. They weren't built to withstand this."

Another crash, closer now. The temple shuddered, the wards flaring bright, then dimming. Idran heard screams from somewhere outside, the wet sound of bodies hitting stone, the shriek of ravagers tearing through flesh.

The shards in his arm burned, reacting to the magic collapsing around them. He hissed, pressed harder, trying to suppress the flare. The blue glow intensified, crawling up his forearm like veins of light.

Eleseth saw it, "They're reacting to something."

"I know," Idran muttered through clenched teeth. "I can feel it."

Eleseth placed a hand on his shoulder, her grip firm. "Then you need to be ready. When the wards fail, we'll need every advantage we have."

Idran looked at her, saw the determination in her eyes, the weight of duty pressing down on her shoulders. She wasn't afraid. Or if she was, she'd buried it so deep it didn't matter anymore.

He wished he could do the same.

The wards flickered again, then shattered, light exploded across the corridor, blinding and sharp, then died. The incantations burned out, leaving nothing but scorched stone.

The ravagers didn't hesitate.

They flooded the outer halls in a black tide, claws scraping stone, jaws snapping, amber eyes blazing in the dim light. The sound was overwhelming, screams, snarls, the wet crunch of bodies being torn apart, the crash of ancient artifacts shattered underfoot.

The refugees panicked.

A woman screamed, clutching her child, scrambling backward. Others surged toward the inner sanctum doors, pushing, shoving, terror overriding reason. An old man stumbled, went down hard, and was trampled before Idran could reach him.

"Stay calm!" Eleseth's voice cut through the chaos, sharp and commanding. "Form lines! Move to the back! Now!"

Her authority held just enough. The crowd didn't stop panicking, but they channeled it, moving toward the rear of the sanctum in ragged clusters instead of blind stampede.

Idran ran to the inner doors, massive slabs of iron-banded wood that hadn't been closed in decades. He grabbed one side, Eleseth the other, both of them hauling with everything they had. The hinges screamed, rust and age fighting them, but the door shifted, inch by grinding inch.

A ravager appeared in the archway, claws raised. Idran didn't think, just thrust out his hand, crystal shard dust flaring. Blue light erupted, a jagged bolt that caught the creature mid-leap. It convulsed, collapsed, smoke rising from charred flesh.

"Keep moving!" Eleseth shouted.

They slammed the door shut, dropped the iron bar across it. It wouldn't hold long. The wood was ancient, the bar corroded, the whole structure built for ceremony, not siege.

Eleseth stepped back, breathing hard, eyes scanning the sanctum. "We need time. Just a few more minutes for the evacuation tunnels to clear."

Idran stared at her. "Tunnels? There are tunnels out of here?"

Eleseth's jaw tightened. She didn't look at him. "Yes."

"Where do they lead?"

"Nowhere safe." Her voice was honest. "Old catacombs. They'll get the refugees out of the sanctum, disperse them through the undercity. It's not safety. But it's all we've got."

Idran's stomach twisted. Not safety. Just a way to scatter, to make the enemy work harder to hunt them down. Better than being trapped in a single room, waiting to die. But not by much.

The door shuddered as something massive slammed into it from the other side. The iron bar groaned, wood splintering at the edges.

Eleseth turned to the crowd, already moving. "Into the tunnels! Move!"

Idran stayed at the door, shards burning in his arm, the blue glow crawling up toward his elbow. He could feel the ravagers on the other side, the weight of their bodies pressing, claws scraping, jaws snapping.

Eleseth ran. She moved with purpose, crossing the sanctum toward a small alcove carved into the far wall. Idran had seen it before, just another shrine, another piece of Fazrum's endless collection of relics and artifacts, most of them dormant, useless, monuments to a past no one understood anymore.

But Eleseth knew exactly what she was looking for.

She reached into the alcove, pulled aside a rough cloth covering, and lifted out the relic.

Idran's breath caught.

It was the same one, faintly glowing, wrapped in the same old velvet he'd seen back when they'd studied it together. The relic his father had used to cling to life, draining himself and everyone around him to stave off death for one more year, one more month, one more breath.

The relic that had broken his family.

"What the hell are you doing with that?" Idran's voice came out sharper than he meant.

Eleseth set the relic on the stone altar in the center of the sanctum, her hands steady despite the chaos pressing in from outside. She kept her incantation stone pressed firmly against it, the only way to touch it directly without the divine energy tearing through unprotected flesh. Even through the stone, Idran could see the strain, her jaw tight, veins standing out on her forearms, sweat beading on her forehead.

"I've been studying it," she said, voice calm, matter-of-fact. "Since it was brought from Karth. Trying to understand how it works, what it was meant for."

Idran moved closer, the shards in his arm pulsing harder now, reacting to the relic's presence. "It's a weapon. That's all it's ever been. My father used it to steal life. To cling to power when he should've let go."

"Your father misused it." Eleseth's gaze didn't leave the relic. "But that doesn't mean it can't be turned to another purpose." She paused, fingers tracing the relic's surface through the stone. "I think I can activate it. Channel its energy outward. Turn it into a weapon, against them."

Idran's stomach dropped. He stared at her, then at the relic, the pieces clicking into place.

"No." His voice final. "Absolutely not."

Eleseth looked at him, something almost like sympathy in her eyes. "It's the only way."

"It'll kill you." Idran grabbed her arm, pulled her away from the altar. "You activate that thing, channel that much energy, it'll drain you. Burn you out from the inside. You know that."

Eleseth pulled free, her grip on the incantation stone unwavering. "I know the cost."

"Then why—" Idran stopped, the weight of her decision landing. "There has to be another way. We can hold the doors longer, buy more time—"

"There isn't time." Eleseth's voice was steady, no hesitation, no fear. "The refugees need minutes we don't have. The doors are failing. The enemy will crash through any ward I can put up." She looked at him, her gaze clear. "This is my duty. I chose to leave the Sages, but I never stopped serving Fazrum. This is how I serve now."

Idran's chest tightened, the shards in his arm burning hotter, brighter, the blue glow crawling past his elbow toward his shoulder. He could feel it, the pull of the relic, the connection between his shardwork and the divine energy pulsing inside the stone.

He could help. Share the burden. Stabilize the relic with his own magic, keep Eleseth from burning out completely.

The shards were already unstable, already reacting to the black tower humming in the distance. Pushing them further, channeling that much power, might kill him. Or worse.

Self-preservation screamed at him to step back. Let her do it alone. Survive.

But duty—

The door shuddered again, the iron bar bending, wood cracking.

Screams echoed from the tunnels, refugees still fleeing, not all of them clear yet.

Idran looked at Eleseth, saw the resolve in her eyes, the certainty that this was the right choice even if it cost everything.

Eleseth didn't wait.

She didn't ask for permission, didn't look back. She pressed both palms against the relic, stone and flesh meeting divine energy, and began pouring her entire will into the stone.

Then the light came.

White and amber, blinding, pure, erupting from the relic like a star tearing itself open. The sanctum flooded with brilliance, every shadow burned away, the air crackling with raw power. The relic sang, a high, keening note that vibrated in Idran's bones, in the shards embedded in his arm.

Wards snapped into place across the sanctum, lines of light etched into stone, crawling up the walls, across the ceiling, sealing every crack, every gap. Ancient magic, older than the city, older than the sages, roaring back to life with a fury that made the air itself shimmer.

The ravagers hit the wards and screamed.

They recoiled, flesh burning where they touched the light, claws sizzling, amber eyes dimming. The ones that had breached the outer halls collapsed, smoke rising from charred bodies. The shades flickered, tried to phase through, and were repelled, torn apart by the wards, dissolving into ash.

Idran saw it immediately, Eleseth's skin cracking, fine lines spreading across her hands, her arms, light bleeding through the fissures like her body was a vessel too fragile to contain what she'd unleashed. Her breath came in short, gasping wheezes, blood trickling from her nose, her eyes wide but unfocused.

"Eleseth—" Idran lunged forward, grabbed her shoulders.

She didn't respond. Just kept channeling, hands locked on the relic, words faint spilling from her lips.

The shards in Idran's arm screamed. Blue light erupted, brighter than it had ever burned, crawling up past his shoulder, across his chest, veins of crystal spreading beneath his skin. He pressed his palm against the relic beside hers, tried to channel his shardwork into the flow, stabilize the energy, share the burden.

The pain was immediate and absolute.

It felt like his arm was being torn apart from the inside, shards grinding against bone, veins on fire, every nerve alight. He gritted his teeth, pushed harder, forced the shardwork to sync with the relic's pulse, to carry some of the weight Eleseth was bearing alone but it wasn't enough.

The relic's power was too vast, divine energy from a time before humanity had learned to shape magic into something controlled. Idran's shardwork was a drop against a flood. He could slow the drain, maybe buy her seconds, but he couldn't stop it.

Eleseth's gaze found his, clarity flickering in her fading eyes. Her lips moved, voice barely a whisper. "Go."

Idran shook his head, grip tightening. "Not yet—"

"Finish your duty." Her voice cracked, blood staining her teeth. "Don't waste this."

The relic pulsed.

Light exploded outward, a final surge that tore through the sanctum like a shockwave. The wards flared white-hot, blindingly bright, and the remaining ravagers outside burned. Not just repelled but obliterated, flesh and bone turning to ash in an instant, shades dissolving into nothing, the entire outer hall scoured clean.

The force threw Idran backward, his grip torn free, body slamming into the stone floor. His vision swam, ears ringing, the taste of blood flooding his mouth.

When he looked up, Eleseth was on the ground.

The relic lay beside her, cracked and dark, the light gone. Her hands were charred, blackened, skin peeling away to reveal bone. The cracks across her arms, her chest, had spread, bleeding light that dimmed even as he watched.

Idran crawled to her, shards still burning in his arm, the pain distant now, drowned out by something worse.

Idran knelt beside her, hands hovering over her body, shaking, unable to touch her. His throat closed, something broken clawing its way up.

He'd hesitated. He'd hesitated, and now—

A hand grabbed his shoulder, hard. A Sage acolyte, one of the survivors, pale and trembling. "The tunnels are clear. We have to go. Now."

Idran didn't move. He stared at Eleseth's body, the charred hands, the cracked skin, the empty eyes.

"Karthian!" The acolyte shook him. "She bought us time. Don't waste it."

The words cut through the fog. Don't waste this.

Idran stood, legs unsteady, the shards in his arm still pulsing, dimmer now but insistent.

He looked at Eleseth one last time. Then he turned away.

The sanctum was collapsing. Stone groaned, cracks spreading across the walls, the wards dying with the relic. Smoke poured in from the outer halls, heat rising, the temple burning.

Idran stumbled toward the tunnels, following the last of the refugees, the Sage pulling him along. Behind him, the sanctum collapsed, burying Eleseth under stone and rubble.

Idran stumbled out of the temple into smoke and ash.

The air was thick, choking, the world reduced to gray haze and distant screams. The temple behind him groaned, stone cracking, the dome collapsing inward with a sound like thunder. Debris rained down, forcing him to shield his face, boots slipping on rubble as he staggered into the street.

Survivors scattered around him, refugees from the tunnels, pale and trembling, some clutching children, others just running, anywhere that wasn't here. A few acolytes tried to organize them, voices hoarse, gesturing toward the inner wards.

Idran couldn't breathe. His chest was tight, lungs burning, the weight of Eleseth's death hitting him like a stone. The shards in his arm pulsed, brighter now, the blue glow spreading up past his shoulder, crawling across his chest in jagged veins of light. It hurt, but distantly, like the pain belonged to someone else.

He stopped in the middle of the street, swaying, vision swimming. The tower loomed ahead, closer than it should be, its hum vibrating in his bones, in his teeth, in the shards embedded in his flesh. It was calling somehow.

Then boots pounded stone, voices shouting, and Saran appeared through the smoke.

She ran toward him, Sekkan beside her, a squad of Karthian warriors fanned out behind, shardwork glowing faint blue in their bodies. Saran's face was streaked with blood and ichor, armor dented, but her eyes were sharp, scanning him, taking in the glow of the shards, the ash covering his clothes, the hollow look in his eyes.

She stopped in front of him, breath coming hard. "Eleseth?"

Idran shook his head. His voice came out hoarse, scraped raw. "Dead."

Saran's jaw tightened, something flickering across her face—grief, or the weight of another loss added to the pile. She nodded once, "Then we move. Inner wards. Regroup with—"

"No." Idran looked past her, toward the tower rising through the smoke. "We go to the tower."

Saran frowned. "What?"

"The tower." Idran gestured, the shards flaring brighter with the movement. "Something's happening there. I can feel it. We need to—"

"How do you know?" Saran's tone was sharp.

Idran looked at her, saw the doubt, the exhaustion, the need for certainty in a world that had none left.

"It's Samric, he's doing...something up there. I can feel it."

Sekkan stepped forward, his gaze fixed on Idran, concern etched into his weathered face. "My lord." His voice was careful, respectful but firm. "You're injured. The shards, they're spreading. You need a healer, not a siege."

Idran shook his head, jaw tight. "I'm fine."

"You're not." Sekkan's tone hardened. "Whatever's happening to you, it's connected to that tower. Going there might kill you."

"Then I die there." Idran met his eyes, saw the worry, the loyalty. Sekkan had followed him out of Karth, trusted him despite everything. But this wasn't about trust. "The tower's the center. Samric's there—" He stopped, swallowed. "Eleseth died buying time. I'm not wasting it running toward safety that doesn't exist."

Sekkan's jaw worked, then he nodded, slow and grudging. "As you say, my lord."

Saran studied Idran, eyes narrowing. Then she exhaled. "Fine. We go to the tower." She turned to Sekkan and the Karthian squad. "You're with us."

Sekkan gestured, and the squad formed up, shardwork flickering.

Saran looked at Idran. "Stay with me. You fall, I'm dragging you back."

Idran almost smiled. "Deal."

They moved through the smoke, boots pounding stone, the city collapsing around them. Fires burned unchecked, buildings sagging into themselves, soldiers fighting in scattered pockets, the horde pressing from every direction.

But the tower loomed ahead, closer with every step, its silhouette cutting through the chaos like a blade. The hum grew louder, drowning out the screams, the clash of steel, the roar of flames. It pressed into Idran's skull, resonating in the shards, pulling harder, insistent.

They rounded a corner, and the tower filled the sky.

26

Darum stood at the inner barricades, watching the outer defenses die.

The line was sandbags and desperation, scavenged timber wedged between collapsed buildings, sharpened stakes driven into broken cobblestones, debris stacked high enough to slow a charge but not stop one. It looked like something built by men who knew they were going to lose but refused to make it easy.

Survivors poured through the gates, a flood of bloodied armor and hollow eyes. Warriors stumbled, limping, some dragging wounded brothers, others just running, discipline shattered, fear driving them toward anything that looked like shelter. The horde pressed close behind, a black tide visible through the smoke.

"Form up!" Darum's voice cut through the chaos, hoarse but steady. "Left flank, fill that gap! Archers, high ground! Anyone too wounded to fight, inner wards, now!"

The survivors responded, muscle memory overriding panic. Warriors moved to positions, shields raised, spears leveled. Archers scrambled up rubble piles, nocking arrows, scanning for targets. The wounded limped toward the inner gates, some carried, others crawling, leaving blood trails across stone.

Darum moved through the chaos, directing traffic, plugging gaps, his hands never far from his sword. His armor was battered, dented across the chest where a ravager's claws had scraped deep but not penetrated. Blood streaked his face, not his, or maybe some of it was, he'd stopped checking a while ago.

Brent appeared beside him, armor cracked across the shoulder, a gash running down his forearm hastily wrapped in cloth already soaked through. But he was standing, blade in hand, eyes clear despite the exhaustion carved into his face.

"Outer wall's gone," Brent said, voice flat. "I couldn't hold it."

Darum nodded. "I know."

Drast limped up from the other flank, one arm bound tight against his ribs, the bandage dark with blood. His face was pale, jaw set against pain, but his grip on his spear was steady.

"Western approach's secure," Drast reported, breath coming short. "For now."

Darum scanned the barricade, took stock. The line was thin, too thin, gaps everywhere, warriors exhausted and bleeding. But they were standing.

The three of them had held lines together before. Years of it, skirmishes on the Karth border, the defense of the outer settlements, the march to Vask and back. They knew each other's rhythms, trusted each other's instincts, moved like parts of the same machine.

But this felt different.

Then the ravagers hit like a breaking wave.

A crushing weight of bodies slamming into the barricades, claws raking wood and stone, jaws snapping at anything that moved. The sound was deafening, a wall of screams and snarls that drowned out everything else.

"HOLD!" Darum roared, sword flashing as he drove it through a ravager's throat. Black ichor sprayed, hot and thick. "Make them pay for every inch!"

The line locked tight, shields overlapping, spears thrusting forward in rhythm. Warriors grunted with effort, boots digging into broken stone, muscles screaming as they pushed back against the tide. The barricade groaned under the pressure, sandbags shifting, stakes snapping, but it held.

Darum fought at the center, blade carving through flesh and bone, his movements economical, no wasted motion. A ravager lunged at his flank. He twisted, caught it across the jaw, felt bone shatter. It collapsed then another took its place.

Brent was beside him, moving with sharp, desperate efficiency. His armor was cracked, his arm bleeding, but his blade didn't waver. He fought like a man with nothing left to lose, every strike driven by something deeper than survival.

A ravager clawed through the line, broke past the shields. Brent stepped into the gap, drove his sword through its chest, yanked it free, and kicked the body back into the horde. "Tighten up! Don't give them space!"

The line shifted, closed the gap. Warriors pressed closer, shields locking, the formation firming despite the exhaustion bleeding through every face.

Down the flank, Drast held the left side together through sheer stubborn refusal to break. His wounded arm hung limp, useless, but his good hand gripped a spear, driving it forward again and again, voice hoarse but steady. "Watch your spacing! Cover each other! Don't let them scatter you!"

The warriors around him responded, movements sharpening, the ragged line firming into something functional. Drast didn't fight pretty. Every strike meant to kill, every order meant to keep the line from collapsing into chaos.

But the stones were failing.

Darum saw it everywhere, acolytes clutching their incantation stones, faces blood dripping from their noses, hands shaking as they tried to pull power that wouldn't come. Wards flickered along the barricade, barely visible, dying before they could form. One acolyte collapsed, stone shattering in his palm, shards embedding in his flesh. He screamed, clutching his hand, blood pouring through his fingers.

Darum's own stone pulsed in his palm, the familiar weight

suddenly wrong. He reached for it, felt the heat radiating through the pouch, hotter than it should be, Then it bit.

Pain lanced through his palm, like the stone was tearing into his flesh from the inside. He hissed, nearly dropped it, his grip faltering. A ravager lunged, claws aimed at his exposed side.

Brent's blade flashed, caught the creature mid-leap, drove it back. "Focus!"

Darum shook his head, forced his grip to steady, shoved the stone back into its pouch. His hand trembled, the pain lingering, a burn that radiated up his arm.

He didn't have time to think about it.

Another ravager came at him. He met it with his blade, felt the impact jar his bones, drove it back. The line held, but only just. Warriors were either bleeding, stumbling or collapsing. The barricade was slick with blood, bodies piling up on both sides.

The line was holding just barely. Then Darum saw the gap.

A narrow alley fed into the barricades from the east, shadowed and choked with rubble. It had seemed defensible, too tight for a mass charge, easy to bottle up. But the ravagers were pouring through it now, a black tide squeezing through the narrow space, bypassing the main barricade, threatening to flank the entire line.

If that alley fell, the horde would be inside the inner ward. The barricade would collapse from behind. Everyone here would be surrounded.

Darum's chest tightened. He started moving. "With me! We plug that gap—"

A hand grabbed his arm, pulled him back.

"I'll take it," Brent said.

Darum stared at him. "You can't hold that alone."

"I'm not holding it." Brent's gaze was clear, "I'm buying time." He met Darum's eyes. "I owe this. Let me pay it."

The words landed heavy. Darum understood immediately, this wasn't about tactics or strategy. This was about redemption. About the forged summons, the breach that let the NineArts through, Ulzaan's death. Brent had carried that weight every day since, and now he was asking for permission to put it down the only way left.

For a moment, Darum's throat was too tight to speak. He wanted to argue, to ask Brent to stay at the main line where they could cover each other. But he saw the resolve in Brent's face, the need to do this, to end it on his terms.

Darum's hand tightened on Brent's arm, then released. "Make it count."

Brent nodded once, he turned, raised his voice. "I need five! Anyone willing to hold a chokepoint!"

Four warriors stepped forward immediately. A fifth followed, younger, barely old enough to have earned his armor. They formed up around Brent, shields raised, blades ready.

Brent looked back at Darum one last time, then he turned and ran toward the alley.

They hit the chokepoint at a dead sprint, boots crunching over rubble, and formed a wall across the narrow gap. Shields locked, spears leveled, five men and Brent standing between the horde and the inner ward.

The ravagers crashed into them like a wave.

Brent's voice cut through the chaos, hoarse but steady. "Ravenblood! Hold the line!"

His blade flashed, carving through the first ravager, then the second. The warriors around him drove their spears forward, shields absorbing impacts, the formation holding tight in the narrow space. The alley worked for them, the ravagers couldn't spread, forced to come at them, funneled into the killing ground.

Darum watched from the main barricade, jaw clenched so hard his teeth ached. He wanted to move, to go, to pull Brent back before it was too late. But the main line was buckling, ravagers pressing everywhere, soldiers shouting for orders, gaps opening faster than he could plug them.

Drast limped up beside him, face pale, blood soaking through his bandage, but his gaze steady. He looked at the chokepoint, then at Darum. "He made his choice."

Ten seconds. Twenty. Brent's blade never stopped moving, driving through flesh and bone, his voice still calling orders, still holding the volunteers together. A ravager's claws raked across his shoulder, tearing through cracked armor. He staggered, caught himself, drove his sword through the creature's skull.

Thirty seconds. The young warrior went down, throat torn open. Another took his place, stepped over the body.

Forty seconds. Brent was bleeding from a dozen cuts, armor hanging in tatters, but he didn't fall. Just kept swinging, kept buying time.

One minute.

A massive ravager, twice the size of the others, slammed into the shield wall. The impact shattered the formation, threw warriors backward, shields splintering. Brent lunged forward, drove his blade through its chest, but it didn't stop. Claws raked across his side, tore through armor and flesh. He went down hard, blood pooling beneath him.

The volunteers collapsed around him, overwhelmed, torn apart.

But the ravagers didn't pour through immediately. They had to climb over the bodies, wade through the blood, navigate the rubble Brent's stand had turned into a charnel house.

And in those seconds, the main line shifted.

Darum barked orders, warriors moving to seal the gap, shields locking across the alley's exit. By the time the ravagers broke through the chokepoint, they hit another wall, this one fresh, ready.

Darum stood at the barricade, staring at the alley, at the bodies piled in the narrow space, at the blood-slick stone. He couldn't see Brent anymore, only the carnage he'd left behind.

His hand tightened on his sword, knuckles white.

"He did his job," Drast said quietly.

Darum nodded, "Always."

The massive ravager that had broken Brent's stand didn't stop. It tore through the chokepoint's exit, claws raking stone, jaws snapping, amber eyes blazing with mindless hunger. Warriors scattered, shields splintering under the weight of its charge.

It locked onto Drast.

He saw it coming and tried to brace, but his wounded arm was useless, his stance off-balance. The ravager's claws swept across his ribs, tore through armor like parchment. Drast's spear clattered to the ground. He went down hard, the impact driving the air from his lungs, blood spreading fast across stone.

"Drast!" Darum lunged forward, but warriors were already moving.

A volley of arrows hissed through the air, punching into the ravager's back. It staggered, roared, twisted toward the archers. Spears drove into its flanks from three directions, warriors swarming it, hacking at legs, arms, anything they could reach.

The creature stumbled, momentum carrying it forward, straight into a ward line etched across the barricade.

An acolyte pressed his palm flat against the stone. Light flared, white-hot, the ward igniting with a sound like thunder. The ravager hit it and convulsed, its flesh burning, smoke rising from charred skin. It collapsed then went still.

The acolyte collapsed too, stone shattering in his hand, blood streaming from his nose.

Darum reached Drast, dropped to his knees beside him. The wound was deep, a ragged gash across his ribs, blood pouring through the gaps in his armor. Not immediately fatal, the claws had missed anything vital, but bad enough. Too much blood loss, and Drast wouldn't last the hour.

Darum pressed a hand to the wound, trying to stem the flow. "Stay still."

Drast grimaced, teeth bared, breath coming in short gasps. "I can still fight."

"You can barely stand."

"Then I'll stand badly." Drast's hand found Darum's arm, gripped it hard. " I'm not leaving this line."

Darum stared at him, saw the stubborn refusal in his eyes, the same thing he'd seen in every warrior who'd ever held ground they knew would break. Was it pride or the refusal to die lying down.

He wanted to argue, get him to a healer, survive this. But he knew the look. Knew the choice had already been made.

Darum exhaled, he helped Drast sit up, propped him against the barricade, blood soaking through both their hands. He grabbed a fallen spear, pressed it into Drast's good hand.

"Don't die on me," Darum said, voice rough.

Drast's grin was bloody, teeth stained red. "You'd have to put me down yourself."

Darum almost smiled. Almost. He stood, checked Drast's position, his back against sandbags, spear angled forward, enough reach to hit anything that got close. Not ideal, but functional.

"Hold here," Darum said. "I'll cover the front."

Drast nodded, breath still coming short, but his grip on the spear was steady. "Go. I've got this."

The horde pulled back, the tide receding to gather strength for the next surge. The ravagers scattered into the smoke, amber eyes glowing in the haze, snarls fading into the distance. The barricade held, warriors gasping, leaning on spears and shields, blood pooling at their feet.

Darum scanned the battlefield, chest heaving, trying to count the living. Too few. The line was thin, held together by spite and muscle memory. Drast still sat propped against the sandbags, spear in hand. The acolytes were mostly dead or burned out, stones shattered, wards gone dark.

Darum saw movement in the smoke, deliberate and unhurried. A figure in a long cloak shifting like smoke, silver hair catching the violet light.

He walked through the chaos with a cadre of shades flickering around him, their forms bending light and shadow. He didn't fight, didn't command. Didn't even acknowledge the battle raging around him. He moved, patiently, heading toward the tower like the rest of the world didn't exist.

Darum's blood froze.

His hand tightened on his sword, every instinct screaming to move, to charge, to cut Samric down before he reached the tower. But the plan had always been to let him reach it. To let him think he'd won, let him complete the ritual, and then stop him when he was vulnerable.

Letting Samric walk away felt like betrayal. Like surrender.

But Darum held his ground.

Samric disappeared into the smoke, the shades flickering after him. The tower loomed in the distance, closer now, its hum vibrating in Darum's chest.

He forced himself to turn away. The line needed him here.

Footsteps came behind him, boots crunching over broken stone. Darum turned, saw Verath moving along the line, armor battered and streaked with blood, a gash across her temple still bleeding, but her stride steady.

She stopped beside him, followed his line of sight toward the tower. "You saw him."

Darum nodded. "He's heading for the tower. Walked right through the battlefield like it wasn't there."

Verath's jaw tightened. "Good. That means the plan's working."

"Doesn't feel like it."

"Never does." She looked at Darum, "I'd go myself if I could to confront him and end it. But I've got a new role now. A responsibility. I can't leave this line."

Darum understood. The weight of command. The burden of staying behind while others went forward. Ulzaan had carried it for decades. Now it was Verath's.

She turned to face him fully. "You need to go. Find Leonard. I saw him heading toward the second barricade, further down the line." She paused, her gaze steady. "He did well today. Plugged a breach when the wall was breaking, kept the flank from collapsing. You should be proud."

Darum's chest tightened. "I am."

"Good." Verath's mouth twitched, almost a smile. "In some ways, you two are alike. Both too stubborn to know when to quit. Too willing to throw yourselves into the breach." Her tone softened, just slightly. "Make sure he survives this. Make sure you both do."

Darum nodded.

Verath clapped a hand on his shoulder, grip firm. "Go. Stop Samric. Finish what Ulzaan started."

Darum glanced back at the line one last time, at Drast, still propped against the barricade, at the warriors holding position, at the bodies piled behind them. Then he turned and ran.

Boots pounding stone, sword in hand, the tower's hum growing louder with every step.

Darum ran through the chaos, lungs burning, boots slipping on blood-slick stone. The city was collapsing around him, buildings sagging into themselves, fires spreading unchecked, soldiers fighting in scattered pockets, the horde pressing from every direction.

He passed a cluster of Ravenblood warriors holding a narrow street, shields locked, spears thrusting in rhythm. Passed refugees fleeing toward the inner wards, some carrying wounded, others just running. Passed bodies, too many bodies, faces he recognized, names he'd known.

The second barricade was just ahead, another desperate line of sandbags and sharpened stakes. Warriors fought at the front, exhausted, bleeding, holding through sheer refusal to break. Darum scanned the line.

He stood near the center, sword dripping ichor, armor battered, face streaked with blood and soot. But he was standing.

Darum pushed through the line, grabbed Leonard's shoulder. "You still breathing?"

Leonard turned, eyes widening. "Darum—"

"Come on. We're moving."

Leonard blinked, exhausted, trying to process. "Where—"

"The tower." Darum's voice was flat, final. "Samric's heading there. We stop him or this whole city burns."

Leonard's jaw tightened. He glanced at the line, at the warriors still fighting, then back at Darum. "What about—"

"Verath's holding the line. Drast's." Darum stopped, swallowed. "He's still standing. For now." He met Leonard's eyes. "But if we don't stop Samric, none of it matters."

Leonard nodded, wiped his blade on his vambrace, sheathed it. "Alright. Let's go."

The tower loomed ahead, closer with every step, its silhouette cutting through the smoke like a blade. The hum was overwhelming now, vibrating in Darum's chest, in his bones, drowning out the noise of the battle behind them.

They reached the city's outskirts, the tower's base just ahead, when Darum saw movement from another street.

More figures, running toward the tower. He tensed, hand on his sword, then recognized them.

Saran led the group, blade in hand, Beside her, Idran stumbled, shards glowing bright blue in his arm, crawling up past his shoulder. Sekkan followed with a handful of Karthian warriors, shardwork flickering.

The two groups converged at the tower's base, boots skidding to a halt on broken stone.

Saran's eyes found Leonard first, relief flickering across her face before she buried it. "You're alive."

"So are you." Leonard's voice was rough.

Darum looked at Idran, saw the glow spreading across his chest, the exhaustion carved into his face. "What happened to you, You alright?"

Idran shook his head. "No. But I'll keep moving."

Saran turned to Darum. "The eastern gate held. Barely. Myran's still there with the Fazrum line, the temple's gone. Eleseth—" She stopped, jaw tight.

Darum nodded, understood without needing the words. Another loss. Another name added to the pile.

"Samric?" Saran asked.

"Inside." Darum gestured at the tower. "Saw him walking through the battlefield like it wasn't there. He's either starting the ritual or already finished."

Leonard stepped forward, staring up at the tower. His voice came out. "He's finishing it. I can feel it."

Idran moved beside him, the shards pulsing in rhythm with the tower's hum. "So can I. It's pulling. Harder than before." He looked at Leonard, something unspoken passing between them. "We're running out of time."

Sekkan stepped forward. "My warriors will hold the base. Keep the horde from following you inside."

Darum nodded. "Appreciated."

Sekkan's gaze found Idran, concern etched into his weathered face. "My lord. Be careful."

Idran's smile was faint, bitter. "Too late for that."

The four of them stood at the tower's entrance, staring into the darkness beyond. The hum pressed down.

Saran drew her blade. "No turning back now."

Leonard checked his sword, his straps, his breathing. "Never was."

Darum looked at each of them in turn, Leonard, the student who'd become more, Saran, the bridge who'd held two armies together, Idran, the prince carrying his father's sins in his flesh. Then he looked at the tower, the black stone rising into the storm.

27

Leonard stood at the threshold with the others, Darum to his left, sword drawn and bloodied. Saran to his right, breathing hard, her armor dented, Idran behind them, shards pulsing faint blue beneath his skin. Sekkan and his Karthian warriors fanned out in a loose semicircle, weapons ready, faces carved from exhaustion and fury.

Behind them, the city burned. Smoke rose in black columns, screams echoing through alleys packed with the dying and the desperate. The siege had bled into the streets, ravagers tearing through barricades, shades flickering through walls. But here, at the tower's base, the air was different.

Leonard felt it first, a pull, deep in his chest, like a hand reaching through his ribs and squeezing. The song was louder now, not a melody but a resonance, thrumming in his skull, colors bleeding into his vision. Amber, violet, blue, all swirling together, synesthetic and sharp.

He staggered, hand shooting out to steady himself against the tower's stone. The surface was warm, pulsing faintly under his palm.

"Leo?" Saran asked.

"Something's—" He tried to find the words, but the song drowned them out. "Something's coming. I can feel—"

The tower roared, a deep, bone-rattling rumble erupted from the core, vibrating through the stone, through the air, through Leonard's teeth. He yanked his hand back, stumbling, and then the shockwave hit.

Light exploded from the summit, a wave of color, blue and violet and amber and something darker, cascading down the tower's face like a waterfall of broken stars. The force of it knocked Leonard to his knees, his ears ringing.

Idran screamed, clutching his arm. The shards embedded in his forearm flared bright, brighter than Leonard had ever seen, cracks spiderwebbing across his skin, light bleeding through. He dropped to one knee, gasping, smoke rising from the shards.

Darum's incantation stone burned. Leonard saw it, the glow in Darum's palm spiking white-hot, then sputtering. Darum swore and yanked his hand back, his skin turned blistered and red.

"Damndable thing!"

The Karthian warriors staggered, eyes wide with panic. Sekkan kept his feet, barely.

The shockwave faded, leaving only the hum, the song that wouldn't stop.

Leonard forced himself up, legs shaking. His amber eyes burned, tears streaming down his face. He wiped them away, and saw the smear of red on his palm. Blood, his nose was bleeding.

"What the hell was that?" Sekkan screamed.

Saran helped Idran to his feet, his arm still smoking, shards dimming but not dead. "The ritual," she said. "Samric just completed it."

Sekkan turned on her, fury blazing. "What? You let him? You let the enemy do what he wanted?"

"It was the plan," Darum rasped, still cradling his burned hand. "Draw him in. Let him think he's won. Then strike when he's vulnerable."

"Vulnerable?" Sekkan gestured at the tower, at the light still flickering at its peak. "That doesn't look vulnerable! That looks like the end of the damn world!"

"It is," Idran muttered, staring at his arm. "And we're out of time."

Before anyone could respond, the tower's door exploded.

Stone shattered, hurled outward in chunks and shrapnel. Leonard threw up an arm, felt something slice his cheek. Saran yanked him back.

Shades. Five, maybe six, flickering in and out of reality, their forms half-solid, half-shadow. And at the front, one larger and more corporeal than the rest, wielding a blade of obsidian black, pulsing with void-light.

When it spoke the voice was layered, like multiple throats speaking at once. "You should not be here."

The shade's gaze, if it could be called that fixed on Leonard. The blade pointed at him. "You were given a chance. A place in the new world. Do not expect mercy now."

Leonard's hand found his sword, drew it on instinct. The blade felt too light against what stood before them.

The shades surged forward.

Sekkan roared, stepping into their path, blade flashing. "Go! Now!"

His warriors moved with him, a wall of Karthian steel and shard-work, crashing into the shades. Light flared, void-energy crackled, steel rang against obsidian.

Darum grabbed Leonard's shoulder, hauled him toward the open door. "Move!"

Leonard didn't argue. He ran, Saran and Idran at his heels, boots pounding stone as they plunged into the tower's maw.

Behind them, Sekkan's voice cut through the chaos one last time. "I gave you my word! Go!"

Leonard felt it the moment they crossed the threshold, reality bending at the edges, the tower's interior warping under the weight of the ritual. The steps spiraled upward, but they didn't stay still. Stone shifted beneath his boots, angles tilting, perspective fracturing.

One moment the stairs were steep, the next shallow, then looping back on themselves like a serpent eating its tail.

Darum led, sword in his good hand, the burned one pressed against his chest. He didn't look back, and kept climbing, trusting the others to follow.

Saran was behind Leonard, her breathing steady, the only anchor in the chaos. "Keep moving," she said, voice cutting through the hum. "Don't look at the walls. Just follow Darum."

Leonard tried. But the walls wanted to be looked at. They pulsed, veins of light crawling through the stone like living things. Colors bled through, amber, violet, blue, shifting and swirling, painting shapes that almost made sense before dissolving into noise.

Idran stumbled, gasped and clutched his arm. The shards were flaring again, brighter than before, cracks spreading across his skin. Smoke rose from the embedded stones, and Leonard smelled burnt flesh.

"Idran—"

"I'm fine," Idran hissed, teeth clenched. "Just, keep moving."

Darum's incantation stone flickered in his palm, sputtering like a dying flame. He cursed under his breath, tried to draw power, but the stone dimmed, the light guttering out. His hand shook.

"Stones are failing," he muttered. "Magic's barely holding."

"Then we do this without magic," Saran said. "We've done worse."

The tower groaned around them, a sound like the world cracking. The stairs buckled, stone splitting, gaps opening into darkness. Leonard jumped, barely cleared the gap, landed hard on the next step. Saran grabbed his arm.

"Don't stop," she said. "We're close."

Leonard looked up. The light was brighter now, bleeding down from above, the hum so loud it drowned out thought. He could feel the summit pulling at him, the song in his head reaching a crescendo.

They climbed faster, desperation overriding exhaustion. The walls warped, reality twitching with every step, but Saran kept them moving, kept them focused, her presence the only solid thing in a world coming apart. And then, finally, they reached the top.

Leonard stepped through the top of the stairwell and stopped, breath catching. The rift dominated the space, a vortex of color and light, spinning impossibly fast. A pillar of energy lanced upward, punching through the clouds, splitting into branch-like beams that stretched toward the horizon. Linking something together. The other towers, Leonard realized. All of them, tied together through the rift.

At the center stood Samric, but he wasn't the same. Leonard had seen him before, at the other tower, regal and composed, silver hair and amber eyes burning with cold purpose. That man was gone.

This thing was barely human looking.

Samric's veins bulged black beneath his skin, pulsing with every beat of the rift. His posture was hunched, shoulders twisted at wrong angles. The energies of the rift wrapped around him like chains, tethering him to the vortex, feeding off him, or maybe feeding him. Leonard couldn't tell.

His eyes found them, amber still, but dimmer, ringed with shadow. Recognition flickered, then hardened into disdain.

"You." His voice was scraped hollow. "You're still here. Still standing."

Darum stepped forward, sword raised. "Disappointed?"

Samric's laugh was bitter, broken. "No. Just tired. Tired of stubborn humans who don't know when to die."

His gaze swept over them, Darum, Saran, Leonard, then stopped on Idran. His expression shifted, something almost like recognition, then anger.

"You," he said, voice sharp. "Those shards in your arm. Do you even know what they are?"

Idran's jaw tightened. "Incantation stones. My father embedded them when I was young."

"Your father was a thief." Samric's voice cracked like a whip. "Those aren't just stones. They're fragments of divine relics, pieces of the old order your people scavenged from the ruins. And now they're rotting inside you, wasted on mortal flesh."

Idran's hand drifted to his arm, shards pulsing faintly. "I didn't ask for them."

"No," Samric said, almost sad. "You didn't. But you carry them anyway. A waste. All of it, a waste."

Darum took another step forward. "You done crying over stones? Or are we going to finish this?"

Samric's gaze snapped back to him, fury igniting. "You mock me. A mortal. A human. You stand before the architect of your world's salvation and you mock me."

"Salvation?" Darum's voice was flat, cold. "You chained yourself to a rift and call it salvation? You look not anything how you once looked, Samric. Whatever divinity you thought you had, it's gone."

Samric's hand twitched, veins pulsing darker. "You don't understand. You can't understand. I did this. I banished my kin to the void. I tore the old order apart because it was broken, because they were weak, because someone had to." His voice cracked. "And now I'm bringing it back. The towers are one again. Linked, like they were before the fall. Before your first king stole what wasn't his, right here on this very tower. "

Leonard's stomach twisted. "You did this because of guilt."

Samric's eyes burned. "I did this because it's right."

Darum spat. "You did this because you're too proud to admit you failed."

Samric's hand found his blade, obsidian black, pulsing with voidlight. He drew it, the vortex behind him roaring louder.

The voidblade cut through the air, faster than it should've been, a black arc that left afterimages burned into Leonard's vision. Darum barely got his sword up in time, steel meeting obsidian with a sound like thunder cracking.

The force of it drove Darum back, boots scraping stone, arms shaking. Samric didn't pause, he twisted and brought the blade around again, aiming for Darum's throat.

Saran was there, blade raised, catching the blow. The impact sent her staggering, but she gave Darum the second he needed to recover.

Leonard circled left, Idran right, both trying to flank. Samric's eyes tracked them, cold and calculating despite the madness crawling under his skin.

"You think numbers will save you?" His voice edged with something that might've been pain. "I've killed armies."

He lunged at Leonard, voidblade flashing. Leonard threw himself sideways, felt the blade pass close enough to cut air, close enough to taste the void-energy crackling off it. He hit the ground, rolled, came up swinging.

His sword caught Samric's side, it should've cut deep, should've drawn blood. But the blade skipped off, barely missing Samric's flesh.

Idran raised his hand, shards flaring bright, crystal shard-dust erupted that screamed across the space. It surrounded Samric and drove him back a step.

For a heartbeat, Leonard thought it worked.

Then Samric straightened, veins pulsing darker, and the rift behind him surged. Energy poured into him, and the wound Idran's magic had opened sealed itself, black veins knitting back together.

"Nice try," Samric said, a smile tugging on his lips and lunged.

He moved like something unmoored from reality, too fast, too fluid. The voidblade carved through the space where Idran had been standing, missed by inches. Idran stumbled back, tripped and went down hard.

Samric raised the blade for a killing blow.

Saran hit him from the side, shoulder-check with her full weight behind it. Samric staggered, blade swinging wide, and Darum was there, sword driving toward his exposed ribs.

The blade bit, just barely, drew a thin line of black blood. Samric snarled, twisted, backhanded Darum across the face. Darum's head snapped sideways, blood spraying, and he went down.

Leonard screamed, he didn't think but moved. He threw himself at Samric, blade high, aiming for the throat. Samric caught his wrist mid-swing, grip like iron, and squeezed.

Leonard felt bone grind, pain spiking white-hot up his arm. His sword clattered to the stone.

Samric pulled him close, amber eyes burning. "You could've been something. You could've stood beside me. Now you're just meat."

He threw Leonard backward. Leonard hit the ground hard, vision swimming, ribs screaming.

Saran was already moving, blade flashing, going for Samric's legs. He blocked, parried, drove her back step by step. She was faster, more precise, but he was stronger, and every blow drove her closer to the edge of the platform.

Idran scrambled to his feet, raised his arm again. The shards flared, brighter, hotter, cracks spreading across his skin. He screamed, poured everything into the next surge.

But this time, the energy didn't flow clean. It warped him. His back arched, muscles bulging, skin splitting at the seams. Black ichor leaked from the cracks, and his face twisted.

He was becoming something else. Something monstrous.

Darum hauled himself up, spat blood, grabbed his sword. "He's tied to that rift. We can't outlast him."

Saran blocked another strike, barely, her sword cracking under the force. "Then we take him down now."

Leonard forced himself to his feet, arm hanging limp, sword forgotten. The song in his head was deafening now, the rift pulling at him, calling him.

Samric lunged again, blade aimed at Leonard's heart.

Darum intercepted it, catching the voidblade, holding it inches from Leonard's chest. "Not today."

Saran came in from the side, blade carving across Samric's leg. He roared, kicked her back, but the wound slowed him, black blood pooling on the stone.

Samric staggered, veins pulsing black, body warping further, but he didn't fall. He braced against the rift, fed off it, the energy pouring into him faster than they could hurt him.

Samric raised his voidblade, eyes fixed on Leonard. Black ichor dripped from his mouth, his veins pulsing so dark they looked like cracks in reality itself. He took a step forward, savoring it.

"You should've taken my offer," Samric rasped. "Now you die with the rest."

The blade came down and stopped. Not because Samric hesitated. Not because Leonard moved. Because someone else was there.

Alistair emerged from the stairwell, hood thrown back, silver hair catching the rift's light like a halo. His amber eyes burned with the rift-light.

Samric froze, the voidblade trembled in his hand, still raised, still poised to kill. But he didn't move. His eyes locked on Alistair, and for the first time since the fight began, Leonard saw something other than rage on Samric's face.

"Brother," Samric breathed, the word cracking like glass.

Alistair didn't answer, stepped forward , boots echoing on stone. The rift pulsed behind Samric, light flaring brighter, but Alistair didn't flinch.

"You're exiled," Samric hissed. "You swore. You swore you'd never interfere."

"I did," Alistair said quietly. "But you broke the world. And I can't let you finish."

Samric's blade lowered, just a fraction. His face twisted, rage, grief, something raw and broken bleeding through the monstrous facade. "You betrayed me. You left me to do this alone."

"And you chose vengeance over wisdom." Alistair's tone was steady, but there was weight underneath, centuries of it. "You banished our kin to the void because you thought they were weak. You tore the old order apart because you couldn't accept that it was dying. And now you chain yourself to this—" He gestured at the rift, at the energy warping Samric's body. "—and call it salvation."

Samric's hand shook, voidblade trembling. "I did what had to be done. I fixed what that human broke."

"You fixed nothing." Alistair's voice cracked, just slightly. "You only made it worse."

For a heartbeat, Samric stood frozen, caught between the brother he'd lost and the monster he'd become. His amber eyes flickered, dimmed, something almost human surfacing beneath the void-energy.

Leonard saw the moment. His legs screamed, ribs grinding, but he pushed through the pain, boots pounding stone. Samric's head started to turn, too slow, still caught in Alistair's presence. Leonard hit him at full speed.

Arms locked around Samric's waist, momentum carrying them both forward. Samric's eyes went wide, realization dawning too late as they both crashed into the rift.

The world dissolved into light and color and sound, amber, violet, blue, all bleeding together, screaming in Leonard's skull. The platform vanished. The tower vanished. Alistair, Darum, Saran, Idran, all gone.

The void had no up or down.

Leonard hit something that wasn't ground, rolled across something that wasn't stone. Light pulsed around him, amber nodes scattered through the darkness like dying stars, each one connected by threads of energy that stretched toward infinity.

He forced himself up, vision swimming. The space twisted, distances collapsing and expanding with every breath. In the distance, or maybe right beside him, space didn't work here, he saw flashes. Ancient battles, towers burning. Figures wreathed in light and shadow, tearing each other apart.

Samric was already on his feet, voidblade in hand, but he wasn't attacking. He was staring at Leonard, eyes wide, black veins pulsing under his skin.

"You—" His voice cracked. "You knew. Alistair told you, didn't he?"

Leonard steadied himself, breathing hard. "He told us enough."

Samric's laugh was bitter, broken. "My brother. The exile. The fool who chose solitude over duty." He took a step forward, blade trembling. "I thought he'd never interfere. I thought—" His voice hitched. "I thought he'd let me fix this."

"You're not fixing anything," Leonard said, backing up. His sword was gone, lost in the fall. He had nothing but his voice and whatever will he had left. "You're just repeating the same mistake. Over and over."

"Mistake?" Samric's fury ignited, veins flaring darker. "I saved our kind! I banished the weak, the corrupt, the ones who would've dragged us all into ruin! And when your king stole the divine power, I —" He stopped, chest heaving. "I did what had to be done."

"And now you're chained to a rift, rotting from the inside out." Leonard's voice was laced with venom. "Was it worth it?"

Samric snarled, raised the voidblade, and lunged.

Leonard dove, rolled, came up empty-handed. Samric's blade carved through the space where he'd been, the energy crackling, bending reality around.it.

"You don't understand!" Samric's voice was ragged. "The towers were meant to bind the divine to the world! Not trap it, not steal it, but channel it! And your king murdered his own son to break that bond, to hoard the power for himself!"

Leonard backed toward one of the amber nodes, the light pulsing brighter as he got closer. "So you're bringing it back. The old order. The divine flood."

"Yes." Samric's eyes burned. "And nothing—nothing will stop me. Not you. Not Alistair. Not—"

A sound cut through the void. A caw, a resonant sound. It echoed through the liminal space, vibrating in Leonard's chest.

Samric froze.

Leonard turned, scanned the darkness. In the distance, or maybe right behind him, distance didn't work, something was moving. Massive. Black wings unfurling, blotting out the amber nodes one by one.

Samric's face went pale. "No. No, not—"

He knew. Whatever it was, he knew, Leonard didn't, but he didn't need to.

The thing in the void drew closer, wings spreading wider, each beat of them collapsing space, drawing them in. Leonard felt the pull, the weight of something vast and old pressing down on the rift.

Samric staggered backward, voidblade forgotten, eyes wide with something Leonard had never seen in him before.

"We have to go," Samric hissed. "Now. Before it—"

"No." Leonard's voice was steady, clearer than it had any right to be.

He turned toward the rift's core, the pulsing amber light that connected all the towers, all the nodes, the entire broken web of the ritual. He raised his arms, palms out, and reached.

Energy poured into him, through him, burning hotter than the stone test, hotter than anything he'd ever felt. His amber eyes flared, brighter than the void, and the song in his head exploded into a roar.

"What are you doing?!" Samric's voice cracked. "You'll kill yourself!"

"Closing it." Leonard's teeth were clenched, sweat and blood streaming down his face. "Ending this."

Samric's eyes went wide. "You can't—if you close it now, with that thing—"

"Then you better run."

The energy surged, and Leonard poured everything into it. His will, his blood, his being. The rift resisted, fought him, but he didn't let go, he couldn't let go.

Images flooded his mind, ancient, impossible, memories that weren't his. Towers standing tall under alien skies. Figures of light and shadow, building, fighting, dying. The first king's blade raised, his son screaming, the divine power torn free and bound to mortal flesh.

Leonard screamed, pushed harder. The rift began to collapse, nodes flickering out one by one, the threads of energy snapping like broken strings.

Samric stumbled, the void-energy feeding him draining. His veins pulsed, dimming, the monstrous changes beginning to recede. He looked at Leonard, at the collapsing rift, at the thing in the darkness drawing closer.

"You're insane," Samric rasped.

"Yeah." Leonard's voice was barely a whisper now, everything burning away. "Probably."

The thing cawed again, closer now, wings blotting out the last of the light.

Samric's eyes met Leonard and he ran.

Bolted toward the edge of the collapsing rift, where reality still bled through to the tower's summit. His form flickered,, but he made it, stumbling through the threshold and disappearing into the world beyond.

Leonard held.

The rift collapsed faster now, spiraling inward, the pressure crushing, the light fading. The thing in the void reached for him, wings spreading wide, but the rift was already closing, sealing itself shut.

Leonard glimpsed it, just for a heartbeat. Black feathers. Eyes like dying stars. A shape too vast to comprehend. Then the rift imploded.

And Leonard was swallowed whole.

28

Leonard hit stone like the world reached up and slammed into him, bones jarring, breath punched out in a wet gasp. His vision whited out, every nerve in his body was screaming.

He couldn't move, he laid there, cheek pressed against cold stone. Behind him, the rift screamed.

The sound was everywhere, a high, keening wail that vibrated in his teeth, in his skull, in the marrow of his bones. The pillar of light guttered, flickered, then collapsed, imploding inward with a sound like the world breaking.

The branch-connections snapped. Leonard felt them go, one by one, the threads of energy linking the towers severing with sharp, violent cracks. The web of the ritual, the binding Samric had spent all this time building, tore itself apart in seconds.

The tower shuddered.

A deep, grinding groan rose from the core, stone cracking, the structure trembling beneath Leonard's body. The light died, amber, violet, blue, all of it snuffed out in an instant, leaving only cold gray dawn bleeding through the smoke.

Leonard dragged in a breath, choked on it, coughed blood onto the stone. His hands scrabbled for purchase, nails scraping, and he forced himself up onto his elbows. His vision swam, then slowly focused.

The summit was dark, empty except for the smoke rising from the rift's remnants; a blackened scar in the stone, still glowing faintly at the edges, dying embers of something vast and ancient.

Samric lay collapsed near the rift, crumpled like a discarded puppet, one hand reaching toward the scar as if he could still touch it. His veins, once black and pulsing, were fading, pale now, almost translucent, the monstrous changes receding. His body shrank inward, muscles deflating, skin sagging, leaving him gaunt and hollow.

Leonard stared, unable to look away. This was the thing that had torn the world apart and now just a man, dying on cold stone.

Samric's amber eyes flickered, then found Leonard. Recognition sparked, followed by something that might've been relief. Or maybe just exhaustion.

"You..." His voice was a rasp, barely audible. "You closed it."

Leonard nodded, too tired to speak.

Samric's hand trembled, fell to the stone. His breathing was shallow, uneven. "The song... it's gone."

Leonard blinked, realized he was right. The resonance in his head, the pull of the rift, the song that had been screaming in his skull for days, all of it was silent now. Only emptiness remained.

Boots pounded stone. Voices shouted, distant but getting closer.

Leonard tried to focus, tried to make sense of the shapes moving toward him through the smoke. His body felt too light, too cold, like something vital had been burned away and all that was left was smoke.

Hands grabbed him, hauled him upright. Saran. She was saying something, words blurred and urgent, but he couldn't make them out over the ringing in his ears.

She cupped his face, forced him to look at her. Her eyes were wide, searching, and then they went wider still.

"Leo, your eyes—"

He blinked, didn't understand what she was trying to say.

"They're blue," she breathed. "They're blue.".

Darum was there too, hand on Leonard's shoulder, checking him over with the efficiency of a man who'd pulled wounded off battlefields his whole life. "Can you stand?"

"Yeah," Leonard rasped. "I think."

Idran stumbled up behind them, shards in his arm dim now, barely glowing. He looked at Leonard, at the dead rift, at Samric's collapsed form, and let out a breathless, broken laugh. "You did it. You actually—"

A sound cut him off, a wet, rasping breath.

Samric was moving, dragging himself up onto his knees. His body was failing, veins pale, skin sagging, every breath a struggle. But his eyes still burned..

"No," he rasped, voice cracking. "No. You don't—you can't—"

Then he lunged, not gracefully but with desperation and rage, one last attempt to tear Leonard apart before the end.

But Darum was already moving, he stepped between Samric and Leonard, blade already rising, and drove it through Samric's chest in one clean thrust.

Samric's eyes went wide, amber flickering and dimmed. He looked down at the blade buried in his ribs, black blood welling around the steel, then up at Darum.

Darum's face was stone. "Not today, I said."

He yanked the blade free, violent and final. Blood sprayed. Samric collapsed, crumpled to the stone, gasping a final breath.

Leonard stepped forward, legs shaking, Saran's hand still gripping his arm. He looked down at the thing that had torn the world apart, the architect of exile and ruin, now just a dying man bleeding out on cold stone.

Samric's eyes found Leonard, then drifted past him, searching. Looking for someone else.

"Brother," he whispered, voice barely audible.

Leonard turned, followed his gaze. Alistair stood at the edge of the platform, watching the events before him unfold. On his face was grief, maybe, or perhaps exhaustion worn smooth by centuries.

Samric's hand trembled, reaching toward him. "Brother... did I... was I..."

Alistair didn't answer.

Samric's hand fell. His breathing hitched, stuttered, then stopped. The amber in his eyes flickered once, then faded to a cold gray.

Leonard swayed, legs giving out. Saran caught him, eased him down to sit, her hand steady on his shoulder.

Alistair moved across the platform, boots silent on stone, until he stood before Leonard. The others gave them space, Darum hovering close, hand resting on his sword hilt, but not interfering. Saran helped Leonard stay upright, then stepped back.

Alistair looked down at Leonard, amber eyes studying him with that same infinite patience, that same weight of centuries pressing down.

"What you did, closing the rift, wasn't just brave. It was necessary." He paused, gaze drifting to the blackened scar where the rift had been. "The divine was never meant to be bound to the mortal world. Not like this. The old gods started this cycle, then perpetuated by the first king and then Samric made an attempt to keep it going. You ended it."

Leonard swallowed, throat raw. "You could've told us. Could've warned us what it would cost."

Alistair crouched beside Samric's body, reached out, and gently closed his eyes. His hand lingered for a moment, fingers trembling just slightly, then he stood.

"He was my brother," Alistair said quietly, voice carrying across the summit. "Despite everything, my own exile, the banishment, the wars—he was still my brother."

Alistair's gaze stayed fixed on Samric's face, pale and still now, all the fury and ambition drained away. "He was right about one thing. The old order was broken, corrupt. Dying from within long before the first king ever raised his blade." He paused."But Samric thought he could rebuild it with blood and chains. He was always too proud to see another way."

Leonard watched him, the same exhaustion Samric had carried but worn differently. Alistair bore it with quiet resignation.

Alistair straightened, turned to face Leonard. His amber eyes swept over the group, Darum, blade still drawn; Saran, vigilant at Leonard's side; Idran, shards dim but alive. Then back to Leonard.

"What happens now?" Leonard asked.

Alistair stepped closer, stopped a few paces away. "The divine is severed from the world. No more relics with true power. No more stones that channel the old gods. The towers are dark. The cycle is broken." He paused, letting the weight of it settle. "Humanity is on its own. Like it should have been when my kind left this world."

Leonard's chest tightened. "That sounds like a curse."

"It's not." Alistair's tone was firm, almost gentle. "It's a gift. The old order kept you bound, kept you dependent, kept you from choosing your own path. Now you can. You'll have to decide what to do with it."

Darum shifted, "And if we fail?"

Alistair's gaze found him. "Then you fail. But it will be your failure, not ours. That's the difference."

Alistair turned, moved toward the stairwell, boots silent on stone. He stopped at the threshold, looked back one last time.

"You'll carry this," he said, eyes on Leonard. "The weight of what you did, what it cost. That's the price of ending gods."

Leonard met his gaze, steady despite the exhaustion pressing down. "I know."

Alistair's mouth quirked, almost a smile. "Good. Then you're wiser than most."

He stepped down the stairwell, into shadow, and was gone as if he'd never been there at all.

Leonard stared at the empty space, Saran's hand found his shoulder, "Come on. We need to get you down."

Leonard nodded, let her help him to his feet. His legs shook, barely holding, but he stayed upright. Darum moved to his other side, ready to catch him if he fell.

Idran lingered near Samric's body, staring down at the corpse. "What do we do with him?"

Darum's voice came. "Leave him. The city can decide if he's worth burying."

All of them prepared to move towards the stairs but then Leonard stopped.

The group paused with him, Saran's hand still on his arm, concern flickering across her face. "What is it?"

"There's something I need from him." he said quietly.

Darum frowned. "Leonard—"

"Just a second." Leonard pulled free of Saran's grip, steadied himself against the wall. "

Leonard climbed. Slower this time, every step agony, but he pushed through. Back up the stairs, back to the summit, back to where Samric lay cold and still in the pale morning light.

He moved over to Samric's lifeless body then reached into his cloak. His fingers found something hard, smooth, warm despite the cold. He pulled it free.

Ulzaan's incantation stone.

The stone was dim now, lifeless, but Leonard could still feel the weight of it, the decades Ulzaan had carried it, the battles fought, the lives saved and lost. He closed his fist around it.

Leonard stood, legs shaking, and held out the stone to Darum. "You hold on to it, please."

Darum crossed the distance slowly, took the stone with hands that trembled just slightly. He looked down at it, jaw clenched so tight Leonard thought it might crack.

"He died with it," Darum said, voice rough. "And this bastard took it."

"Now it's back." Leonard's voice was steady. "Where it belongs."

Darum's fingers closed around the stone, knuckles white, then turned and walked back toward the stairs.

Leonard followed, slower, the weight of what he'd reclaimed settling over him.

They descended together, rejoining Saran and Idran at the base. Sekkan was still there, bloodied, leaning on his sword, his surviving warriors scattered around him in various states of collapse.

He looked up as they approached, saw Leonard's face, the exhaustion carved into every line. "What the hell happened up there? The tower's dead. The whole damn thing just.. stopped."

"It's over," Darum said, voice flat. "Samric's dead. The ritual's broken."

Sekkan blinked, processed, then let out a long, ragged breath. "Good. Then maybe we can stop dying for a few hours."

They moved through the city, slower now, injuries catching up. The streets were chaos, refugees emerging from hiding, soldiers stumbling through rubble, the wounded being carried toward makeshift infirmaries. But the enemy was scattering. Ravagers fled into alleys, shades flickered and died, the horde collapsing without Samric's will holding them together.

Leonard barely registered it. He focused on moving, one step at a time, Saran and Darum flanking him, keeping him upright.

They found Verath near the inner ward, armor cracked and bloodied, barking orders to a cluster of ravenblood warriors. She saw them coming, eyes sweeping over the group and her posture shifted, just slightly.

She moved to them, stopped in front of Leonard. "It's done?"

Leonard nodded, too tired to speak.

Verath's gaze lingered on him for a moment, something almost like approval flickering there. "Then we hold what's left."

She turned back to the warriors, already moving, already coordinating the next phase.

Drast limped up from the side, one arm in a makeshift sling, He saw Darum and managed something that might've been a smile. "Still standing, old man."

Darum snorted. "Barely."

Drast's gaze found Leonard, swept over him, then nodded once. "Good work, kid."

Leonard almost laughed. "Thanks."

They kept moving, deeper into the inner ward, where the worst of the fighting had been. Bodies everywhere, ravenblood, Karthian, civilians who'd been caught in the crossfire. Leonard tried not to look, tried not to count.

But he saw them. Every one of them.

The sun climbed higher, bleeding light across the broken city. The tower stood dark and silent behind them, no longer humming, no longer calling.

Leonard leaned against a wall, let himself slide down to sit, legs finally giving out. Saran dropped beside him, close enough that their shoulders touched.

The sun climbed higher, bleeding light across the broken city. The tower stood dark and silent behind them, no longer humming, no longer calling.

Leonard leaned against a wall, let himself slide down to sit, legs finally giving out. Saran dropped beside him, close enough that their shoulders touched.

Darum stood for a moment longer, surveying the ruins, the bodies, the scattered warriors still hauling wounded toward the inner ward. Then, with a grunt, he lowered himself down on Leonard's other side, back against the stone, sword laid across his knees.

For a long time, none of them spoke. They sat there, listening to the distant sounds of the city pulling itself back together. Shouts, hammers, the creak of carts being wheeled through rubble.

Darum spoke first "Didn't think we'd make it."

Saran snorted softly. "Neither did I."

Leonard looked down at his hands, scarred, bloodied, trembling faintly. "I kept waiting for it to go wrong. For one of us to—" He stopped, throat tight.

Saran's hand found his, fingers lacing through his. "We didn't."

Darum's gaze drifted to Ulzaan's stone, still clutched in his palm. His thumb traced the edge, slow and deliberate. "He'd be proud. Stubborn old bastard." His voice cracked, just slightly. "All of them would be."

Leonard thought of Tomas. Marel. Theran. Ulzaan. Eleseth. Brent. All the names carved into memory, all the faces he'd never forget.

"We're still here," he said quietly. "That has to count for something."

Darum looked at him, something unguarded in his eyes. "It counts for everything." He reached out, clapped a hand on Leonard's shoulder, grip firm. "You did good, Leonard, better than good."

Leonard's eyes burned, but he didn't look away. "I had help."

"Damn right you did." Saran leaned into him, head resting against his shoulder. "You're not getting rid of us that easy."

Darum's hand stayed on Leonard's shoulder for a moment longer, then he pulled back, settled against the wall. "So what now?"

Leonard exhaled, the question hanging in the air, "I don't know. Rebuild, I guess. Figure out what's left."

"Together," Saran said.

"Together," Leonard agreed.

Darum nodded, eyes distant. "I can work with that."

They sat in silence again, the three of them pressed shoulder to shoulder, watching the sun climb higher over the broken city. No more gods. No more prophecies. No more songs in their heads.

It wasn't much. But it was enough.

EPILOGUE

Dawn broke over Fazrum, like the city wasn't sure it deserved another day.

Leonard walked through streets that had learned to live again. The noise was different now. Hammers rang against stone as workers hauled scaffolding into place, shoring up damaged buildings. Merchants called out prices from reopened stalls, voices hoarse but steady. Somewhere, a child laughed, the sound startling against the backdrop of reconstruction.

The scars were everywhere. Scorched walls where fire had climbed during the siege. Cracked cobblestones, gaps in the rows where buildings used to stand. Empty spaces that would take years to fill, if they ever did.

Leonard passed a cluster of refugees, former refugees, he corrected himself. Residents now. They were repairing a storefront, arguing good-naturedly about whether the sign should hang crooked or straight. One of them glanced up, caught Leonard's eye, and nodded. Leonard nodded back.

His reflection caught in a shop window, and he stopped. Blue eyes stared back at him.

The divine was gone. Severed when the rift collapsed, torn out of him along with the song, the pull, the weight of something older than stone. He was just Leonard now.

People noticed. Some nodded in recognition, he was still Ravenblood. Others avoided his gaze, uncertain what to make of the boy who'd closed the rift and survived it.

He kept walking.

The Ravenblood barracks rose ahead, quieter than it used to be. Fewer warriors on the walls, fewer voices echoing through the training yards. But the raven sigil still hung above the door, black and defiant, battered but unbroken.

Leonard's path curved away, taking him toward the black tower.

The tower had been sealed, runes carved into the base, heavy chains wrapped around the door. Ravenblood guards stood watch, not because it was dangerous anymore, but because it was a grave. A monument to what had been lost, and what had been saved.

Leonard stopped at the edge of the plaza, staring up.

The tower didn't hum anymore. It was just stone now, the rift inside collapsed into nothing. No light bled from the cracks. No song echoed in his mind.

He remembered the climb. The warped stairs, reality bending under the weight of the ritual. Samric at the summit, chained to the rift, more monster than man. Alistair's arrival. The moment Leonard had tackled Samric into the void.

He didn't remember how he'd gotten out. Just waking up on the summit floor, the rift gone, the tower silent. Saran's face above him, Darum's hand gripping his shoulder, holding him together.

He didn't linger at the tower. Turned away and kept walking.

The memorial ground lay outside the city walls, rows of graves stretching across a field that had once been farmland. Simple stones, wooden markers, some with names carved deep, others left blank because no one knew who lay beneath.

Leonard walked the rows slowly, boots crunching frost.

He stopped at Ulzaan's grave.

The stone was larger than the others, the raven sigil carved deep into the surface. Ulzaan's incantation stone was embedded in the marker, Darum's doing, Leonard knew. The stone was dark now, but it caught the morning light and held it.

Leonard knelt, brushed dirt from the base of the marker. His throat tightened, words catching before he forced them out.

"We're still standing," he said quietly. "Thought you'd want to know."

He stayed there for a moment longer, then stood and moved on.

Eleseth's grave was smaller, Fresh flowers lay at the base, someone had been here recently. Idran, maybe, before he left.

Leonard crouched, adjusted the flowers, fingers lingering on the petals. "You were right," he murmured. "About duty. About sacrifice. I get it now."

Then Brent's grave, a name and dates carved into weathered wood. Leonard paused, remembering how he was told about the chokepoint, the last stand, the man who'd sought redemption and found it in blood.

"You did good," Leonard said. "For what it's worth."

He walked the rows after that, stopping at graves of warriors he'd known. Tomas. Marel. Others whose names blurred together but whose faces he'd never forget. Each one a life, a choice, a piece of the cost they'd paid.

Near the far edge of the graveyard, he found Darum.

He was knelt by a cluster of newer graves, out of armor for the first time Leonard could remember. Plain clothes, worn and simple, sleeves rolled up to his elbows. His hands moved methodically, pulling weeds, straightening markers, brushing dirt from stones.

Leonard approached quietly.

"Wondered when you'd show," Darum said.

Leonard sat beside him, picked up a spare rag, started cleaning a nearby marker. "How's the retired life?"

Darum snorted. "Retired. That's one word for it." He gestured at the graves. "Someone has to tend them. Verath's got the Pact. I've got this."

They worked in silence for a while, hands moving in sync, the only sound the scrape of cloth on stone and the distant murmur of the city.

"How are you doing?" Darum asked finally, not looking at Leonard.

Leonard paused, considered. "The silence is strange. No song in my head anymore. No pull. It's... quieter."

"Quieter good or quieter bad?"

"Just quieter." Leonard wiped dirt from his hands. "I'm adjusting."

Darum nodded, pulled another weed, tossed it aside. "Ulzaan would've been proud."

Leonard's chest tightened. "You think?"

"I know." Darum's tone left no room for argument. "You did what you had to. That's all he ever wanted, for the job to get done, no matter the cost."

Leonard looked at Ulzaan's grave in the distance. "Sometimes I wonder if he knew. If he saw it coming."

"Probably." Darum's smile was faint, sad. "He saw most things. Just didn't always say."

Silence stretched. Leonard broke it. "You ever regret stepping back? Letting Verath take the Pact?"

Darum shook his head. "I've done my part. Fought my wars. Time to let the next generation figure it out." He glanced at Leonard. "That includes you."

Leonard huffed a dry laugh. "I'm not leading anything."

"Didn't say you had to. Just said you're part of it. Whether you like it or not."

They worked a while longer, then Darum stood, brushed dirt from his knees. He pulled something from his pocket, a flask, dented and worn. Took a sip and offered it to Leonard.

Leonard took it and drank.

"Idran's leaving today, isn't he?" Darum asked.

Leonard nodded. "Yeah. Thought I'd see him off."

Darum's hand found Leonard's shoulder, gripped once, firm and grounding. "Then don't keep him waiting. And tell Saran I'll see her later."

Leonard stood, met Darum's gaze. "You going to be alright?"

Darum's smile was crooked, tired, but real. "Always."

Leonard left him there, still tending the graves, quiet and at peace in a way Leonard had never seen before.

The Ravenblood courtyard was quiet, the morning sun slanting across worn cobblestones. Most of the warriors were out on patrol or sleeping off night watch. Just Leonard and the sound of a horse stamping.

Idran stood beside the animal, a Karthian mare with shardwork woven into her tack, faint blue glimmers along the saddle. He was moving saddlebags into place.

His arms were wrapped in fresh bandages from wrist to elbow. Clean white linen, stained faintly with old blood where it pressed against the skin beneath. The fabric bulged slightly in places, uneven, and Leonard knew without asking what lay underneath.

Idran looked thinner, paler, like he'd been hollowed out and was only now learning to stand upright again. But there was something steadier in the way he moved, the way he held himself. Like a weight had been lifted, even if the cost had carved him open.

Leonard stopped a few paces away, hands in his pockets. "You're really going."

Idran glanced up, managed a tired smile. "Can't stay. Too much history here." He tugged the strap tighter and tightened the knot. "And Karth needs me. Or I need it. Haven't figured out which yet."

Leonard's gaze dropped to the bandages. "The shards?"

Idran flexed his fingers, slow and careful, wincing as the motion pulled at something beneath the linen. "Gone. Took a Karthian surgeon, a lot of wine, and more screaming than I'd like to admit." He paused, stared at his hands like they were foreign things. "But they're out. I can breathe now. First time since I was a kid."

Leonard nodded, didn't push. He knew what it cost to carry something you didn't ask for. "What's waiting for you in Karth?"

Idran snorted, bitter. "Chaos, probably. My family's court is a bloodbath. My sister is holding it together, but barely. Someone has to step in, clean up the mess my father left behind." He looked at Leonard, something raw flickering in his gaze. "Might as well be me."

"You don't have to go back," Leonard said quietly. "You could stay. Help rebuild here."

Idran shook his head. "No. I need to figure out who I am without the shards. Without all of this." He gestured vaguely at the barracks, the city, the war they'd left behind. "Karth's a mess, but it's my mess. I owe it that much."

Leonard understood. He'd felt the same pull, the need to step away, to find something that wasn't defined by blood. "You think you'll come back?"

"I don't know." Idran's voice was honest. "Maybe. If there's anything left worth coming back to."

"You saved my life," Idran said quietly. "More than once. I won't forget that."

Leonard almost deflected, the old instinct to brush it off rising. Then he stopped, let the words settle. "You saved mine too. We're even."

Idran laughed. "Even. Yeah. That's one way to put it."

He extended his hand. Leonard took it, gripped firm. Idran's palm was rough, trembling just slightly from the pain still radiating up his arm.

Then Idran pulled him into a brief, awkward embrace. Leonard stiffened, then relaxed, let it happen. When they pulled back, Idran's eyes were bright, not quite tears but close.

"Take care of yourself, Leonard," Idran said. "And tell Saran—" He stopped, searched for words. "—tell her I'll miss the arguments but not her fists."

Leonard smiled faintly. "I will."

Idran turned, mounted the horse with a wince, settled into the saddle slow and careful. He looked down at Leonard, something final in his gaze, the knowledge that this might be the last time they saw each other, that paths diverged here and might never cross again.

"One step at a time," Idran said quietly.

Leonard nodded. "One step."

Idran turned the horse, urged her forward. Hooves clattered on cobblestones, the sound echoing through the empty courtyard. Leonard watched him ride toward the gate, silhouette shrinking against the morning light.

Then he was gone. Just a speck on the horizon, then nothing.

Leonard climbed the stone steps to the ramparts, boots scraping against worn edges smoothed by decades of patrols.

He found Saran standing at the wall, looking out over the city.

She was out of armor, just practical clothes, dark and worn, a blade at her hip more out of habit than necessity. Her hair hung loose for once, falling past her shoulders instead of pulled back in the tight braid she'd always worn. The wind caught it, lifted it, and she didn't bother pushing it back.

She didn't turn when he approached, but shifted slightly and made room.

Leonard leaned against the wall beside her, elbows resting on cold stone. "Idran left."

Saran nodded, gaze still on the city. "Figured. Saw him packing earlier." She paused, glanced at him. "You okay?"

Leonard considered, let the question settle. "Yeah. I think so."

They stood in comfortable silence, watching Fazrum wake up below them. Workers hauled timber through the streets, merchants called out from reopened stalls, children chased each other through alleys that had been battlegrounds weeks ago. The city was scarred, broken in places, but it was alive.

"Verath's restructuring the Pact," Saran said finally. "Less doctrine, more practical defense. Turns out when the stones die, people care more about skill than prophecy."

Leonard almost smiled. "Would Ulzaan have, After the war?."

"Ulzaan would've adapted." Saran's tone was matter-of-fact. "He always did."

Leonard nodded, "What about you? What are you doing now?"

Saran shrugged, rolled her shoulders like shaking off weight. "Coordinating between Fazrum and Karth. Making sure the peace holds. Someone has to. Might as well be me." She glanced at him, grin tugging at the corner of her mouth. "Besides, I'm good at telling people they're idiots. Turns out that's a valuable diplomatic skill."

Leonard huffed a quiet laugh. "Yeah. I bet."

Saran spoke. "Darum's doing alright?"

"Yeah. He's tending graves. Out of armor, finally." Leonard's chest tightened, but it didn't hurt. "He earned his rest. Let him have it."

Saran nodded, something soft flickering in her gaze. "Good. He deserves it."

Then Saran's voice shifted. "What about you? The eyes, does it feel different? Being fully human now?"

Leonard looked down at his hands, flexed his fingers. No pull toward the rift. No song in his head. "It does," he admitted. "Quieter, it's not bad, I like it."

Saran studied him. Then she reached out, bumped his shoulder with hers. "You know you don't have to carry this alone, right? Whatever comes next."

Leonard met her eyes, saw the weight she carried too, grief, exhaustion, the scars that didn't show. "I know. I've got you. Darum, even the pact. That's more than enough."

Saran's head tilted, rested against his shoulder. The contact was warm. "So what now?"

Leonard looked out over the city No more gods pulling strings. No more prophecies. But people, figuring it out one day at a time.

"We keep going," he said quietly. "One step at a time."

Saran leaned into him, shoulder to shoulder. "We've done worse."

Leonard almost laughed, the sound rough but real. "Yeah. We have."

They stood together, watching the sun climb higher, the city waking up below them. The black tower loomed in the distance. Beyond the walls, the graves stretched across the field.

Saran squeezed his hand, pulled him back to the present. "Come on. Verath wants us at the council meeting. Something about assigning new patrols."

Leonard groaned. "Already?"

Saran grinned, sharp and teasing. "Already. Welcome to peacetime."

She pushed off the wall, started walking back toward the stairs. Leonard glanced back once, at the tower, at the graves, at the horizon where Idran had disappeared.

Then he turned forward and followed Saran, boots scraping stone, the city spreading out below them. And whatever came next, they'd face it together.

One step at a time.

AFTERWORD

If you've made it this far, thank you for sticking with it and reaching the end.

Finishing this duology, Ravenblood: Amber & Glass has been one of the most rewarding things I've ever done. It's been quite the journey through broken cities, bitter silences, brutal choices, and the companionship that survives all of it. I made this for the kind of reader who doesn't need clean answers or perfect heroes but something that feels real, even if it's wrapped in a dark fantasy novel.

You might have noticed I don't like to hold readers' hands. I prefer stories that trust you to find the thread, even if it's frayed. Some people will bounce off that. Some won't and that's fine. If you're reading this now, chances are you didn't bounce, and for that I'm grateful. You're exactly the kind of person I made this story for.

This story was always meant to be two books. Nothing drawn out, no trilogy just because. Just a beginning, a middle, and an end. As a reader, you gave it time. You walked with these characters. You let them be complicated. That matters to me more than you probably realize.

Where I go from here, I'm not sure, but for any updates or announcements on future projects, head over to my website, there you'll find a sign up for my newsletter as well. Ravenblood.org.

Thanks for walking this road with me.

— Lukas

www.ingramcontent.com/pod-product-compliance
Lightning Source LLC
LaVergne TN
LVHW091109080826
845145LV00008B/1854

* 9 7 8 9 0 9 0 4 1 5 1 7 8 *